Andrew Barton Paterson was born near Orange in 1864. He always considered himself a country boy at heart, despite moving to Sydney as a young boy to live with his grandmother, Emily Barton, while he attended Sydney Grammar School. Paterson spent his school holidays on the family property, "Illalong", near Yass in New South Wales, until he became an articled clerk and then a solicitor in Sydney.

A.B. Paterson was a correspondent for the *Sydney Morning Herald* and the Melbourne *Argus* during the Boer War, and both his verse and prose show his commitment to portraying the experiences of Australian soldiers abroad. Upon returning to Australia after his correspondent years, Paterson married Alice Walker, and they and their two children settled on a property on the upper Murrumbidgee. When the First World War broke out Paterson again hoped to work as a correspondent in Europe, but instead joined the ambulance corps in France. Back in Australia after the war, the family moved to Sydney where Paterson worked as a freelance writer until his death in 1941.

# Banjo Paterson

## Complete Poems

A&R Classics
An imprint of HarperCollins*Publishers*

**A&R Classics**
An imprint of HarperCollins*Publishers*, Australia

This A&R Classics edition published in 2001
by HarperCollins*Publishers* Pty Limited
ABN 36 009 913 517
A member of the HarperCollins*Publishers* (Australia) Pty Limited Group
www.harpercollins.com.au

Published by arrangement with Retusa Pty Ltd

Poems by A.B. Paterson first published in 1983 © Retusa Pty Ltd 1983: "A Grain of
Desert Sand"; "Bandy Burke"; "Barney Devine"; "Campin' Round Coonamble";
"Cape Mounted Rifles"; "Castlebar"; "General Drought and General Rain"; "Here's
Luck"; "I Joined a Contingent"; "Johnny Riley's Cow"; "Maxims of War"; "No
Class"; "Our Own Flag"; "Our Underpaid Army"; "Queensland Mounted Infantry";
"Song of Murray's Brigade"; "Ten Little Jackaroos"; "The Ballad of Ashantie
Pagoda"; "The Uplift"; "They Met in a Hall at a Charity Ball"; "To George Lambert".

**HarperCollins*Publishers***
25 Ryde Road, Pymble, Sydney NSW 2073, Australia
31 View Road, Glenfield, Auckland 10, New Zealand
77–85 Fulham Palace Road, London W6 8JB, United Kingdom
Hazelton Lanes, 55 Avenue Road, Suite 2900, Toronto, Ontario, M5R 3L2
*and* 1995 Markham Road, Scarborough, Ontario, M1B 5M8, Canada
10 East 53rd Street, New York NY 10022, USA

National Library of Australia Cataloguing-in-Publication data:

Paterson, A. B. (Andrew Barton), 1864–1941.
The complete poems.
Includes index.
ISBN 0 207 19867 5.
I. Title. (Series: A&R classics).
A821.2

Cover design: Russell Jeffery, HarperCollins Design Studio
Cover image: Coo-ee Historical Picture Library
Printed and bound in Australia by Griffin Press on 70gsm Bulky Book Ivory

7 6 5 4 3 2 1     01 02 03 04

# Contents

## *Saltbush Bill, J.P., and Other Verses*

# Publisher's Preface

When verses written by 'The Banjo' started appearing in the *Bulletin* in the 1880s, they were greeted with warm approval. His first collection, *The Man from Snowy River and Other Verses*, was published in 1895, and the mysterious 'Banjo's' identity was revealed as Andrew Barton 'Banjo' Paterson, a young Sydney solicitor. The volume went on to sell over 100 000 copies, confirming that there was both a source and a market for Australian writing.

A.B. Paterson is regarded as one of Australia's finest bush balladists who, having grown up in rural New South Wales, had ample personal experience to inform his predominantly romanticised and comic bush mythology. While Paterson is best known for his ballads depicting the Australian bush and its characters, his verse and prose show his broad interests, ranging from cultural obsessions (such as horse racing and bicycle riding), to a general championing of the underdog, and his responses to war. Aside from writing verse, Paterson wrote prose, in the form of dispatches and journalism, as well as longer fictional works, such as his novel *The Shearer's Colt* (1936).

This A&R Classics edition of A.B. Paterson's verse is based on the grouping of his first compiled collection, comprising the previously published *The Man from Snowy River and Other Verses*; *Rio Grande's Last Race and Other Verses*; and *Saltbush Bill, J.P., and Other Verses*. This 1921 collection was revised and expanded in 1986 to include 'A Late Collection', and these additional poems are included here, along with Paterson's collection of children's verse, *The Animals Noah Forgot*, and other uncollected verse.

Sydney, 2001

# Chronology

17 February 1864  Andrew Barton Paterson born at "Narrambla", near Orange, N.S.W.

1864–1870  Family lived at "Buckinbah", near Obley, N.S.W., then moved to "Illalong", near Yass, N.S.W. in 1870.

1874  Moved to Sydney to live with grandmother, E.M. Barton, at Gladesville, N.S.W., to attend Sydney Grammar School.

1885  First poem, "El Mahdi to the Australian Troops", published in the *Bulletin*.

1886  Admitted as an attorney, solicitor and proctor of the Supreme Court of N.S.W.

1889  Publication of "Clancy of The Overflow" in the *Bulletin*.

1890  Publication of "The Man from Snowy River" in the *Bulletin*.

1895  Publication of first collection of poetry, *The Man from Snowy River and Other Verses*.

1889–1902  Boer War.

October 1899–July 1900  War correspondent reporting on the Boer War for the *Sydney Morning Herald* and the Melbourne *Argus*.

May 1900  Publication of serialised novel *An Outback Marriage*, under the title, *In No Man's Land*.

1902  Publication of *Rio Grande's Last Race and Other Verses*.

1903  Married Alice Emily Walker.

1903–1906  Editor of the *Evening News*.

1904  Birth of daughter, Grace.

1906  Birth of son, Hugh Barton.

1906–1908  Editor of the *Town and Country Journal*.

1908–1912  Lived at "Coodra Vale" near Wee Jasper, N.S.W.

1912  Moved to property at Grenfell, N.S.W.

1914–1918  World War I.

September 1914  To England seeking work as war correspondent, but unsuccessful.

1915  Ambulance driver in France. Returned to Australia and commissioned as Lieutenant in Remount Division.

1915–1919  Served in A.I.F., rose to the rank of Major. Served in the Middle East.

1917  Publication of *Saltbush Bill, J.P., and Other Verses*.
      Publication of prose sketches *Three Elephant Power and Other Stories*.
1921  First publication of *Collected Verse*.
1922–1930  Editor of the *Sydney Sportsman*.
1933 Publication of *The Animals Noah Forgot*.
1934 Publication of *Happy Dispatches* (personal reminiscences).
1936 Publication of *The Shearer's Colt*, a novel.
1 January 1939 Appointed Commander of the British Empire.
5 February 1941 Died in Sydney.

# THE MAN FROM SNOWY RIVER AND OTHER VERSES

# Prelude

I have gathered these stories afar,
    In the wind and the rain,
In the land where the cattle camps are,
    On the edge of the plain.
On the overland routes of the West,
    When the watches were long,
I have fashioned in earnest and jest
    These fragments of song.

They are just the rude stories one hears
    In sadness and mirth,
The records of wandering years,
    And scant is their worth.
Though their merits indeed are but slight,
    I shall not repine,
If they give you one moment's delight,
    Old comrades of mine.

# The Man from Snowy River

There was movement at the station, for the word had passed around
That the colt from old Regret had got away,
And had joined the wild bush horses — he was worth a thousand pound,
So all the cracks had gathered to the fray.
All the tried and noted riders from the stations near and far
Had mustered at the homestead overnight,
For the bushmen love hard riding where the wild bush horses are,
And the stock horse snuffs the battle with delight.

There was Harrison, who made his pile when Pardon won the cup,
The old man with his hair as white as snow;
But few could ride beside him when his blood was fairly up —
He would go wherever horse and man could go.
And Clancy of the Overflow came down to lend a hand,
No better horseman ever held the reins;
For never horse could throw him while the saddle girths would stand,
He learnt to ride while droving on the plains.

And one was there, a stripling on a small and weedy beast,
He was something like a racehorse undersized,
With a touch of Timor pony — three parts thoroughbred at least —
And such as are by mountain horsemen prized.
He was hard and tough and wiry — just the sort that won't say die —
There was courage in his quick impatient tread;
And he bore the badge of gameness in his bright and fiery eye,
And the proud and lofty carriage of his head.

But still so slight and weedy, one would doubt his power to stay,
And the old man said, "That horse will never do
For a long and tiring gallop — lad, you'd better stop away,
Those hills are far too rough for such as you."
So he waited sad and wistful — only Clancy stood his friend —
"I think we ought to let him come," he said;
"I warrant he'll be with us when he's wanted at the end,
For both his horse and he are mountain bred.

"He hails from Snowy River, up by Kosciusko's side,
Where the hills are twice as steep and twice as rough,

4

Where a horse's hoofs strike firelight from the flint stones every stride,
The man that holds his own is good enough.
And the Snowy River riders on the mountains make their home,
Where the river runs those giant hills between;
I have seen full many horsemen since I first commenced to roam,
But nowhere yet such horsemen have I seen."

So he went — they found the horses by the big mimosa clump —
They raced away towards the mountain's brow,
And the old man gave his orders, "Boys, go at them from the jump,
No use to try for fancy riding now.
And, Clancy, you must wheel them, try and wheel them to the right.
Ride boldly, lad, and never fear the spills,
For never yet was rider that could keep the mob in sight,
If once they gain the shelter of those hills."

So Clancy rode to wheel them — he was racing on the wing
Where the best and boldest riders take their place,
And he raced his stockhorse past them, and he made the ranges ring
With the stockwhip, as he met them face to face.
Then they halted for a moment, while he swung the dreaded lash,
But they saw their well-loved mountain full in view,
And they charged beneath the stockwhip with a sharp and sudden dash,
And off into the mountain scrub they flew.

Then fast the horsemen followed, where the gorges deep and black
Resounded to the thunder of their tread,
And the stockwhips woke the echoes, and they fiercely answered back
From cliffs and crags that beetled overhead.
And upward, ever upward, the wild horses held their way,
Where mountain ash and kurrajong grew wide;
And the old man muttered fiercely, "We may bid the mob good day,
*No* man can hold them down the other side."

When they reached the mountain's summit, even Clancy took a pull,
It well might make the boldest hold their breath,
The wild hop scrub grew thickly, and the hidden ground was full
Of wombat holes, and any slip was death.
But the man from Snowy River let the pony have his head,
And he swung his stockwhip round and gave a cheer,
And he raced him down the mountain like a torrent down its bed,
While the others stood and watched in very fear.

He sent the flint stones flying, but the pony kept his feet,
He cleared the fallen timber in his stride,
And the man from Snowy River never shifted in his seat —
It was grand to see that mountain horseman ride.
Through the stringybarks and saplings, on the rough and broken ground,
Down the hillside at a racing pace he went;
And he never drew the bridle till he landed safe and sound,
At the bottom of that terrible descent.

He was right among the horses as they climbed the further hill,
And the watchers on the mountain standing mute,
Saw him ply the stockwhip fiercely, he was right among them still,
As he raced across the clearing in pursuit.
Then they lost him for a moment, where two mountain gullies met
In the ranges, but a final glimpse reveals
On a dim and distant hillside the wild horses racing yet,
With the man from Snowy River at their heels.

And he ran them single-handed till their sides were white with foam.
He followed like a bloodhound on their track,
Till they halted cowed and beaten, then he turned their heads for home,
And alone and unassisted brought them back.
But his hardy mountain pony he could scarcely raise a trot,
He was blood from hip to shoulder from the spur;
But his pluck was still undaunted, and his courage fiery hot,
For never yet was mountain horse a cur.

And down by Kosciusko, where the pine-clad ridges raise
Their torn and rugged battlements on high,
Where the air is clear as crystal, and the white stars fairly blaze
At midnight in the cold and frosty sky,
And where around The Overflow the reed beds sweep and sway
To the breezes, and the rolling plains are wide,
The man from Snowy River is a household word today,
And the stockmen tell the story of his ride.

# Old Pardon the Son
## of Reprieve

Y ou never heard tell of the story?
    Well, now, I can hardly believe!
Never heard of the honour and glory
    Of Pardon, the son of Reprieve?
But maybe you're only a Johnnie
    And don't know a horse from a hoe?
Well, well, don't get angry, my sonny,
    But, really, a young 'un should know.

They bred him out back on the "Never",
    His mother was Mameluke breed.
To the front — and then stay there — was ever
    The root of the Mameluke creed.
He seemed to inherit their wiry
    Strong frames — and their pluck to receive —
As hard as a flint and as fiery
    Was Pardon, the son of Reprieve.

We ran him at many a meeting
    At crossing and gully and town,
And nothing could give him a beating —
    As least when our money was down.
For weight wouldn't stop him, nor distance,
    Nor odds, though the others were fast,
He'd race with a dogged persistence,
    And wear them all down at the last.

At the Turon the Yattendon filly
    Led by lengths at the mile and a half,
And we all began to look silly,
    While *her* crowd were starting to laugh;
But the old horse came faster and faster,
    His pluck told its tale, and his strength,
He gained on her, caught her, and passed her,
    And won it, hands down, by a length.

And then we swooped down on Menindie
    To run for the President's Cup —
Oh! that's a sweet township — a shindy
    To them is board, lodging, and sup.
Eye-openers they are, and their system
    Is never to suffer defeat;
It's "win, tie, or wrangle" — to best 'em
    You must lose 'em, or else it's "dead heat".

We strolled down the township and found 'em
    At drinking and gaming and play;
If sorrows they had, why they drowned 'em,
    And betting was soon under way.
Their horses were good 'uns and fit 'uns,
    There was plenty of cash in the town;
They backed their own horses like Britons,
    And Lord! how *we* rattled it down!

With gladness we thought of the morrow,
    We counted our wagers with glee,
A simile homely to borrow —
    "There was plenty of milk in our tea".
You see we were green; and we never
    Had even a thought of foul play,
Though we well might have known that the clever
    Division would "put us away".

Experience "*docet*", they tell us,
    At least so I've frequently heard,
But, "dosing" or "stuffing", those fellows
    Were up to each move on the board;
They got to his stall — it is sinful
    To think what such villains would do —
And they gave him a regular skinful
    Of barley — green barley — to chew.

He munched it all night, and we found him
    Next morning as full as a hog —
The girths wouldn't nearly meet round him;
    He looked like an overfed frog.
We saw we were done like a dinner —
    The odds were a thousand to one

Against Pardon turning up winner,
    'Twas cruel to ask him to run.

We got to the course with our troubles,
    A crestfallen couple were we;
And we heard the "books" calling the doubles —
    A roar like the surf of the sea;
And over the tumult and louder
    Rang, "Any price Pardon, I lay!"
Says Jimmy, "The children of Judah
    Are out on the warpath to-day."

Three miles in three heats: Ah, my sonny
    The horses in those days were stout,
They had to run well to win money;
    I don't see such horses about.
Your six-furlong vermin that scamper
    Half a mile with their featherweight up;
They wouldn't earn much of their damper
    In a race like the President's Cup.

The first heat was soon set a-going;
    The Dancer went off to the front;
The Don on his quarters was showing,
    With Pardon right out of the hunt.
He rolled and he weltered and wallowed —
    You'd kick your hat faster, I'll bet;
They finished all bunched, and he followed
    All lathered and dripping with sweat.

But troubles came thicker upon us,
    For while we were rubbing him dry
The stewards came over to warn us:
    "We hear you are running a bye!
If Pardon don't spiel like tarnation
    And win the next heat — if he can —
He'll earn a disqualification;
    Just think over *that*, now, my man!"

Our money all gone and our credit,
    Our horse couldn't gallop a yard;
And then people thought that *we* did it!
    It really was terribly hard.

We were objects of mirth and derision
    To folk in the lawn and the stand,
And the yells of the clever division
    Of "Any price, Pardon!" were grand.

We still had a chance for the money,
    Two heats still remained to be run;
If both fell to us — why, my sonny,
    The clever division were done.
And Pardon was better, we reckoned,
    His sickness was passing away,
So he went to the post for the second
    And principal heat of the day.

They're off and away with a rattle,
    Like dogs from the leashes let slip,
And right at the back of the battle
    He followed them under the whip.
They gained ten good lengths on him quickly,
    He dropped right away from the pack;
I tell you it made me feel sickly
    To see the blue jacket fall back.

Our very last hope had departed —
    We thought the old fellow was done,
When all of a sudden he started
    To go like a shot from a gun.
His chances seemed slight to embolden
    Our hearts; but, with teeth firmly set,
We thought, "Now or never! The old 'un
    May reckon with some of 'em yet."

Then loud rose the warcry for Pardon;
    He swept like the wind down the dip,
And over the rise by the garden,
    The jockey was done with the whip;
The field were at sixes and sevens —
    The pace at the first had been fast —
And hope seemed to drop from the heavens,
    For Pardon was coming at last.

And how he did come! It was splendid;
    He gained on them yards every bound,

Stretching out like a greyhound extended,
    His girth laid right down on the ground.
A shimmer of silk in the cedars
    As into the running they wheeled,
And out flashed the whips on the leaders,
    For Pardon had collared the field.

Then right through the ruck he came sailing —
    I knew that the battle was won —
The son of Haphazard was failing,
    The Yattendon filly was done;
He cut down the Don and the Dancer,
    He raced clean away from the mare —
He's in front! Catch him now if you can, sir!
    And up went my hat in the air!

Then loud from the lawn and the garden
    Rose offers of "Ten to one *on*!"
"Who'll bet on the field? I back Pardon!"
    No use; all the money was gone.
He came for the third heat light-hearted,
    A-jumping and dancing about;
The others were done ere they started
    Crestfallen, and tired, and worn out.

He won it, and ran it much faster
    Than even the first, I believe;
Oh, he was the daddy, the master,
    Was Pardon, the son of Reprieve.
He showed 'em the method to travel —
    The boy sat as still as a stone —
They never could see him for gravel;
    He came in hard-held and alone.

\* \* \* \*

But he's old — and his eyes are grown hollow;
    Like me, with my thatch of the snow;
When he dies, then I hope I may follow,
    And go where the racehorses go,
I don't want no harping nor singing —
    Such things with my style don't agree;
Where the hoofs of the horses are ringing
    There's music sufficient for me.

And surely the thoroughbred horses
    Will rise up again and begin
Fresh races on faraway courses
    And p'raps they might let me slip in.
It would look rather well the race card on
    'Mongst cherubs and seraphs and things,
"Angel Harrison's black gelding Pardon,
    Blue halo, white body and wings".

And if they have racing hereafter,
    (And who is to say they will not?)
When the cheers and the shouting and laughter
    Proclaim that the battle grows hot;
As they come down the racecourse a-steering,
    He'll rush to the front, I believe;
And you'll hear the great multitude cheering
    For Pardon, the son of Reprieve.

# Clancy of The Overflow

I had written him a letter which I had, for want of better
  Knowledge, sent to where I met him down the Lachlan, years ago;
He was shearing when I knew him, so I sent the letter to him,
    Just "on spec", addressed as follows: "Clancy, of The Overflow".

And an answer came directed in a writing unexpected,
    (And I think the same was written with a thumbnail dipped in tar);
'Twas his shearing mate who wrote it, and *verbatim* I will quote it:
    "Clancy's gone to Queensland droving, and we don't know where he are."

\* \* \* \*

In my wild erratic fancy visions come to me of Clancy
    Gone a-droving "down the Cooper" where the Western drovers go;
As the stock are slowly stringing, Clancy rides behind them singing,
    For the drover's life has pleasures that the townsfolk never know.

And the bush hath friends to meet him, and their kindly voices greet him
    In the murmur of the breezes and the river on its bars,
And he sees the vision splendid of the sunlit plains extended,
    And at night the wondrous glory of the everlasting stars.

\* \* \* \*

I am sitting in my dingy little office, where a stingy
    Ray of sunlight struggles feebly down between the houses tall,
And the foetid air and gritty of the dusty, dirty city
    Through the open window floating, spreads its foulness over all.

And in place of lowing cattle, I can hear the fiendish rattle
    Of the tramways and the buses making hurry down the street,
And the language uninviting of the gutter children fighting
    Comes fitfully and faintly through the ceaseless tramp of feet.

And the hurrying people daunt me, and their pallid faces haunt me
    As they shoulder one another in their rush and nervous haste,
With their eager eyes and greedy, and their stunted forms and weedy,
    For townsfolk have no time to grow, they have no time to waste.

And I somehow rather fancy that I'd like to change with Clancy,
    Like to take a turn at droving where the seasons come and go,
While he faced the round eternal of the cashbook and the journal —
    But I doubt he'd suit the office, Clancy, of "The Overflow".

# Conroy's Gap

This was the way of it, don't you know —
    Ryan was "wanted" for stealing sheep,
And never a trooper, high or low,
    Could find him — catch a weasel asleep!
Till Trooper Scott, from the Stockman's Ford —
    A bushman, too, as I've heard them tell —
Chanced to find him drunk as a lord
    Round at the Shadow of Death Hotel.

D' you know the place? It's a wayside inn,
    A low grog-shanty — a bushman trap,
Hiding away in its shame and sin
    Under the shelter of Conroy's Gap —
Under the shade of that frowning range,
    The roughest crowd that ever drew breath —
Thieves and rowdies, uncouth and strange,
    Were mustered round at the Shadow of Death.

The trooper knew that his man would slide
    Like a dingo pup, if he saw the chance;
And with half a start on the mountain side
    Ryan would lead him a merry dance.
Drunk as he was when the trooper came,
    To him that did not matter a rap —
Drunk or sober, he was the same,
    The boldest rider in Conroy's Gap.

"I want you, Ryan," the trooper said,
    "And listen to me, if you dare resist,
So help me heaven, I'll shoot you dead!"
    He snapped the steel on his prisoner's wrist,
And Ryan, hearing the handcuffs click,
    Recovered his wits as they turned to go,
For fright will sober a man as quick
    As all the drugs that the doctors know.

There was a girl in that rough bar
    Went by the name of Kate Carew,

Quiet and shy as the bush girls are,
    But ready-witted and plucky, too.
She loved this Ryan, or so they say,
    And passing by, while her eyes were dim
With tears, she said in a careless way,
    "The Swagman's round in the stable, Jim."

Spoken too low for the trooper's ear,
    Why should she care if he heard or not?
Plenty of swagmen far and near,
    And yet to Ryan it meant a lot.
That was the name of the grandest horse
    In all the district from east to west;
In every show ring, on every course
    They always counted the Swagman best.

He was a wonder, a raking bay —
    One of the grand old Snowdon strain —
One of the sort that could race and stay
    With his mighty limbs and his length of rein.
Born and bred on the mountain side,
    He could race through scrub like a kangaroo,
The girl herself on his back might ride,
    And the Swagman would carry her safely through.

He would travel gaily from daylight's flush
    Till after the stars hung out their lamps,
There was never his like in the open bush,
    And never his match on the cattle camps.
For faster horses might well be found
    On racing tracks, or a plain's extent,
But few, if any, on broken ground
    Could see the way that the Swagman went.

When this girl's father, old Jim Carew,
    Was droving out on the Castlereagh
With Conroy's cattle, a wire came through
    To say that his wife couldn't live the day.
And he was a hundred miles from home,
    As flies the crow, with never a track,
Through plains as pathless as ocean's foam,
    He mounted straight on the Swagman's back.

He left the camp by the sundown light,
      And the settlers out on the Marthaguy
Awoke and heard, in the dead of night,
      A single horseman hurrying by.
He crossed the Bogan at Dandaloo,
      And many a mile of the silent plain
That lonely rider behind him threw
      Before they settled to sleep again.

He rode all night and he steercd his course
      By the shining stars with a bushman's skill,
And every time that he pressed his horse
      The Swagman answered him gamely still.
He neared his home as the east was bright,
      The doctor met him outside the town:
"Carew! How far did you come last night?"
      "A hundred miles since the sun went down."

And his wife got round, and an oath he passed,
      So long as he or one of his breed
Could raise a coin, though it took their last
      The Swagman never should want a feed.
And Kate Carew, when her father died,
      She kept the horse and she kept him well:
The pride of the district far and wide,
      He lived in style at the bush hotel.

Such was the Swagman; and Ryan knew
      Nothing about could pace the crack;
Little he'd care for the man in blue
      If once he got on the Swagman's back.
But how to do it? A word let fall
      Gave him the hint as the girl passed by;
Nothing but "Swagman — stable-wall;
      Go to the stable and mind your eye."

He caught her meaning, and quickly turned
      To the trooper: "Reckon you'll gain a stripe
By arresting me, and it's easily earned;
      Let's go to the stable and get my pipe,
The Swagman has it." So off they went,
      And soon as ever they turned their backs

16

The girl slipped down, on some errand bent
    Behind the stable, and seized an axe.

The trooper stood at the stable door
    While Ryan went in quite cool and slow,
And then (the trick had been played before)
    The girl outside gave the wall a blow.
Three slabs fell out of the stable wall —
    'Twas done 'fore ever the trooper knew —
And Ryan, as soon as he saw them fall,
    Mounted the Swagman and rushed him through.

The trooper heard the hoofbeats ring
    In the stable yard, and he slammed the gate,
But the Swagman rose with a mighty spring
    At the fence, and the trooper fired too late,
As they raced away and his shots flew wide
    And Ryan no longer need care a rap,
For never a horse that was lapped in hide
    Could catch the Swagman in Conroy's Gap.

And that's the story. You want to know
    If Ryan came back to his Kate Carew;
Of course he should have, as stories go,
    But the worst of it is, this story's true:
And in real life it's a certain rule,
    Whatever poets and authors say
Of high-toned robbers and all their school,
    These horse thief fellows aren't built that way.

Come back! Don't hope it — the slinking hound,
    He sloped across to the Queensland side,
And sold the Swagman for fifty pound,
    And stole the money, and more beside.
And took to drink, and by some good chance
    Was killed — thrown out of a stolen trap.
And that was the end of this small romance,
    The end of the story of Conroy's Gap.

# *Our New Horse*

The boys had come back from the races
    All silent and down on their luck;
They'd backed 'em, straight out and for places,
    But never a winner they struck.
They lost their good money on Slogan,
    And fell most uncommonly flat,
When Partner, the pride of the Bogan,
    Was beaten by Aristocrat.

And one said, "I move that instanter
    We sell out our horses and quit,
The brutes ought to win in a canter,
    Such trials they do when they're fit.
The last one they ran was a snorter —
    A gallop to gladden one's heart —
Two-twelve for a mile and a quarter,
    And finished as straight as a dart.

"And then when I think that they're ready
    To win me a nice little swag,
They are licked like the veriest neddy —
    They're licked from the fall of the flag.
The mare held her own to the stable,
    She died out to nothing at that,
And Partner he never seemed able
    To pace it with Aristocrat.

"And times have been bad, and the seasons
    Don't promise to be of the best;
In short, boys, there's plenty of reasons
    For giving the racing a rest.
The mare can be kept on the station —
    Her breeding is good as can be —
But Partner, his next destination
    Is rather a trouble to me.

"We can't sell him here, for they know him
    As well as the clerk of the course;

He's raced and won races till, blow him,
    He's done as a handicap horse.
A jady, uncertain performer,
    They weight him right out of the hunt,
And clap it on warmer and warmer
    Whenever he gets near the front.

"It's no use to paint him or dot him
    Or put any 'fake' on his brand,
For bushmen are smart, and they'd spot him
    In any saleyard in the land.
The folk about here could all tell him,
    Could swear to each separate hair;
Let us send him to Sydney and sell him,
    There's plenty of Jugginses there.

"We'll call him a maiden, and treat 'em
    To trials will open their eyes,
We'll run their best horses and beat 'em,
    And then won't they think him a prize.
I pity the fellow that buys him,
    He'll find in a very short space,
No matter how highly he tries him,
    The beggar won't *race* in a race."

* * * *

Next week, under "Seller and Buyer",
    Appeared in the *Daily Gazette*:
"A racehorse for sale, and a flyer;
    Has never been started as yet;
A trial will show what his pace is;
    The buyer can get him in light,
And win all the handicap races.
    Apply here before Wednesday night."

He sold for a hundred and thirty,
    Because of a gallop he had
One morning with Bluefish and Bertie,
    And donkey-licked both of 'em bad.
And when the old horse had departed,
    The life on the station grew tame;
The racetrack was dull and deserted,
    The boys had gone back on the game.

19

The winter rolled by, and the station
    Was green with the garland of spring,
A spirit of glad exultation
    Awoke in each animate thing.
And all the old love, the old longing,
    Broke out in the breasts of the boys,
The visions of racing came thronging
    With all its delirious joys.

The rushing of floods in their courses,
    The rattle of rain on the roofs
Recalled the fierce rush of the horses,
    The thunder of galloping hoofs.
And soon one broke out: "I can suffer
    No longer the life of a slug,
The man that don't race is a duffer,
    Let's have one more run for the mug.

"Why, *everything* races, no matter
    Whatever its method may be:
The waterfowl hold a regatta;
    The possums run heats up a tree;
The emus are constantly sprinting
    A handicap out on the plain;
It seems like all nature was hinting,
    'Tis time to be at it again.

"The cockatoo parrots are talking
    Of races to faraway lands;
The native companions are walking
    A go-as-you-please on the sands;
The little foals gallop for pastime;
    The wallabies race down the gap;
Let's try it once more for the last time,
    Bring out the old jacket and cap.

"And now for a horse; we might try one
    Of those that are bred on the place,
But I think it better to buy one,
    A horse that has proved he can race.
Let us send down to Sydney to Skinner,
    A thorough good judge who can ride,

And ask him to buy us a spinner
    To clean out the whole countryside."

They wrote him a letter as follows:
    "We want you to buy us a horse;
He must have the speed to catch swallows,
    And stamina with it of course.
The price aint a thing that'll grieve us,
    It's getting a bad 'un annoys
The undersigned blokes, and believe us,
    We're yours to a cinder, 'The boys'."

He answered: "I've bought you a hummer,
    A horse that has never been raced;
I saw him run over the Drummer,
    He held him outclassed and outpaced.
His breeding's not known, but they state he
    Is born of a thoroughbred strain,
I paid them a hundred and eighty,
    And started the horse in the train."

They met him — alas, that these verses
    Aren't up to the subject's demands —
Can't set forth their eloquent curses,
    *For Partner was back on their hands.*
They went in to meet him in gladness,
    They opened his box with delight —
A silent procession of sadness
    They crept to the station at night.

And life has grown dull on the station,
    The boys are all silent and slow;
Their work is a daily vexation,
    And sport is unknown to them now.
Whenever they think how they stranded,
    They squeal just like guinea-pigs squeal;
They bit their own hook, and were landed
    With fifty pounds' loss on the deal.

# An Idyll of Dandaloo

On Western plains, where shade is not,
    'Neath summer skies of cloudless blue,
Where all is dry and all is hot,
        There stands the town of Dandaloo —
A township where life's total sum
Is sleep, diversified with rum.

Its grass-grown streets with dust are deep,
    'Twere vain endeavour to express
The dreamless silence of its sleep,
        Its wide, expansive drunkenness.
The yearly races mostly drew
A lively crowd to Dandaloo.

There came a sportsman from the East,
    The eastern land where sportsmen blow,
And brought with him a speedy beast —
        A speedy beast as horses go.
He came afar in hope to "do"
The little town of Dandaloo.

Now this was weak of him, I wot —
    Exceeding weak, it seemed to me —
For we in Dandaloo were not
        The Jugginses we seemed to be;
In fact, we rather thought we knew
Our book by heart in Dandaloo.

We held a meeting at the bar,
    And met the question fair and square —
"We've stumped the country near and far
        To raise the cash for races here;
We've got a hundred pounds or two —
Not half so bad for Dandaloo.

"And now, it seems, we have to be
    Cleaned out by this here Sydney bloke,
With his imported horse; and he
        Will scoop the pool and leave us broke.

Shall we sit still, and make no fuss
While this chap climbs all over us?"

* * * *

The races came to Dandaloo,
        And all the cornstalks from the West,
On ev'ry kind of moke and screw,
        Came forth in all their glory drest.
The stranger's horse, as hard as nails,
Look'd fit to run for New South Wales.

He won the race by half a length —
        *Quite* half a length, it seemed to me —
But Dandaloo, with all its strength,
        Roared out, "Dead heat!" most fervently;
And, after hesitation meet,
The judge's verdict was "Dead heat!"

And many men there were could tell
        What gave the verdict extra force:
The stewards, and the judge as well —
        They all had backed the second horse.
For things like this they sometimes do
In larger towns than Dandaloo.

They ran it off; the stranger won,
        Hands down, by near a hundred yards.
He smiled to think his troubles done;
        But Dandaloo held all the cards.
They went to scale and — cruel fate! —
His jockey turned out underweight.

Perhaps they'd tampered with the scale!
        I cannot tell. I only know
It weighed him *out* all right. I fail
        To paint that Sydney sportsman's woe.
He said the stewards were a crew
Of low-lived thieves in Dandaloo.

He lifted up his voice, irate,
        And swore till all the air was blue;
So then we rose to vindicate
        The dignity of Dandaloo.

"Look here," said we, "you must not poke
Such oaths at us poor country folk."

We rode him softly on a rail,
    We shied at him, in careless glee,
Some large tomatoes, rank and stale,
    And eggs of great antiquity —
Their wild, unholy fragrance flew
About the town of Dandaloo.

He left the town at break of day,
    He led his racehorse through the streets,
And now he tells the tale, they say,
    To every racing man he meets.
And Sydney sportsmen all eschew
The atmosphere of Dandaloo.

# The Geebung Polo Club

It was somewhere up the country, in a land of rock and scrub,
That they formed an institution called the Geebung Polo Club.
They were long and wiry natives from the rugged mountainside,
And the horse was never saddled that the Geebungs couldn't ride;
But their style of playing polo was irregular and rash —
They had mighty little science, but a mighty lot of dash:
And they played on mountain ponies that were muscular and strong,
Though their coats were quite unpolished, and their manes and tails
      were long.
And they used to train those ponies wheeling cattle in the scrub:
They were demons, were the members of the Geebung Polo Club.

It was somewhere down the country, in a city's smoke and steam,
That a polo club existed, called the Cuff and Collar Team.
As a social institution 'twas a marvellous success,
For the members were distinguished by exclusiveness and dress.
They had natty little ponies that were nice, and smooth, and sleek,
For their cultivated owners only rode 'em once a week.
So they started up the country in pursuit of sport and fame,
For they meant to show the Geebungs how they ought to play the game;
And they took their valets with them — just to give their boots a rub
Ere they started operations on the Geebung Polo Club.

Now my readers can imagine how the contest ebbed and flowed,
When the Geebung boys got going it was time to clear the road;
And the game was so terrific that ere half the time was gone
A spectator's leg was broken — just from merely looking on.
For they waddied one another till the plain was strewn with dead,
While the score was kept so even that they neither got ahead.
And the Cuff and Collar captain, when he tumbled off to die,
Was the last surviving player — so the game was called a tie.

Then the captain of the Geebungs raised him slowly from the ground,
Though his wounds were mostly mortal, yet he fiercely gazed around;
There was no one to oppose him — all the rest were in a trance,
So he scrambled on his pony for his last expiring chance,
For he meant to make an effort to get victory to his side;
So he struck at goal — and missed it — then he tumbled off and died.

\* \* \* \*

By the old Campaspe River, where the breezes shake the grass,
There's a row of little gravestones that the stockmen never pass,
For they bear a crude inscription saying, "Stranger, drop a tear,
For the Cuff and Collar players and the Geebung boys lie here."
And on misty moonlit evenings, while the dingoes howl around,
You can see their shadows flitting down that phantom polo ground;
You can hear the loud collisions as the flying players meet,
And the rattle of the mallets, and the rush of ponies' feet,
Till the terrified spectator rides like blazes to the pub —
He's been haunted by the spectres of the Geebung Polo Club.

# The Travelling Post Office

The roving breezes come and go, the reed beds sweep and sway,
The sleepy river murmurs low, and loiters on its way,
It is the land of lots o' time along the Castlereagh.

\* \* \* \*

The old man's son had left the farm, he found it dull and slow,
He drifted to the great North-west where all the rovers go.
"He's gone so long," the old man said, "he's dropped right out of mind,
But if you'd write a line to him I'd take it very kind;
He's shearing here and fencing there, a kind of waif and stray,
He's droving now with Conroy's sheep along the Castlereagh.
The sheep are travelling for the grass, and travelling very slow;
They may be at Mundooran now, or past the Overflow,
Or tramping down the black soil flats across by Waddiwong,
But all those little country towns would send the letter wrong,
The mailman, if he's extra tired, would pass them in his sleep,
It's safest to address the note to 'Care of Conroy's sheep',
For five and twenty thousand head can scarcely go astray,
You write to 'Care of Conroy's sheep along the Castlereagh'."

\* \* \* \*

By rock and ridge and riverside the western mail has gone,
Across the great Blue Mountain Range to take that letter on.
A moment on the topmost grade while open fire doors glare,
She pauses like a living thing to breathe the mountain air,
Then launches down the other side across the plains away
To bear that note to "Conroy's sheep along the Castlereagh".

And now by coach and mailman's bag it goes from town to town,
And Conroy's Gap and Conroy's Creek have marked it "further down".
Beneath a sky of deepest blue where never cloud abides,
A speck upon the waste of plain the lonely mailman rides.
Where fierce hot winds have set the pine and myall boughs asweep
He hails the shearers passing by for news of Conroy's sheep.
By big lagoons where wildfowl play and crested pigeons flock,
By campfires where the drovers ride around their restless stock,
And past the teamster toiling down to fetch the wool away
My letter chases Conroy's sheep along the Castlereagh.

# Saltbush Bill

Now this is the law of the Overland that all in the West obey,
A man must cover with travelling sheep a six-mile stage a day;
But this is the law which the drovers make, right easily understood,
They travel their stage where the grass is bad, but they camp where
      the grass is good;
They camp, and they ravage the squatter's grass till never a blade remains,
Then they drift away as the white clouds drift on the edge of the
      saltbush plains,
From camp to camp and from run to run they battle it hand to hand,
For a blade of grass and the right to pass on the track of the Overland.

For this is the law of the Great Stock Routes, 'tis written in
      white and black —
The man that goes with a travelling mob must keep to a half-mile track;
And the drovers keep to a half-mile track on the runs where the
      grass is dead,
But they spread their sheep on a well-grassed run till they go with
      a two-mile spread.
So the squatters hurry the drovers on from dawn till the fall of night,
And the squatters' dogs and the drovers' dogs get mixed in a
      deadly fight;
Yet the squatters' men, though they hunt the mob, are willing the
      peace to keep,
For the drovers learn how to use their hands when they go with the
      travelling sheep;
But this is the tale of a Jackaroo that came from a foreign strand,
And the fight that he fought with Saltbush Bill, the King of the Overland.

Now Saltbush Bill was a drover tough, as ever the country knew,
He had fought his way on the Great Stock Routes from the sea to
      the Big Barcoo;
He could tell when he came to a friendly run that gave him a chance
      to spread,
And he knew where the hungry owners were that hurried his sheep ahead;
He was drifting down in the Eighty drought with a mob that
      could scarcely creep,
(When the kangaroos by the thousands starve, it is rough on the
      travelling sheep.)

And he camped one night at the crossing place on the edge of the
      Wilga run,
"We must manage a feed for them here," he said, "or the half of
      the mob are done!"

So he spread them out when they left the camp wherever they liked to go,
Till he grew aware of a Jackaroo with a station hand in tow,
And they set to work on the straggling sheep, and with many a
      stockwhip crack
They forced them in where the grass was dead in the space of the
      half-mile track;
So William prayed that the hand of fate might suddenly strike him blue
But he'd get some grass for his starving sheep in the teeth of that Jackaroo.
So he turned and he cursed the Jackaroo, he cursed him alive or dead,
From the soles of his great unwieldy feet to the crown of his ugly head,
With an extra curse on the moke he rode and the cur at his heels that ran,
Till the Jackaroo from his horse got down and he went for the drover man;
With the station hand for his picker-up, though the sheep ran loose
      the while,
They battled it out on the saltbush plain in the regular prize ring style.

Now, the new chum fought for his honour's sake and the pride of
      the English race,
But the drover fought for his daily bread with a smile on his bearded face;
So he shifted ground and he sparred for wind and he made it a lengthy mill,
And from time to time as his scouts came in they whispered to Saltbush Bill —
"We have spread the sheep with a two-mile spread, and the grass it is
      something grand,
You must stick to him, Bill, for another round for the pride of the
      Overland."

The new chum made it a rushing fight, though never a blow got home,
Till the sun rode high in the cloudless sky and glared on
      the brick-red loam,
Till the sheep drew in to the shelter trees and settled them down to rest,
Then the drover said he would fight no more and he gave his opponent best.
So the new chum rode to the homestead straight and he told them
      a story grand
Of the desperate fight that he fought that day with the King of
      the Overland.
And the tale went home to the public schools of the pluck of
      the English swell,

How the drover fought for his very life, but blood in the end must tell.
But the travelling sheep and the Wilga sheep were boxed on
      the Old Man Plain.
'Twas a full week's work ere they drafted out and hunted them off again,
With a week's good grass in their wretched hides, with a curse and a
      stockwhip crack,
They hunted them off on the road once more to starve on the half-mile track.
And Saltbush Bill, on the Overland, will many a time recite
How the best day's work that ever he did was the day that he lost the fight.

# A Mountain Station

I bought a run a while ago,
  On country rough and ridgy,
Where wallaroos and wombats grow —
  The Upper Murrumbidgee.
The grass is rather scant, it's true,
  But this a fair exchange is,
The sheep can see a lovely view
  By climbing up the ranges.

And "She-oak Flat" 's the station's name,
  I'm not surprised at that, sirs:
The oaks were there before I came,
  And I supplied the flat, sirs.
A man would wonder how it's done,
  The stock so soon decreases —
They sometimes tumble off the run
  And break themselves to pieces.

I've tried to make expenses meet,
  But wasted all my labours,
The sheep the dingoes didn't eat
  Were stolen by the neighbours.
They stole my pears — my native pears —
  Those thrice-convicted felons,
And ravished from me unawares
  My crop of paddymelons.

And sometimes under sunny skies,
  Without an explanation,
The Murrumbidgee used to rise
  And overflow the station.
But this was caused (as now I know)
  When summer sunshine glowing
Had melted all Kiandra's snow
  And set the river going.

And in the news, perhaps you read:
  "Stock passings. Puckawidgee,
Fat cattle: Seven hundred head

Swept down the Murrumbidgee;
Their destination's quite obscure,
    But, somehow, there's a notion,
Unless the river falls, they're sure
    To reach the Southern Ocean."

So after that I'll give it best;
    No more with Fate I'll battle.
I'll let the river take the rest,
    For those were all my cattle.
And with one comprehensive curse
    I close my brief narration,
And advertise it in my verse —
    "For Sale! A Mountain Station".

# Been There Before

There came a stranger to Walgett town,
    To Walgett town when the sun was low,
And he carried a thirst that was worth a crown,
    Yet how to quench it he did not know;
But he thought he might take those yokels down,
The guileless yokels of Walgett town.

They made him a bet in a private bar,
    In a private bar when the talk was high,
And they bet him some pounds no matter how far
    He could pelt a stone, yet he could not shy
A stone right over the river so brown,
The Darling River at Walgett town.

He knew that the river from bank to bank
    Was fifty yards, and he smiled a smile
As he trundled down, but his hopes they sank
    For there wasn't a stone within fifty mile;
For the saltbush plain and the open down
Produce no quarries in Walgett town.

The yokels laughed at his hopes o'erthrown,
    And he stood awhile like a man in a dream;
Then out of his pocket he fetched a stone,
    And pelted it over the silent stream —
He had been there before: he had wandered down
On a previous visit to Walgett town.

# The Man Who Was Away

The widow sought the lawyer's room with children three in tow,
She told the lawyer man her tale in tones of deepest woe.
Said she, "My husband took to drink for pains in his inside,
And never drew a sober breath from then until he died.

"He never drew a sober breath, he died without a will,
And I must sell the bit of land the childer's mouths to fill.
There's some is grown and gone away, but some is childer yet,
And times is very bad indeed — a livin's hard to get.

"There's Min and Sis and little Chris, they stops at home with me,
And Sal has married Greenhide Bill that breaks for Bingeree.
And Fred is drovin' Conroy's sheep along the Castlereagh,
And Charley's shearin' down the Bland, and Peter is away."

The lawyer wrote the details down in ink of legal blue —
"There's Minnie, Susan, Christopher, they stop at home with you;
There's Sarah, Frederick and Charles, I'll write to them to-day,
But what about the other one — the one who is away?

"You'll have to furnish his consent to sell the bit of land."
The widow shuffled in her seat, "Oh, don't you understand?
I thought a lawyer ought to know — I don't know what to say —
You'll have to do without him, boss, for Peter is away."

But here the little boy spoke up — said he, "We thought you knew;
He's done six months in Goulburn gaol — he's got six more to do."
Thus in one comprehensive flash he made it clear as day,
The mystery of Peter's life — the man who was away.

# The Man from Ironbark

It was the man from Ironbark who struck the Sydney town,
He wandered over street and park, he wandered up and down.
He loitered here, he loitered there, till he was like to drop,
Until at last in sheer despair he sought a barber's shop.
" 'Ere! shave my beard and whiskers off, I'll be a man of mark,
I'll go and do the Sydney toff up home in Ironbark."

The barber man was small and flash, as barbers mostly are,
He wore a strike-your-fancy sash, he smoked a huge cigar;
He was a humorist of note and keen at repartee,
He laid the odds and kept a "tote", whatever that may be,
And when he saw our friend arrive, he whispered, "Here's a lark!
Just watch me catch him all alive, this man from Ironbark."

There were some gilded youths that sat along the barber's wall.
Their eyes were dull, their heads were flat, they had no brains at all;
To them the barber passed the wink, his dexter eyelid shut,
"I'll make this bloomin' yokel think his bloomin' throat is cut."
And as he soaped and rubbed it in he made a rude remark:
"I s'pose the flats is pretty green up there in Ironbark."

A grunt was all reply he got; he shaved the bushman's chin,
Then made the water boiling hot and dipped the razor in.
He raised his hand, his brow grew black, he paused awhile to gloat,
Then slashed the red-hot razor-back across his victim's throat;
Upon the newly-shaven skin it made a livid mark —
No doubt it fairly took him in — the man from Ironbark.

He fetched a wild up-country yell might wake the dead to hear,
And though his throat, he knew full well, was cut from ear to ear,
He struggled gamely to his feet, and faced the murd'rous foe:
"You've done for me! you dog, I'm beat! one hit before I go!
I only wish I had a knife, you blessed murdering shark!
But you'll remember all your life the man from Ironbark."

He lifted up his hairy paw, with one tremendous clout
He landed on the barber's jaw, and knocked the barber out.
He set to work with nail and tooth, he made the place a wreck;
He grabbed the nearest gilded youth, and tried to break his neck.

And all the while his throat he held to save his vital spark,
And "Murder! Bloody murder!" yelled the man from Ironbark.

A peelerman who heard the din came in to see the show;
He tried to run the bushman in, but he refused to go.
And when at last the barber spoke, and said " 'Twas all in fun —
'Twas just a little harmless joke, a trifle overdone."
"A joke!" he cried, "By George, that's fine; a lively sort of lark;
I'd like to catch that murdering swine some night in Ironbark."

And now while round the shearing floor the list'ning shearers gape,
He tells the story o'er and o'er, and brags of his escape.
"Them barber chaps what keeps a tote, By George, I've had enough,
One tried to cut my bloomin' throat, but thank the Lord it's tough."
And whether he's believed or no, there's one thing to remark,
That flowing beards are all the go way up in Ironbark.

# The Open Steeplechase

I had ridden over hurdles up the country once or twice,
By the side of Snowy River with a horse they called "The Ace".
And we brought him down to Sydney, and our rider, Jimmy Rice,
Got a fall and broke his shoulder, so they nabbed me in a trice —
Me, that never wore the colours, for the Open Steeplechase.

"Make the running," said the trainer, "it's your only chance whatever,
Make it hot from start to finish, for the old black horse can stay,
And just think of how they'll take it, when they hear on Snowy River
That the country boy was plucky, and the country horse was clever.
You must ride for old Monaro and the mountain boys today."

"Are you ready?" said the starter, as we held the horses back,
All ablazing with impatience, with excitement all aglow;
Before us like a ribbon stretched the steeplechasing track,
And the sunrays glistened brightly on the chestnut and the black
As the starter's words came slowly, "Are — you — ready? Go!"

Well, I scarcely knew we'd started, I was stupid-like with wonder
Till the field closed up beside me and a jump appeared ahead.
And we flew it like a hurdle, not a baulk and not a blunder,
As we charged it all together, and it fairly whistled under,
And then some were pulled behind me and a few shot out and led.

So we ran for half the distance, and I'm making no pretences
When I tell you I was feeling very nervous-like and queer,
For those jockeys rode like demons; you would think they'd lost their senses
If you saw them rush their horses at those rasping five foot fences —
And in place of making running I was falling to the rear.

Till a chap came racing past me on a horse they called "The Quiver",
And said he, "My country joker, are you going to give it best?
Are you frightened of the fences? Does their stoutness make you shiver?
Have they come to breeding cowards by the side of Snowy River?
Are there riders on Monaro? —" but I never heard the rest.

For I drove The Ace and sent him just as fast as he could pace it,
At the big black line of timber stretching fair across the track,
And he shot beside The Quiver. "Now," said I, "my boy, we'll race it.

You can come with Snowy River if you're only game to face it;
Let us mend the pace a little and we'll see who cries a crack."

So we raced away together, and we left the others standing,
And the people cheered and shouted as we settled down to ride,
And we clung beside The Quiver. At his taking off and landing
I could see his scarlet nostril and his mighty ribs expanding,
And The Ace stretched out in earnest and we held him stride for stride.

But the pace was so terrific that they soon ran out their tether —
They were rolling in their gallop, they were fairly blown and beat —
But they both were game as pebbles — neither one would show the feather.
And we rushed them at the fences, and they cleared them both together,
Nearly every time they clouted but they somehow kept their feet.

Then the last jump rose before us, and they faced it game as ever —
We were both at spur and whipcord, fetching blood at every bound —
And above the people's cheering and the cries of "Ace" and "Quiver",
I could hear the trainer shouting, "One more run for Snowy River".
Then we struck the jump together and came smashing to the ground.

Well, The Quiver ran to blazes, but The Ace stood still and waited,
Stood and waited like a statue while I scrambled on his back.
There was no one next or near me for the field was fairly slated,
So I cantered home a winner with my shoulder dislocated,
While the man that rode The Quiver followed limping down the track.

And he shook my hand and told me that in all his days he never
Met a man who rode more gamely, and our last set to was prime,
And we wired them on Monaro how we chanced to beat The Quiver.
And they sent us back an answer, "Good old sort from Snowy River;
Send us word each race you start in and we'll back you every time."

# The Amateur Rider

*H*im going to ride for us! *Him* — with the pants and the eyeglass and all.
Amateur! don't he just look it — it's twenty to one on a fall.
Boss must be gone off his head to be sending our steeplechase crack
Out over fences like these with an object like that on his back.

Ride! Don't tell *me* he can ride. With his pants just as loose as balloons,
How can he sit on his horse? And his spurs like a pair of harpoons;
Ought to be under the Dog Act, he ought, and be kept off the course.
Fall! why, he'd fall off a cart, let alone off a steeplechase horse.

\* \* \* \*

Yessir! the 'orse is all ready — I wish you'd have rode him before;
Nothing like knowing your 'orse, sir, and this chap's a terror to bore;
Battleaxe always could pull, and he rushes his fences like fun —
Stands off his jump twenty feet, and then springs like a shot from a gun.

Oh, he can jump 'em all right, sir, you make no mistake, 'e's a toff;
Clouts 'em in earnest, too, sometimes, you mind that he don't clout you off —
Don't seem to mind how he hits 'em, his shins is as hard as a nail,
Sometimes you'll see the fence shake and the splinters fly up from the rail.

All you can do is to hold him and just let him jump as he likes,
Give him his head at the fences, and hang on like death if he strikes;
Don't let him run himself out — you can lie third or fourth in the race —
Until you clear the stone wall, and from that you can put on the pace.

Fell at that wall once, he did, and it gave him a regular spread,
Ever since that time he flies it — he'll stop if you pull at his head,
Just let him race — you can trust him — he'll take first-class care he don't
fall,
And I think that's the lot — but remember, *he must have his head at the wall.*

\* \* \* \*

Well, he's down safe as far as the start, and he seems to sit on pretty neat,
Only his baggified breeches would ruinate anyone's seat —
They're away — here they come — the first fence, and he's head over heels
for a crown!
Good for the new chum, he's over, and two of the others are down!

39

Now for the treble, my hearty — By Jove, he can ride, after all;
Whoop, that's your sort — let him fly them! He hasn't much fear of a fall.
Who in the world would have thought it? And aren't they just going a pace?
Little Recruit in the lead there will make it a stoutly run race.

Lord! But they're racing in earnest — and down goes Recruit on his head,
Rolling clean over his boy — it's a miracle if he ain't dead.
Battleaxe, Battleaxe yet! By the Lord, he's got most of 'em beat —
Ho! did you see how he struck, and the swell never moved in his seat?

Second time round, and, by Jingo! he's holding his lead of 'em well;
Hark to him clouting the timber! It don't seem to trouble the swell.
Now for the wall — let him rush it. A thirty-foot leap, I declare —
Never a shift in his seat, and he's racing for home like a hare.

What's that that's chasing him — Rataplan — regular demon to stay!
Sit down and ride for your life now! Oh, good, that's the style — come away!
Rataplan's certain to beat you, unless you can give him the slip;
Sit down and rub in the whalebone now — give him the spurs and the whip!

Battleaxe, Battleaxe, yet — and it's Battleaxe wins for a crown;
Look at him rushing the fences, he wants to bring t'other chap down.
Rataplan never will catch him if only he keeps on his pins;
Now! the last fence! and he's over it! Battleaxe, Battleaxe wins!

* * * *

Well, sir, you rode him just perfect — I knew from the first you could ride.
Some of the chaps said you couldn't, an' I says just like this a' one side:
Mark me, I says, that's a tradesman — the saddle is where he was bred.
Weight! you're all right, sir, and thank you; and them was the words that I said.

# On Kiley's Run

The roving breezes come and go
    On Kiley's Run,
The sleepy river murmurs low,
And far away one dimly sees
Beyond the stretch of forest trees —
Beyond the foothills dusk and dun —
The ranges sleeping in the sun
    On Kiley's Run.

'Tis many years since first I came
    To Kiley's Run,
More years than I would care to name
Since I, a stripling, used to ride
For miles and miles at Kiley's side,
The while in stirring tones he told
The stories of the days of old
    On Kiley's Run.

I see the old bush homestead now
    On Kiley's Run,
Just nestled down beneath the brow
Of one small ridge above the sweep
Of river flat, where willows weep
And jasmine flowers and roses bloom,
The air was laden with perfume
    On Kiley's Run.

We lived the good old station life
    On Kiley's Run,
With little thought of care or strife.
Old Kiley seldom used to roam,
He liked to make the Run his home,
The swagman never turned away
With empty hand at close of day
    From Kiley's Run.

We kept a racehorse now and then
    On Kiley's Run,
And neighb'ring stations brought their men

To meetings where the sport was free,
And dainty ladies came to see
Their champions ride; with laugh and song
The old house rang the whole night long
    On Kiley's Run.

The station hands were friends I wot
    On Kiley's Run,
A reckless, merry-hearted lot —
All splendid riders, and they knew
The "boss" was kindness through and through.
Old Kiley always stood their friend,
And so they served him to the end
    On Kiley's Run.

But droughts and losses came apace
    To Kiley's Run,
Till ruin stared him in the face;
He toiled and toiled while lived the light,
He dreamed of overdrafts at night:
At length, because he could not pay,
His bankers took the stock away
    From Kiley's Run.

Old Kiley stood and saw them go
    From Kiley's Run.
The well-bred cattle marching slow;
His stockmen, mates for many a day,
They wrung his hand and went away.
Too old to make another start,
Old Kiley died — of broken heart,
    On Kiley's Run.

The owner lives in England now
    Of Kiley's Run.
He knows a racehorse from a cow;
But that is all he knows of stock:
His chiefest care is how to dock
Expenses, and he sends from town
To cut the shearers' wages down
    On Kiley's Run.

There are no neighbours anywhere
    Near Kiley's Run.
The hospitable homes are bare,
The gardens gone; for no pretence
Must hinder cutting down expense:
The homestead that we held so dear
Contains a half-paid overseer
    On Kiley's Run.

All life and sport and hope have died
    On Kiley's Run.
No longer there the stockmen ride;
Four sour-faced boundary riders creep
On mongrel horses after sheep,
Through ranges where, at racing speed,
Old Kiley used to "wheel the lead"
    On Kiley's Run.

There runs a lane for thirty miles
    Through Kiley's Run.
On either side the herbage smiles,
But wretched trav'lling sheep must pass
Without a drink or blade of grass
Thro' that long lane of death and shame:
The weary drovers curse the name
    Of Kiley's Run.

The name itself is changed of late
    Of Kiley's Run.
They call it "Chandos Park Estate".
The lonely swagman through the dark
Must hump his swag past Chandos Park.
The name is English, don't you see,
The old name sweeter sounds to me
    Of "Kiley's Run".

I cannot guess what fate will bring
    To Kiley's Run —
For chances come and changes ring —
I scarcely think 'twill always be
Locked up to suit an absentee;
And if he lets it out in farms
His tenants soon will carry arms
    On Kiley's Run.

# *Frying Pan's Theology*

SCENE: On Monaro.
   *Dramatis Personae*:
Shock-headed blackfellow,
   Boy (on a pony).
Snowflakes are falling
   So gentle and slow,
Youngster says, "Frying Pan,
   What makes it snow?"
Frying Pan confident
   Makes the reply —
"Shake 'em big flour bag
   Up in the sky!"

"What! when there's miles of it!
   Surely that's brag.
Who is there strong enough
   Shake such a bag?"
"What parson tellin' you,
   Ole Mister Dodd,
Tell you in Sunday-school?
   Big feller God!
He drive His bullock dray,
   Then thunder go,
He shake His flour bag —
   Tumble down snow!"

# The Two Devines

It was shearing time at the Myall Lake,
   And there rose the sound thro' the livelong day
Of the constant clash that the shear blades make
   When the fastest shearers are making play,
But there wasn't a man in the shearers' lines
That could shear a sheep with the two Devines.

They had rung the sheds of the east and west,
   Had beaten the cracks of the Walgett side,
And the Cooma shearers had giv'n them best —
   When they saw them shear, they were satisfied.
From the southern slopes to the western pines
They were noted men, were the two Devines.

'Twas a wether flock that had come to hand,
   Great struggling brutes, that the shearers shirk,
For the fleece was filled with the grass and sand,
   And seventy sheep was a big day's work.
"At a pound a hundred it's dashed hard lines
To shear such sheep," said the two Devines.

But the shearers knew that they'd make a cheque
   When they came to deal with the station ewes;
They were bare of belly and bare of neck
   With a fleece as light as a kangaroo's.
"We will show the boss how a shear blade shines
When we reach those ewes," said the two Devines.

But it chanced next day when the stunted pines
   Were swayed and stirred with the dawn wind's breath,
That a message came for the two Devines
   That their father lay at the point of death.
So away at speed through the whispering pines
Down the bridle track rode the two Devines.

It was fifty miles to their father's hut,
   And the dawn was bright when they rode away;
At the fall of night when the shed was shut
   And the men had rest from the toilsome day,

To the shed once more through the dark'ning pines
On their weary steeds came the two Devines.

"Well, you're back right sudden," the super. said;
    "Is the old man dead and the funeral done?"
"Well, no, sir, he ain't not exactly dead,
    But as good as dead," said the eldest son —
"And we couldn't bear such a chance to lose,
So we came straight back to tackle the ewes."

They are shearing ewes at the Myall Lake,
    And the shed is merry the livelong day
With the clashing sound that the shear blades make
    When the fastest shearers are making play,
And a couple of "hundred and ninety-nines"
Are the tallies made by the two Devines.

# In the Droving Days

"Only a pound," said the auctioneer,
   "Only a pound; and I'm standing here
Selling this animal, gain or loss.
Only a pound for the drover's horse;
One of the sort that was ne'er afraid,
One of the boys of the Old Brigade;
Thoroughly honest and game, I'll swear,
Only a little the worse for wear;
Plenty as bad to be seen in town,
Give me a bid and I'll knock him down;
Sold as he stands, and without recourse,
Give me a bid for the drover's horse."

Loitering there in an aimless way
Somehow I noticed the poor old grey,
Weary and battered and screwed, of course,
Yet when I noticed the old grey horse,
The rough bush saddle, and single rein
Of the bridle laid on his tangled mane,
Straightway the crowd and the auctioneer
Seemed on a sudden to disappear,
Melted away in a kind of haze,
For my heart went back to the droving days.

Back to the road, and I crossed again
Over the miles of the saltbush plain —
The shining plain that is said to be
The dried-up bed of an inland sea,
Where the air so dry and so clear and bright
Refracts the sun with a wondrous light,
And out in the dim horizon makes
The deep blue gleam of the phantom lakes.

At dawn of day we would feel the breeze
That stirred the boughs of the sleeping trees,
And brought a breath of the fragrance rare
That comes and goes in that scented air;
For the trees and grass and the shrubs contain

A dry sweet scent on the saltbush plain.
For those that love it and understand,
The saltbush plain is a wonderland.
A wondrous country, where nature's ways
Were revealed to me in the droving days.

We saw the fleet wild horses pass,
And the kangaroos through the Mitchell grass,
The emu ran with her frightened brood
All unmolested and unpursued.
But there rose a shout and a wild hubbub
When the dingo raced for his native scrub,
And he paid right dear for his stolen meals
With the drovers' dogs at his wretched heels.
For we ran him down at a rattling pace,
While the pack horse joined in the stirring chase.
And a wild halloo at the kill we'd raise —
We were light of heart in the droving days.

'Twas a drover's horse, and my hand again
Made a move to close on a fancied rein.
For I felt the swing and the easy stride
Of the grand old horse that I used to ride
In drought or plenty, in good or ill,
That same old steed was my comrade still;
The old grey horse with his honest ways
Was a mate to me in the droving days.

When we kept our watch in the cold and damp,
If the cattle broke from the sleeping camp,
Over the flats and across the plain,
With my head bent down on his waving mane,
Through the boughs above and the stumps below
On the darkest night I would let him go
At a racing speed; he would choose his course,
And my life was safe with the old grey horse.
But man and horse had a favourite job,
When an outlaw broke from a station mob,
With a right good will was the stockwhip plied,
As the old horse raced at the straggler's side,
And the greenhide whip such a weal would raise,
We could use the whip in the droving days.

"Only a pound!" and was this the end —
Only a pound for the drover's friend.
The drover's friend that had seen his day,
And now was worthless, and cast away
With a broken knee and a broken heart
To be flogged and starved in a hawker's cart.
Well, I made a bid for a sense of shame
And the memories dear of the good old game.

"Thank you? Guinea! and cheap at that!
Against you there in the curly hat!
Only a guinea, and one more chance,
Down he goes if there's no advance,
Third, and the last time, one! two! three!"
And the old grey horse was knocked down to me.
And now he's wandering, fat and sleek,
On the lucerne flats by the Homestead Creek;
I dare not ride him for fear he'd fall,
But he does a journey to beat them all,
For though he scarcely a trot can raise,
He can take me back to the droving days.

# Lost

"He ought to be home," said the old man, "without there's
    something amiss.
He only went to the Two-mile — he ought to be back by this.
He *would* ride the Reckless filly, he *would* have his wilful way;
And, here, he's not back at sundown — and what will his mother say?

"He was always his mother's idol, since ever his father died;
And there isn't a horse on the station that he isn't game to ride.
But that Reckless mare is vicious, and if once she gets away
He hasn't got strength to hold her — and what will his mother say?"

The old man walked to the sliprail, and peered up the dark'ning track,
And looked and longed for the rider that would never more come back;
And the mother came and clutched him, with sudden, spasmodic fright:
"What has become of my Willie? Why isn't he home tonight?"

Away in the gloomy ranges, at the foot of an ironbark,
The bonnie, winsome laddie was lying stiff and stark;
For the Reckless mare had smashed him against a leaning limb,
And his comely face was battered, and his merry eyes were dim.

And the thoroughbred chestnut filly, the saddle beneath her flanks,
Was away like fire through the ranges to join the wild mob's ranks;
And a broken-hearted woman and an old man worn and grey
Were searching all night in the ranges till the sunrise brought the day.

And the mother kept feebly calling, with a hope that would not die,
"Willie! where are you, Willie?" But how can the dead reply;
And hope died out with the daylight, and the darkness brought despair,
God pity the stricken mother, and answer the widow's prayer!

Though far and wide they sought him, they found not where he fell;
For the ranges held him precious, and guarded their treasure well.
The wattle blooms above him, and the bluebells blow close by,
And the brown bees buzz the secret, and the wild birds sing reply.

But the mother pined and faded, and cried, and took no rest,
And rode each day to the ranges on her hopeless, weary quest.
Seeking her loved one ever, she faded and pined away,
But with strength of her great affection she still sought every day.

"I know that sooner or later I shall find my boy," she said.
But she came not home one evening, and they found her lying dead,
And stamped on the poor pale features, as the spirit homeward pass'd,
Was an angel smile of gladness — she had found the boy at last.

# Over the Range

Little bush maiden, wondering-eyed,
  Playing alone in the creek bed dry,
In the small green flat on every side
  Walled in by the Moonbi Ranges high;
Tell us the tale of your lonely life,
  'Mid the great grey forests that know no change.
"I never have left my home," she said,
  "I have never been over the Moonbi Range.

"Father and mother are both long dead,
  And I live with granny in yon wee place."
"Where are your father and mother?" we said.
  She puzzled awhile with thoughtful face,
Then a light came into the shy brown eye,
  And she smiled, for she thought the question strange
On a thing so certain — "When people die
  They go to the country over the range."

"And what is this country like, my lass?"
  "There are blossoming trees and pretty flowers,
And shining creeks where the golden grass
  Is fresh and sweet from the summer showers.
They never need work, nor want, nor weep;
  No troubles can come their hearts to estrange.
Some summer night I shall fall asleep,
  And wake in the country over the range."

Child, you are wise in your simple trust,
  For the wisest man knows no more than you.
Ashes to ashes, and dust to dust:
  Our views by a range are bounded too;
But we know that God hath this gift in store,
  That when we come to the final change,
We shall meet with our loved ones gone before
  To the beautiful country over the range.

# Only a Jockey

*"Richard Bennison, a jockey, aged 14, while riding William Tell
in his training, was thrown and killed.
The horse is luckily uninjured." Melbourne wire*

Out in the grey cheerless chill of the morning light,
    Out on the track where the night shades still lurk;
Ere the first gleam of the sun god's returning light,
    Round come the racehorses early at work.

Reefing and pulling and racing so readily,
    Close sit the jockey boys holding them hard,
"Steady the stallion there — canter him steadily,
    Don't let him gallop so much as a yard."

Fiercely he fights while the others run wide of him,
    Reefs at the bit that would hold him in thrall,
Plunges and bucks till the boy that's astride of him
    Goes to the ground with a terrible fall.

"Stop him there! Block him there! Drive him in carefully,
    Lead him about till he's quiet and cool.
Sound as a bell! though he's blown himself fearfully,
    Now let us pick up this poor little fool.

"Stunned? Oh, by Jove, I'm afraid it's a case with him;
    Ride for the doctor! keep bathing his head!
Send for a cart to go down to our place with him" —
    No use! One long sigh and the little chap's dead.

Only a jockey boy! foul-mouthed and bad you see,
    Ignorant, heathenish, gone to his rest.
Parson or Presbyter, Pharisee, Sadducee,
    What did you do for him? — bad was the best.

Negroes and foreigners, all have a claim on you;
    Yearly you send your well-advertised hoard,
But the poor jockey boy — shame on you, shame on you,
    "Feed ye my little ones" — What said the Lord?

Him ye held less than the outer barbarian,
    Left him to die in his ignorant sin;
Have you no principles, humanitarian?
    Have you no precept — "Go gather them in"?

* * * *

Knew he God's name? In his brutal profanity,
    That name was an oath — out of many but one —
What did he get from our famed Christianity?
    Where has his soul — if he had any — gone?

Fourteen years old, and what was he taught of it?
    What did he know of God's infinite grace?
Draw the dark curtain of shame o'er the thought of it,
    Draw the shroud over the jockey boy's face.

# How M'Ginnis Went Missing

L et us cease our idle chatter,
    Let the tears bedew our cheek,
For a man from Tallangatta
Has been missing for a week.

Where the roaring, flooded Murray
Covered all the lower land,
There he started in a hurry,
With a bottle in his hand.

And his fate is hid for ever,
But the public seem to think
That he slumbered by the river,
'Neath the influence of drink.

And they scarcely seem to wonder
That the river, wide and deep,
Never woke him with its thunder,
Never stirred him in his sleep.

As the crashing logs came sweeping,
And their tumult filled the air,
Then M'Ginnis murmured, sleeping,
" 'Tis a wake in ould Kildare."

So the river rose and found him
Sleeping softly by the stream,
And the cruel waters drowned him
Ere he wakened from his dream.

And the blossom-tufted wattle,
Blooming brightly on the lea
Saw M'Ginnis and the bottle
Going drifting out to sea.

# A Voice from the Town

*A sequel to "A Voice from the Bush"*

I thought, in the days of the droving,
  Of steps I might hope to retrace,
To be done with the bush and the roving
  And settle once more in my place.
With a heart that was well nigh to breaking,
  In the long, lonely rides on the plain,
I thought of the pleasure of taking
  The hand of a lady again.

I am back into civilisation,
  Once more in the stir and the strife,
But the old joys have lost their sensation —
  The light has gone out of my life;
The men of my time they have married,
  Made fortunes or gone to the wall;
Too long from the scene I have tarried,
  And, somehow, I'm out of it all.

For I go to the balls and the races
  A lonely companionless elf,
And the ladies bestow all their graces
  On others less grey than myself;
While the talk goes around I'm a dumb one
  'Midst youngsters that chatter and prate,
And they call me "the Man who was Someone
  Way back in the year Sixty-eight".

And I look, sour and old, at the dancers
  That swing to the strains of the band,
And the ladies all give me the Lancers,
  No waltzes — I quite understand.
For matrons intent upon matching
  Their daughters with infinite push,
Would scarce think him worthy the catching,
  The broken-down man from the bush.

New partners have come and new faces,
  And I, of the bygone brigade,

56

Sharply feel that oblivion my place is —
    I must lie with the rest in the shade.
And the youngsters, fresh-featured and pleasant,
    They lived as we lived — fairly fast;
But I doubt if the men of the present
    Are as good as the men of the past.

Of excitement and praise they are chary,
    There is nothing much good upon earth;
Their watchword is *nil admirari,*
    They are bored from the days of their birth.
Where the life that we led was a revel
    They "wince and relent and refrain" —
I could show them the road — to the devil,
    Were I only a youngster again.

I could show them the road where the stumps are
    The pleasures that end in remorse,
And the game where the Devil's three trumps are,
    The woman, the card, and the horse.
Shall the blind lead the blind — shall the sower
    Of wind reap the storm as of yore?
Though they get to their goal somewhat slower,
    They march where we hurried before.

For the world never learns — just as we did,
    They gallantly go to their fate,
Unheeded all warnings, unheeded
    The maxims of elders sedate.
As the husbandman, patiently toiling,
    Draws a harvest each year from the soil,
So the fools grow afresh for the spoiling,
    And a new crop of thieves for the spoil.

But a truce to this dull moralising,
    Let them drink while the drops are of gold,
I have tasted the dregs — 'twere surprising
    Were the new wine to me like the old;
And I weary for lack of employment
    In idleness day after day,
For the key to the door of enjoyment
    Is Youth — and I've thrown it away.

57

# A Bunch of Roses

R oses ruddy and roses white,
  What are the joys that my heart discloses?
Sitting alone in the fading light
Memories come to me here to-night
  With the wonderful scent of the big red roses.

Memories come as the daylight fades
  Down on the hearth where the firelight dozes;
Flicker and flutter the lights and shades,
And I see the face of a queen of maids
  Whose memory comes with the scent of roses.

Visions arise of a scene of mirth,
  And a ballroom belle that superbly poses —
A queenly woman of queenly worth,
And I am the happiest man on earth
  With a single flower from a bunch of roses.

Only her memory lives tonight —
  God in His wisdom her young life closes;
Over her grave may the turf be light,
Cover her coffin with roses white —
  She was always fond of the big white roses.

Such are the visions that fade away —
  Man proposes and God disposes;
Look in the glass and I see to-day
Only an old man, worn and grey,
  Bending his head to a bunch of roses.

# Black Swans

As I lie at rest on a patch of clover
In the Western Park when the day is done,
I watch as the wild black swans fly over
With their phalanx turned to the sinking sun;
And I hear the clang of their leader crying
To a lagging mate in the rearward flying,
And they fade away in the darkness dying,
Where the stars are mustering one by one.

Oh! ye wild black swans, 'twere a world of wonder
For a while to join in your westward flight,
With the stars above and the dim earth under,
Through the cooling air of the glorious night.
As we swept along on our pinions winging,
We should catch the chime of a church-bell ringing,
Or the distant note of a torrent singing,
Or the far-off flash of a station light.

From the northern lakes with the reeds and rushes,
Where the hills are clothed with a purple haze,
Where the bellbirds chime and the songs of thrushes
Make music sweet in the jungle maze,
They will hold their course to the westward ever,
Till they reach the banks of the old grey river,
Where the waters wash, and the reed beds quiver
In the burning heat of the summer days.

Oh! ye strange wild birds, will ye bear a greeting
To the folk that live in that western land?
Then for every sweep of your pinions beating,
Ye shall bear a wish to the sunburnt band,
To the stalwart men who are stoutly fighting
With the heat and drought and dust storm smiting,
Yet whose life somehow has a strange inviting,
When once to the work they have put their hand.

Facing it yet! Oh, my friend stout-hearted,
What does it matter for rain or shine,
For the hopes deferred and the gain departed?

Nothing could conquer that heart of thine.
And thy health and strength are beyond confessing
As the only joys that are worth possessing.
May the days to come be as rich in blessing
As the days we spent in the auld lang syne.

I would fain go back to the old grey river,
To the old bush days when our hearts were light,
But, alas! those days they have fled for ever,
They are like the swans that have swept from sight.
And I know full well that the strangers' faces
Would meet us now in our dearest places;
For our day is dead and has left no traces
But the thoughts that live in my mind tonight.

There are folk long dead, and our hearts would sicken —
We would grieve for them with a bitter pain,
If the past could live and the dead could quicken,
We then might turn to that life again.
But on lonely nights we would hear them calling,
We should hear their steps on the pathways falling,
We should loathe the life with a hate appalling
In our lonely rides by the ridge and plain.

* * * *

In the silent park is a scent of clover,
And the distant roar of the town is dead,
And I hear once more as the swans fly over
Their far-off clamour from overhead.
They are flying west by their instinct guided,
And for man likewise is his fate decided,
And griefs apportioned and joys divided
By a mighty power — with a purpose dread.

# The All Right 'Un

He came from "further out",
That land of heat and drought
And dust and gravel.
He got a touch of sun,
And rested at the run
Until his cure was done,
And he could travel.

When spring had decked the plain,
He flitted off again
As flit the swallows.
And from that western land,
When many months were spanned,
A letter came to hand,
Which read as follows:

"Dear Sir, I take my pen
In hopes that all your men
And you are hearty.
You think that I've forgot
Your kindness, Mr Scott,
Oh, no, dear sir, I'm not
That sort of party.

"You sometimes bet, I know,
Well, now you'll have a show
The 'books' to frighten.
Up here at Wingadee
Young Billy Fife and me
We're training Strife, and he
Is a all right 'un.

"Just now we're running byes,
But, sir, first time he tries
I'll send you word of.
And running 'on the crook'
Their measures we have took,
It is the deadest hook
You ever heard of.

"So when we lets him go,
Why, then, I'll let you know,
And you can have a show
To put a mite on.
Now, sir, my leave I'll take,
Yours truly, William Blake.
P. S. Make no mistake,
*He's a all right 'un.*"

\* \* \* \*

By next week's *Riverine*
I saw my friend had been
A bit too cunning.
I read: "The racehorse Strife
And jockey William Fife
Disqualified for life —
Suspicious running."
But though they spoilt his game,
I reckon all the same
I fairly ought to claim
My friend a white 'un.
For though he wasn't straight,
His deeds would indicate
His heart at any rate
Was "a all right 'un".

# The Boss of the Admiral Lynch

Did you ever hear tell of Chile? I was readin' the other day
 Of President Balmaceda and of how he was sent away.
It seems that he didn't suit 'em — they thought that they'd like a change,
So they started an insurrection and chased him across the range.
They seem to be restless people — and, judging by what you hear,
They raise up these revolutions 'bout two or three times a year;
And the man that goes out of office, he goes for the boundary *quick*,
For there isn't no vote by ballot — it's bullets that does the trick.
And it ain't like a real battle, where the prisoners' lives are spared,
And they fight till there's one side beaten and then there's a truce declared,
And the man that has got the licking goes down like a blooming lord
To hand in his resignation and give up his blooming sword,
And the other man bows and takes it, and everything's all polite —
This wasn't that kind of a picnic, this wasn't that sort of a fight.
For the pris'ners they took — they shot 'em; no odds were they small
  or great,
If they'd collared old Balmaceda, they reckoned to shoot him straight.
A lot of bloodthirsty devils they were — but there ain't a doubt
They must have been real plucked 'uns — the way that they fought it out,
And the king of 'em all, I reckon, the man that could stand a pinch,
Was the boss of a one-horse gunboat. They called her the *Admiral Lynch*.
Well, he was for Balmaceda, and after the war was done,
And Balmaceda was beaten and his troops had been forced to run,
The other man fetched his army and proceeded to do things brown,
He marched 'em into the fortress and took command of the town.
Cannon and guns and horses troopin' along the road,
Rumblin' over the bridges, and never a foeman showed
Till they came in sight of the harbour, and the very first thing they see
Was this mite of a one-horse gunboat a-lying against the quay,
And there as they watched they noticed a flutter of crimson rag,
And under their eyes he hoisted old Balmaceda's flag.
Well, I tell you it fairly knocked 'em — it just took away their breath,
For he must ha' known if they caught him, 'twas nothin' but sudden death.
An' he'd got no fire in his furnace, no chance to put out to sea,
So he stood by his gun and waited with his vessel against the quay.
Well, they sent him a civil message to say that the war was done,
And most of his side were corpses, and all that were left had run;

And blood had been spilt sufficient, so they gave him a chance to decide
If he'd haul down his bit of bunting and come on the winning side.
He listened and heard their message, and answered them all polite,
That he was a Spanish hidalgo, and the men of his race *must* fight!
A gunboat against an army, and with never a chance to run,
And them with their hundred cannon and him with a single gun:
The odds were a trifle heavy — but he wasn't the sort to flinch,
So he opened fire on the army, did the boss of the *Admiral Lynch*.
They pounded his boat to pieces, they silenced his single gun,
And captured the whole consignment, for none of 'em cared to run;
And it don't say whether they shot him — it don't even give his name —
But whatever they did I'll wager that he went to his graveyard game.
I tell you those old hidalgos so stately and so polite,
They turn out the real Maginnis when it comes to an uphill fight.
There was General Alcantara, who died in the heaviest brunt,
And General Alzereca was killed in the battle's front;
But the king of 'em all, I reckon — the man that could stand a pinch —
Was the man who attacked the army with the gunboat *Admiral Lynch*.

# A Bushman's Song

I'm travellin' down the Castlereagh, and I'm a station hand,
I'm handy with the ropin' pole, I'm handy with the brand,
And I can ride a rowdy colt, or swing the axe all day,
But there's no demand for a station hand along the Castlereagh.

So it's shift, boys, shift, for there isn't the slightest doubt
That we've got to make a shift to the stations further out;
With the packhorse runnin' after, for he follows like a dog,
We must strike across the country at the old jig jog.

This old black horse I'm riding — if you'll notice what's
        his brand,
He wears the crooked R, you see — none better in the land.
He takes a lot of beatin', and the other day we tried,
For a bit of a joke, with a racing bloke, for twenty
        pounds aside.

It was shift, boys, shift, for there wasn't the slightest doubt,
That I had to make him shift, for the money was nearly out;
But he cantered home a winner, with the other one at the flog —
He's a red-hot sort to pick up with his old jig jog.

I asked a cove for shearin' once along the Marthaguy:
"We shear non-union, here," says he. "I call it scab," says I.
I looked along the shearin' floor before I turned to go —
There were eight or ten dashed Chinamen a-shearin'
        in a row.

It was shift, boys, shift, for there wasn't the slightest doubt
It was time to make a shift with the leprosy about.
So I saddled up my horses, and I whistled to my dog,
And I left his scabby station at the old jig-jog.

I went to Illawarra where my brother's got a farm,
He has to ask his landlord's leave before he lifts his arm;
The landlord owns the countryside — man, woman,
        dog, and cat,
They haven't the cheek to dare to speak without they
        touch their hat.

It was shift, boys, shift, for there wasn't the slightest doubt
Their little landlord god and I would soon have fallen out;
Was I to touch my hat to him? — was I his bloomin' dog?
So I makes for up the country at the old jig-jog.

But it's time that I was movin', I've a mighty way to go
Till I drink artesian water from a thousand feet below;
Till I meet the overlanders with the cattle comin' down,
And I'll work a while till I make a pile, then have a
      spree in town.

So, it's shift, boys, shift, for there isn't the slightest doubt
We've got to make a shift to the stations further out;
The packhorse runs behind us, for he follows like a dog,
And we cross a lot of country at the old jig-jog.

# How Gilbert Died

There's never a stone at the sleeper's head,
  There's never a fence beside,
And the wandering stock on the grave may tread
  Unnoticed and undenied,
But the smallest child on the Watershed
  Can tell you how Gilbert died.

For he rode at dusk, with his comrade Dunn
  To the hut at the Stockman's Ford,
In the waning light of the sinking sun
  They peered with a fierce accord.
They were outlaws both — and on each man's head
  Was a thousand pounds reward.

They had taken toll of the country round,
  And the troopers came behind
With a black that tracked like a human hound
  In the scrub and the ranges blind:
He could run the trail where a white man's eye
  No sign of a track could find.

He had hunted them out of the One Tree Hill
  And over the Old Man Plain,
But they wheeled their tracks with a wild beast's skill,
  And they made for the range again.
Then away to the hut where their grandsire dwelt,
  They rode with a loosened rein.

And their grandsire gave them a greeting bold:
  "Come in and rest in peace,
No safer place does the country hold —
  With the night pursuit must cease,
And we'll drink success to the roving boys,
  And to hell with the black police."

But they went to death when they entered there,
  In the hut at the Stockman's Ford,
For their grandsire's words were as false as fair —
  They were doomed to the hangman's cord.

He had sold them both to the black police
    For the sake of the big reward.

In the depth of night there are forms that glide
    As stealthy as serpents creep,
And around the hut where the outlaws hide
    They plant in the shadows deep,
And they wait till the first faint flush of dawn
    Shall waken their prey from sleep.

But Gilbert wakes while the night is dark —
    A restless sleeper, aye,
He has heard the sound of a sheepdog's bark,
    And his horse's warning neigh,
And he says to his mate, "There are hawks abroad,
    And it's time that we went away."

Their rifles stood at the stretcher head,
    Their bridles lay to hand,
They wakened the old man out of his bed,
    When they heard the sharp command:
"In the name of the Queen lay down your arms,
    Now, Dunn and Gilbert, stand!"

Then Gilbert reached for his rifle true
    That close at his hand he kept,
He pointed it straight at the voice and drew,
    But never a flash outleapt,
For the water ran from the rifle breach —
    It was drenched while the outlaws slept.

Then he dropped the piece with a bitter oath,
    And he turned to his comrade Dunn:
"We are sold," he said, "we are dead men both,
    But there may be a chance for one;
I'll stop and I'll fight with the pistol here,
    You take to your heels and run."

So Dunn crept out on his hands and knees
    In the dim, half-dawning light,
And he made his way to a patch of trees,
    And vanished among the night,

And the trackers hunted his tracks all day,
    But they never could trace his flight.

But Gilbert walked from the open door
    In a confident style and rash;
He heard at his side the rifles roar,
    And he heard the bullets crash.
But he laughed as he lifted his pistol-hand,
    And he fired at the rifle flash.

Then out of the shadows the troopers aimed
    At his voice and the pistol sound,
With the rifle flashes the darkness flamed,
    He staggered and spun around,
And they riddled his body with rifle balls
    As it lay on the blood-soaked ground.

There's never a stone at the sleeper's head
    There's never a fence beside,
And the wandering stock on the grave may tread
    Unnoticed and undenied,
But the smallest child on the Watershed
    Can tell you how Gilbert died.

# The Flying Gang

*A Railroad Song*

I served my time, in the days gone by,
In the railway's clash and clang,
And I worked my way to the end, and I
Was the head of the "Flying Gang".
'Twas a chosen band that was kept at hand
In case of an urgent need,
Was it south or north we were started forth
And away at our utmost speed.
   If word reached town that a bridge was down,
   The imperious summons rang —
   "Come out with the pilot engine sharp,
   And away with the flying gang."

Then a piercing scream and a rush of steam
As the engine moved ahead,
With a measured beat by the slum and street
Of the busy town we fled,
By the uplands bright and the homesteads white,
With the rush of the western gale,
And the pilot swayed with the pace we made
As she rocked on the ringing rail.
   And the country children clapped their hands
   As the engine's echoes rang,
   But their elders said, "There is work ahead
   When they send for the flying gang."

Then across the miles of the saltbush plain
That gleamed with the morning dew,
Where the grasses waved like the ripening grain
The pilot engine flew,
A fiery rush in the open bush
Where the grade marks seemed to fly,
And the order sped on the wires ahead,
The pilot *must* go by.

    The Governor's special must stand aside,
    And the fast express go hang,
    Let your orders be that the line is free
    For the boys of the flying gang.

# *Shearing at Castlereagh*

The bell is set aringing, and the engine gives a toot,
There's five and thirty shearers here are shearing for the loot,
So stir yourselves, you penners-up and shove the sheep along,
The musterers are fetching them a hundred thousand strong,
And make your collie dogs speak up — what would the buyers say
In London if the wool was late this year from Castlereagh?

The man that "rung" the Tubbo shed is not the ringer here,
That stripling from the Cooma side can teach him how to shear.
They trim away the ragged locks, and rip the cutter goes,
And leaves a track of snowy fleece from brisket to the nose;
It's lovely how they peel it off with never stop nor stay,
They're racing for the ringer's place this year at Castlereagh.

The man that keeps the cutters sharp is growling in his cage,
He's always in a hurry and he's always in a rage —
"You clumsy-fisted muttonheads, you'd turn a fellow sick,
You pass yourselves as shearers? You were born to swing a pick!
Another broken cutter here, that's two you've broke today,
It's awful how such crawlers come to shear at Castlereagh."

The youngsters picking up the fleece enjoy the merry din,
They throw the classer up the fleece, he throws it to the bin;
The pressers standing by the rack are waiting for the wool,
There's room for just a couple more, the press is nearly full;
Now jump upon the lever, lads, and heave and heave away,
Another bale of golden fleece is branded "Castlereagh".

# The Wind's Message

There came a whisper down the Bland between the dawn and dark,
    Above the tossing of the pines, above the river's flow;
It stirred the boughs of giant gums and stalwart ironbark;
It drifted where the wild ducks played amid the swamps below;
It brought a breath of mountain air from off the hills of pine,
A scent of eucalyptus trees in honey-laden bloom;
And drifting, drifting far away along the southern line
It caught from leaf and grass and fern a subtle strange perfume.

It reached the toiling city folk, but few there were that heard —
The rattle of their busy life had choked the whisper down;
And some but caught a fresh-blown breeze with scent of
        pine that stirred
A thought of blue hills far away beyond the smoky town;
And others heard the whisper pass, but could not understand
The magic of the breeze's breath that set their hearts aglow,
Nor how the roving wind could bring across the Overland
A sound of voices silent now and songs of long ago.

But some that heard the whisper clear were filled with vague unrest;
The breeze had brought its message home, they could not fixed abide;
Their fancies wandered all the day towards the blue hills' breast,
Towards the sunny slopes that lie along the riverside,
The mighty rolling western plains are very fair to see,
Where waving to the passing breeze the silver myalls stand,
But fairer are the giant hills, all rugged though they be,
From which the two great rivers rise that run along the Bland.

Oh! rocky range and rugged spur and river running clear,
That swings around the sudden bends with swirl of snow-white foam,
Though we, your sons, are far away, we sometimes seem to hear
The message that the breezes bring to call the wanderers home.
The mountain peaks are white with snow that feeds a thousand rills,
Along the river banks the maize grows tall on virgin land,
And we shall live to see once more those sunny southern hills,
And strike once more the bridle track that leads along the Bland.

# Johnson's Antidote

Down along the Snakebite River, where the
    overlanders camp,
Where the serpents are in millions, all of the most
    deadly stamp;
Where the station cook in terror, nearly every time
    he bakes,
Mixes up among the doughboys half a dozen poison snakes:
Where the wily free selector walks in armour-plated pants,
And defies the stings of scorpions, and the bites of
    bulldog ants:
Where the adder and the viper tear each other by the
    throat,
There it was that William Johnson sought his
    snakebite Antidote.

Johnson was a free selector, and his brain went
    rather queer,
For the constant sight of serpents filled him with a
    deadly fear;
So he tramped his free selection, morning, afternoon
    and night,
Seeking for some great specific that would cure the
    serpent's bite.
Till King Billy, of the Mooki, chieftain of the flour
    bag head,
Told him, "Spos'n snake bite pfeller, pfeller mostly
    drop down dead;
Spos'n snake bite old goanna, then you watch a
    while you see,
Old goanna cure himself with eating little pfeller tree."
"That's the cure," said William Johnson, "point me
    out this plant sublime",
But King Billy, feeling lazy, said he'd go another time.
Thus it came to pass that Johnson, having got the
    tale by rote,
Followed every stray goanna, seeking for the antidote.

* * * *

Loafing once beside the river, while he thought his
          heart would break,
There he saw a big goanna, fighting with a tiger snake,
In and out they rolled and wriggled, bit each other,
          heart and soul,
Till the valiant old goanna swallowed his opponent whole.
Breathless, Johnson sat and watched him, saw him
          struggle up the bank,
Saw him nibbling at the branches of some bushes, green
          and rank;
Saw him, happy and contented, lick his lips, as off he crept,
While the bulging in his stomach showed where his
          opponent slept.
Then a cheer of exultation burst aloud from Johnson's
          throat;
"Luck at last," said he, "I've struck it! 'tis the famous
          antidote.

"Here it is, the Grand Elixir, greatest blessing ever
          known,
Twenty thousand men in India die each year of snakes
          alone.
Think of all the foreign nations, negro, chow, and
          blackamoor,
Saved from sudden expiration, by my wondrous
          snakebite cure.
It will bring me fame and fortune! In the happy days to be,
Men of every clime and nation will be round to gaze
          on me —
Scientific men in thousands, men of mark and men
          of note,
Rushing down the Mooki River, after Johnson's Antidote.
It will cure *delirium tremens*, when the patient's
          eyeballs stare
At imaginary spiders, snakes which really are not there.
When he thinks he sees them wriggle, when he
          thinks he sees them bloat,
It will cure him just to think of Johnson's Snakebite Antidote."

Then he rushed to the museum, found a scientific man —
"Trot me out a deadly serpent, just the deadliest you can;
I intend to let him bite me, all the risk I will endure,
Just to prove the sterling value of my wondrous
      snakebite cure.
Even though an adder bit me, back to life again I'd float;
Snakes are out of date, I tell you, since I've found
      the antidote."
Said the scientific person, "If you really want to die,
Go ahead — but, if you're doubtful, let your
      sheepdog have a try.
Get a pair of dogs and try it, let the snake give both
      a nip;
Give your dog the snakebite mixture, let the other
      fellow rip;
If he dies and yours survives him, then it proves the
      thing is good.
Will you fetch your dog and try it?" Johnson rather
      thought he would.
So he went and fetched his canine, hauled him
      forward by the throat.
"Stump, old man," says he, "we'll show them we've
      the genwine antidote."

Both the dogs were duly loaded with the poison
      gland's contents;
Johnson gave his dog the mixture, then sat down to
      wait events.
"Mark," he said, "in twenty minutes Stump'll be
      a-rushing round,
While the other wretched creature lies a corpse upon
      the ground."
But, alas for William Johnson! ere they'd watched a
      half-hour's spell
Stumpy was as dead as mutton, t'other dog was live
      and well.
And the scientific person hurried off with utmost speed,
Tested Johnson's drug and found it was a deadly
      poison weed;

Half a tumbler killed an emu, half a spoonful killed
      a goat,
All the snakes on earth were harmless to that awful
      antidote.

\* \* \* \*

Down along the Mooki River, on the overlanders' camp,
Where the serpents are in millions, all of the most
      deadly stamp,
Wanders, daily, William Johnson, down among
      those poisonous hordes,
Shooting every stray goanna, calls them "black and
      yaller frauds".
And King Billy, of the Mooki, cadging for the cast-
      off coat,
Somehow seems to dodge the subject of the
      snakebite antidote.

# Ambition and Art

## Ambition

I am the maid of the lustrous eyes
  Of great fruition,
Whom the sons of men that are over-wise
  Have called Ambition.

And the world's success is the only goal
  I have within me;
The meanest man with the smallest soul
  May woo and win me.

For the lust of power and the pride of place
  To all I proffer.
Wilt thou take thy part in the crowded race
  For what I offer?

The choice is thine, and the world is wide —
  Thy path is lonely.
I may not lead and I may not guide —
  I urge thee only.

I am just a whip and a spur that smites
  To fierce endeavour.
In the restless days and the sleepless nights
  I urge thee ever.

Thou shalt wake from sleep with a startled cry,
  In fright upleaping
At a rival's step as it passes by
  Whilst thou art sleeping.

Honour and truth shall be overthrown
  In fierce desire;
Thou shalt use thy friend as a stepping-stone
  To mount thee higher.

When the curtain falls on the sordid strife
  That seemed so splendid,

Thou shalt look with pain on the wasted life
    That thou hast ended.

Thou hast sold thy life for a guerdon small
    In fitful flashes;
There has been reward — but the end of all
    Is dust and ashes.

For the night has come and it brings to naught
    Thy projects cherished,
And thine epitaph shall in brass be wrought —
    "He lived and perished."

## *Art*

I wait for thee at the outer gate,
    My love, mine only;
Wherefore tarriest thou so late
    While I am lonely?

Thou shalt seek my side with a footstep swift,
    In thee implanted
Is the love of Art and the greatest gift
    That God has granted.

And the world's concerns with its rights and wrongs
    Shall seem but small things —
Poet or painter, a singer of songs,
    Thine art is all things.

For the wine of life is a woman's love
    To keep beside thee;
But the love of Art is a thing above —
    A star to guide thee.

As the years go by with thy love of Art
    All undiminished,
Thou shalt end thy days with a quiet heart —
    Thy work is finished.

So the painter fashions a picture strong
    That fadeth never,
And the singer singeth a wondrous song
    That lives for ever.

# In Defence of the Bush

So you're back from up the country, Mister Lawson, where you went,
And you're cursing all the business in a bitter discontent;
Well, we grieve to disappoint you, and it makes us sad to hear
That it wasn't cool and shady — and there wasn't plenty beer,
And the loony bullock snorted when you first came into view;
Well, you know it's not so often that he sees a swell like you;
And the roads were hot and dusty, and the plains were burnt and brown,
And no doubt you're better suited drinking lemon squash in town.

Yet, perchance, if you should journey down the very track you went
In a month or two at furthest you would wonder what it meant,
Where the sunbaked earth was gasping like a creature in its pain
You would find the grasses waving like a field of summer grain,
And the miles of thirsty gutters blocked with sand and choked with mud,
You would find them mighty rivers with a turbid, sweeping flood;
For the rain and drought and sunshine make no changes in the street,
In the sullen line of buildings and the ceaseless tramp of feet;
But the bush hath moods and changes, as the seasons rise and fall,
And the men who know the bush land — they are loyal through it all.

\* \* \* \*

But you found the bush was dismal and a land of no delight,
Did you chance to hear a chorus in the shearers' huts at night?
Did they "rise up, William Riley" by the camp-fire's cheery blaze?
Did they rise him as we rose him in the good old droving days?
And the women of the homesteads and the men you chanced to meet —
Were their faces sour and saddened like the "faces in the street",
And the "shy selector children" — were they better now or worse
Than the little city urchins who would greet you with a curse?
Is not such a life much better than the squalid street and square
Where the fallen women flaunt it in the fierce electric glare,
Where the sempstress plies her sewing till her eyes are sore and red
In a filthy, dirty attic toiling on for daily bread?
Did you hear no sweeter voices in the music of the bush
Than the roar of trams and buses, and the war whoop of "the push"?
Did the magpies rouse your slumbers with their carol sweet and strange?
Did you hear the silver chiming of the bellbirds on the range?

But, perchance, the wild birds' music by your senses was despised,
For you say you'll stay in townships till the bush is civilised.
Would you make it a tea garden and on Sundays have a band
Where the "blokes" might take their "donahs", with a "public"
      close at hand?
You had better stick to Sydney and make merry with the "push",
For the bush will never suit you, and you'll never suit the bush.

# Last Week

Oh, the new chum went to the backblock run,
But he should have gone there last week.
He tramped ten miles with a loaded gun,
But of turkey or duck he saw never a one,
For he should have been there last week,
    They said,
There were flocks of 'em there last week.

He wended his way to a waterfall,
And he should have gone there last week.
He carried a camera, legs and all,
But the day was hot, and the stream was small,
For he should have gone there last week,
    They said,
They drowned a man there last week.

He went for a drive, and he made a start,
Which should have been made last week,
For the old horse died of a broken heart;
So he footed it home and he dragged the cart —
But the horse was all right last week,
    They said,
He trotted a match last week.

So he asked the bushies who came from far
To visit the town last week,
If they'd dine with him, and they said, "Hurrah!"
But there wasn't a drop in the whisky jar —
"You should have been here last week,"
    He said,
"I drank it all up last week!"

# Those Names

The shearers sat in the firelight, hearty and hale and strong,
After the hard day's shearing, passing the joke along:
The "ringer" that shore a hundred, as they never were shorn before,
And the novice who, toiling bravely, had tommyhawked half a score,
The tar boy, the cook, and the slushy, the sweeper that swept the board,
The picker-up, and the penner, with the rest of the shearing horde.
There were men from the inland stations where the skies like a furnace glow,
And men from the Snowy River, the land of the frozen snow;
There were swarthy Queensland drovers who reckoned all
       land by miles,
And farmers' sons from the Murray, where many a vineyard smiles.
They started at telling stories when they wearied of cards and games,
And to give these stories a flavour they threw in some local names,
And a man from the bleak Monaro, away on the tableland,
He fixed his eyes on the ceiling, and he started to play his hand.

He told them of Adjintoothbong, where the pine-clad mountains freeze,
And the weight of the snow in summer breaks branches off the trees,
And, as he warmed to the business, he let them have it strong —
Nimitybelle, Conargo, Wheeo, Bongongolong;
He lingered over them fondly, because they recalled to mind
A thought of the old bush homestead, and the girl that he left behind.
Then the shearers all sat silent till a man in the corner rose;
Said he, "I've travelled aplenty but never heard names like those,
Out in the western districts, out on the Castlereagh
Most of the names are easy — short for a man to say.
You've heard of Mungrybambone and the Gundabluey pine,
Quobbotha, Girilambone, and Terramungamine,
Quambone, Eunonyhareenyha, Wee Waa, and Buntijo —"
But the rest of the shearers stopped him, "For the sake of your jaw, go slow,
If you reckon those names are short ones out where such names prevail,
Just try and remember some long ones before you begin the tale."

And the man from the western district, though never a word he said,
Just winked with his dexter eyelid, and then he retired to bed.

# A Bush Christening

On the outer Barcoo where the churches are few,
    And men of religion are scanty,
On a road never cross'd 'cept by folk that are lost,
    One Michael Magee had a shanty.

Now this Mike was the dad of a ten-year-old lad,
    Plump, healthy, and stoutly conditioned;
He was strong as the best, but poor Mike had no rest
    For the youngster had never been christened.

And his wife used to cry, "If the darlin' should die
    Saint Peter would not recognise him."
But by luck he survived till a preacher arrived,
    Who agreed straightaway to baptise him.

Now the artful young rogue, while they held their collogue,
    With his ear to the keyhole was listenin',
And he muttered in fright while his features turned white,
    "What the divil and all is this christenin'?"

He was none of your dolts, he had seen them brand colts,
    And it seemed to his small understanding,
If the man in the frock made him one of the flock,
    It must mean something very like branding.

So away with a rush he set off for the bush,
    While the tears in his eyelids they glistened —
" 'Tis outrageous," says he, "to brand youngsters like me,
    I'll be dashed if I'll stop to be christened!"

Like a young native dog he ran into a log,
    And his father with language uncivil,
Never heeding the "praste" cried aloud in his haste,
    "Come out and be christened, you divil!"

But he lay there as snug as a bug in a rug,
    And his parents in vain might reprove him,
Till his reverence spoke (he was fond of a joke)
    "I've a notion," says he, "that'll move him."

"Poke a stick up the log, give the spalpeen a prog;
  Poke him aisy — don't hurt him or maim him,
'Tis not long that he'll stand, I've the water at hand,
  As he rushes out this end I'll name him.

"Here he comes, and for shame! ye've forgotten the name —
  Is it Patsy or Michael or Dinnis?"
Here the youngster ran out, and the priest gave a shout —
  Take your chance, anyhow, wid 'Maginnis'!"

As the howling young cub ran away to the scrub
  Where he knew that pursuit would be risky,
The priest, as he fled, flung a flask at his head
  That was labelled "Maginnis's Whisky!"

And Maginnis Magee has been made a J.P.,
  And the one thing he hates more than sin is
To be asked by the folk who have heard of the joke,
  How he came to be christened "Maginnis"!

# How the Favourite Beat Us

" Aye," said the boozer, "I tell you it's true, sir,
    I once was a punter with plenty of pelf,
But gone is my glory, I'll tell you the story
    How I stiffened my horse and got stiffened myself.

" 'Twas a mare called the Cracker, I came down to back her,
    But found she was favourite all of a rush,
The folk just did pour on to lay six to four on,
    And several bookies were killed in the crush.

"It seems old Tomato was stiff, though a starter;
    They reckoned him fit for the Caulfield to keep.
The Bloke and the Donah were scratched by their owner,
    He only was offered three-fourths of the sweep.

"We knew Salamander was slow as a gander,
    The mare could have beat him the length of the straight,
And old Manumission was out of condition,
    And most of the others were running off weight.

"No doubt someone 'blew it', for everyone knew it,
    The bets were all gone, and I muttered in spite,
'If I can't get a copper, by Jingo, I'll stop her,
    Let the public fall in, it will serve the brutes right.'

"I said to the jockey, 'Now, listen, my cocky,
    You watch as you're cantering down by the stand,
I'll wait where that toff is and give you the office,
    You're only to win if I lift up my hand.'

"I then tried to back her — 'What price is the Cracker?'
    'Our books are all full, sir,' each bookie did swear;
My mind, then, I made up, my fortune I played up
    I bet every shilling against my own mare.

"I strolled to the gateway, the mare in the straight way
    Was shifting and dancing, and pawing the ground,
The boy saw me enter and wheeled for his canter,
    When a darned great mosquito came buzzing around.

"They breed 'em at Hexham, it's risky to vex 'em,
    They suck a man dry at a sitting, no doubt,
But just as the mare passed, he fluttered my hair past,
    I lifted my hand, and I flattened him out.

"I was stunned when they started, the mare simply darted
    Away to the front when the flag was let fall,
For none there could match her, and none tried to catch her —
    She finished a furlong in front of them all.

"You bet that I went for the boy, whom I sent for
    The moment he weighed and came out of the stand —
'Who paid you to win it? Come, own up this minute.'
    'Lord love yer,' said he, 'why, you lifted your hand.'

" 'Twas true, by St Peter, that cursed 'muskeeter'
    Had broke me so broke that I hadn't a brown,
And you'll find the best course is when dealing with horses
    To win when you're able, and *keep your hands down*."

# The Great Calamity

MacFierce'un came to Whiskeyhurst
 When summer days were hot,
And bided there wi' Jock McThirst,
 A brawny brother Scot.
Gude Faith! They made the whiskey fly,
 Like Highland chieftains true,
And when they'd drunk the beaker dry
 They sang, "We are nae fou!"

"There is nae folk like oor ain folk,
 Sae gallant and sae true."
They sang the only Scottish joke
 Which is, "We are nae fou."

Said bold McThirst, "Let Saxons jaw
 Aboot their great concerns,
But bonny Scotland beats them a',
 The land o' cakes and Burns,
The land o' partridge, deer, and grouse,
 Fill up your glass, I beg,
There's muckle whuskey i' the house,
 Forbye what's in the keg."

And here a hearty laugh he laughed,
 "Just come wi' me, I beg."
MacFierce'un saw with pleasure daft
 A fifty-gallon keg.

"Losh, man, that's grand," MacFierce'un cried,
 "Saw ever man the like?
Now, wi' the daylight, I maun ride
 To meet a Southron tyke,
But I'll be back ere summer's gone,
 So bide for me, I beg,
We'll make a grand assault upon
 Yon deevil of a keg."

\* \* \* \*

MacFierce'un rode to Whiskeyhurst,
    When summer days were gone,
And there he met with Jock McThirst
    Was greetin' all alone.
"McThirst, what gars ye look sae blank?
    Have all yer wits gane daft?
Has that accursed Southron bank
    Called up your overdraft?
Is all your grass burnt up wi' drouth?
    Is wool and hides gone flat?"
McThirst replied, "Gude friend, in truth,
    'Tis muckle waur than that."

"Has sair misfortune cursed your life
    That you should weep sae free?
Is harm upon your bonny wife,
    The children at your knee?
Is scaith upon your house and hame?"
    McThirst upraised his head:
"My bairns hae done the deed of shame —
    'Twere better they were dead.

"To think my bonny infant son
    Should do the deed o' guilt —
*He let the whuskey spigot run,*
    *And a' the whuskey's spilt!"*

                    * * * *

Upon them both these words did bring
    A solemn silence deep,
Gude faith, it is a fearsome thing
    To see two strong men weep.

# Come-by-Chance

As I pondered very weary o'er a volume long and dreary —
For the plot was void of interest — 'Twas that Postal Guide, in fact,
There I learnt the true location, distance, size, and population
Of each township, town, and village in the radius of the Act.

And I learnt that Puckawidgee stands beside the Murrumbidgee,
And that Booleroi and Bumble get their letters twice a year,
Also that the post inspector, when he visited Collector,
Closed the office up instanter, and re-opened Dungalear.

But my languid mood forsook me, when I found a name that took me,
Quite by chance I came across it — "Come-by-Chance" was what I read;
No location was assigned it, not a thing to help one find it,
Just an "N" which stood for northward, and the rest was all unsaid.

I shall leave my home, and forthward wander stoutly to the northward
Till I come by chance across it, and I'll straightway settle down,
For there can't be any hurry, nor the slightest cause for worry
Where the telegraph don't reach you nor the railways run to town.

And one's letters and exchanges come by chance across the ranges,
Where a wiry young Australian leads a pack horse once a week,
And the good news grows by keeping, and you're spared the pain of weeping
Over bad news when the mailman drops the letters in the creek.

But I fear, and more's the pity, that there's really no such city,
For there's not a man can find it of the shrewdest folk I know,
"Come-by-Chance", be sure it never means a land of fierce endeavour,
It is just the careless country where the dreamers only go.

\* \* \* \*

Though we work and toil and hustle in our life of haste and bustle,
All that makes our life worth living comes unstriven for and free;
Man may weary and importune, but the fickle goddess Fortune
Deals him out his pain or pleasure careless what his worth may be.

All the happy times entrancing, days of sport and nights of dancing,
Moonlit rides and stolen kisses, pouting lips and loving glance:
When you think of these be certain you have looked behind the curtain,
You have had the luck to linger just a while in "Come-by-Chance".

# Under the Shadow of Kiley's Hill

This is the place where they all were bred;
Some of the rafters are standing still;
Now they are scattered and lost and dead,
Every one from the old nest fled,
Out of the shadow of Kiley's Hill.

Better it is that they ne'er came back —
Changes and chances are quickly rung;
Now the old homestead is gone to rack,
Green is the grass on the well-worn track
Down by the gate where the roses clung.

Gone is the garden they kept with care;
Left to decay at its own sweet will,
Fruit trees and flower beds eaten bare,
Cattle and sheep where the roses were,
Under the shadow of Kiley's Hill.

Where are the children that throve and grew
In the old homestead in days gone by?
One is away on the far Barcoo
Watching his cattle the long year through,
Watching them starve in the droughts and die.

One in the town where all cares are rife,
Weary with troubles that cramp and kill,
Fain would be done with the restless strife,
Fain would go back to the old bush life,
Back to the shadow of Kiley's Hill.

One is away on the roving quest,
Seeking his share of the golden spoil,
Out in the wastes of the trackless west,
Wandering ever he gives the best
Of his years and strength to the hopeless toil.

What of the parents? That unkempt mound
Shows where they slumber united still;
Rough is their grave, but they sleep as sound
Out on the range as on holy ground,
Under the shadow of Kiley's Hill.

# Jim Carew

Born of a thoroughbred English race,
    Well-proportioned and closely knit,
Neat of figure and handsome face,
    Always ready and always fit,
Hard and wiry of limb and thew,
That was the ne'er-do-well Jim Carew.

One of the sons of the good old land —
    Many a year since his like was known;
Never a game but he took command,
    Never a sport but he held his own;
Gained at his college a triple blue —
Good as they make them was Jim Carew.

Came to grief — was it card or horse?
    Nobody asked and nobody cared;
Ship him away to the bush of course,
    Ne'er-do-well fellows are easily spared;
Only of women a tolerable few
Sorrowed at parting with Jim Carew.

Gentleman Jim on the cattle camp,
    Sitting his horse with an easy grace;
But the reckless living has left its stamp
    In the deep drawn lines of that handsome face,
And a harder look in those eyes of blue:
Prompt at a quarrel is Jim Carew.

Billy the Lasher was out for gore —
    Twelve-stone navvy with chest of hair,
When he opened out with a hungry roar,
    On a ten-stone man it was hardly fair;
But his wife was wise if his face she knew
By the time you were done with him, Jim Carew.

Gentleman Jim in the stockmen's hut
    Works with them, toils with them, side by side;
As to his past — well, his lips are shut.
    "Gentleman once," say his mates with pride;
And the wildest cornstalk can ne'er outdo
In feats of recklessness, Jim Carew.

What should he live for? A dull despair!
    Drink is his master and drags him down,
Water of Lethe that drowns all care.
    Gentleman Jim has a lot to drown,
And he reigns as king with a drunken crew,
Sinking to misery, Jim Carew.

Such is the end of the ne'er-do-well —
    Jimmy the Boozer, all down at heel;
But he straightens up when he's asked to tell
    His name and race, and a flash of steel
Still lightens up in those eyes of blue —
"I am, or — no, I *was* — Jim Carew."

# The Swagman's Rest

We buried old Bob where the bloodwoods wave
    At the foot of the Eaglehawk;
We fashioned a cross on the old man's grave,
    For fear that his ghost might walk;
We carved his name on a bloodwood tree,
    With the date of his sad decease,
And in place of "Died from effects of spree",
    We wrote, "May he rest in peace".

For Bob was known on the Overland,
    A regular old bush wag,
Tramping along in the dust and sand,
    Humping his well worn swag.
He would camp for days in the river bed,
    And loiter and "fish for whales".
"I'm into the swagman's yard", he said,
    "And I never shall find the rails."

But he found the rails on that summer night
    For a better place — or worse,
As we watched by turns in the flickering light
    With an old black gin for nurse.
The breeze came in with the scent of pine,
    The river sounded clear,
When a change came on, and we saw the sign
    That told us the end was near.

But he spoke in a cultured voice and low —
    "I fancy they've 'sent the route';
I once was an army man, you know,
    Though now I'm a drunken brute;
But bury me out where the bloodwoods wave,
    And if ever you're fairly stuck,
Just take and shovel me out of the grave,
    And, maybe, I'll bring you luck.

"For I've always heard —" here his voice fell weak,
  His strength was well-nigh sped,
He gasped and struggled and tried to speak,
  Then fell in a moment — dead.
Thus ended a wasted life and hard,
  Of energies misapplied —
Old Bob was out of the "swagman's yard"
  And over the Great Divide.

* * * *

The drought came down on the field and flock,
  And never a raindrop fell,
Though the tortured moans of the starving stock
  Might soften a fiend from hell.
And we thought of the hint that the swagman gave
  When he went to the Great Unseen —
We shovelled the skeleton out of the grave
  To see what his hint might mean.

We dug where the cross and the graveposts were,
  We shovelled away the mould,
When sudden a vein of quartz lay bare
  All gleaming with yellow gold.
'Twas a reef with never a fault nor baulk
  That ran from the range's crest,
And the richest mine on the Eaglehawk
  Is known as "The Swagman's Rest".

# The Daylight is Dying

The daylight is dying
　　Away in the west,
The wild birds are flying
　　In silence to rest;
In leafage and frondage
　　Where shadows are deep,
They pass to its bondage —
　　The kingdom of sleep.
And watched in their sleeping
　　By stars in the height,
They rest in your keeping,
　　Oh, wonderful night.

When night doth her glories
　　Of starshine unfold,
'Tis then that the stories
　　Of bushland are told.
Unnumbered I hold them
　　In memories bright,
But who could unfold them,
　　Or read them aright?
Beyond all denials
　　The stars in their glories
The breeze in the myalls
　　Are part of these stories.
The waving of grasses,
　　The song of the river

That sings as it passes
　　For ever and ever,
The hobble chain's rattle,
　　The calling of birds,
The lowing of cattle
　　Must blend with the words.

Without these, indeed, you
    Would find it ere long,
As though I should read you
    The words of a song
That lamely would linger
    When lacking the rune,
The voice of the singer,
    The lilt of the tune.

But, as one half-hearing
    An old-time refrain,
With memory clearing,
    Recalls it again,
These tales, roughly wrought of
    The bush and its ways,
May call back a thought of
    The wandering days,
And, blending with each
    In the mem'ries that throng,
There haply shall reach
    You some echo of song.

# Rio Grande and Other Verses

# Rio Grande's Last Race

Now this was what Macpherson told
    While waiting in the stand;
A reckless rider, over-bold,
The only man with hands to hold
    The rushing Rio Grande.

He said, "This day I bid goodbye
    To bit and bridle rein,
To ditches deep and fences high,
For I have dreamed a dream, and I
    Shall never ride again.

"I dreamed last night I rode this race
    That I to-day must ride,
And cant'ring down to take my place
I saw full many an old friend's face
    Come stealing to my side.

"Dead men on horses long since dead,
    They clustered on the track;
The champions of the days long fled,
They moved around with noiseless tread —
    Bay, chestnut, brown, and black.

"And one man on a big grey steed
    Rode up and waved his hand;
Said he, 'We help a friend in need,
And we have come to give a lead
    To you and Rio Grande.

" 'For you must give the field the slip,
    So never draw the rein,
But keep him moving with the whip,
And if he falter — set your lip
    And rouse him up again.

" 'But when you reach the big stone wall,
    Put down your bridle hand

And let him sail — he cannot fall —
But don't you interfere at all;
    You trust old Rio Grande.'

"We started, and in front we showed,
    The big horse running free:
Right fearlessly and game he strode,
And by my side those dead men rode
    Whom no one else could see.

"As silently as flies a bird,
    They rode on either hand;
At every fence I plainly heard
The phantom leader give the word,
    'Make room for Rio Grande!'

"I spurred him on to get the lead,
    I chanced full many a fall;
But swifter still each phantom steed
Kept with me, and at racing speed
    We reached the big stone wall.

"And there the phantoms on each side
    Drew in and blocked his leap;
'Make room! make room!' I loudly cried,
But right in front they seemed to ride —
    I cursed them in my sleep.

"He never flinched, he faced it game,
    He struck it with his chest,
And every stone burst out in flame,
And Rio Grande and I became
    As phantoms with the rest.

"And then I woke, and for a space
    All nerveless did I seem;
For I have ridden many a race,
But never one at such a pace
    As in that fearful dream.

"And I am sure as man can be
    That out upon the track,
Those phantoms that men cannot see
Are waiting now to ride with me,
    And I shall not come back.

"For I must ride the dead men's race,
    And follow their command;
'Twere worse than death, the foul disgrace
If I should fear to take my place
    Today on Rio Grande."

He mounted, and a jest he threw,
    With never sign of gloom;
But all who heard the story knew
That Jack Macpherson, brave and true,
    Was going to his doom.

They started, and the big black steed
    Came flashing past the stand;
All single-handed in the lead
He strode along at racing speed,
    The mighty Rio Grande.

But on his ribs the whalebone stung,
    A madness it did seem!
And soon it rose on every tongue
That Jack Macpherson rode among
    The creatures of his dream.

He looked to left and looked to right,
    As though men rode beside;
And Rio Grande, with foam-flecks white,
Raced at his jumps in headlong flight
    And cleared them in his stride.

But when they reached the big stone wall,
    Down went the bridle hand,
And loud we heard Macpherson call,
"Make room, or half the field will fall!
    Make room for Rio Grande!"

"He's down! he's down!" And horse and man
    Lay quiet side by side!
No need the pallid face to scan,
We knew with Rio Grande he ran
    The race the dead men ride.

# With French to Kimberley

The Boers were down on Kimberley with siege and Maxim gun;
The Boers were down on Kimberley, their numbers ten to one!
Faint were the hopes the British had to make the struggle good,
Defenceless in an open plain the Diamond City stood.
They built them forts from bags of sand, they fought from roof and wall,
They flashed a message to the south, "Help! or the town must fall!"
And down our ranks the order ran to march at dawn of day,
For French was off to Kimberley to drive the Boers away.

He made no march along the line; he made no front attack
Upon those Magersfontein heights that drove the Scotchmen back;
But eastward over pathless plains by open veldt and vley,
Across the front of Cronje's force his troopers held their way.
The springbuck, feeding on the flats where Modder River runs,
Were startled by his horses' hoofs, the rumble of his guns.
The Dutchman's spies that watched his march from every rocky wall
Rode back in haste: "He marches east! He threatens Jacobsdal!"
Then north he wheeled as wheels the hawk and showed to their dismay,
That French was off to Kimberley to drive the Boers away.

His column was five thousand strong — all mounted men — and guns:
There met, beneath the world-wide flag, the world-wide Empire's sons;
They came to prove to all the earth that kinship conquers space,
And those who fight the British Isles must fight the British race!
From far New Zealand's flax and fern, from cold Canadian snows,
From Queensland plains, where hot as fire the summer sunshine glows;
And in the front the Lancers rode that New South Wales had sent:
With easy stride across the plain their long, lean Walers went.
Unknown, untried, those squadrons were, but proudly out they drew
Beside the English regiments that fought at Waterloo.
From every coast, from every clime, they met in proud array,
To go with French to Kimberley to drive the Boers away.

He crossed the Reit and fought his way towards the Modder bank.
The foemen closed behind his march, and hung upon the flank.
The long, dry grass was all ablaze, and fierce the veldt fire runs;
He fought them through a wall of flame that blazed around the guns!
Then limbered up and drove at speed, though horses fell and died;

We might not halt for man nor beast on that wild, daring ride.
Black with the smoke and parched with thirst, we pressed the livelong day
Our headlong march to Kimberley to drive the Boers away.

We reached the drift at fall of night, and camped across the ford.
Next day from all the hills around the Dutchman's cannons roared.
A narrow pass between the hills, with guns on either side;
The boldest man might well turn pale before that pass he tried,
For if the first attack should fail then every hope was gone:
But French looked once, and only once, and then he said, "Push on!"
The gunners plied their guns amain; the hail of shrapnel flew;
With rifle fire and lancer charge their squadrons back we threw;
And through the pass between the hills we swept in furious fray,
And French was through to Kimberley to drive the Boers away.

Ay, French was through to Kimberley! And ere the day was done
We saw the Diamond City stand, lit by the evening sun:
Above the town the heliograph hung like an eye of flame:
Around the town the foemen camped — they knew not that we came;
But soon they saw us, rank on rank; they heard our squadrons' tread;
In panic fear they left their tents, in hopeless rout they fled;
And French rode into Kimberley; the people cheered amain,
The women came with tear-stained eyes to touch his bridle rein,
The starving children lined the streets to raise a feeble cheer,
The bells rang out a joyous peal to say "Relief is here!"
Ay! we that saw that stirring march are proud that we can say
We went with French to Kimberley to drive the Boers away.

# By the Grey Gulf-water

Far to the Northward there lies a land,
  A wonderful land that the winds blow over,
And none may fathom nor understand
  The charm it holds for the restless rover;
A great grey chaos — a land half made,
  Where endless space is and no life stirreth;
And the soul of a man will recoil afraid
  From the sphinx-like visage that Nature weareth.
But old Dame Nature, though scornful, craves
  Her dole of death and her share of slaughter;
Many indeed are the nameless graves
  Where her victims sleep by the Grey Gulf-water.

Slowly and slowly those grey streams glide,
  Drifting along with a languid motion,
Lapping the reed beds on either side,
  Wending their way to the Northern Ocean.
Grey are the plains where the emus pass
  Silent and slow, with their staid demeanour;
Over the dead men's graves the grass
  Maybe is waving a trifle greener.
Down in the world where men toil and spin
  Dame Nature smiles as man's hand has taught her;
Only the dead men her smiles can win
  In the great lone land by the Grey Gulf-water.

For the strength of man is an insect's strength,
  In the face of that mighty plain and river,
And the life of a man is a moment's length
  To the life of the stream that will run for ever.
And so it cometh they take no part
  In small-world worries; each hardy rover
Rideth abroad and is light of heart,
  With the plains around and the blue sky over.
And up in the heavens the brown lark sings
  The songs that the strange wild land has taught her;
Full of thanksgiving her sweet song rings —
  And I wish I were back by the Grey Gulf-water.

# With the Cattle

The drought is down on field and flock,
  The river bed is dry;
And we must shift the starving stock
  Before the cattle die.
We muster up with weary hearts
  At breaking of the day,
And turn our heads to foreign parts,
  To take the stock away.
    And it's hunt 'em up and dog 'em,
    And it's get the whip and flog 'em,
For it's weary work is droving when they're
    dying every day;
    By stock routes bare and eaten,
    On dusty roads and beaten,
With half a chance to save their lives we
    take the stock away.

We cannot use the whip for shame
  On beasts that crawl along;
We have to drop the weak and lame,
  And try to save the strong;
The wrath of God is on the track,
  The drought fiend holds his sway,
With blows and cries and stockwhip crack
  We take the stock away.
    As they fall we leave them lying,
    With the crows to watch them dying,
Grim sextons of the Overland that fasten on their prey;
    By the fiery dust storm drifting,
    And the mocking mirage shifting,
In heat and drought and hopeless pain we
    take the stock away.

In dull despair the days go by
  With never hope of change,
But every stage we draw more nigh
  Towards the mountain range;

And some may live to climb the pass,
    And reach the great plateau,
And revel in the mountain grass,
    By streamlets fed with snow.
        As the mountain wind is blowing
        It starts the cattle lowing,
And calling to each other down the dusty long array;
        And there speaks a grizzled drover:
        "Well, thank God, the worst is over,
The creatures smell the mountain grass that's
        twenty miles away."

They press towards the mountain grass,
    They look with eager eyes
Along the rugged stony pass,
    That slopes towards the skies;
Their feet may bleed from rocks and stones,
    But though the blood-drop starts,
They struggle on with stifled groans,
    For hope is in their hearts.
        And the cattle that are leading,
        Though their feet are worn and bleeding,
Are breaking to a kind of run — pull up, and let them go!
        For the mountain wind is blowing,
        And the mountain grass is growing,
They settle down by running streams ice-cold with melted snow.

The days are done of heat and drought
    Upon the stricken plain;
The wind has shifted right about,
    And brought the welcome rain;
The river runs with sullen roar,
    All flecked with yellow foam,
And we must take the road once more,
    To bring the cattle home.
        And it's "Lads! we'll raise a chorus,
        There's a pleasant trip before us."
And the horses bound beneath us as we start
    them down the track;
        And the drovers canter, singing,
        Through the sweet green grasses springing,

Towards the far-off mountain land, to bring the
    cattle back.

Are these the beasts we brought away
    That move so lively now?
They scatter off like flying spray
    Across the mountain's brow;
And dashing down the rugged range
    We hear the stockwhip crack,
Good faith, it is a welcome change
    To bring such cattle back.
        And it's "Steady down the lead there!"
        And it's "Let 'em stop and feed there!"
For they're wild as mountain eagles and
        their sides are all afoam;
        But they're settling down already,
        And they'll travel nice and steady,
With cheery call and jest and song we fetch
    the cattle home.

We have to watch them close at night
    For fear they'll make a rush,
And break away in headlong flight
    Across the open bush;
And by the campfire's cheery blaze,
    With mellow voice and strong,
We hear the lonely watchman raise
    The Overlander's song:
        "Oh! it's when we're done with roving,
        With the camping and the droving,
It's homeward down the Bland we'll go,
        and never more we'll roam";
        While the stars shine out above us,
        Like the eyes of those who love us —
The eyes of those who watch and wait to greet
    the cattle home.

The plains are all awave with grass,
    The skies are deepest blue;
And leisurely the cattle pass
    And feed the long day through;

But when we sight the station gate,
　　We make the stockwhips crack,
A welcome sound to those who wait
　　To greet the cattle back:
　　　　And through the twilight falling
　　　　We hear their voices calling,
As the cattle splash across the ford and
　　　　churn it into foam;
　　　　And the children run to meet us,
　　　　And our wives and sweethearts greet us,
Their heroes from the Overland who brought
　　　　the cattle home.

# The First Surveyor

### His Widow Speaks

"The opening of the railway line! The Governor and all!
With flags and banners down the street, a banquet and a ball.
Hark to 'em at the station now! They're raising cheer on cheer!
'The man who brought the railway through — our friend the engineer!'

"They cheer *his* pluck and enterprise and engineering skill!
'Twas my old husband found the pass behind that big red hill.
Before the engineer was grown we settled with our stock
Behind that great big mountain chain, a line of range and rock —
A line that kept us starving there in weary weeks of drought,
With ne'er a track across the range to let the cattle out.

" 'Twas then, with horses starved and weak and scarcely fit to crawl,
My husband went to find a way across that rocky wall.
He vanished in the wilderness, God knows where he was gone,
He hunted till his food gave out, but still he battled on.
His horses strayed — 'twas well they did — they made towards the grass,
And down behind that big red hill they found an easy pass.

"He followed up and blazed the trees, to show the safest track,
Then drew his belt another hole and turned and started back.
His horses died — just one pulled through with nothing much to spare;
God bless the beast that brought him home, the old white Arab mare!
We drove the cattle through the hills, along the new-found way,
And this was our first camping ground — just where I live to-day.

"Then others came across the range and built the township here,
And then there came the railway line and this young engineer.
He drove about with tents and traps, a cook to cook his meals,
A bath to wash himself at night, a chain-man at his heels.
And that was all the pluck and skill for which he's cheered and praised,
For after all he took the track, the same my husband blazed!

"My poor old husband, dead and gone with never feast nor cheer;
He's buried by the railway line! — I wonder can he hear
When down the very track he marked, and close to where he's laid,
The cattle trains go roaring down the one-in-thirty grade.

111

I wonder does he hear them pass and can he see the sight,
When through the dark the fast express goes flaming by at night?

"I think 'twould comfort him to know there's someone left to care,
I'll take some things this very night and hold a banquet there!
The hard old fare we've often shared together, him and me,
Some damper and a bite of beef, a pannikin of tea:
We'll do without the bands and flags, the speeches and the fuss,
We know who *ought* to get the cheers and that's enough for us.

"What's that? They wish that I'd come down — the oldest settler here!
Present me to the Governor and that young engineer!
Well, just you tell his Excellence and put the thing polite,
I'm sorry, but I can't come down — I'm dining out tonight!"

## Mulga Bill's Bicycle

'Twas Mulga Bill, from Eaglehawk, that caught the cycling craze;
He turned away the good old horse that served him many days;
He dressed himself in cycling clothes, resplendent to be seen;
He hurried off to town and bought a shining new machine;
And as he wheeled it through the door, with air of lordly pride,
The grinning shop assistant said, "Excuse me, can you ride?"

"See here, young man," said Mulga Bill, "from Walgett to the sea,
From Conroy's Gap to Castlereagh, there's none can ride like me.
I'm good all round at everything, as everybody knows,
Although I'm not the one to talk — I *hate* a man that blows.
But riding is my special gift, my chiefest, sole delight;
Just ask a wild duck can it swim, a wildcat can it fight.
There's nothing clothed in hair or hide, or built of flesh or steel,
There's nothing walks or jumps, or runs, on axle, hoof, or wheel,
But what I'll sit, while hide will hold and girth and straps are tight:
I'll ride this here two-wheeled concern right straight away at sight."

'Twas Mulga Bill, from Eaglehawk, that sought his own abode,
That perched above the Dead Man's Creek, beside the mountain road.
He turned the cycle down the hill and mounted for the fray,
But ere he'd gone a dozen yards it bolted clean away.
It left the track, and through the trees, just like a silver streak,
It whistled down the awful slope towards the Dead Man's Creek.

It shaved a stump by half an inch, it dodged a big white box:
The very wallaroos in fright went scrambling up the rocks,
The wombats hiding in their caves dug deeper underground,
As Mulga Bill, as white as chalk, sat tight to every bound.
It struck a stone and gave a spring that cleared a fallen tree,
It raced beside a precipice as close as close could be;
And then as Mulga Bill let out one last despairing shriek
It made a leap of twenty feet into the Dead Man's Creek.

'Twas Mulga Bill, from Eaglehawk, that slowly swam ashore:
He said, "I've had some narrer shaves and lively rides before;
I've rode a wild bull round a yard to win a five-pound bet,
But this was the most awful ride that I've encountered yet.
I'll give that two-wheeled outlaw best; it's shaken all my nerve
To feel it whistle through the air and plunge and buck and swerve.
It's safe at rest in Dead Man's Creek, we'll leave it lying still;
A horse's back is good enough henceforth for Mulga Bill."

# The Pearl Diver

Kanzo Makame, the diver, sturdy and small Japanee,
  Seeker of pearls and of pearl shell down in the depths of the sea,
Trudged o'er the bed of the ocean, searching industriously.

Over the pearl grounds, the lugger drifted — a little white speck:
Joe Nagasaki, the "tender", holding the life line on deck,
Talked through the rope to the diver, knew when to drift or to check.

Kanzo was king of his lugger, master and diver in one,
Diving wherever it pleased him, taking instructions from none;
Hither and thither he wandered, steering by stars and by sun.

Fearless he was beyond credence, looking at death eye to eye:
This was his formula always, "All man go dead by and by —
S'posing time come no can help it — s'pose time no come, then no die."

Dived in the depths of the Darnleys, down twenty fathom and five;
Down where by law and by reason, men are forbidden to dive;
Down in a pressure so awful that only the strongest survive:

Sweated four men at the air pumps, fast as the handles could go,
Forcing the air down that reached him, heated, and tainted, and slow —
Kanzo Makame the diver stayed seven minutes below;

Came up on deck like a dead man, paralysed body and brain;
Suffered, while blood was returning, infinite tortures of pain:
Sailed once again to the Darnleys — laughed and descended again!

* * * *

Scarce grew the shell in the shallows, rarely a patch could they touch;
Always the take was so little, always the labour so much;
Always they thought of the Islands held by the lumbering Dutch,

Islands where shell was in plenty lying in passage and bay,
Islands where divers could gather hundreds of shell in a day:
But the lumbering Dutch, with their gunboats, hunted the divers away.

Joe Nagasaki, the "tender", finding the profits grow small,
Said, "Let us go to the Islands, try for a number one haul!
If we get caught, go to prison — let them take lugger and all!"

115

Kanzo Makame, the diver — knowing full well what it meant —
Fatalist, gambler, and stoic, smiled a broad smile of content,
Flattened in mainsail and foresail, and off to the Islands they went.

Close to the headlands they drifted, picking up shell by the ton,
Piled up on deck were the oysters, opening wide in the sun,
When, from the lee of the headland, boomed the report of a gun.

Once that the diver was sighted, pearl shell and lugger must go.
Joe Nagasaki decided — quick was the word and the blow —
Cut both the pipe and the life line, leaving the diver below!

Kanzo Makame, the diver, failing to quite understand,
Pulled the "haul up" on the life line, found it was slack in his hand;
Then, like a little brown stoic, lay down and died on the sand.

Joe Nagasaki, the "tender", smiling a sanctified smile,
Headed her straight for the gunboat — throwing out shells all the while —
Then went aboard and reported, "No makee dive in three mile!

"Dress no have got and no helmet — diver go shore on the spree;
Plenty wind come and break rudder — lugger get blown out to sea:
Take me to Japanee Consul, he help a poor Japanee!"

\* \* \* \*

So the Dutch let him go, and they watched him, as off from the Islands he ran,
Doubting him much, but what would you? You have to be sure of your man
Ere you wake up that nest full of hornets — the little brown men of Japan.

Down in the ooze and the coral, down where earth's wonders are spread,
Helmeted, ghastly, and swollen, Kanzo Makame lies dead:
Joe Nagasaki, his "tender", is owner and diver instead.

Wearer of pearls in your necklace, comfort yourself if you can,
These are the risks of the pearling — these are the ways of Japan,
"Plenty more Japanee diver, plenty more little brown man!"

# The City of Dreadful Thirst

The stranger came from Narromine and made his little joke —
"They say we folks in Narromine are narrow-minded folk.
But all the smartest men down here are puzzled to define
A kind of new phenomenon that came to Narromine.

"Last summer up in Narromine 'twas gettin' rather warm —
Two hundred in the water bag, and lookin' like a storm —
We all were in the private bar, the coolest place in town,
When out across the stretch of plain a cloud came rollin' down,

"We don't respect the clouds up there, they fill us with disgust,
They mostly bring a Bogan shower — three raindrops
     and some dust;
But each man, simultaneous-like, to each man said, 'I think
That cloud suggests it's up to us to have another drink!'

"There's clouds of rain and clouds of dust — we'd heard
     of them before,
And sometimes in the daily press we read of 'clouds of war':
But — if this ain't the Gospel truth I hope that I may burst —
That cloud that came to Narromine was just a cloud of thirst.

"It wasn't like a common cloud, 'twas more a sort of haze;
It settled down about the streets, and stopped for days and days,
And not a drop of dew could fall and not a sunbeam shine
To pierce that dismal sort of mist that hung on Narromine.

"Oh, Lord! we had a dreadful time beneath that cloud of thirst!
We all chucked-up our daily work and went upon the burst.
The very blacks about the town that used to cadge for grub,
They made an organised attack and tried to loot the pub.

"We couldn't leave the private bar no matter how we tried;
Shearers and squatters, union men and blacklegs side by side
Were drinkin' there and dursn't move, for each was sure, he said,
Before he'd get a half a mile the thirst would strike him dead!

"We drank until the drink gave out, we searched from
        room to room,
And round the pub, like drunken ghosts, went howling
        through the gloom.
The shearers found some kerosene and settled down again,
But all the squatter chaps and I, we staggered to the train.

"And, once outside the cloud of thirst, we felt as right as pie,
But while we stopped about the town we had to drink or die.
But now I hear it's safe enough, I'm going back to work
Because they say the cloud of thirst has shifted on to Bourke.

"But when you see those clouds about — like this one over here —
All white and frothy at the top, just like a pint of beer,
It's time to go and have a drink, for if that cloud should burst
You'd find the drink would all be gone, for that's a cloud of thirst!"

                    * * * *

We stood the man from Narromine a pint of half-and-half;
He drank it off without a gasp in one tremendous quaff;
"I joined some friends last night," he said, "in what
        *they* called a spree;
But after Narromine 'twas just a holiday to me."

And now beyond the Western Range, where sunset skies are red,
And clouds of dust, and clouds of thirst, go drifting overhead,
The railway train is taking back, along the Western Line,
That narrow-minded person on his road to Narromine.

# Saltbush Bill's Gamecock

'Twas Saltbush Bill, with his travelling sheep, was making his
    way to town;
He crossed them over the Hard Times Run, and he came to the Take 'Em Down;
He counted through at the boundary gate, and camped at the drafting yard:
For Stingy Smith, of the Hard Times Run, had hunted him rather hard.
He bore no malice to Stingy Smith — 'Twas simply the hand of fate
That caused his waggon to swerve aside and shatter old Stingy's gate;
And, being only the hand of fate, it follows, without a doubt,
It wasn't the fault of Saltbush Bill that Stingy's sheep got out.
So Saltbush Bill, with an easy heart, prepared for what might befall,
Commenced his stages on Take 'Em Down, the station of Rooster Hall.

'Tis strange how often the men outback will take to some curious craft,
Some ruling passion to keep their thoughts away from the overdraft;
And Rooster Hall, of the Take 'Em Down, was widely known to fame
As breeder of champion fighting cocks — his *forte* was the British Game.
The passing stranger within his gates that camped with old Rooster Hall
Was forced to talk about fowls all night, or else not talk at all.
Though droughts should come, and though sheep should die, his fowls were
    his sole delight;
He left his shed in the flood of work to watch two gamecocks fight.
He held in scorn the Australian Game, that long-legged child of sin;
In a desperate fight, with the steel-tipped spurs, the British Game must win!
The Australian bird was a mongrel bird, with a touch of the jungle cock;
The want of breeding must find him out, when facing the English stock;
For British breeding, and British pluck, must triumph it over all —
And that was the root of the simple creed that governed old Rooster Hall.

\* \* \* \*

'Twas Saltbush Bill to the station rode ahead of his travelling sheep,
And sent a message to Rooster Hall that wakened him out of his sleep —
A crafty message that fetched him out, and hurried him as he came —
"A drover has an Australian Bird to match with your British Game."
'Twas done, and done in half a trice; a five-pound note aside;
Old Rooster Hall, with his champion bird, and the drover's bird untried.
"Steel spurs, of course?" said old Rooster Hall; "you'll need 'em,
    without a doubt!"

119

"You stick the spurs on your bird," said Bill, "but mine fights best without."
"Fights best without?" said old Rooster Hall; "he can't fight best unspurred!
You must be crazy!" But Saltbush Bill said, "Wait till you see my bird!"

So Rooster Hall to his fowl yard went, and quickly back he came,
Bearing a clipt and a shaven cock, the pride of his English Game.
With an eye as fierce as an eaglehawk, and a crow like a trumpet call,
He strutted about on the garden walk, and cackled at Rooster Hall.
Then Rooster Hall sent off a boy with word to his cronies two,
McCrae (the boss of the Black Police) and Father Donahoo.
Full many a cockfight old McCrae had held in his empty Court,
With Father D. as a picker-up — a regular all-round Sport!

They got the message of Rooster Hall, and down to his run they came,
Prepared to scoff at the drover's bird, and to bet on the English Game;
They hied them off to the drover's camp, while Saltbush rode before —
Old Rooster Hall was a blithesome man, when he thought of the treat in store.
They reached the camp, where the drover's cook, with countenance all serene,
Was boiling beef in an iron pot, but never a fowl was seen.

"Take off the beef from the fire," said Bill, "and wait till you see the fight;
There's something fresh for the bill-of-fare — there's game-fowl stew to-night!
For Mister Hall has a fighting cock, all feathered and clipped and spurred;
And he's fetched him here, for a bit of sport, to fight our Australian bird.
I've made a match that our pet will win, though he's hardly a fighting cock,
But he's game enough, and it's many a mile that he's tramped with the
        travelling stock."
The cook he banged on a saucepan lid; and, soon as the sound was heard,
Under the dray, in the shadows hid, a something moved and stirred:
A great tame Emu strutted out. Said Saltbush, "Here's our bird!"
But Rooster Hall, and his cronies two, drove home without a word.

The passing stranger within his gates that camps with old Rooster Hall
Must talk about something else than fowls, if he wishes to talk at all.
For the record lies in the local Court, and filed in its deepest vault,
That Peter Hall, of the Take 'Em Down, was tried for a fierce assault
On a stranger man, who, in all good faith, and prompted by what he heard,
Had asked old Hall if a British Game could beat an Australian bird;
And old McCrae, who was on the Bench, as soon as the case was tried,
Remarked, "Discharged with a clean discharge — the assault was justified!"

# Hay and Hell and Booligal

"You come and see me, boys," he said;
    "You'll find a welcome and a bed
    And whisky any time you call;
Although our township hasn't got
The name of quite a lively spot —
    You see, I live in Booligal.

"And people have an awful down
Upon the district and the town —
    Which worse than hell itself they call;
In fact, the saying far and wide
Along the Riverina side
    Is 'Hay and Hell and Booligal'.

"No doubt it suits 'em very well
To say it's worse than Hay or Hell,
    But don't you heed their talk at all;
Of course, there's heat — no one denies —
And sand and dust and stacks of flies,
    And rabbits, too, at Booligal.

"But such a pleasant, quiet place,
You never see a stranger's face —
    They hardly ever care to call;
The drovers mostly pass it by;
They reckon that they'd rather die
    Than spend a night in Booligal.

"The big mosquitoes frighten some —
You'll lie awake to hear 'em hum —
    And snakes about the township crawl;
But shearers, when they get their cheque,
They never come along and wreck
    The blessed town of Booligal.

"But down in Hay the shearers come
And fill themselves with fighting rum,
     And chase blue devils up the wall,
And fight the snaggers every day,
Until there is the deuce to pay —
     There's none of that in Booligal.

"Of course, there isn't much to see —
The billiard table used to be
     The great attraction for us all,
Until some careless, drunken curs
Got sleeping on it in their spurs,
     And ruined it, in Booligal.

"Just now there is a howling drought
That pretty near has starved us out —
     It never seems to rain at all;
But, if there *should* come any rain,
You couldn't cross the black soil plain —
     You'd have to stop in Booligal."

* * * *

"*We'd have to stop!*" With bated breath
We prayed that both in life and death
     Our fate in other lines might fall:
"Oh, send us to our just reward
In Hay or Hell, but, gracious Lord,
     Deliver us from Booligal!"

# A Walgett Episode

The sun strikes down with a blinding glare,
  The skies are blue and the plains are wide,
The saltbush plains that are burnt and bare
  By Walgett out on the Barwon side —
The Barwon River that wanders down
In a leisurely manner by Walgett Town.

There came a stranger — a "cockatoo" —
  The word means farmer, as all men know
Who dwell in the land where the kangaroo
  Barks loud at dawn, and the white-eyed crow
Uplifts his song on the stockyard fence
As he watches the lambkins passing hence.

The sunburnt stranger was gaunt and brown,
  But it soon appeared that he meant to flout
The iron law of the country town,
  Which is — that the stranger has got to shout:
"If he will not shout we must take him down,"
Remarked the yokels of Walgett Town.

They baited a trap with a crafty bait,
  With a crafty bait, for they held discourse
Concerning a new chum who of late
  Had bought such a thoroughly lazy horse;
They would wager that no one could ride him down
The length of the city of Walgett Town.

The stranger was born on a horse's hide;
  So he took the wagers, and made them good
With his hard-earned cash — but his hopes they died,
  For the horse was a clothes-horse, made of wood!
'Twas a well-known horse that had taken down
Full many a stranger in Walgett Town.

The stranger smiled with a sickly smile —
  'Tis a sickly smile that the loser grins —
And he said he had travelled for quite a while
  In trying to sell some marsupial skins.

"And I thought that perhaps, as you've took me
    down,
You would buy them from me, in Walgett Town!"

He said that his home was at Wingadee,
    At Wingadee where he had for sale
Some fifty skins and would guarantee
    They were full-sized skins, with the ears and tail
Complete, and he sold them for money down
To a venturesome buyer in Walgett Town.

Then he smiled a smile as he pouched the pelf,
    "I'm glad that I'm quit of them, win or lose:
You can fetch them in when it suits yourself,
    And you'll find the skins — on the kangaroos!"
Then he left — and the silence settled down
Like a tangible thing upon Walgett Town.

# Father Riley's Horse

'Twas the horse thief, Andy Regan, that was hunted like a dog
    By the troopers of the upper Murray side,
They had searched in every gully — they had looked in every log,
    But never sight or track of him they spied,
Till the priest at Kiley's Crossing heard a knocking very late
    And a whisper "Father Riley — come across!"
So his Rev'rence in pyjamas trotted softly to the gate
    And admitted Andy Regan — and a horse!

"Now, it's listen, Father Riley, to the words I've got to say,
    For it's close upon my death I am tonight.
With the troopers hard behind me I've been hiding all the day
    In the gullies keeping close and out of sight.
But they're watching all the ranges till there's not a bird could fly,
    And I'm fairly worn to pieces with the strife,
So I'm taking no more trouble, but I'm going home to die,
    'Tis the only way I see to save my life.

"Yes, I'm making home to mother's, and I'll die o' Tuesday next
    An' be buried on the Thursday — and, of course,
I'm prepared to meet my penance, but with one thing I'm perplexed
    And it's — Father, it's this jewel of a horse!
He was never bought nor paid for, and there's not a man can swear
    To his owner or his breeder, but I know,
That his sire was by Pedantic from the Old Pretender mare
    And his dam was close related to The Roe.

"And there's nothing in the district that can race him for a step,
    He could canter while they're going at their top:
He's the king or all the leppers that was ever seen to lep,
    A five-foot fence — he'd clear it in a hop!
So I'll leave him with you, Father, till the dead shall rise again,
    'Tis yourself that knows a good 'un; and, of course,
You can say he's got by Moonlight out of Paddy Murphy's plain
    If you're ever asked the breeding of the horse!

"But it's getting on to daylight and it's time to say goodbye,
    For the stars above the east are growing pale.
And I'm making home to mother — and it's hard for me to die!
    But it's harder still, is keeping out of gaol!
You can ride the old horse over to my grave across the dip
    Where the wattle bloom is waving overhead.
Sure he'll jump them fences easy — you must never raise the whip
    Or he'll rush 'em! — now, goodbye!" and he had fled!

So they buried Andy Regan, and they buried him to rights,
    In the graveyard at the back of Kiley's Hill;
There were five-and-twenty mourners who had five-and-twenty fights
    Till the very boldest fighters had their fill.
There were fifty horses racing from the graveyard to the pub,
    And their riders flogged each other all the while.
And the lashin's of the liquor! And the lavin's of the grub!
    Oh, poor Andy went to rest in proper style.

Then the races came to Kiley's — with a steeplechase and all,
    For the folk were mostly Irish round about,
And it takes an Irish rider to be fearless of a fall,
    They were training morning in and morning out.
But they never started training till the sun was on the course
    For a superstitious story kept 'em back,
That the ghost of Andy Regan on a slashing chestnut horse,
    Had been training by the starlight on the track.

And they read the nominations for the races with surprise
    And amusement at the Father's little joke,
For a novice had been entered for the steeplechasing prize,
    And they found that it was Father Riley's moke!
He was neat enough to gallop, he was strong enough to stay!
    But his owner's views of training were immense,
For the Reverend Father Riley used to ride him every day,
    And he never saw a hurdle nor a fence.

And the priest would join the laughter: "Oh," said he, "I put him in,
   For there's five-and-twenty sovereigns to be won.
And the poor would find it useful, if the chestnut chanced to win,
   And he'll maybe win when all is said and done!"
He had called him Faugh-a-ballagh, which is French for "clear the course",
   And his colours were a vivid shade of green:
All the Dooleys and O'Donnells were on Father Riley's horse,
   While the Orangemen were backing Mandarin!

It was Hogan, the dog poisoner — aged man and very wise,
   Who was camping in the racecourse with his swag,
And who ventured the opinion, to the township's great surprise,
   That the race would go to Father Riley's nag.
"You can talk about your riders — and the horse has not been schooled,
   And the fences is terrific, and the rest!
When the field is fairly going, then ye'll see ye've all been fooled,
   And the chestnut horse will battle with the best.

"For there's some has got condition, and they think the race is sure,
   And the chestnut horse will fall beneath the weight,
But the hopes of all the helpless, and the prayers of all the poor,
   Will be running by his side to keep him straight.
And it's what's the need of schoolin' or of workin' on the track,
·    Whin the saints are there to guide him round the course!
I've prayed him over every fence — I've prayed him out and back!
   And I'll bet my cash on Father Riley's horse!"

                         * * * *

Oh, the steeple was a caution! They went tearin' round and round,
   And the fences rang and rattled where they struck.
There was some that cleared the water — there was more fell in and
   drowned,
   Some blamed the men and others blamed the luck!
But the whips were flying freely when the field came into view,
   For the finish down the long green stretch of course,
And in front of all the flyers — jumpin' like a kangaroo,
   Came the rank outsider — Father Riley's horse!

Oh, the shouting and the cheering as he rattled past the post!
    For he left the others standing, in the straight;
And the rider — well they reckoned it was Andy Regan's ghost,
    And it beat 'em how a ghost would draw the weight!
But he weighed in, nine stone seven, then he laughed and disappeared,
    Like a banshee (which is Spanish for an elf),
And old Hogan muttered sagely, "If it wasn't for the beard
    They'd be thinking it was Andy Regan's self!"

And the poor of Kiley's Crossing drank the health at Christmastide
    Of the chestnut and his rider dressed in green.
There was never such a rider, not since Andy Regan died,
    And they wondered who on earth he could have been.
But they settled it among 'em, for the story got about,
    'Mongst the bushmen and the people on the course,
That the Devil had been ordered to let Andy Regan out
    For the steeplechase on Father Riley's horse!

# The Scotch Engineer

With eyes that searched in the dark,
  Peering along the line,
Stood the grim Scotchman, Hector Clark,
Driver of "Forty-nine",
And the veldt fire flamed on the hills ahead,
Like a blood-red beacon sign.

There was word of a fight to the north,
And a column hard-pressed,
So they started the Highlanders forth,
Without food, without rest.

But the pipers gaily played,
Chanting their fierce delight,
And the armoured carriages rocked and swayed,
Laden with men of the Scotch Brigade,
Hurrying up to the fight,
And the grim, grey Highland engineer,
Driving them into the night.

Then a signal light glowed red,
And a picket came to the track.
"Enemy holding the line ahead,
Three of our mates we have left for dead,
Only we two got back."
And far to the north through the still night air,
They heard the rifles crack.

And the boom of a gun rang out,
Like the sound of a deep appeal,
And the picket stood in doubt
By the side of the driving wheel.

But the Engineer looked down,
With his hand on the starting-bar,
"Ride ye back to the town,
Ye know what my orders are,
Maybe they're wanting the Scotch Brigade
Up on those hills afar.

"I am no soldier at all,
Only an engineer,
But I could not bear that the folk should say,
Over in Scotland — Glasgow way —
That Hector Clark stayed here
With the Scotch Brigade till the foe were gone,
With ever a rail to run her on.
Ready behind! Stand clear!

"Fireman, get you gone
Into the armoured train,
I will drive her alone;
One more trip — and perhaps the last —
With a well-raked fire and an open blast —
Hark to the rifles again."

* * * *

On through the choking dark,
Never a lamp nor a light,
Never an engine spark,
Showing her hurried flight.
Over the lonely plain
Rushed the great armoured-train,
Hurrying up to the fight.

Then with her living freight
Onto the foe she came,
And the rifles snapped their hate,
And the darkness spouted flame.

Over the roar of the fray
The hungry bullets whined,
As she dashed through the foe that lay
Loading and firing blind,
Till the glare of the furnace burning clear
Showed them the form of the engineer,
Sharply and well defined.

Through! They were safely through!
Hark to the column's cheer!
Surely the driver knew
He was to halt her here;
But he took no heed of the signals red,
And the fireman found, when he climbed ahead,
There on the floor of his engine — dead,
Lay the Scotch Engineer!

# Song of the Future

'Tis strange that in a land so strong,
  So strong and bold in mighty youth,
We have no poet's voice of truth
To sing for us a wondrous song.

Our chiefest singer yet has sung
In wild, sweet notes a passing strain,
All carelessly and sadly flung
To that dull world he thought so vain.

"I care for nothing, good nor bad,
My hopes are gone, my pleasures fled,
I am but sifting sand," he said:
What wonder Gordon's songs were sad!

And yet, not always sad and hard;
In cheerful mood and light of heart
He told the tale of Britomarte,
And wrote the Rhyme of Joyous Guard.

And some have said that Nature's face
To us is always sad; but these
Have never felt the smiling grace
Of waving grass and forest trees
On sunlit plains as wide as seas.

"A land where dull Despair is king
O'er scentless flower and songless bird!"
But we have heard the bellbirds ring
Their silver bells at eventide,
Like fairies on the mountain side,
The sweetest note man ever heard.

The wild thrush lifts a note of mirth;
The bronzewing pigeons call and coo
Beside their nests the long day through;
The magpie warbles clear and strong
A joyous, glad, thanksgiving song,
For all God's mercies upon earth.

132

And many voices such as these
Are joyful sounds for those to tell,
Who know the Bush and love it well,
With all its hidden mysteries.

We cannot love the restless sea,
That rolls and tosses to and fro
Like some fierce creature in its glee;
For human weal or human woe
It has no touch of sympathy.

For us the bush is never sad:
Its myriad voices whisper low,
In tones the bushmen only know,
Its sympathy and welcome glad.

For us the roving breezes bring
From many a blossom-tufted tree —
Where wild bees murmur dreamily —
The honey-laden breath of Spring.

* * * *

We have no tales of other days,
No bygone history to tell;
Our tales are told where campfires blaze
At midnight, when the solemn hush
Of that vast wonderland, the Bush,
Hath laid on every heart its spell.

Although we have no songs of strife,
Of bloodshed reddening the land,
We yet may find achievements grand
Within the bushman's quiet life.

Lift ye your faces to the sky
Ye far blue mountains of the West,
Who lie so peacefully at rest
Enshrouded in a haze of blue;
'Tis hard to feel that years went by
Before the pioneers broke through
Your rocky heights and walls of stone,
And made your secrets all their own.

For years the fertile Western plains
Were hid behind your sullen walls,

Your cliffs and crags and waterfalls
All weatherworn with tropic rains.

Between the mountains and the sea,
Like Israelites with staff in hand,
The people waited restlessly:
They looked towards the mountains old
And saw the sunsets come and go
With gorgeous golden afterglow,
That made the West a fairyland,
And marvelled what that West might be
Of which such wondrous tales were told.

For tales were told of inland seas
Like sullen oceans, salt and dead,
And sandy deserts, white and wan,
Where never trod the foot of man,
Nor bird went winging overhead,
Nor ever stirred a gracious breeze
To wake the silence with its breath —
A land of loneliness and death.

At length the hardy pioneers
By rock and crag found out the way,
And woke with voices of today,
A silence kept for years and years.

Upon the Western slope they stood
And saw — a wide expanse of plain
As far as eye could stretch or see
Go rolling westward endlessly.
The native grasses, tall as grain,
Were waved and rippled in the breeze;
From boughs of blossom-laden trees
The parrots answered back again.

They saw the land that it was good,
A land of fatness all untrod,
And gave their silent thanks to God.

The way is won! The way is won!
And straightway from the barren coast
There came a westward-marching host,
That aye and ever onward prest

With eager faces to the West,
Along the pathway of the sun.

The mountains saw them marching by:
They faced the all-consuming drought,
They would not rest in settled land:
But, taking each his life in hand,
Their faces ever westward bent
Beyond the farthest settlement,
Responding to the challenge cry
Of "better country further out".

And lo a miracle! the land
But yesterday was all unknown,
The wild man's boomerang was thrown
Where now great busy cities stand.

It was not much, you say, that these
Should win their way where none withstood;
In sooth there was not much of blood —
No war was fought between the seas.

It was not much! but we who know
The strange capricious land they trod —
At times a stricken, parching sod,
At times with raging floods beset —
Through which they found their lonely way,
Are quite content that you should say
It was not much, while we can feel
That nothing in the ages old,
In song or story written yet
On Grecian urn or Roman arch,
Though it should ring with clash of steel,
Could braver histories unfold
Than this bush story, yet untold —
The story of their westward march.

* * * *

But times are changed, and changes rung
From old to new — the olden days,
The old bush life and all its ways
Are passing from us all unsung.

The freedom, and the hopeful sense

135

Of toil that brought due recompense,
Of room for all, has passed away,
And lies forgotten with the dead.
Within our streets men cry for bread
In cities built but yesterday.

About us stretches wealth of land,
A boundless wealth of virgin soil
As yet unfruitful and untilled!
Our willing workmen, strong and skilled
Within our cities idle stand,
And cry aloud for leave to toil.

The stunted children come and go
In squalid lanes and alleys black;
We follow but the beaten track
Of other nations, and we grow
In wealth for some — for many, woe.

And it may be that we who live
In this new land apart, beyond
The hard old world grown fierce and fond
And bound by precedent and bond,
May read the riddle right and give
New hope to those who dimly see
That all things may be yet for good,
And teach the world at length to be
One vast united brotherhood.

* * * *

So may it be, and he who sings
In accents hopeful, clear, and strong,
The glories which that future brings
Shall sing, indeed, a wondrous song.

# Anthony Considine

Out in the wastes of the West countrie,
    Out where the white stars shine,
Grim and silent as such men be,
Rideth a man with a history —
    Anthony Considine.

For the ways of men they are manifold
    As their differing views in life;
For some are sold for the lust of gold
    And some for the lust of strife:
But this man counted the world well lost
    For the love of his neighbour's wife.

They fled together, as those must flee
    Whom all men hold in blame;
Each to the other must all things be
Who cross the gulf of iniquity
    And live in the land of shame.

But a light-o'-love, if she sins with one,
    She sinneth with ninety-nine:
The rule holds good since the world begun —
Since ever the streams began to run
    And the stars began to shine.
The rule holds true, and he found it true —
    Anthony Considine.

A nobler spirit had turned in scorn
    From a love that was stained with mire;
A weaker being might mourn and mourn
    For the loss of his Heart's Desire:
But the anger of Anthony Considine
    Blazed up like a flaming fire.

And she, with her new love, presently
    Came past with her eyes ashine;
And God so willed it, and God knows why,
She turned and laughed as they passed him by —
    Anthony Considine.

Her laughter stung as a whip might sting;
    And mad with his wounded pride
He turned and sprang with a panther's spring
    And struck at his rival's side:
And only the woman, shuddering,
    Could tell how the dead man died!

She dared not speak — and the mystery
    Is buried in auld lang syne,
But out on the wastes of the West countrie,
Grim and silent as such men be,
Rideth a man with a history —
    Anthony Considine.

# Song of the Artesian Water

Now the stock have started dying, for the Lord has sent a drought;
But we're sick of prayers and Providence — we're going to do without;
With the derricks up above us and the solid earth below,
We are waiting at the lever for the word to let her to.
    Sinking down, deeper down,
    Oh, we'll sink it deeper down:
As the drill is plugging downward at a thousand feet of level,
If the Lord won't send us water, oh, we'll get it from the devil;
     Yes, we'll get it from the devil deeper down.

Now, our engine's built in Glasgow by a very canny Scot,
And he marked it twenty horsepower, but he don't know what is what:
When Canadian Bill is firing with the sun-dried gidgee logs,
She can equal thirty horses and a score or so of dogs.
    Sinking down, deeper down,
    Oh, we're going deeper down:
If we fail to get the water then it's ruin to the squatter,
For the drought is on the station and the weather's growing hotter,
     But we're bound to get the water deeper down.

But the shaft has started caving and the sinking's very slow,
And the yellow rods are bending in the water down below,
And the tubes are always jamming and they can't be made to shift
Till we nearly burst the engine with a forty horsepower lift.
    Sinking down, deeper down,
    Oh, we're going deeper down:
Though the shaft is always caving, and the tubes are always jamming,
Yet we'll fight our way to water while the stubborn drill is ramming —
     While the stubborn drill is ramming deeper down.

But there's no artesian water, though we've passed three thousand feet,
And the contract price is growing and the boss is nearly beat.
But it must be down beneath us, and it's down we've got to go,
Though she's bumping on the solid rock four thousand feet below.
    Sinking down, deeper down,
    Oh, we're going deeper down:

And it's time they heard us knocking on the roof of Satan's dwellin';
But we'll get artesian water if we cave the roof of Hell in —
 Oh! we'll get artesian water deeper down.

But it's hark! the whistle's blowing with a wild, exultant blast,
And the boys are madly cheering, for they've struck the flow at last,
And it's rushing up the tubing from four thousand feet below
Till it spouts above the casing in a million-gallon flow.
 And its down, deeper down,
 Oh, it comes from deeper down;
It is flowing, ever flowing, in a free, unstinted measure
From the silent hidden places where the old earth hides her treasure —
 Where the old earth hides her treasure deeper down.

And it's clear away the timber, and it's let the water run:
How it glimmers in the shadow, how it flashes in the sun!
By the silent belts of timber, by the miles of blazing plain
It is bringing hope and comfort to the thirsty land again.
 Flowing down, further down;
 It is flowing further down
To the tortured thirsty cattle, bringing gladness in its going;
Through the droughty days of summer it is flowing, ever flowing —
 It is flowing, ever flowing, further down.

# A Disqualified Jockey's Story

You see, the thing was this way — there was me,
That rode Panoppoly, the Splendour mare,
And Ikey Chambers on the Iron Dook,
And Smith, the half-caste rider, on Regret,
And that long bloke from Wagga — him what rode
Veronikew, the Snowy River horse.
Well, none of them had chances — not a chance
Among the lot, unless the rest fell dead
Or wasn't trying — for a blind man's dog
Could see Enchantress was a certain cop,
And all the books was layin' six to four.

They brought her out to show our lot the road,
Or so they said; but, then, Gord's truth! you know,
You can't believe 'em, though they took an oath
On forty Bibles that they'd tell the truth.
But anyhow, an amateur was up
On this Enchantress, and so Ike and me,
We thought that we might frighten him a bit
By asking if he minded riding rough —
"Oh, not at all," says he, "oh, not at all!
I learnt at Robbo Park, and if it comes
To bumping I'm your Moses! Strike me blue!"
Says he, "I'll bump you over either rail,
The inside rail or outside — which you choose
Is good enough for me" — which settled Ike;
For he was shaky since he near got killed
From being sent a buster on the rail,
When some chap bumped his horse and
          fetched him down
At Stony Bridge, so Ikey thought it best
To leave this bloke alone, and I agreed.

So all the books was layin' six to four
Against the favourite, and the amateur
Was walking this Enchantress up and down,
And me and Smithy backed him; for we thought
We might as well get something for ourselves,

141

Because we knew our horses couldn't win.
But Ikey wouldn't back him for a bob;
Because he said he reckoned he was stiff,
And all the books was layin' six to four.

Well, anyhow, before the start, the news
Got round that this here amateur was stiff,
And our good stuff was blued, and all the books
Was in it, and the prices lengthened out,
And every book was bustin' of his throat,
And layin' five to one the favourite.
So there was we that couldn't win ourselves,
And this here amateur that wouldn't try,
And all the books was layin' five to one.

So Smithy says to me, "You take a hold
Of that there moke of yours, and round the turn
Come up behind Enchantress with the whip
And let her have it; that long bloke and me
Will wait ahead, and when she comes to us
We'll pass her on and belt her down the straight,
And Ikey'll flog her home, because his boss
Is judge and steward and the Lord knows what,
And so he won't be touched — and, as for us,
We'll swear we only hit her by mistake!"
And all the books was layin' five to one.

Well, off we went, and comin' to the turn
I saw the amateur was holding back
And poking into every hole he could
To get her blocked, and so I pulled behind
And drew the whip and dropped it on the mare —
I let her have it twice, and then she shot
Ahead of me, and Smithy opened out
And let her up beside him on the rails,
And kept her there a-beltin' her like smoke
Until she struggled past him pullin' hard
And came to Ike; but Ikey drew his whip
And hit her on the nose and sent her back
And won the race himself — for, after all,
It seems he had a fiver on the Dook
And never told us — so our stuff was lost.

And then they had us up for ridin' foul,
And warned us off the tracks for twelve months each,
To get our livin' any way we could;
But Ikey wasn't touched, because his boss
Was judge and steward and the Lord knows what.

But Mister — if you'll lend us half-a-crown,
I know three certain winners at the Park —
Three certain cops as no one knows but me;
And — thank you, Mister, come an' have a beer
(I always like a beer about this time) ...
Well, so long, Mister, till we meet again.

# The Road to Gundagai

The mountain road goes up and down,
From Gundagai to Tumut town.

And branching off there runs a track,
Across the foothills grim and black,

Across the plains and ranges grey
To Sydney city far away.

\* \* \* \*

It came by chance one day that I
From Tumut rode to Gundagai.

And reached about the evening tide
The crossing where the roads divide;

And, waiting at the crossing place,
I saw a maiden fair of face,

With eyes of deepest violet blue,
And cheeks to match the rose in hue —

The fairest maids Australia knows
Are bred among the mountain snows.

Then, fearing I might go astray,
I asked if she could show the way.

Her voice might well a man bewitch —
Its tones so supple, deep, and rich.

"The tracks are clear," she made reply,
"And this goes down to Sydney town,
And that one goes to Gundagai."

Then slowly, looking coyly back,
She went along the Sydney track.
And I for one was well content
To go the road the lady went;

But round the turn a swain she met —
The kiss she gave him haunts me yet!

* * * *

I turned and travelled with a sigh
The lonely road to Gundagai.

## *Saltbush Bill's Second Fight*

The news came down on the Castlereagh, and went to the world at large,
That twenty thousand travelling sheep, with Saltbush Bill in charge,
Were drifting down from a dried-out run to ravage the Castlereagh;
And the squatters swore when they heard the news, and wished they
   were well away:
For the name and the fame of Saltbush Bill were over the countryside
For the wonderful way that he fed his sheep, and the dodges and
   tricks he tried.
He would lose his way on a main stock route, and stray to the
   squatters' grass;
He would come to a run with the boss away, and swear he had leave to pass;
And back of all and behind it all, as well the squatters knew,
If he had to fight, he would fight all day, so long as his sheep got through:
But this is the story of Stingy Smith, the owner of Hard Times Hill,
And the way that he chanced on a fighting man to reckon with Saltbush Bill.

    \* \* \* \*

'Twas Stingy Smith on his stockyard sat, and prayed for an early spring,
When he started at sight of a clean-shaved tramp, who walked
   with jaunty swing;
For a clean-shaved tramp with a jaunty walk a-swinging along the track
Is as rare a thing as a feathered frog on the desolate roads outback.
So the tramp he made for the travellers' hut, and asked could he
   camp the night;
But Stingy Smith had a bright idea, and he said to him, "Can you fight?"
"Why, what's the game?" said the clean-shaved tramp, as he looked
   at him up and down —
"If you want a battle, get off that fence, and I'll kill you for half-a-crown!
But, Boss, you'd better not fight with me, it wouldn't be fair nor right;
I'm Stiffener Joe, from the Rocks Brigade, and I killed a man in a fight:
I served two years for it, fair and square, and now I'm a trampin' back,
To look for a peaceful quiet life away on the outside track —"
"Oh, it's not myself, but a drover chap," said Stingy Smith with glee;
"A bullying fellow, called Saltbush Bill — and you are the man for me.
He's on the road with his hungry sheep, and he's certain to raise a row,
For he's bullied the whole of the Castlereagh till he's got them under cow —
Just pick a quarrel and raise a fight, and leather him good and hard,

146

And I'll take good care that his wretched sheep don't wander a half a yard.
It's a five-pound job if you belt him well — do anything short of kill,
For there isn't a beak on the Castlereagh will fine you for Saltbush Bill."
"I'll take the job," said the fighting man, "and hot as this cove appears,
He'll stand no chance with a bloke like me, what's lived on the game
      for years;
For he's maybe learnt in a boxing school, and sparred for a round or so,
But I've fought all hands in a ten foot ring each night in a travelling show;
They earnt a pound if they stayed three rounds, and they tried for it
      every night —
In a ten foot ring! Oh, that's the game that teaches a bloke to fight,
For they'd rush and clinch, it was Dublin Rules, and we drew
      no colour line;
And they all tried hard for to earn the pound, but they got no
      pound of mine:
If I saw no chance in the opening round I'd slog at their wind, and wait
Till an opening came — and it *always* came — and I settled 'em,
      sure as fate;
Left on the ribs and right on the jaw — and, when the chance comes,
      *make sure*!
And it's there a professional bloke like me gets home on an amateur:

"For it's my experience every day, and I make no doubt it's yours,
That a third-class pro is an over-match for the best of the amateurs —"
"Oh, take your swag to the travellers' hut," said Smith, "for you waste
      your breath;
You've a first-class chance, if you lose the fight, of talking your man to death.
I'll tell the cook you're to have your grub, and see that you eat your fill,
And come to the scratch all fit and well to leather this Saltbush Bill."

           \* \* \* \*

'Twas Saltbush Bill, and his travelling sheep were wending their weary way
On the Main Stock Route, through the Hard Times Run, on their six-mile
      stage a day;
And he strayed a mile from the Main Stock Route, and started to feed along,
And, when Stingy Smith came up, Bill said that the Route was
      surveyed wrong;
And he tried to prove that the sheep had rushed and strayed from
      their camp at night,
But the fighting man he kicked Bill's dog, and of course that meant a fight:

So they sparred and fought, and they shifted ground and never
      a sound was heard

But the thudding fists on their brawny ribs, and the seconds'
       muttered word,
Till the fighting man shot home his left on the ribs with a mighty clout,
And his right flashed up with a half-arm blow — and Saltbush Bill
       "went out".
He fell face down, and towards the blow; and their hearts with
       fear were filled,
For he lay as still as a fallen tree, and they thought that he must be killed.

So Stingy Smith and the fighting man, they lifted him from the ground,
And sent to home for a brandy flask, and they slowly fetched him round;
But his head was bad, and his jaw was hurt — in fact,
       he could scarcely speak —
So they let him spell till he got his wits, and he camped on the run a week,
While the travelling sheep went here and there, wherever they
       liked to stray,
Till Saltbush Bill was fit once more for the track to the Castlereagh.

* * * *

Then Stingy Smith he wrote a note, and gave to the fighting man:
'Twas writ to the boss of the neighbouring run, and thus the missive ran:
"The man with this is a fighting man, one Stiffener Joe by name;
He came near murdering Saltbush Bill, and I found it a costly game:
But it's worth your while to employ the chap, for there isn't
       the slightest doubt
You'll have no trouble from Saltbush Bill while this man hangs about —"
But an answer came by the next week's mail, with news that
       might well appal:
"The man you sent with a note is not a fighting man at all!
He has shaved his beard, and has cut his hair, but I spotted him at a look;
He is Tom Devine, who has worked for years for Saltbush Bill as cook.
Bill coached him up in the fighting yarn, and taught him the tale by rote,
And they shammed to fight, and they got your grass and divided
       your five-pound note.
'Twas a clean take-in, and you'll find it wise — 'twill save you
       a lot of pelf —
When next you're hiring a fighting man, just fight him a round yourself."

* * * *

And the teamsters out on the Castlereagh, when they meet with
       a week of rain,
And the waggon sinks to its axle-tree, deep down in the black soil plain,
When the bullocks wade in a sea of mud, and strain at the load of wool,

And the cattle dogs at the bullocks' heels are biting to make them pull,
When the offside driver flays the team, and curses them while he flogs,
And the air is thick with the language used, and the clamour
      of men and dogs —
The teamsters say, as they pause to rest and moisten each hairy throat,
They wish they could swear like Stingy Smith when he read
      that neighbour's note.

# Hard Luck

I left the course, and by my side
   There walked a ruined tout —
A hungry creature evil-eyed,
   Who poured this story out.

"You see," he said, "there came a swell
   To Kensington today,
And if I picked the winners well,
   A crown at least he'd pay.

"I picked three winners straight, I did,
   I filled his purse with pelf,
And then he gave me half a quid,
   To back one for myself.

"A half a quid to me he cast,
   I wanted it indeed.
So help me Bob, for two days past
   I haven't had a feed.

"But still I thought my luck was in,
   I couldn't go astray,
I put it all on Little Min,
   And lost it straightaway.

"I haven't got a bite or bed,
   I'm absolutely stuck,
So keep this lesson in your head:
   Don't over-trust your luck!"

The folks went homeward, near and far,
   The tout, Oh! where was he?
Ask where the empty boilers are,
   Beside the Circular Quay.

# Song of the Federation

As the nations sat together, grimly waiting —
  The fierce old nations battle-scarred —
Grown grey in their lusting and their hating,
  Ever armed and ever ready keeping guard,
Through the tumult of their warlike preparation
  And the half-stilled clamour of the drums
Came a voice crying, "Lo! a new-made nation,
  To her place in the sisterhood she comes!"

And she came — she was beautiful as morning,
  With the bloom of the roses in her mouth,
Like a young queen lavishly adorning
  Her charms with the splendours of the South.
And the fierce old nations, looking on her,
  Said, "Nay, surely she were quickly overthrown,
Hath she strength for the burden laid upon her,
  Hath she power to protect and guard her own?"

Then she spoke, and her voice was clear and ringing
  In the ears of the nations old and grey,
Saying, "Hark, and ye shall see my children singing
  Their war song in countries far away.
They are strangers to the tumult of the battle,
  They are few but their hearts are very strong,
'Twas but yesterday they called unto the cattle,
  But they now sing Australia's marching song."

## Song of the Australians in Action

*For the honour of Australia, our mother,*
  *Side by side with our kin from over sea,*
*We have fought and we have tested one another,*
  *And enrolled among the brotherhood are we.*

*There was never post of danger but we sought it*
  *In the fighting, through the fire, and through the flood.*
*There was never prize so costly but we bought it,*
  *Though we paid for its purchase with our blood.*

*Was there any road too rough for us to travel?*
*Was there any path too far for us to tread?*
*You can track us by the blood drops on the gravel*
*On the roads that we milestoned with our dead!*

*And for you, oh our young and anxious mother,*
*O'er your great gains keeping watch and ward,*
*Neither fearing nor despising any other,*
*We will hold your possessions with the sword.*

\* \* \* \*

Then they passed to the place of world-long sleeping,
    The grey-clad figures with their dead,
To the sound of their women softly weeping
    And the Dead March moaning at their head:
And the Nations, as the grim procession ended,
    Whispered, "Child! But ye have seen the price we pay,
From War may we ever be defended,
    Kneel ye down, new-made Sister — Let us Pray!"

# The Old Australian Ways

The London lights are far abeam
    Behind a bank of cloud,
Along the shore the gas lights gleam,
    The gale is piping loud;
And down the Channel, groping blind,
    We drive her through the haze
Towards the land we left behind —
The good old land of "never mind",
    And old Australian ways.

The narrow ways of English folk
    Are not for such as we;
They bear the long-accustomed yoke
    Of staid conservancy:
But all our roads are new and strange
    And through our blood there runs
The vagabonding love of change
That drove us westward of the range
    And westward of the suns.

The city folk go to and fro
    Behind a prison's bars,
They never feel the breezes blow
    And never see the stars;
They never hear in blossomed trees
    The music low and sweet
Of wild birds making melodies,
Nor catch the little laughing breeze
    That whispers in the wheat.

Our fathers came of roving stock
    That could not fixed abide:
And we have followed field and flock
    Since e'er we learnt to ride;
    By miner's camp and shearing shed,
    In land of heat and drought,
We followed where our fortunes led,
With fortune always on ahead
    And always further out.

The wind is in the barley grass,
    The wattles are in bloom;
The breezes greet us as they pass
    With honey-sweet perfume;
The parakeets go screaming by
    With flash of golden wing,
And from the swamp the wild ducks cry
Their long-drawn note of revelry,
    Rejoicing at the spring.

So throw the weary pen aside
    And let the papers rest,
For we must saddle up and ride
    Towards the blue hill's breast;
And we must travel far and fast
    Across their rugged maze,
To find the Spring of Youth at last,
And call back from the buried past
    The old Australian ways.

When Clancy took the drover's track
    In years of long ago,
He drifted to the outer back
    Beyond the Overflow;
By rolling plain and rocky shelf,
    With stockwhip in his hand,
He reached at last, oh lucky elf,
The Town of Come-and-Help-Yourself
    In Rough-and-Ready Land.

And if it be that you would know
    The tracks he used to ride,
Then you must saddle up and go
    Beyond the Queensland side —
Beyond the reach of rule or law,
    To ride the long day through,
In Nature's homestead — filled with awe:
You then might see what Clancy saw
    And know what Clancy knew.

# *The Ballad of the* Calliope

By the far Samoan shore,
    Where the league-long rollers pour
All the wash of the Pacific on the coral-guarded bay,
    Riding lightly at their ease,
    In the calm of tropic seas,
The three great nations' warships at their anchors
        proudly lay.


    Riding lightly, head to wind,
    With the coral reefs behind
Three German and three Yankee ships were mirrored
      in the blue;
    And on one ship unfurled
    Was the flag that rules the world —
For on the old *Calliope* the flag of England flew.


    When the gentle offshore breeze,
    That had scarcely stirred the trees,
Dropped down to utter stillness, and the glass began to fall,
    Away across the main
    Lowered the coming hurricane,
And far away to seaward hung the cloud wrack like a pall.


    If the word had passed around,
    "Let us move to safer ground;
Let us steam away to seaward" — then this tale were not to tell!
    But each Captain seemed to say
    "If the others stay, I stay!"
And they lingered at their moorings till the shades of evening fell.


    Then the cloud wrack neared them fast,
    And there came a sudden blast,
And the hurricane came leaping down a thousand miles of main!
    Like a lion on its prey,
    Leapt the storm fiend on the bay,
And the vessels shook and shivered as their cables felt the strain.

As the surging seas came by,
  That were running mountains high,
The vessels started dragging, drifting slowly to the lee;
  And the darkness of the night
  Hid the coral reefs from sight,
And the Captains dared not risk the chance to grope
      their way to sea.

In the dark they dared not shift!
  They were forced to wait and drift;
All hands stood by uncertain would the anchors hold or no.
  But the men on deck could see
  If a chance of hope might be —
There was little chance of safety for the men who were below.

Through that long, long night of dread,
  While the storm raged overhead,
They were waiting by their engines, with the furnace fires aroar.
  So they waited, staunch and true,
  Though they knew, and well they knew,
They must drown like rats imprisoned if the vessel
      touched the shore.

When the grey dawn broke at last,
  And the long, long night was past,
While the hurricane redoubled, lest its prey should steal away,
  On the rocks, all smashed and strewn,
  Were the German vessels thrown,
While the Yankees, swamped and helpless, drifted
      shorewards down the bay.

Then at last spoke Captain Kane,
  "All our anchors are in vain,
And the Germans and the Yankees they have drifted to the lee!
  Cut the cables at the bow!
  We must trust the engines now!
Give her steam, and let her have it, lads, we'll fight
      her out to sea!"

And the answer came with cheers
  From the stalwart engineers,

From the grim and grimy firemen at the furnaces below;
    And above the sullen roar
    Of the breakers on the shore
Came the throbbing of the engines as they laboured to and fro.


    If the strain should find a flaw,
    Should a bolt or rivet draw,
Then — God help them! for the vessel were a plaything in the tide!
    With a face of honest cheer,
    Quoth an English engineer,
"I will answer for the engines that were built on old Thames side!


    "For the stays and stanchions taut,
    For the rivets truly wrought,
For the valves that fit their faces as a glove should fit the hand.
    Give her every ounce of power,
    If we make a knot an hour
Then it's way enough to steer her and we'll drive her from the land."


    Like a foam-flake tossed and thrown,
    She could barely hold her own,
While the other ships all helplessly were drifting to the lee.
    Through the smother and the rout
    The *Calliope* steamed out —
And they cheered her from the *Trenton* that was foundering in the sea.


    Aye! drifting shoreward there,
    All helpless as they were,
Their vessel hurled upon the reefs as weed ashore is hurled.
    Without a thought of fear
    The Yankees raised a cheer —
A cheer that English-speaking folk should echo round the world.

# Do They Know?

Do they know? At the turn to the straight
    Where the favourites fail,
And every atom of weight
    Is telling its tale;
As some grim old stayer hard-pressed
    Runs true to his breed,
And with head just in front of the rest
    Fights on in the lead;
When the jockeys are out with the whips,
    With a furlong to go;
And the backers grow white to the lips —
    Do you think *they* don't know?

Do they know? As they come back to weigh
    In a whirlwind of cheers,
Though the spurs have left marks of the fray,
    Though the sweat on the ears
Gathers cold, and they sob with distress
    As they roll up the track,
They know just as well their success
    As the man on their back.
As they walk through a dense human lane,
    That sways to and fro,
And cheers them again and again,
    Do you think *they* don't know?

# The Passing of Gundagai

I'll introdooce a friend!" he said,
   "And if you've got a vacant pen
You'd better take him in the shed
And start him shearing straight ahead,
      He's one of these here quiet men.

"He never strikes — that aint his game;
      No matter what the others try
*He* goes on shearing just the same.
I never rightly knew his name —
      We always call him 'Gundagai!' "

Our flashest shearer then had gone
      To train a racehorse for a race,
And while his sporting fit was on
He couldn't be relied upon,
      So "Gundagai" shore in his place.

Alas for man's veracity!
      For reputations false and true!
This "Gundagai" turned out to be,
For strife and all-round villainy,
      The very worst I ever knew!

He started racing Jack Devine,
      And grumbled when I made him stop.
The pace he showed was extra fine,
But all those pure-bred ewes of mine
      Were bleeding like a butcher's shop.

He cursed the sheep, he cursed the shed,
      From roof to rafter, floor to shelf;
As for my mongrel ewes, he said,
I ought to get a razor blade
      And shave the blooming things myself.

On Sundays he controlled a "school",
  And played "two-up" the livelong day;
And many a young confiding fool
He shore of his financial wool;
  And when he lost he would not pay.

He organised a shearers' race,
  And "touched" me to provide the prize.
His packhorse showed surprising pace
And won hands down — he was The Ace,
  A well-known racehorse in disguise.

Next day the bruiser of the shed
  Displayed an opal-tinted eye,
With large contusions on his head.
He smiled a sickly smile, and said
  He'd "had a cut at 'Gundagai!' "

But just as we were getting full
  Of "Gundagai" and all his ways,
A telegram for "Henry Bull"
Arrived. Said he, "That's me — all wool!
  Let's see what this here message says."

He opened it, his face grew white,
  He dropped the shears and turned away.
It ran, "Your wife took bad last night;
Come home at once — no time to write,
  We fear she may not last the day."

He got his cheque — I didn't care
  To dock him for my mangled ewes;
His store account — we "called it square".
Poor wretch! he had enough to bear,
  Confronted by such dreadful news.

The shearers raised a little purse
  To help a mate, as shearers will,
"To pay the doctor and the nurse,
And if there should be something worse —
  To pay the undertaker's bill."

They wrung his hand in sympathy,
    He rode away without a word,
His head hung down in misery.
A wandering hawker passing by
    Was told of what had just occurred.

"Well! that's a curious thing," he said,
    "I've known that feller all his life —
He's had the loan of this here shed!
I know his wife ain't nearly dead,
    Because he *hasn't got a wife!*"

            \* \* \* \*

You should have heard the whipcord crack
    As angry shearers galloped by,
In vain they tried to fetch him back.
A little dust along the track
    Was all they saw of "Gundagai".

# The Wargeilah Handicap

Wargeilah town is very small,
    There's no cathedral nor a club,
In fact the township, all in all,
    Is just one unpretentious pub;
And there, from all the stations round,
The local sportsmen can be found.

The sportsmen of Wargeilah side
    Are very few but very fit:
There's scarcely any sport been tried
    But what they held their own at it.
In fact, to search their records o'er,
They held their own and something more.

'Twas round about Wargeilah town
    An English new chum did infest:
He used to wander up and down
    In baggy English breeches drest —
His mental aspect seemed to be
Just stolid self-sufficiency.

The local sportsmen vainly sought
    His tranquil calm to counteract,
By urging that he should be brought
    Within the Noxious Creatures Act.
"Nay, harm him not," said one more wise,
"He is a blessing in disguise!

"You see, he wants to buy a horse,
    To ride, and hunt, and steeplechase,
And carry ladies, too, of course,
    And pull a cart and win a race.
Good gracious! he must be a flat
To think he'll get a horse like that!

"But since he has so little sense
    And such a lot of cash to burn,
We'll sell him some experience
    By which alone a fool can learn.

Suppose we let him have The Trap
To win Wargeilah Handicap!"

And here, I must explain to you
     That, round about Wargeilah run,
There lived a very aged screw
     Whose days of brilliancy were done:
A grand old warrior in his prime —
But age will beat us all in time.

A trooper's horse in seasons past
     He did his share to keep the peace,
But took to falling, and at last
     Was cast for age from the Police.
A publican at Conroy's Gap
Then bought and christened him The Trap.

When grass was good, and horses dear,
     He changed his owner now and then
At prices ranging somewhere near
     The neighbourhood of two pound ten:
And manfully he earned his keep
By yarding cows and ration sheep.

They brought him in from off the grass
     And fed and groomed the old horse up;
His coat began to shine like glass —
     You'd think he'd win the Melbourne Cup.
And when they'd got him fat and flash
They asked the new chum — fifty — cash!

And when he said the price was high,
     Their indignation knew no bounds.
They said, "It's seldom you can buy
     A horse like that for fifty pounds!
We'll refund twenty if The Trap
Should fail to win the handicap!"

The deed was done, the price was paid,
     The new chum put the horse in train:
The local sports were much afraid
     That he would sad experience gain,
By racing with some shearer's hack,
Who'd beat him halfway round the track.

So, on this guileless English spark
    They did most fervently impress
That he must keep the matter dark,
    And not let any person guess
That he was purchasing The Trap
To win Wargeilah Handicap.

They spoke of "spielers from the Bland",
    And "champions from the Castlereagh",
And gave the youth to understand
    That all of these would stop away,
And spoil the race, if they should hear
That they had got The Trap to fear.

"Keep dark! They'll muster thick as flies
    When once the news gets sent around
We're giving such a splendid prize —
    A Snowdon horse worth fifty pound!
They'll come right in from Dandaloo,
And find — that it's a gift to you!"

The race came on — with no display,
    Nor any calling of the card,
But round about the pub all day
    A crowd of shearers, drinking hard,
And using language in a strain
'Twere flattery to call profane.

Our hero, dressed in silk attire —
    Blue jacket and a scarlet cap —
With boots that shone like flames of fire,
    Now did his canter on The Trap,
And walked him up and round about,
Until the other steeds came out.

He eyed them with a haughty look,
    But saw a sight that caught his breath!
It was! Ah John! The Chinee cook!
    In boots and breeches! Pale as death!
Tied with a rope, like any sack,
Upon a piebald pony's back!

The next, a colt — all mud and burrs!
    Half-broken, with a black boy up,

Who said, "You gim'me pair o' spurs,
    I win the bloomin' Melbourne Cup!"
These two were to oppose The Trap
For the Wargeilah Handicap!

They're off! The colt whipped down his head,
    And humped his back and gave a squeal,
And bucked into the drinking shed,
    Revolving like a Cath'rine wheel!
Men ran like rats! The atmosphere
Was filled with oaths and pints of beer!

But up the course the bold Ah John
    Beside The Trap raced neck and neck:
The boys had tied him firmly on,
    Which ultimately proved his wreck,
The saddle turned, and, like a clown,
He rode some distance upside down.

His legs around the horse were tied,
    His feet towards the heavens were spread,
He swung and bumped at every stride
    And ploughed the ground up with his head!
And when they rescued him, The Trap
Had won Wargeilah Handicap!

And no enquiries we could make
    Could tell by what false statements swayed
Ah John was led to undertake
    A task so foreign to his trade!
He only smiled and said, "Hoo Ki!
I stop topside, I win all 'li!"

But never, in Wargeilah Town,
    Was heard so eloquent a cheer
As when the President came down,
    And toasted, in Colonial Beer,
"The finest rider on the course!
The winner of the Snowdon Horse!"

"You go and get your prize," he said,
    "He's with a wild mob, somewhere round
The mountains near The Watershed;
    He's honestly worth fifty pound,

A noble horse, indeed, to win,
But none of *us* can run him in!

"We've chased him poor, we've chased him fat,
    We've run him till our horses dropped,
But by such obstacles as that
    A man like you will not be stopped,
You'll go and yard him any day,
So here's your health! Hooray! Hooray!"

\* \* \* \*

The day wound up with booze and blow
    And fights till all were well content,
But of the new chum, all I know
    Is shown by this advertisement —
"For Sale, the well-known racehorse Trap,
He won Wargeilah Handicap!"

# Any Other Time

A ll of us play our very best game —
    Any other time.
Golf or billiards, it's all the same —
    Any other time.
Lose a match and you always say,
"Just my luck! I was 'off' to-day!
I could have beaten him quite halfway —
    Any other time!"

After a fiver you ought to go —
    Any other time.
Every man that you ask says "Oh,
    Any *other* time.
Lend you a fiver! I'd lend you two,
But I'm overdrawn and my bills are due,
Wish you'd ask me — now, mind you do —
    Any other time!"

Fellows will ask you out to dine —
    Any other time.
"Not tonight, for we're twenty-nine —
    Any other time.
Not tomorrow, for cook's on strike —
Not next day, I'll be out on the bike —
Just drop in whenever you like —
    Any other time!"

Seasick passengers like the sea —
    Any other time.
"Something ... I ate ... disagreed ... with me!
    Any other time
Ocean-trav'lling is ... simply bliss,
Must be my ... liver ... has gone amiss ...
Why, I would laugh ... at a sea ... like this —
    Any other time."

Most of us mean to be better men —
    Any other time:

Regular upright characters then —
    Any other time.
Yet somehow as the years go by
Still we gamble and drink and lie,
When it comes to the last we'll want to die —
    Any other time!

# The Last Trump

"You led the trump," the old man said
 With fury in his eye,
"And yet you hope my girl to wed!
Young man! your hopes of love are fled,
 'Twere better she should die!

"My sweet young daughter sitting there,
 So innocent and plump!
You don't suppose that she would care
To wed an outlawed man who'd dare
 To lead the thirteenth trump!

"If you had drawn their leading spade
 It meant a certain win!
But no! By Pembroke's mighty shade
The thirteenth trump you went and played
 And let their diamonds in!

"My girl! Return at my command
 His presents in a lump!
Return his ring! For understand
No man is fit to hold your hand
 Who leads a thirteenth trump!

"But hold! Give every man his due
 And every dog his day.
Speak up and say what made you do
This dreadful thing — that is, if you
 Have anything to say!"

He spoke. "I meant at first," said he,
 "To give their spades a bump:
Or lead the hearts, but then you see
I thought against us there might be,
 Perhaps, a fourteenth trump!"

\* \* \* \*

They buried him at dawn of day
　　Beside a ruined stump:
And there he sleeps the hours away
And waits for Gabriel to play
　　The last — the fourteenth — trump.

# Tar and Feathers

Oh, the circus swooped down
   On the Narrabri town,
For the Narrabri populace moneyed are;
   And the circus man smiled
   At the folk he beguiled
To come all the distance from Gunnedah.

But a juvenile smart,
   Who objected to "part",
Went in "on the nod", and to do it he
   Crawled in through a crack
   In the tent at the back,
For the boy had no slight ingenuity.

Says he, with a grin,
   "*That's* the way to get in,
But I reckon I'd better be quiet, or
   They'll spiflicate me" —
   And he chuckled, for he
Had the loan of the circus proprietor.

But the showman astute
   On that wily galoot,
Soon dropped, and you'll say that he leathered him.
   Not he! With a grim
   Sort of humorous whim
He took him and tarred him and feathered him.

Says he, "You can go
   As a star with Jo Jo,
And knock ev'ry Injun and Arab wry,
   With your name and your trade
   On the posters displayed,
'The Feathered What Is It from Narrabri!' "

Next day for his freak
By a Narrabri beak
He was jawed with a deal of verbosity.
For his only appeal
Was "professional zeal" —
"He wanted another monstrosity."

Said his worship, "Begob!
You are fined for-r-r-ty bob!
An' six shillin's costs to the *clurk*," he says;
Yet the Narrabri Joy,
Half-bird and half-boy,
Has a "down" on himself and on circuses.

# It's Grand

It's grand to be a squatter
　　And sit upon a post,
And watch your little ewes and lambs
　　A-giving up the ghost.

It's grand to be a "cockie"
　　With wife and kids to keep,
And find an all-wise Providence
　　Has mustered all your sheep.

It's grand to be a western man,
　　With shovel in your hand,
To dig your little homestead out
　　From underneath the sand.

It's grand to be a shearer,
　　Along the Darling side,
And pluck the wool from stinking sheep
　　That some days since have died.

It's grand to be a rabbit
　　And breed till all is blue,
And then to die in heaps because
　　There's nothing left to chew.

It's grand to be a Minister
　　And travel like a swell,
And tell the central district folk
　　To go to — Inverell.

It's grand to be a Socialist
　　And lead the bold array
That marches to prosperity
　　At seven bob a day.

It's grand to be an unemployed
　　And lie in the Domain,
And wake up every second day
　　And go to sleep again.

It's grand to borrow English tin
        To pay for wharves and Rocks,
And then to find it isn't in
        The little money-box.

It's grand to be a democrat
        And toady to the mob,
For fear that if you told the truth
        They'd hunt you from your job.

It's grand to be a lot of things
        In this fair southern land,
But if the Lord would send us rain,
        That would, indeed, be grand!

# Out of Sight

They held a polo meeting at a little country town,
  And all the local sportsmen came to win themselves renown.
There came two strangers with a horse, and I am much afraid
They both belonged to what is called "the take-you-down brigade".

They said their horse could jump like fun, and asked an amateur
To ride him in the steeplechase, and told him they were sure,
The last time round, he'd sail away with such a swallow's flight
The rest would never see him go — he'd finish out of sight.

So out he went; and, when folk saw the amateur was up,
Some local genius called the race "the dude-in-danger cup".
The horse was known as "Who's Afraid", by "Panic" from "The Fright",
But still his owners told the jock he'd finish out of sight.

And so he did; for "Who's Afraid", without the least pretence,
Disposed of him by rushing through the very second fence;
And when they ran the last time round the prophecy was right —
For he was in the ambulance, and safely "out of sight".

# The Road to Old Man's Town

The fields of youth are filled with flowers,
  The wine of youth is strong:
What need have we to count the hours?
    The summer days are long.

But soon we find to our dismay
    That we are drifting down
The barren slopes that fall away
Towards the foothills grim and grey
    That lead to Old Man's Town.

And marching with us on the track
    Full many friends we find:
We see them looking sadly back
    For those that dropped behind.

But God forbid a fate so dread —
    *Alone* to travel down
The dreary road we all must tread,
With faltering steps and whitening head,
    The road to Old Man's Town!

# The Old Timer's Steeplechase

The sheep were shorn and the wool went down
    At the time of our local racing:
And I'd earned a spell — I was burnt and brown —
So I rolled my swag for a trip to town
    And a look at the steeplechasing.

'Twas rough and ready — an uncleared course
    As rough as the blacks had found it;
With barbed wire fences, topped with gorse,
And a water jump that would drown a horse,
    And the steeple three times round it.

There was never a fence the tracks to guard —
    Some straggling posts defined 'em:
And the day was hot, and the drinking hard,
Till none of the stewards could see a yard
    Before nor yet behind 'em!

But the bell was rung and the nags were out,
    Excepting an old outsider
Whose trainer started an awful rout,
For his boy had gone on a drinking bout
    And left him without a rider.

"Is there not one man in the crowd," he cried,
    "In the whole of the crowd so clever,
Is there not one man that will take a ride
On the old white horse from the northern side
    That was bred on the Mooki River?"

'Twas an old white horse that they called The Cow,
    And a cow would look well beside him;
But I was pluckier then than now
(And I wanted excitement anyhow),
    So at last I agreed to ride him.

And the trainer said, "Well, he's dreadful slow,
    And he hasn't a chance whatever;

But I'm stony broke, so it's time to show
A trick or two that the trainers know
    Who train by the Mooki River.

"The first time round at the further side,
    With the trees and the scrub about you,
Just pull behind them and run out wide
And then dodge into the scrub and hide,
    And let them go round without you.

"At the third time round, for the final spin
    With the pace, and the dust to blind 'em,
They'll never notice if you chip in
For the last half-mile — you'll be sure to win,
    And they'll think you raced behind 'em.

"At the water jump you may have to swim —
    He hasn't a hope to clear it —
Unless he skims like the swallows skim
At full speed over, but not for him!
    He'll never go next or near it.

"But don't you worry — just plunge across,
    For he swims like a well-trained setter.
Then hide away in the scrub and gorse
The rest will be far ahead of course —
    The further ahead the better.

"You must rush the jumps in the last half-round
    For fear that he might refuse 'em;
He'll try to baulk with you, I'll be bound,
Take whip and spurs on the mean old hound,
    And don't be afraid to use 'em.

"At the final round, when the field are slow
    And you are quite fresh to meet 'em,
Sit down, and hustle him all you know
With the whip and spurs, and he'll have to go —
    Remember, you've *got* to beat 'em!"

\* \* \* \*

The flag went down and we seemed to fly,
    And we made the timbers shiver
Of the first big fence, as the stand flashed by,
And I caught the ring of the trainer's cry:
    "Go on! For the Mooki River!"

I jammed him in with a well-packed crush,
    And recklessly — out for slaughter —
Like a living wave over fence and brush
We swept and swung with a flying rush,
    Till we came to the dreaded water.

Ha, ha! I laugh at it now to think
    Of the way I contrived to work it.
Shut in amongst them, before you'd wink,
He found himself on the water's brink,
    With never a chance to shirk it!

The thought of the horror he felt beguiles
    The heart of this grizzled rover!
He gave a snort you could hear for miles,
And a spring would have cleared the Channel Isles
    And carried me safely over!

Then we neared the scrub, and I pulled him back
    In the shade where the gum leaves quiver:
And I waited there in the shadows black
While the rest of the horses, round the track,
    Went on like a rushing river!

At the second round, as the field swept by,
    I saw that the pace was telling;
But on they thundered, and by and by
As they passed the stand I could hear the cry
    Of the folk in the distance, yelling!

Then the last time round! And the hoofbeats rang!
    And I said, "Well, it's now or never!"
And out on the heels of the throng I sprang,
And the spurs bit deep and the whipcord sang
    As I rode! For the Mooki River!

We raced for home in a cloud of dust
    And the curses rose in chorus.
'Twas flog, and hustle, and jump you must!
And The Cow ran well — but to my disgust
    There was one got home before us.

'Twas a big black horse, that I had not seen
    In the part of the race I'd ridden;
And his coat was cool and his rider clean,
And I thought that perhaps I had not been
    The only one that had hidden.

And the trainer came with a visage blue
    With rage, when the race concluded:
Said he, "I thought you'd have pulled us through,
But the man on the black horse planted too,
    *And nearer to home than you did!*"

* * * *

Alas to think that those times so gay
    Have vanished and passed forever!
You don't believe in the yarn you say?
Why, man! 'Twas a matter of every day
    When we raced on the Mooki River!

# *In the Stable*

What! You don't like him; well, maybe — we all have our
    fancies, of course:
Brumby to look at you reckon? Well, no: he's a thoroughbred horse;
Sired by a son of old Panic — look at his ears and his head —
Lop-eared and Roman-nosed, ain't he? — well, that's how the Panics are bred.
Gluttonous, ugly and lazy, rough as a tip-cart to ride,
Yet if you offered a sovereign apiece for the hairs on his hide
That wouldn't buy him, nor twice that; while I've a pound to the good,
This here old stager stays by me and lives like a thoroughbred should:
Hunt him away from his bedding, and sit yourself down by the wall,
Till you hear how the old fellow saved me from Gilbert, O'Maley and Hall.

* * * *

Gilbert and Hall and O'Maley, back in the bushranging days,
Made themselves kings of the district — ruled it in old-fashioned ways —
Robbing the coach and the escort, stealing our horses at night,
Calling sometimes at the homesteads and giving the women a fright:
Came to the station one morning — and why they did this no one knows —
Took a brood mare from the paddock — wanting some fun, I suppose —
Fastened a bucket beneath her, hung by a strap round her flank,
Then turned her loose in the timber back of the seven-mile tank.

Go! She went mad! She went tearing and screaming with fear through the trees,
While the curst bucket beneath her was banging her flanks and her knees.
Bucking and racing and screaming she ran to the back of the run,
Killed herself there in a gully; by God, but they paid for their fun!
Paid for it dear, for the black boys found tracks, and the bucket, and all,
And I swore that I'd live to get even with Gilbert, O'Maley and Hall.

Day after day then I chased them — 'course they had friends on the sly,
Friends who were willing to sell them to those who were willing to buy.
Early one morning we found them in camp at the Cockatoo Farm
One of us shot at O'Maley and wounded him under the arm:
Ran them for miles in the ranges, till Hall, with his horse fairly beat,
Took to the rocks and we lost him — the others made good their retreat.
It was war to the knife then, I tell you, and once, on the door of my shed,
They nailed up a notice that offered a hundred reward for my head!

181

Then we heard they were gone from the district, they stuck up
    a coach in the West,
And I rode by myself in the paddocks, taking a bit of a rest,
Riding this colt as a youngster — awkward, half-broken and shy,
He wheeled round one day on a sudden; I looked, but I couldn't see why,
But I soon found out why, for before me, the hillside rose up like a wall,
And there on the top with their rifles were Gilbert, O'Maley and Hall!

'Twas a good three-mile run to the homestead — bad going,
    with plenty of trees —
So I gathered the youngster together, and gripped at his ribs with my knees.
'Twas a mighty poor chance to escape them! It puts a man's nerve to the test
On a half-broken colt to be hunted by the best mounted men in the West.
But the half-broken colt was a racehorse! He lay down to work with a will,
Flashed through the scrub like a clean-skin — by Heavens we
    *flew* down the hill!
Over a twenty-foot gully he swept with the spring of a deer
And they fired as we jumped, but they missed me — a bullet sang close to
    my ear —
And the jump gained us ground, for they shirked it: but I saw as we raced
    through the gap
That the rails at the homestead were fastened — I was caught like a rat in
    a trap.
Fenced with barbed wire was the paddock — barbed wire that
    would cut like a knife —
How was a youngster to clear it that never had jumped in his life?

Bang went a rifle behind me — the colt gave a spring, he was hit;
Straight at the sliprails I rode him — I felt him take hold of the bit;
Never a foot to the right or the left did he swerve in his stride,
Awkward and frightened, but honest, the sort it's a pleasure to ride!
Straight at the rails, where they'd fastened barbed wire on the top of the post,
Rose like a stag and went over, with hardly a scratch at the most;
Into the homestead I darted, and snatched down my gun from the wall,
And I tell you I made them step lively, Gilbert, O'Maley and Hall!

Yes! There's the mark of the bullet — he's got it inside of him yet
Mixed up somehow with his victuals, but bless you he don't seem to fret!
Gluttonous, ugly, and lazy — eats any thing he can bite;
Now, let us shut up the stable, and bid the old fellow goodnight:
Ah! We can't breed 'em, the sort that were bred when we old 'uns were
    young.

Yes, I was saying, these bushrangers, none of 'em lived to be hung,
Gilbert was shot by the troopers, Hall was betrayed by his friend,
Campbell disposed of O'Maley, bringing the lot to an end.

But you can talk about riding — I've ridden a lot in the past —
Wait till there's rifles behind you, you'll know what it means to go fast!
I've steeplechased, raced, and "run horses", but I think the most dashing of
    all
Was the ride when the old fellow saved me from Gilbert, O'Maley and Hall!

## "He Giveth His Beloved Sleep"

The long day passes with its load of sorrow:
    In slumber deep
I lay me down to rest until tomorrow —
    Thank God for sleep.

Thank God for all respite from weary toiling,
    From cares that creep
Across our lives like evil shadows, spoiling
    God's kindly sleep.

We plough and sow, and, as the hours grow later,
    We strive to reap,
And build our barns, and hope to build them greater
    Before we sleep.

We toil and strain and strive with one another
    In hopes to heap
Some greater share of profit than our brother
    Before we sleep.

What will it profit that with tears or laughter
    Our watch we keep?
Beyond it all there lies the Great Hereafter!
    Thank God for sleep!

For, at the last, beseeching Christ to save us,
    We turn with deep
Heartfelt thanksgiving unto God, who gave us
    The Gift of Sleep.

# Driver Smith

'Twas Driver Smith of Battery A was anxious to see a fight;
He thought of the Transvaal all the day, he thought of it all the night —
"Well, if the battery's left behind, I'll go to the war," says he,
"I'll go a-driving an ambulance in the ranks of the A.M.C.

"I'm fairly sick of these here parades, it's want of a change that kills
A-charging the Randwick Rifle Range and aiming at Surry Hills.
And I think if I go with the ambulance I'm certain to find a show,
For they have to send the medical men wherever the troops can go.

"Wherever the rifle bullets flash and the Maxims raise a din,
It's there you'll find the medical men a-raking the wounded in —
A-raking 'em in like human flies — and a driver smart like me
Will find some scope for his extra skill in the ranks of the A.M.C."

So Driver Smith he went to the war a-cracking his driver's whip,
From ambulance to collecting base they showed him his regular trip.
And he said to the boys that were marching past, as he gave his whip a crack,
"You'll walk yourselves to the fight," says he — "Lord spare me, I'll drive
        you back."

Now, the fight went on in the Transvaal hills for the half of a day or more,
And Driver Smith he worked his trip — all aboard for the seat of war!
He took his load from the stretcher men and hurried 'em homeward fast
Till he heard a sound that he knew full well — a battery rolling past.

He heard the clink of the leading chains and the roll of the guns behind —
He heard the crack of the drivers' whips, and he says to 'em, "Strike me blind,
I'll miss me trip with this ambulance, although I don't care to shirk,
But I'll take the car off the line to-day and follow the guns at work."

Then up the Battery Colonel came a-cursing 'em black in the face.
"Sit down and shift 'em, you drivers there, and gallop 'em into place."
So off the Battery rolled and swung, a-going a merry dance,
And holding his own with the leading gun goes Smith with his ambulance.

They opened fire on the mountainside, a-peppering by and large,
When over the hill above their flank the Boers came down at the charge;
They rushed the guns with a daring rush, a-volleying left and right,
And Driver Smith with his ambulance moved up to the edge of the fight.

The gunners stuck to their guns like men, and fought like the wild cats fight,
For a Battery man don't leave his gun with ever a hope in sight;
But the bullets sang and the Mausers cracked and the Battery men gave way,
Till Driver Smith with his ambulance drove into the thick of the fray.

He saw the head of the Transvaal troop a-thundering to and fro,
A hard old face with a monkey beard — a face that he seemed to know;
"Now, who's that leader," said Driver Smith, "I've seen him before to-day.
Why, bless my heart, but it's Kruger's self," and he jumped for him straight
        away.

He collared old Kruger round the waist and hustled him into the van.
It wasn't according to stretcher drill for raising a wounded man;
But he forced him in and said: "All aboard, we're off for a little ride,
And you'll have the car to yourself," says he, "I reckon we're full inside."

He wheeled his team on the mountainside and set 'em a merry pace,
A-galloping over the rocks and stones, and a lot of the Boers gave chase;
But Driver Smith had a fairish start, and he said to the Boers, "Good-day,
You have Buckley's chance for to catch a man that was trained in Battery
        A."

He drove his team to the hospital and said to the P.M.O.,
"Beg pardon, sir, but I missed a trip, mistaking the way to go;
And Kruger came to the ambulance and asked could we spare a bed,
So I fetched him here, and we'll take him home to show for a bob a head."

So the word went round to the English troops to say they need fight no more,
For Driver Smith with his ambulance had ended the blooming war:
And in London now at the music halls he's starring it every night,
And drawing a hundred pounds a week to tell how he won the fight.

# There's Another Blessed Horse Fell Down

When you're lying in your hammock, sleeping soft and
 sleeping sound,
 Without a care or trouble on your mind,
And there's nothing to disturb you but the engines going round,
 And you're dreaming of the girl you left behind;
In the middle of your joys you'll be wakened by a noise,
 And a clatter on the deck above your crown,
And you'll hear the corporal shout as he turns the picket out,
 "There's another blessed horse fell down."

You can see 'em in the morning, when you're cleaning out the stall,
 A-leaning on the railings nearly dead,
And you reckon by the evening they'll be pretty sure to fall,
 And you curse them as you tumble into bed.
Oh, you'll hear it pretty soon, "Pass the word for Denny Moon,
 There's a horse here throwing handsprings like a clown";
And it's "Shove the others back or he'll cripple half the pack,
 There's another blessed horse fell down."

And when the war is over and the fighting all is done,
 And you're all at home with medals on your chest,
And you've learnt to sleep so soundly that the firing of a gun
 At your bedside wouldn't rob you of your rest;
As you lie in slumber deep, if your wife walks in her sleep,
 And tumbles down the stairs and breaks her crown,
Oh, it won't awaken you, for you'll say, "It's nothing new,
 It's another blessed horse fell down."

# On the Trek

Oh, the weary, weary journey on the trek, day after day,
   With sun above and silent veldt below;
And our hearts keep turning homeward to the youngsters far away,
   And the homestead where the climbing roses grow.
Shall we see the flats grow golden with the ripening of the grain?
   Shall we hear the parrots calling on the bough?
Ah! the weary months of marching ere we hear them call again,
   For we're going on a long job now.

In the drowsy days on escort, riding slowly half asleep,
   With the endless line of waggons stretching back,
While the khaki soldiers travel like a mob of travelling sheep,
   Plodding silent on the never-ending track,
While the constant snap and sniping of the foe you never see
   Makes you wonder will your turn come — when and how?
As the Mauser ball hums past you like a vicious kind of bee —
   Oh! we're going on a long job now.

When the dash and the excitement and the novelty are dead,
   And you've seen a load of wounded once or twice,
Or you've watched your old mate dying — with the vultures overhead,
   Well, you wonder if the war is worth the price.
And down along Monaro now they're starting out to shear,
   I can picture the excitement and the row;
But they'll miss me on the Lachlan when they call the roll this year,
   For we're going on a long job now.

# The Last Parade

With never a sound of trumpet,
  With never a flag displayed,
The last of the old campaigners
  Lined up for the last parade.

Weary they were and battered,
  Shoeless, and knocked about;
From under their ragged forelocks
  Their hungry eyes looked out.

And they watched as the old commander
  Read out, to the cheering men,
The Nation's thanks and the orders
  To carry them home again.

And the last of the old campaigners,
  Sinewy, lean, and spare —
He spoke for his hungry comrades:
  "Have we not done our share?

"Starving and tired and thirsty
  We limped on the blazing plain;
And after a long night's picket
  You saddled us up again.

"We froze on the windswept kopjes
  When the frost lay snowy white.
Never a halt in the daytime,
  Never a rest at night!

"We knew when the rifles rattled
  From the hillside bare and brown,
And over our weary shoulders
  We felt warm blood run down.

"As we turned for the stretching gallop,
  Crushed to the earth with weight;
But we carried our riders through it —
  Carried them p'raps too late.

"Steel! We were steel to stand it —
     We that have lasted through,
We that are old campaigners
     Pitiful, poor, and few.

"Over the sea you brought us,
     Over the leagues of foam:
Now we have served you fairly
     Will you not take us home?

"Home to the Hunter River,
     To the flats where the lucerne grows;
Home where the Murrumbidgee
     Runs white with the melted snows.

"This is a small thing, surely!
     Will not you give command
That the last of the old campaigners
     Go back to their native land?"

\* \* \* \*

They looked at the grim commander,
     But never a sign he made.
"Dismiss!" and the old campaigners
     Moved off from their last parade.

# Johnny Boer

Men fight all shapes and sizes as the racing horses run,
And no man knows his courage till he stands before a gun.
At mixed-up fighting, hand to hand, and clawing men about
They reckon Fuzzy-wuzzy is the hottest fighter out.
But Fuzzy gives himself away — his style is out of date,
He charges like a driven grouse that rushes on its fate;
You've nothing in the world to do but pump him full of lead:
But when you're fighting Johnny Boer you have to use your head;
He don't believe in front attacks or charging at the run,
He fights you from a kopje with his little Maxim gun.

For when the Lord He made the earth, it seems uncommon clear,
He gave the job of Africa to some good engineer,
Who started building fortresses on fashions of his own —
Lunettes, redoubts, and counterscarps all made of rock and stone.
The Boer needs only bring a gun, for ready to his hand
He finds these heaven-built fortresses all scattered through the land;
And there he sits and winks his eye and wheels his gun about,
And we must charge across the plain to hunt the beggar out.
It ain't a game that grows on us, there's lots of better fun
Than charging at old Johnny with his little Maxim gun.

On rocks a goat could scarcely climb, steep as the walls of Troy,
He wheels a four-point-seven about as easy as a toy;
With bullocks yoked and drag ropes manned, he lifts her up the rocks
And shifts her every now and then, as cunning as a fox.
At night you mark her right ahead, you see her clean and clear,
Next day at dawn — "What, ho! she bumps" — from somewhere in the rear.
Or else the keenest-eyed patrol will miss him with the glass —
He's lying hidden in the rocks to let the leaders pass;
But when the main guard comes along he opens up the fun,
There's lots of ammunition for the little Maxim gun.

But after all the job is sure, although the job is slow,
We have to see the business through, the Boer has got to go.
With Nordenfeldt and lyddite shell it's certain, soon or late,
We'll hunt him from his kopjes and across the Orange State;
And then across those open flats you'll see the beggar run,
And we'll be running after with *our* little Maxim gun.

# *Right in Front of the Army*

"Where 'ave you been this week or more,
    'Aven't seen you about the war?
Thought perhaps you was at the rear
Guarding the waggons." "What, us? No fear!
Where have we been? Why, bless my heart,
Where have we been since the bloomin' start?
    Right in the front of the army,
        Battling day and night!
    Right in the front of the army,
        Teaching 'em how to fight!"
    Every separate man you see,
    Sapper, gunner, and C.I.V.,
    Every one of 'em seems to be
    Right in the front of the army!

Most of the troops to the camp had gone,
When we met with a cow gun toiling on;
And we said to the boys, as they walked her past,
"Well, thank goodness, you're here at last!"
"Here at last! Why, what d'yer mean?
Ain't we just where we've always been?
    Right in the front of the army,
        Battling day and night!
    Right in the front of the army,
        Teaching 'em how to fight!"
    Correspondents and vets in force,
    Mounted foot and dismounted horse,
    All of them were, as a matter of course,
    Right in the front of the army.

Old Lord Roberts will have to mind
If ever the enemy get behind;
For they'll smash him up with a rear attack,
Because his army has got no back!
Think of the horrors that might befall
An army without any rear at all!
    Right in the front of the army,
        Battling day and night!
    Right in the front of the army,
        Teaching 'em how to fight!
    Swede attachés and German counts,
    Yeomen (known as De Wet's remounts),
    All of them were by their own accounts
    Right in the front of the army!

# *That V.C.*

'Twas in the days of front attack,
 This glorious truth we'd yet to learn it —
That every "front" had got a back,
 And French was just the man to turn it.

A wounded soldier on the ground
 Was lying hid behind a hummock;
He proved the good old proverb sound —
 An army travels on its stomach.

He lay as flat as any fish,
 His nose had worn a little furrow;
He only had one frantic wish,
 That like an ant-bear he could burrow.

The bullets whistled into space,
 The pom-pom gun kept up its braying,
The four-point-seven supplied the bass —
 You'd think the devil's band was playing.

A valiant comrade, crawling near,
 Observed his most supine behaviour,
And crept towards him, "Hey! what cheer?
 Buck up," said he, "I've come to save yer.

"You get up on my shoulders, mate,
 And if we live beyond the firing,
I'll get the V.C. sure as fate,
 Because our blokes is all retiring.

"It's fifty pounds a year," says he,
 "I'll stand you lots of beer and whisky."
"No," says the wounded man, "not me,
 I'll not be saved, it's far too risky.

"I'm fairly safe behind this mound,
 I've worn a hole that seems to fit me;
But if you lift me off the ground,
 It's fifty pounds to one they'll hit me."

194

So back towards the firing line
    Our friend crept slowly to the rear, oh!
Remarking, "What a selfish swine!
    He might have let me be a hero."

# *Jock*

There's a soldier that's been doing of his share
In the fighting up and down and round about.
He's continually marching here and there
And he's fighting, morning in and morning out.

The Boer, you see, he generally runs;
But sometimes when he hides behind a rock,
And we can't make no impression with the guns,
Oh, then you'll hear the order, "Send for Jock!"

Yes, it's Jock — Scotch Jock.
He's the fellow that can give or take a knock.
For he's hairy and he's hard,
And his feet are by the yard,
And his face is like the face what's on a clock.
But when the bullets fly you will mostly hear the cry —
"Send for Jock!"

The Cavalry have gun and sword and lance,
Before they choose their weapon, why, they're dead.
The Mounted Fut are hampered in advance
By holding of their helmets on their head.

And when the Boer has dug himself a trench
And placed his Maxim gun behind a rock,
These mounted heroes — pets of Johnny French —
They have to sit and wait and send for Jock!

Yes, the Jocks — Scotch Jocks,
With their music that'd terrify an ox!
When the bullets kick the sand
You can hear the sharp command —
"Forty-Second! At the double! Charge the rocks!"
And the charge is like a flood
When they've warmed the Highland blood
Of the Jocks!

# *Santa Claus*

Halt! Who goes there? The sentry's call
Rose on the midnight air
Above the noises of the camp,
The roll of wheels, the horses' tramp.
The challenge echoed over all —
Halt! Who goes there?

A quaint old figure clothed in white,
He bore a staff of pine,
An ivy wreath was on his head.
"Advance, oh friend," the sentry said,
"Advance, for this is Christmas night,
And give the countersign."

"No sign nor countersign have I,
Through many lands I roam
The whole world over far and wide,
To exiles all at Christmastide,
From those who love them tenderly
I bring a thought of home.

"From English brook and Scottish burn,
From cold Canadian snows,
From those far lands ye hold most dear
I bring you all a greeting here,
A frond of a New Zealand fern,
A bloom of English rose.

"From faithful wife and loving lass
I bring a wish divine,
For Christmas blessings on your head."
"I wish you well," the sentry said,
"But here, alas! you may not pass
Without the countersign."

He vanished — and the sentry's tramp
Re-echoed down the line.
It was not till the morning light
The soldiers knew that in the night
Old Santa Claus had come to camp
Without the countersign.

# SALTBUSH BILL, J.P., AND OTHER VERSES

# Song of the Wheat

We have sung the song of the droving days,
  Of the march of the travelling sheep;
By silent stages and lonely ways
  Thin, white battalions creep.
But the man who now by the land would thrive
  Must his spurs to a ploughshare beat.
Is there ever a man in the world alive
  To sing the song of the Wheat!

It's west by south of the Great Divide
  The grim grey plains run out,
Where the old flock masters lived and died
  In a ceaseless fight with drought.
Weary with waiting and hope deferred
  They were ready to own defeat,
Till at last they heard the master-word
  And the master-word was Wheat.

Yarran and Myall and Box and Pine —
  'Twas axe and fire for all;
They scarce could tarry to blaze the line
  Or wait for the trees to fall,
Ere the team was yoked and the gates flung wide,
  And the dust of the horses' feet
Rose up like a pillar of smoke to guide
  The wonderful march of Wheat.

Furrow by furrow, and fold by fold,
  The soil is turned on the plain;
Better than silver and better than gold
  Is the surface-mine of the grain.
Better than cattle and better than sheep
  In the fight with the drought and heat.
For a streak of stubbornness wide and deep
  Lies hid in a grain of Wheat.

When the stock is swept by the hand of fate,
    Deep down in his bed of clay
The brave brown Wheat will lie and wait
    For the resurrection day:
Lie hid while the whole world thinks him dead;
    But the spring rain, soft and sweet,
Will over the steaming paddocks spread
    The first green flush of the Wheat.

Green and amber and gold it grows
    When the sun sinks late in the West
And the breeze sweeps over the rippling rows
    Where the quail and the skylark nest.
Mountain or river or shining star,
    There's never a sight can beat —
Away to the skyline stretching far —
    A sea of the ripening Wheat.

When the burning harvest sun sinks low,
    And the shadows stretch on the plain,
The roaring strippers come and go
    Like ships on a sea of grain;
Till the lurching, groaning waggons bear
    Their tale of the load complete.
Of the world's great work he has done his share
    Who has gathered a crop of Wheat.

Princes and Potentates and Czars,
    They travel in regal state,
But old King Wheat has a thousand cars
    For his trip to the water-gate;
And his thousand steamships breast the tide
    And plough thro' the wind and sleet
To the lands where the teeming millions bide
    That say, "Thank God for Wheat!"

# Brumby's Run

*The Aboriginal term for a wild horse is "brumby". At a recent
trial in Sydney a Supreme Court Judge, hearing of
"brumby horses", asked "Who is Brumby, and where is his run?"*

It lies beyond the western pines
    Towards the sinking sun,
And not a survey mark defines
    The bounds of "Brumby's run".

On odds and ends of mountain land
    On tracks of range and rock,
Where no one else can make a stand,
    Old Brumby rears his stock —

A wild, unhandled lot they are
    Of every shape and breed,
They venture out 'neath moon and star
    Along the flats to feed.

But when the dawn makes pink the sky
    And steals along the plain,
The Brumby horses turn and fly
    Towards the hills again.

The traveller by the mountain track
    May hear their hoofbeats pass,
And catch a glimpse of brown and black,
    Dim shadows on the grass.

The eager stock horse pricks his ears
    And lifts his head on high
In wild excitement when he hears
    The Brumby mob go by.

Old Brumby asks no price or fee
    O'er all his wide domains:
The man who yards his stock is free
    To keep them for his pains.

So, off to scour the mountainside
    With eager eyes aglow,
To strongholds where the wild mobs hide
    The gully-rakers go.

A rush of horses through the trees,
    A red shirt making play;
A sound of stockwhips on the breeze,
    They vanish far away!

* * * *

Ah, me! before our day is done
    We long with bitter pain
To ride once more on Brumby's run
    And yard his mob again.

# Saltbush Bill on the Patriarchs

Come all ye little rouseabouts and climb upon my knee;
To-day, ye see, is Christmas Day, and so it's up to me
To give you some instruction like — a kind of Christmas tale —
So name your yarn, and off she goes. What, "Jonah and the Whale"?

Well, whales is sheep I've never shore; I've never been to sea,
So all them great Leviathans is mysteries to me;
But there's a tale the Bible tells I fully understand,
About the time the Patriarchs were settling on the land.

Those Patriarchs of olden time, when all is said and done,
They lived the same as far-out men on many a Queensland run —
A lot of roving, droving men that drifted to and fro,
The same we did out Queensland way a score of years ago.

Now Isaac was a squatter man, and Jacob was his son,
And when the boy grew up, you see, he wearied of the run.
You know the way that boys grow up — there's some that stick at home.
But any boy that's worth his salt will roll his swag and roam;

So Jacob caught the roving fit and took the drovers' track
To where his uncle had a run, beyond the outer back;
You see they made for outback runs for room to stretch and grow,
The same we did out Queensland way, a score of years ago.

Now, Jacob knew the ways of stock — that's most uncommon clear —
For when he got to Laban's Run, they made him overseer.
He didn't ask a pound a week, but bargained for his pay,
To take the roan and strawberry calves — the same we'd take today.

The duns and blacks and "Goulburn roans" (that's brindles), coarse and hard,
He branded them with Laban's brand, in Old Man Laban's yard;
So, when he'd done the station work for close on seven year,
Why, all the choicest stock belonged to Laban's overseer.

It's often so with overseers — I've seen the same thing done
By many a Queensland overseer on many a Queensland run —
But when the mustering time came on old Laban acted straight.
He gave him country of his own outside the bound'ry gate.

He gave him stock, and offered him his daughter's hand in troth;
And Jacob first he married one, and then he married both.
You see, they weren't particular about a wife or so;
No more were we up Queensland way a score of years ago.

But when the stock were strong and fat with grass and lots of rain,
Then Jacob felt the call to take the homeward road again.
It's strange in every creed and clime, no matter where you roam,
There comes a day when every man would like to make for home.

So off he set, with sheep and goats — a mighty moving band —
To battle down the homeward track along the Overland.
It's droving mixed-up mobs like that, that makes men cut their throats.
I've travelled rams, which Lord forget, but never travelled goats.

But Jacob knew the ways of stock, for, so the story goes,
When battlin' through the Philistines — selectors, I suppose —
He thought he'd have to fight his way, an awkward sort of job;
So what did Old Man Jacob do — of course, he split the mob.

He sent the strong stock on ahead to battle out the way;
He couldn't hurry lambing ewes — no more you could today —
And down the road, from run to run, his hand 'gainst every hand,
He moved that mighty mob of stock across the Overland.

The thing is made so clear and plain, so solid in and out,
There isn't any room at all for any kind of doubt.
It's just a plain straightforward tale — a tale that lets you know
The way they lived in Palestine three thousand years ago.

It's strange to read it all today, the shifting of the stock;
You'd think you see the caravans that loaf behind the flock.
The little donkeys and the mules, the sheep that slowly spread,
And maybe Dan or Naphthali a-ridin' on ahead;

The long, dry, dusty summer days, the smouldering fires at night;
The stir and bustle of the camp at break of morning light;
The little kids that skipped about, the camels' dead-slow tramp —
I wish I'd done a week or two in Old Man Jacob's camp!

But if I keep the narrer path, some day, perhaps, I'll know
How Jacob bred them strawberry calves three thousand years ago.

# The Reverend Mullineux

I'd reckon his weight at eight-stun-eight,
  And his height at five-foot-two,
With a face as plain as an eight-day clock
And a walk as brisk as a bantam-cock —
    Game as a bantam, too,
Hard and wiry and full of steam,
That's the boss of the English team,
    The Reverend Mullineux.

Makes no row when the game gets rough —
    None of your "Strike me blue!
You's want smacking across the snout!"
Plays like a gentleman out-and-out —
    Such as he ought to do.
"Kindly remove from off my face!"
That's the way that he states his case —
    Reverend Mullineux.

Kick! He can kick like an army mule —
    Runs like a kangaroo!
Hard to get by as a lawyer plant,
Tackles his man like a bulldog ant —
    Fetches him over too!
*Didn't* the public cheer and shout
Watchin' him chuckin' big blokes about —
    Reverened Mullineux.

Scrimmage was packed on his prostrate form.
    Somehow the ball got through.
Who was it tackled our big half-back,
Flinging him down like an empty sack,
    Right on our goal line too?
Who but the man that we thought was dead,
Down with a score of 'em on his head —
    Reverend Mullineux.

# Wisdom of Hafiz

*The Philosopher Takes to Racing*

My son, if you go to the races to battle with Ikey and Mo,
Remember, it's seldom the pigeon can pick out the eye of the crow;
Remember, they live by the business; remember, my son, and go slow!

If ever an owner should tell you, "Back mine" — don't you be such a flat.
He knows his own cunning no doubt — does he know what the others are at?
Find out what he's frightened of most, and invest a few dollars on that.

Walk not in the track of the trainer, nor hang round the rails at his stall.
His wisdom belongs to his patron — shall he give it to one and to all?
When the stable is served he may tell you — and his words are like jewels
    let fall.

Run wide of the tipster, who whispers that Borak is sure to be first,
He tells the next mug that he meets with a tale with the placings reversed;
And, remember, of judges of racing, the jockey's the absolute worst.

When they lay three to one on the field, and the runners are twenty-and-two,
Take a pull at yourself; take a pull — it's a mighty big field to get through.
Is the club handicapper a fool? If a fool is about, perhaps it's you!

Beware of the critic who tells you the handicap's absolute rot,
For this is chucked in, and that's hopeless, and somebody ought to be shot.
How is it he can't make a fortune himself when he knows such a lot?

From tipsters, and jockeys, and trials, and gallops, the glory has gone,
For this is the wisdom of Hafiz that sages have pondered upon,
"The very best tip in the world is to see the commission go on!"

# Saltbush Bill, J.P.

B eyond the land where Leichhardt went,
    Beyond Sturt's western track,
The rolling tide of change has sent
    Some strange J.P.s out back.

And Saltbush Bill, grown old and grey,
    And worn with want of sleep,
Received the news in camp one day
    Behind the travelling sheep,

That Edward Rex, confiding in
    His known integrity,
By hand and seal on parchment skin
    Had made him a J.P.

He read the news with eager face
    But found no word of pay.
"I'd like to see my sister's place
    And kids on Christmas Day.

"I'd like to see green grass again,
    And watch clear water run,
Away from this unholy plain,
    And flies, and dust, and sun."

At last one little clause he found
    That might some hope inspire,
"A magistrate may charge a pound
    For inquest on a fire."

A big blacks' camp was built close by
    And Saltbush Bill, says he,
"I think that camp might well supply
    A job for a J.P."

That night, by strange coincidence,
    A most disastrous fire
Destroyed the country residence
    Of Jacky Jack, Esquire.

'Twas mostly leaves, and bark, and dirt;
    The party most concerned
Appeared to think it wouldn't hurt
    If forty such were burned.

Quite otherwise thought Saltbush Bill,
    Who watched the leaping flame.
"The home is small," said he, "but still
    The principle's the same.

" 'Midst palaces though you should roam,
    Or follow pleasure's tracks,
You'll find," he said, "no place like home,
    At least like Jacky Jack's.

"Tell every man in camp 'Come quick',
    Tell every black Maria,
I give tobacco half a stick —
    Hold inquest long-a fire."

Each juryman received a name
    Well suited to a Court.
"Long Jack" and "Stumpy Bill" became
    "John Long" and "William Short".

While such as "Tarpot", "Bullock Dray",
    And "Tommy Wait-a-While",
Became, for ever and a day,
    "Scott", "Dickens", and "Carlyle".

And twelve good sable men and true
    Were soon engaged upon
The conflagration that o'erthrew
    The home of John A. John.

Their verdict, "Burnt by act of fate",
    They scarcely had returned
When, just behind the magistrate,
    Another humpy burned!

The jury sat again and drew
    Another stick of plug.
Said Saltbush Bill, "It's up to you
    Put some one long-a jug."

"I'll camp the sheep," he said, "and sift
    The evidence about."
For quite a week he couldn't shift,
    The way the fires broke out.

The jury thought the whole concern
    As good as any play.
They used to "take him oath" and earn
    Three sticks of plug a day.

At last the tribe lay down to sleep
    Homeless, beneath a tree;
And onward with his travelling sheep
    Went Saltbush Bill, J.P.

The sheep delivered, safe and sound,
    His horse to town he turned,
And drew some five-and-twenty pound
    For fees that he had earned.

And where Monaro's ranges hide
    Their little farms away,
His sister's children by his side,
    He spent his Christmas Day.

The next J.P. that went outback
    Was shocked, or pained, or both
At hearing every pagan black
    Repeat the juror's oath.

No matter though he turned and fled
    They followed faster still,
"You make it inkwich, boss," they said
    "All same like Saltbush Bill."

They even said they'd let him see
    The fires originate.
When he refused they said that he
    Was "No good magistrate".

And out beyond Sturt's Western track,
    And Leichhardt's furthest tree,
They wait till fate shall send them back
    Their Saltbush Bill, J.P.

# The Riders in the Stand

There's some that ride the Robbo style, and bump at every stride;
 While others sit a long way back, to get a longer ride.
There's some that ride like sailors do, with legs, and arms, and teeth;
And some ride on the horse's neck, and some ride underneath.

But all the finest horsemen out — the men to beat the band —
You'll find amongst the crowd that ride their races in the stand.
They'll say, "He had the race in hand, and lost it in the straight".
They'll show how Godby came too soon, and Barden came too late.

They'll say Chevalley lost his nerve, and Regan lost his head;
They'll tell how one was "livened up" and something else was "dead" —
In fact, the race was never run on sea, or sky, or land,
But what you'd get it better done by riders in the stand.

The rule holds good in everything in life's uncertain fight:
You'll find the winner can't go wrong, the loser can't go right.
You ride a slashing race, and lose — by one and all you're banned!
Ride like a bag of flour, and win — they'll cheer you in the stand.

# *Waltzing Matilda*

*Carrying a Swag*

Oh there once was a swagman camped in the billabongs,
   Under the shade of a Coolibah tree;
And he sang as he looked at the old billy boiling,
   "Who'll come a-waltzing Matilda with me."

   Who'll come a-waltzing Matilda, my darling,
      Who'll come a-waltzing Matilda with me.
   Waltzing Matilda and leading a water-bag,
      Who'll come a-waltzing Matilda with me.

Up came the jumbuck to drink at the waterhole,
   Up jumped the swagman and grabbed him in glee;
And he sang as he put him away in his tucker-bag,
   "You'll come a-waltzing Matilda with me."

   Who'll come a-waltzing Matilda, my darling,
      Who'll come a-waltzing Matilda with me.
   Waltzing Matilda and leading a water-bag,
      Who'll come a-waltzing Matilda with me.

Up came the squatter a-riding his thoroughbred;
   Up came policemen — one, two, and three.
"Whose is the jumbuck you've got in the tucker-bag?
   You'll come a-waltzing Matilda with we."

   Who'll come a-waltzing Matilda, my darling,
      Who'll come a-waltzing Matilda with me.
   Waltzing Matilda and leading a water-bag,
      Who'll come a-waltzing Matilda with me.

Up sprang the swagman and jumped in the waterhole,
   Drowning himself by the Coolibah tree;
And his voice can be heard as it sings in the billabongs,
   "Who'll come a-waltzing Matilda with me?"

   Who'll come a-waltzing Matilda, my darling,
      Who'll come a-waltzing Matilda with me.
   Waltzing Matilda and leading a water-bag,
      Who'll come a-waltzing Matilda with me.

# An Answer to Various Bards

Well, I've waited mighty patient while they all came rolling in,
    Mister Lawson, Mister Dyson, and the others of their kin,
With their dreadful, dismal stories of the overlander's camp,
How his fire is always smoky, and his boots are always damp;
And they paint it so terrific it would fill one's soul with gloom,
But you know they're fond of writing about "corpses" and "the tomb"
So, before they curse the bushland they should let their fancy range,
And take something for their livers, and be cheerful for a change.

Now, for instance, Mister Lawson — well, of course, we almost cried
At the sorrowful description how his "little 'Arvie" died.
And we wept in silent sorrow when "His Father's Mate" was slain;
Then he went and killed the father, and we had to weep again.
Ben Duggan and Jack Denver, too, he caused them to expire,
And he went and cooked the gander of Jack Dunn, of Nevertire;
And he spoke in terms prophetic of a revolution's beat,
When the world should hear the clamour of those people in the street;
But the shearer chaps who start it — why, he rounds on them in blame,
And he calls 'em "agitators" who are living on the game.
So, no doubt, the bush is wretched if you judge it by the groan
Of the sad and soulful poet with a graveyard of his own.

But I "over-write" the bushmen! Well, I own without a doubt
That I always see a hero in the "man from furthest out".
I could never contemplate him through an atmosphere of gloom,
And a bushman never struck me as a subject for "the tomb"
If it ain't all "golden sunshine" where the "wattle branches wave",
Well, it ain't all damp and dismal, and it ain't all "lonely grave".
And, of course, there's no denying that the bushman's life is rough,
But a man can easy stand it if he's built of sterling stuff;
Tho' it's seldom that the drover gets a bed of eiderdown,
Yet the man who's born a bushman, he gets mighty sick of town,
For he's jotting down the figures, and he's adding up the bills
While his heart is simply aching for a sight of southern hills.
Then he hears a wool team passing with a rumble and a lurch,
And although the work is pressing yet it brings him off his perch.

214

For it stirs him like a message from his station friends afar
And he seems to sniff the ranges in the scent of wool and tar;
And it takes him back in fancy, half in laughter, half in tears,

To a sound of other voices and a thought of other years,
When the woolshed rang with bustle from the dawning of the day,
And the shear blades were a-clicking to the cry of "wool away!"
When his face was somewhat browner and his frame was firmer set,
And he feels his flabby muscles with a feeling of regret.
Then the wool team slowly passes and his eyes go sadly back
To the dusty little table and the papers in the rack,
And his thoughts go to the terrace where his sickly children squall,
And he thinks there's something healthy in the bush life after all.

But we'll go no more a-droving in the wind or in the sun,
For our fathers' hearts have failed us and the droving days are done.
There's a nasty dash of danger where the long-horned bullock wheels,
And we like to live in comfort and to get our reg'lar meals.
And to hang about the townships suits us better, you'll agree,
For a job at washing bottles is the job for such as we.
Let us herd into the cities, let us crush and crowd and push
Till we lose the love of roving and we learn to hate the bush;
And we'll turn our aspirations to a city life and beer,
And we'll sneak across to England — it's a nicer place than here;
For there's not much risk of hardship where all comforts are in store,
And the theatres are plenty and the pubs are more and more.

But that ends it, Mister Lawson, and it's time to say good-bye,
We must agree to differ in all friendship, you and I;
And our personal opinions — well, they're scarcely worth a rush,
For there's some that like the city and there's some that like the bush;
And there's no one quite contented, as I've always heard it said,
Except one favoured person, and *he* turned out to be dead.
So we'll work our own salvation with the stoutest hearts we may,
And if fortune only favours we will take the road some day,
And go droving down the river 'neath the sunshine and the stars,
And then we'll come to Sydney and vermilionise the bars.

# T.Y.S.O.N.

Across the Queensland border line
    The mobs of cattle go;
They travel down in sun and shine
    On dusty stage, and slow.
The drovers, riding slowly on
    To let the cattle spread,
Will say, "Here's one old landmark gone,
    For old man Tyson's dead."

What tales there'll be in every camp
    By men that Tyson knew;
The swagmen, meeting on the tramp,
    Will yarn the long day through,
And tell of how he passed as "Brown",
    And fooled the local men.
"But not for me — I struck the town,
And passed the message further down;
    That's T.Y.S.O.N.!"

There stands a little country town
    Beyond the border line,
Where dusty roads go up and down,
    And banks with pubs combine.
A stranger came to cash a cheque,
    Few were the words he said;
A handkerchief about his neck,
    An old hat on his head.

A long, grey stranger, eagle-eyed,
    "You know me? Of course you do."
"It's not my work," the boss replied,
    "To know such tramps as you."
"Well, look here, Mister, don't be flash,"
    Replied the stranger then,
"I never care to make a splash,
I'm simple — but I've got the cash,
    I'm T.Y.S.O.N."

But in that last great drafting yard,
    Where Peter keeps the gate,
And souls of sinners find it barred,
    And go to meet their fate;
There's one who ought to enter in,
    For good deeds done on earth;
Such deeds as merit ought to win,
    Kind deeds of sterling worth.

Not by the straight and narrow gate,
    Reserved for wealthy men,
But through the big gate, opened wide,
The grizzled figure, eagle-eyed,
    Will travel through — and then
Old Peter'll say, "We pass him through,
There's many a thing he used to do,
Good-hearted things that no one knew;
    That's T.Y.S.O.N."

# As Long as Your Eyes are Blue

Wilt thou love me, sweet, when my hair is grey,
    And my cheeks shall have lost their hue?
When the charms of youth shall have passed away,
    Will your love as of old prove true?
For the looks may change, and the heart may range,
    And the love be no longer fond;
Wilt thou love with truth in the years of youth
    And away to the years beyond?

Oh, I love you, sweet, for your locks of brown
    And the blush on your cheek that lies —
But I love you most for the kindly heart
    That I see in your sweet blue eyes —
For the eyes are signs of the soul within,
    Of the heart that is leal and true,
And mine own sweetheart, I shall love you still,
    Just as long as your eyes are blue.

For the locks may bleach, and the cheeks of peach
    May be reft of their golden hue;
But mine own sweetheart, I shall love you still,
    Just as long as your eyes are blue.

# The "Bottle-oh" Man

I ain't the kind of bloke as takes to any steady job —
    I drives a bottle cart around the town.
A man what keeps his eye about need never want a bob —
    I couldn't bear to work for every brown.
There's lots of 'andy things about in everybody's yard,
    There's cocks and 'ens a-running to and fro,
And little dorgs what comes and barks — we takes 'em off their guard;
    And we puts 'em with the Empty Bottle, oh!

    So it's "Any empty bottles, any empty bottles, oh!"
    You can hear us shout for half a mile or so;
    You can see the women rushing
    To take in the Monday's washing
    When they hear the cry of "Empty Bottle, oh!"

I'm driving down by Wexford Street, and up a window goes —
    A girl puts out 'er 'ead and looks at me,
An all right tart with ginger hair and freckles on 'er nose —
    I stops the cart and walks across to see.
"There ain't no bottles 'ere;" says she, "since father took the pledge."
    "No bottles 'ere?" says I. "I'd like to know
Wot right you 'ave to stick your 'ead outside the winder-ledge,
    If you 'aven't got no Empty Bottle, oh!"

I sometimes gives the 'orse a spell, and then the push and me
    We takes a little trip to Chowder Bay;
Oh, ain't it nice the 'ole day long a-gazing at the sea
    And a-hiding of the tanglefoot away!
But when the booze gets 'old of us and fellers starts to "scrap",
    There's some what likes blue metal for to throw!
But as for me, I always says, for laying out a trap,
    Oh, there's nothing like an Empty Bottle, oh!

# The Story of Mongrel Grey

This is the story the stockman told,
    On the cattle camp, when the stars were bright;
The moon rose up like a globe of gold
    And flooded the plain with her mellow light.
We watched the cattle till dawn of day
And he told me the story of Mongrel Grey.

"He was a knock-about station hack,
    Spurred and walloped, and banged and beat;
Ridden all day with a sore on his back,
    Left all night with nothing to eat.
That was a matter of everyday —
Common occurrence to Mongrel Grey.

"Pr'aps we'd have sold him, but someone heard
    He was bred out back on a flooded run,
Where he learnt to swim like a water bird,
    Midnight or midday were all as one.
In the flooded ground he could find his way,
Nothing could puzzle old Mongrel Grey.

" 'Tis a special gift that some horses learn,
    When the floods are out they will splash along
In girth-deep water, and twist and turn
    From hidden channel and billabong.
Never mistaking the road to go,
For a man may guess — but the horses *know.*

"I was camping out with my youngest son
    — Bit of a nipper just learnt to speak —
In an empty hut on the lower run,
    Shooting and fishing in Conroy's Creek.
The youngster toddled about all day,
And with our horses was Mongrel Grey.

"All of a sudden the flood came down
    Fresh from the hills with the mountain rain,
Roaring and eddying, rank and brown,
    Over the flats and across the plain.

Rising and falling — fall of night —
Nothing but water appeared in sight!

" 'Tis a nasty place when the floods are out,
    Even in daylight, for all around
Channels and billabongs twist about,
    Stretching for miles in the flooded ground.
And to move was a hopeless thing to try
In the dark, with the water just racing by.

"I had to try it. I heard a roar,
    And the wind swept down with the blinding rain;
And the water rose till it reached the floor
    Of our highest room, and 'twas very plain
The way the water was sweeping down
We must shift for the highlands at once, or drown.

"Off to the stable I splashed, and found
    The horses shaking with cold and fright;
I led them down to the lower ground,
    But never a yard would they swim that night!
They reared and snorted and turned away,
And none would face it but Mongrel Grey.

"I bound the child on the horse's back,
    And we started off with a prayer to Heaven,
Through the rain and the wind and the pitchy black,
    For I knew that the instinct God has given
To guide His creatures by night and day
Would lead the footsteps of Mongrel Grey.

"He struck deep water at once and swam —
    I swam beside him and held his mane —
Till we touched the bank of the broken dam
    In shallow water — then off again,
Swimming in darkness across the flood,
Rank with the smell of the drifting mud.

"He turned and twisted across and back,
    Choosing the places to wade or swim,
Picking the safest and shortest track,
    The pitchy darkness was clear to him.
Did he strike the crossing by sight or smell?
The Lord that led him alone could tell!

"He dodged the timber whene'er he could,
    But the timber brought us to grief at last;
I was partly stunned by a log of wood,
    That struck my head as it drifted past;
And I lost my grip of the brave old grey,
And in half a second he swept away.

"I reached a tree, where I had to stay,
    And did a perish for two days hard;
And lived on water — but Mongrel Grey,
    He walked right into the homestead yard
At dawn next morning, and grazed around,
With the child on top of him safe and sound.

"We keep him now for the wife to ride,
    Nothing too good for him now of course;
Never a whip on his fat old hide,
    For she owes the child to that old grey horse.
And not Old Tyson himself could pay
The purchase money of Mongrel Grey."

# Gilhooley's Estate

*A ballad concerning the amalgamation of the legal profession*

Oh, Mr Gilhooley he turned up his toes,
    As most of us do, soon or late;
And Jones was a lawyer, as everyone knows,
    So they took him Gilhooley's estate.

Gilhooley in life had been living so free
    'Twas thought his possessions were great,
So Jones, with a smile, says, "There's many a fee
    For me in Gilhooley's estate."

They made out a list of his property fine,
    It totalled a thousand and eight;
But the debts were nine hundred and ninety and nine —
    The debts of Gilhooley's estate.

So Mrs Gilhooley says, "Jones, my dear man,
    My childer have little to ait:
Just keep the expenses as low as you can
    Against poor Gilhooley's estate."

But Jones says, "The will isn't clear in its terms,
    I fear it will need some debate,
And the law won't allow me (attorneys are worms)
    To appear in Gilhooley's estate."

So a barrister man, with a wig on his head,
    And a brief in his hand quite elate,
Went up to the Court where they bury the dead,
    Just to move in Gilhooley's estate.

But His Honour the judge said, "I think that the joint
    Legatees must be called to *probate* —
*Ex parte* Pokehorney is clear on the point —
    The point of Gilhooley's estate.

"I order a suit to be brought just to try
    If this is correct that I state —
A nice friendly suit, and the costs, by and by,
    Must be borne by Gilhooley's estate."

So Mrs Gilhooley says, "Jones, you'll appear!
    Thim barristers' fees is too great;
The suit is but friendly." "Attorneys, my dear,
    Can't be heard in Gilhooley's estate."

From Barristers' Court there's a mighty hurrah
    Arises both early and late:
It's only the whoop of the Junior Bar
    Dividing Gilhooley's estate.

# The Road to Hogan's Gap

Now look, y' see, it's this way like,
    Y' cross the broken bridge
And run the crick down till y' strike
    The second right-hand ridge.

The track is hard to see in parts,
    But still it's pretty clear;
There's been two Injin hawkers' carts
    Along that road this year.

Well, run that right-hand ridge along,
    It ain't, to say, too steep.
There's two fresh tracks might put y' wrong
    Where blokes went out with sheep.

But keep the crick upon your right,
    And follow pretty straight
Along the spur, until y' sight
    A wire and sapling gate.

Well, that's where Hogan's old grey mare
    Fell off and broke her back;
You'll see her carcase layin' there,
    Jist down below the track.

And then you drop two mile, or three,
    It's pretty steep and blind;
You want to go and fall a tree
    And tie it on behind.

And then you'll pass a broken cart
    Below a granite bluff;
And that is where you strike the part
    They reckon pretty rough.

But by the time you've got that far
    It's either cure or kill,
So turn your horses round the spur
    And face 'em up the hill.

For, look, if you should miss the slope
    And get below the track,
You haven't got the whitest hope
    Of ever gettin' back.

An' halfway up you'll see the hide
    Of Hogan's brindled bull;
Well, mind and keep the right-hand side,
    The left's too steep a pull.

And both the banks is full of cracks;
    An' just about at dark
You'll see the last year's bullock tracks
    Where Hogan drew the bark.

The marks is old and pretty faint
    And grown with scrub and such;
Of course the track to Hogan's ain't
    A road that's travelled much.

But turn and run the tracks along
    For half a mile or more,
And then, of course, you can't go wrong —
    You're right at Hogan's door.

When first you come to Hogan's gate
    He mightn't show, perhaps;
He's pretty sure to plant and wait
    To see it ain't the traps.

I wouldn't call it good enough
    To let your horses out;
There's some that's pretty extra rough
    Is livin' round about.

It's likely if your horses did
    Get feedin' near the track,
It's goin' to cost at least a quid
    Or more to get them back.

So, if you find they're off the place,
    It's up to you to go
And flash a quid in Hogan's face —
    He'll know the blokes that know.

But, listen, if you're feelin' dry,
    Just see there's no one near,
And go and wink the other eye
    And ask for ginger beer.

The blokes come in from near and far
    To sample Hogan's pop;
They reckon once they breast the bar
    They stay there till they drop.

On Sundays you can see them spread
    Like flies around the tap.
It's like that song "The Livin' Dead"
    Up there at Hogan's Gap.

They like to make it pretty strong
    Whenever there's a charnce;
So when a stranger comes along
    They always holds a darnce.

There's recitations, songs, and fights,
    They do the thing a treat.
There's one long bloke up there recites
    As well as e'er you'd meet.

They're lively blokes all right up there,
    It's never dull a day.
I'd go meself if I could spare
    The time to get away.

* * * *

The stranger turned his horses, quick,
    He didn't cross the bridge.
He didn't go along the crick
    To strike the second ridge.

He didn't make the trip, because
    He wasn't feeling fit.
His business up at Hogan's was
    To serve him with a writ.

He reckoned if he faced the pull
    And climbed the rocky stair,
The next to come might find his hide
    A landmark on the mountain side,
Along with Hogan's brindled bull
    And Hogan's old grey mare!

# A Singer of the Bush

There is waving of grass in the breeze
    And a song in the air,
And a murmur of myriad bees
    That toil everywhere.
There is scent in the blossom and bough,
    And the breath of the spring
Is as soft as a kiss on a brow —
    And springtime I sing.

There is drought on the land, and the stock
    Tumble down in their tracks
Or follow — a tottering flock —
    The scrub-cutter's axe.
While ever a creature survives
    The axes shall swing;
We are fighting with fate for their lives —
    And the combat I sing.

# "Shouting" for a Camel

It was over at Coolgardie that a mining speculator,
  Who was going down the township just to make a bit o' chink,
Went off to hire a camel from a camel propagator,
  And the Afghan said he'd lend it if he'd stand the beast a drink.
Yes, the only price he asked him was to stand the beast a drink.
He was cheap, very cheap, as the dromedaries go.

So the mining speculator made the bargain, proudly thinking
  He had bested old Mahomet, he had done him in the eye.
Then he clambered on the camel, and the while the beast was drinking
  He explained the situation to the miners standing by.
That 'twas cheap, very cheap, as the dromedaries go.

But the camel kept on drinking and he filled his hold with water,
  And the more he had inside him yet the more he seemed to need,
For he drank it by the gallon, and his girths grew taut and tauter,
  And the miners muttered softly, "Yes, he's very dry indeed!
But he's cheap, very cheap, as the dromedaries go."

So he drank up twenty buckets — it was weird to watch him suck it,
  And the market price for water was per bucket half a crown.
Then the speculator stopped him, saying, "Not another bucket —
  If I give him any more there'll be a famine in the town.
Take him back to old Mahomet and I'll tramp it through the town."
He was cheap, very cheap, as the speculators go.

There's a moral to this story — in your hat you ought to paste it —
  Be careful whom you shout for when a camel is about,
And there's plenty human camels who, before they'll see you waste it,
  Will drink up all you'll pay for if you're fool enough to shout:
If you chance to strike a camel when you're fool enough to shout,
You'll be cheap, very cheap, as the speculators go.

# Mulligan's Mare

Oh, Mulligan's bar was the deuce of a place
To drink and to fight, and to gamble and race;
The height of choice spirits from near and from far
Were all concentrated on Mulligan's bar.

There was "Jerry the Swell", and the jockey boy Ned,
"Dog-bite-me" — so called from the shape of his head —
And a man whom the boys, in their musical slang,
Designed as the "Gaffer of Mulligan's Gang".

Now, Mulligan's Gang had a racer to show,
A bad 'un to look at, a good 'un to go;
Whenever they backed her you safely might swear
She'd walk in a winner, would Mulligan's mare.

But Mulligan, having some radical views,
Neglected his business and got "on the booze";
He took up with runners — a treacherous troop —
Who gave him away and he "fell in the soup".

And so it turned out on a fine summer day,
A bailiff turned up with a writ of "*fi fa*";
He walked to the bar with a manner serene,
"I levy," said he, "in the name of the Queen."

Then Mulligan wanted, in spite of the law,
To pay out the bailiff with "*one* in the jaw";
He drew out to hit him, but, ere you could wink,
He changed his intentions and stood him a drink.

A great consultation there straightway befell
'Twixt jockey boy Neddy and Jerry the Swell,
And the man with the head, who remarked, "Why, you bet!
Dog-bite-me!" said he, "but we'll diddle 'em yet.

"We'll slip out the mare from her stall in a crack,
And put in her place the old broken-down hack;
The hack is so like her, I'm ready to swear
The bailiff will think he has Mulligan's mare.

"So out with the racer and in with the screw,
We'll show him what Mulligan's talent can do;
And if he gets nasty and dares to say much
I'll knock him as stiff as my grandmother's crutch."

Then off to the town went the mare and the lad;
The bailiff came out, never dreamt he was "had";
But marched to the stall with a confident air —
"I levy," said he, "upon Mulligan's mare."

He never would let her go out of his sight,
He watched her by day and he watched her by night,
For races were coming away in the West
And Mulligan's mare had a chance with the best.

And, thinking to quietly serve his own ends,
He sent off a wire to some bookmaking friends:
"Get all you can borrow, beg, snavel, or snare
And lay the whole lot against Mulligan's mare."

The races came round, and a crowd on the course
Were laying the mare till they made themselves hoarse,
And Mulligan's party, with ardour intense,
They backed her for pounds and for shillings and pence.

And think of the grief of the bookmaking host
At sound of the summons to go to the post —
For down to the start with her thoroughbred air
As fit as a fiddle pranced Mulligan's mare!

They started, and off went the boy to the front,
He cleared out at once, and he made it a hunt;
He steadied as rounding the corner they wheeled,
Then gave her her head and she smothered the field.

The race put her owner right clear of his debts,
He landed a fortune in stakes and in bets,
He paid the old bailiff the whole of his pelf,
And gave him a hiding to keep for himself.

So all you bold sportsmen take warning, I pray,
Keep clear of the running, you'll find it don't pay;
For the very best rule that you'll hear in a week —
Is never to bet on a thing that can speak.

And whether you're lucky or whether you lose,
Keep clear of the cards and keep clear of the booze,
And fortune in season will answer your prayer,
And send you a flyer like Mulligan's mare.

# The Mountain Squatter

Here in my mountain home,
    On rugged hills and steep,
I sit and watch you come,
    Oh Riverina Sheep!

You come from fertile plains
    Where saltbush (sometimes) grows,
And flats that (when it rains)
    Will blossom like the rose.

But when the summer sun
    Gleams down like burnished brass
You have to leave your run
    And hustle off for grass.

'Tis then that — forced to roam —
    You come to where I keep,
Here in my mountain home,
    A boarding-house for sheep.

Around me where I sit
    The wary wombat goes,
A beast of little wit
    But what he knows, he *knows.*

The very same remark
    Applies to me also,
I don't give out a spark,
    But what I know, I *know.*

My brain perhaps would show
    No convolutions deep;
But anyhow I know
    The way to handle sheep.

These Riverina cracks,
    They do not care to ride
The half-inch hanging tracks
    Along the mountain side.

Their horses shake with fear
    When loosened boulders go,
With leaps, like startled deer,
    Down to the gulfs below.

Their very dogs will shirk,
    And drop their tails in fright
When asked to go and work
    A mob that's out of sight.

My little collie pup
    Works silently and wide,
You'll see her climbing up
    Along the mountain side.

As silent as a fox
    You'll see her come and go
A shadow through the rocks
    Where ash and messmate grow.

Then, lost to sight and sound
    Behind some rugged steep,
She works her way around
    And gathers up the sheep.

And working wide and shy,
    She holds them rounded up.
The cash ain't coined to buy
    That little collie pup.

And so I draw a screw
    For self and dog and keep
To boundary ride for you,
    Oh Riverina Sheep!

And when the autumn rain
    Has made the herbage grow,
You travel off again,
    And glad — no doubt — to go!

But some are left behind
    Around the mountain's spread,
For those we cannot find
    We put them down as dead.

But when we say *adieu*
 And close the boarding job,
I always find a few
 Fresh earmarks in my mob.

So what with those I sell,
 And what with those I keep,
You pay me pretty well,
 Oh Riverina Sheep!

It's up to me to shout
 Before we say goodbye —
"Here's to a howlin' drought
 All west of Gundagai!"

# *Pioneers*

They came of bold and roving stock that would not fixed abide;
They were the sons of field and flock since e'er they learned to ride;
We may not hope to see such men in these degenerate years
As those explorers of the bush — the brave old pioneers.

'Twas they who rode the trackless bush in heat and storm and drought;
'Twas they that heard the master-word that called them further out;
'Twas they that followed up the trail the mountain cattle made
And pressed across the mighty range where now their bones are laid.

But now the times are dull and slow, the brave old days are dead
When hardy bushmen started out, and forced their way ahead
By tangled scrub and forests grim towards the unknown west,
And spied the far-off promised land from off the ranges' crest.

Oh! ye, that sleep in lonely graves by far-off ridge and plain,
We drink to you in silence now as Christmas comes again,
The men who fought the wilderness through rough, unsettled years —
The founders of our nation's life, the brave old pioneers.

# Santa Claus in the Bush

It chanced out back at the Christmas time,
  When the wheat was ripe and tall,
A stranger rode to the farmer's gate,
    A sturdy man, and a small.

"Run down, run down, my little son Jack,
    And bid the stranger stay;
And we'll hae a crack for the 'Auld Lang Syne',
    For tomorrow is Christmas Day."

"Nay now, nay now," said the dour gude wife,
    "But ye should let him be;
He's maybe only a drover chap
    From the land o' the Darling Pea.

"Wi' a drover's tales, and a drover's thirst
    To swiggle the whole night through;
Or he's maybe a life assurance carle,
    To talk ye black and blue."

"Gude wife, he's never a drover chap,
    For their swags are neat and thin;
And he's never a life assurance carle,
    Wi' the brick dust burnt in his skin.

"Gude wife, gude wife, be not so dour,
    For the wheat stands ripe and tall,
And we shore wi' a seven-pound fleece this year,
    Ewes and weaners and all.

"There is grass to spare, and the stock are fat,
    When they whiles are gaunt and thin,
And we owe a tithe to the travelling poor,
    So we must ask him in.

"You can set him a chair to the table side,
    And give him a bite to eat;
An omelette made of a new-laid egg,
    Or a tasty piece of meat."

"But the native cats have taken the fowls,
     They have na' left a leg;
And he'll get no omelette here at all
     Till the emu lays an egg!"

"Run down, run down, my little son Jack,
     To where the emus bide,
Ye shall find the old hen on the nest,
     While the old cock sits beside.

"But speak them fair, and speak them soft,
     Lest they kick ye a fearsome jolt,
Ye can give them a feed of thae half-inch nails,
     Or a rusty carriage bolt."

So little son Jack ran blithely down,
     With the rusty nails in hand,
Till he came where the emus fluffed and scratched,
     By their nest in the open sand.

And there he has gathered the new-laid egg,
     Would feed three men or four,
And the emus came for the half-inch nails,
     Right up to the settler's door.

"A waste of food," said the dour gude wife,
     As she took the egg, wi' a frown.
"But he gets no meat,  unless ye run
     A paddymelon down."

"Gae oot, gae oot, my little son Jack,
     Wi' your twa-three doggies small;
Gin ye come not back wi' a paddymelon,
     Then come not back at all."

So little son Jack he raced and he ran,
     And he was bare o' the feet,
And soon he captured the paddymelon,
     Was gorged wi' the stolen wheat.

"Sit down, sit down, my bonny wee man,
     To the best that the house can do —
An omelette made of the emu egg
     And a paddymelon stew."

" 'Tis well, 'tis well," said the bonny wee man;
    "I have eaten the wide world's meat,
But the food that is given wi' a right good will
    Is the sweetest food to eat.

"But the night draws on to the Christmas Day
    And I must rise and go,
For I have a mighty way to ride
    To the land of the Esquimaux.

"And it's there I must load my sledges up
    With the reindeers four-in-hand,
That go to the North, South, East, and West,
    To every Christian land."

"To the Esquimaux," said the dour good wife,
    "Ye suit my husband well!
For when he gets up on his journey horse
    He's a bit of a liar himsel'."

Then out wi' a laugh went the bonny wee man
    To his old horse grazing nigh,
And away like a meteor flash they went
    Far off to the Northern sky.

\* \* \* \*

When the children woke on the Christmas morn
    They chattered might and main —
Wi' a sword and gun for little son Jack,
    And a braw new doll for Jane,
And a packet o' nails for the twa emus;
    But the dour gude wife got nane.

# "In re *a Gentleman, One*"

*When an attorney is called before the Full Court to
answer for any alleged misconduct it is not usual to
publish his name until he is found guilty; until then the
matter appears in the papers as, "In re a Gentleman,
One of the Attorneys of the Supreme Court", or, more
shortly, "In re a Gentleman, One".*

We see it each day in the paper,
    And know that there's mischief in store;
That some unprofessional caper
    Has landed a shark on the shore.
We know there'll be plenty of trouble
    Before they get through with the fun,
Because he's been coming the double
    On clients, has "Gentleman, One".

Alas! for the gallant attorney,
    Intent upon cutting a dash,
Sets out on life's perilous journey
    With rather more cunning than cash.
And fortune at first is inviting —
    He struts his brief hour in the sun —
But, lo! on the wall is the writing
    Of Nemesis, "Gentleman, One".

For soon he runs short of the dollars,
    He fears he must go to the wall;
So Peter's trust-money he collars
    To pay off his creditor, Paul;
Then robs right and left — for he goes it
    In earnest when once he's begun.
*Descensus averni* — he knows it;
    It's easy for "Gentleman, One".

The crash comes as sure as the seasons;
    He loses his coin in a mine,
Or booming in land, or for reasons
    Connected with women and wine.

Or maybe the cards or the horses
  A share of the damage have done.
No matter; the end of the course is
  The same: "*Re* a Gentleman, One".

He struggles a while to keep going,
  To stave off detection and shame;
But creditors clamorous growing
  Ere long put an end to the game.
At length the poor soldier of Satan
  His course to a finish has run —
And just think of Windeyer waiting
  To deal with "a Gentleman, One!"

And some face it boldly, and brazen
  The shame and the utter disgrace;
While others, more sensitive, hasten
  Their names and their deeds to efface.
They snap the frail thread which the Furies
  And Fates have so cruelly spun.
May the Great Final Judge and His juries
  Have mercy on "Gentleman, One!"

# At the Melting of the Snow

There's a sunny southern land,
  And it's there that I would be
Where the big hills stand,
  In the South Countrie!
When the wattles bloom again,
  Then it's time for us to go
To the old Monaro country
  At the melting of the snow.

To the East or to the West,
  Or wherever you may be,
You will find no place
  Like the South Countrie.
For the skies are blue above,
  And the grass is green below,
In the old Monaro country
  At the melting of the snow.

Now the team is in the plough,
  And the thrushes start to sing,
And the pigeons on the bough
  Are rejoicing at the Spring.
So come my comrades all,
  Let us saddle up and go
To the old Monaro country
  At the melting of the snow.

# A Dream of the Melbourne Cup

*A Long Way After Gordon*

Bring me a quart of colonial beer
And some doughy damper to make good cheer,
 I must make a heavy dinner;
Heavily dine and heavily sup
Of indigestible things full-up,
Next month they run the Melbourne Cup,
 And I have to dream the winner.

Stoke it in, boys! the half-cooked ham,
The rich ragout and the charming cham,
 I've got to mix my liquor;
Give me a gander's gaunt hind leg,
Hard and tough as a wooden peg,
And I'll grease it down with a hard-boiled egg,
 'Twill make me dream the quicker.

Now I am full of fearful feed,
Now I may dream a race indeed,
 In my restless troubled slumber;
While the nightmares race through my heated brain
And their devil riders spur amain,
The tip for the Cup will reward my pain,
 And I'll spot the winning number.

Thousands and thousands and thousands more,
Like sands on the white Pacific shore,
 The crowding people cluster;
For evermore it's the story old,
While races are bought and backers are sold,
Drawn by the greed of the gain of gold,
 In their thousands still they muster.

\* \* \* \*

And the bookies' cries grow fierce and hot,
"I'll lay the Cup! The double, if not!"
 "Five monkeys, Littlejohn, sir!"
"Here's fives bar one, I lay, I lay!"

And so they shout through the live-long day,
And stick to the game that is sure to pay,
    While fools put money on, sir!

And now in my dream I seem to go
And bet with a "book" that I seem to know —
    A Hebrew moneylender;
A million to five is the price I get —
Not bad! but before I book the bet
The horse's name I clean forget,
    His number and even gender.

Now for the start, and here they come,
And the hoof-strokes roar like a mighty drum
    Beat by a hand unsteady;
They come like a rushing, roaring flood,
Hurrah for the speed of the Chester blood!
For Acme is making the pace so good
    There are some of 'em done already.

But round the back she begins to tire,
And a mighty shout goes up: "Crossfire!"
    The magpie jacket's leading;
And Crossfire challenges fierce and bold,
And the lead she'll have and the lead she'll hold,
But at length gives way to the black and gold,
    Which away to the front is speeding.

Carry them on and keep it up —
A flying race is the Melbourne Cup,
    You must race and stay to win it;
And old Commotion, Victoria's pride,
Now takes the lead with his raking stride,
And a mighty roar goes far and wide —
    "There's only Commotion in it!"

But one draws out from the beaten ruck,
And up on the rails by a piece of luck
    He comes in a style that's clever;
"It's Trident! Trident! Hurrah for Hales!
Go at 'em now while their courage fails";
"Trident! Trident! for New South Wales!"
    "The blue and white for ever!"

Under the whip! With the ears flat back,
Under the whip! Though the sinews crack,
    No sign of the base white feather;
Stick to it now for your breeding's sake,
Stick to it now though your hearts should break,
While the yells and roars make the grandstand shake,
    They come down the straight together.

Trident slowly forges ahead,
The fierce whips cut and the spurs are red,
    The pace is undiminished;
Now for the Panics that never fail!
But many a backer's face grows pale
As old Commotion swings his tail
    And swerves — and the Cup is finished.

* * * *

And now in my dream it all comes back:
I bet my coin on the Sydney crack,
    A million I've won, no question!
Give me my money, you hook-nosed hog!
Give me my money, bookmaking dog!
But he disappears in a kind of fog,
    And I wake with "the indigestion".

# The Gundaroo Bullock

Oh, there's some that breeds the Devon that's as solid as a stone,
And there's some that breeds the brindle which they call the "Goulburn
Roan";
But amongst the breeds of cattle there are very, very few
Like the hairy-whiskered bullock that they bred at Gundaroo.

Far away by Grabben Gullen, where the Murrumbidgee flows,
There's a block of broken countryside where no one ever goes;
For the banks have gripped the squatters, and the free selectors too,
And their stock are always stolen by the men of Gundaroo.

There came a low informer to the Grabben Gullen side,
And he said to Smith the squatter, "You must saddle up and ride,
For your bullock's in the harness-cask of Morgan Donahoo —
He's the greatest cattle-stealer that abides in Gundaroo."

"Oh, ho!" said Smith, the owner of the Grabben Gullen run,
"I'll go and get the troopers by the sinking of the sun,
And down into his homestead tonight we'll take a ride,
With warrants to identify the carcase and the hide."

That night rode down the troopers, the squatter at their head,
They rode into the homestead, and pulled Morgan out of bed.
"Now, show to us the carcase of the bullock that you slew —
The great marsupial bullock that you killed in Gundaroo."

They peered into the harness-cask, and found it wasn't full,
But down among the brine they saw some flesh and bits of wool.
"What's this?" exclaimed the trooper — "an infant, I declare."
Said Morgan, " 'Tis the carcase of an old man native bear.
I heard that ye were coming, so an old man bear I slew,
Just to give you kindly welcome to my home in Gundaroo.

"The times is something awful, as you can plainly see,
The banks have broke the squatters, and they've broke the likes of me;
We can't afford a bullock — such expense would never do —
So an old man bear for breakfast is a treat in Gundaroo."

And along by Grabben Gullen where the rushing river flows;
In the block of broken country where there's no one ever goes,
On the Upper Murrumbidgee they're a hospitable crew,
But you mustn't ask for "bullock" when you go to Gundaroo.

# Lay of the Motor Car

We're away! and the wind whistles shrewd
    In our whiskers and teeth;
And the granite-like grey of the road
    Seems to slide underneath.
As an eagle might sweep through the sky,
    So we sweep through the land;
And the pallid, pedestrians fly
    When they hear us at hand.

We outpace, we outlast, we outstrip!
    Not the fast-fleeing hare,
Nor the racehorses under the whip,
    Nor the birds of the air
Can compete with our swiftness sublime,
    Our ease and our grace.
We annihilate chickens and time
    And policemen and space.

Do you mind that fat grocer who crossed?
    How he dropped down to pray
In the road when he saw he was lost;
    How he melted away
Underneath, and there rang through the fog
    His earsplitting squeal
As he went — Is that he or a dog,
    That stuff on the wheel?

# The Corner Man

I dreamed a dream at the midnight deep,
  When fancies come and go
To vex a man in his soothing sleep
  With thoughts of awful woe —
I dreamed that I was the corner man
  Of a nigger minstrel show.

I cracked my jokes, and the building rang
  With laughter loud and long;
I hushed the house as I softly sang
  An old plantation song —
A tale of the wicked slavery days
  Of cruelty and wrong.

A small boy sat on the foremost seat —
  A mirthful youngster he,
He beat the time with his restless feet
  To each new melody,
And he picked me out as the brightest star
  Of the black fraternity.

"Oh, father," he said, "what *would* we do
  If the corner man should die?
I never saw such a man — did you?
  He makes the people cry,
And then, when he likes, he makes them laugh."
  The old man made reply:

"We each of us fill a very small space
  On the great creation's plan,
If a man don't keep his lead in the race
  There's plenty more that can;
The world can very soon fill the place
  Of even a corner man."

\* \* \* \*

I woke with a jump, rejoiced to find
    Myself at home in bed,
And I framed a moral in my mind
    From the words the old man said.
The world will jog along just the same
    When its corner men are dead.

# When Dacey Rode the Mule

'Twas in a small, up-country town,
    When we were boys at school,
There came a circus with a clown
    And with a bucking mule.
The clown announced a scheme they had —
    The mule was such a king —
They'd give a crown to any lad
    Who'd ride him round the ring.
And, gentle reader, do not scoff
    Nor think the man a fool,
To buck a porous plaster off
    Was pastime to that mule.

The boys got on — he bucked like sin —
    He threw them in the dirt,
And then the clown would raise a grin
    By asking, "Were they hurt?"
But Johnny Dacey came one night,
    The crack of all the school,
Said he, "I'll win the crown all right,
    Bring in your bucking mule."
The elephant went off his trunk,
    The monkey played the fool
And all the band got blazing drunk
    When Dacey rode the mule.

But soon there rose an awful shout
    Of laughter, when the clown,
From somewhere in his pants drew out
    A little paper crown.
He placed the crown on Dacey's head,
    While Dacey looked a fool,
"Now, there's your crown, my lad," he said,
    "For riding of the mule!"
The band struck up with "Killaloe",
    And "Rule Britannia, Rule",
And "Young Man from the Country", too,
    When Dacey rode the mule.

Then Dacey, in a furious rage,
    For vengeance on the show
Ascended to the monkeys' cage
    And let the monkeys go;
The blue-tailed ape and chimpanzee
    He turned abroad to roam;
Good faith! It was a sight to see
    The people step for home.
For big baboons with canine snout
    Are spiteful, as a rule,
The people didn't sit it out
    When Dacey rode the mule.

And from the beasts that did escape
    The bushmen all declare
Were born some creatures partly ape
    And partly native bear.
They're rather few and far between;
    The race is nearly spent;
But some of them may still be seen
    In Sydney Parliament.
And when those legislators fight,
    And drink, and act the fool —
It all commenced that wretched night
    When Dacey rode the mule.

# The Mylora Elopement

By the winding Wollondilly where the weeping willows weep,
And the shepherd with his billy half awake and half asleep
Folds his fleecy flocks that linger homewards in the setting sun,
Lived my hero, Jim the Ringer, "cocky" on Mylora Run.

Jimmy loved the super's daughter, Miss Amelia Jane McGrath,
Long and earnestly he sought her, but he feared her stern papa;
And Amelia loved him truly — but the course of love, if true,
Never yet ran smooth or duly, as it ought, I think, to do.

Watching with his slow affection once Jim saw McGrath the boss
Riding out by Jim's selection, looking for a station 'oss
That was running in the ranges with a mob of outlaws wild,
Old McGrath "Good day" exchanges — off goes Jim to see his child;

Says, "The old man's after Stager, which he'll find is no light job,
And tomorrow I will wager he will try and yard the mob.
Will you come with me tomorrow, I will let the parson know,
And for ever joy, or sorrow, he will join us here below!

"I will bring my nags so speedy, Crazy Jane and Tambourine,
One more kiss — don't think I'm greedy — goodbye, lass, before I'm seen —
Just one more — God bless you, dearie!
Don't forget to meet me here,
Life without you is but weary! now, once more goodbye, my dear."

> The daylight shines on figures twain
> That ride across Mylora plain,
> Laughing and talking — Jim and Jane.
> "Steadily, darling. There's lots of time,
> Didn't we slip the old man prime!
> I knew he'd tackle that Bowneck mob,
> I reckon he'll find it too big a job.
> They've beaten us all. I had a try,
> But the warrigal devils seem to fly.
> That Sambo's a real good bit of stuff
> No doubt, but not quite good enough.
> He'll have to gallop the livelong day,
> To cut and come, to race and stay.

I hope he yards 'em; 'twill do him good,
To see us going I don't think would."
A turn in the road, and fair and square,
They meet the old man standing there.
"What's up?" "Why, running away, of course,"
Says Jim, emboldened. The old man turned,
His eye with wild excitement burned.
"I've raced all day through the scorching heat
After old Bowneck: now I'm beat.
But over that range I think you'll find
The Bowneck mob all run stone-blind.
Will you go and leave the mob behind?
Which will you do? Take the girl away,
Or ride like a white man should today,
And yard old Bowneck? Go or stay?"
Says Jim, "I can't throw this away,
We can bolt some other day, of course,
Amelia Jane, get off that horse.
Up you get, old man. Whoop, halloo,
Here goes to put old Bowneck through!"
Two distant specks on the mountainside,
Two stockwhips echoing far and wide.
Amelia Jane sat down and cried.
"Sakes, Amelia, what's up now,
Leading old Sambo, too, I vow,
And him dead beat. Where have you been?
Bolted with Jim! What *do* you mean?
Met the old man with Sambo licked
From running old Bowneck. Well, I'm kicked.
Run 'em till Sambo nearly dropped?
What did Jim do when you were stopped?
Did you bolt from father across the plain?
Jim made you get off Crazy Jane!
And father got on, and away again.
The two of 'em went in the ranges grim.
Good boy, Jimmy! Well done, Jim!
They're sure to get them now, of course,
That Tambourine is a spanking horse.
And Crazy Jane is good as gold.

And Jim, they say, rides pretty bold;
Not like your father, but very fair.
Jim will have to follow the mare."
"It never was yet in father's hide
To best my Jim on the mountainside.
Jim can rally, and Jim can ride."
But here again Amelia cried.

The sound of a whip comes faint and far,
A rattle of hoofs, and here they are,
In all their tameless pride.
The fleet wild horses snort with fear,
And wheel and break as the yard draws near.
Now, Jim the Ringer, ride!
Wheel 'em! Wheel 'em! Wo back there, wo!
And the foam-flakes fly like the driven snow,
As under the whip the horses go
Adown the mountain side.
And Jim, hands down, and teeth firm set,
On a horse that never has failed him yet,
Is after them down the range.
Well ridden, well ridden, they wheel, wo back,
And long and loud the stockwhips crack.
Their flying course they change.
"Steadily does it — let Sambo go!
Open those sliprails down below.
Smart! or you'll be too late.
They'll follow old Sambo up — look out!
Wheel that black horse — give Sam a clout.
They're in! Make fast the gate."

The mob is safely in the yard;
The old man mounts delighted guard.
No eyes had he but for his prize.
Jim catches poor Amelia's eyes.
"Will you come with me after all I've done?
Here's Crazy Jane is fit to run
For a prince's life — now, don't say no;
Slip on while the old man's down below

        At the inner yard, and away we'll go.
        Will you come, my girl?" "I will, you bet,
        We'll manage this here elopement yet."

By the winding Wollondilly stands the hut of Ringer Jim.
And his loving little Meely makes a perfect god of him.
He has stalwart sons and daughters, and, I think, before he's done,
There'll be numerous "six-fortys" taken on Mylora Run.

# The Pannikin Poet

There's nothing here sublime,
But just a roving rhyme,
Run off to pass the time,
    With nought titanic in
The theme that it supports
And, though it treats of quarts,
It's bare of golden thoughts —
    It's just a pannikin.

I think it's rather hard
That each Australian bard —
Each wan, poetic card —
    With thoughts galvanic in
His fiery soul alight,
In wild aerial flight,
Will sit him down and write
    About a pannikin.

He makes some new chum fare
From out his English lair
To hunt the native bear,
    That curious mannikin;
And then when times get bad
That wand'ring English lad
Writes out a message sad
    Upon his pannikin:

"Oh, mother, think of me
Beneath the wattle tree."
(For you may bet that he
    Will drag the wattle in.)
"Oh, mother, here I think
That I shall have to sink
There ain't a single drink
    The water bottle in."

The dingo homeward hies,
The sooty crows uprise
And caw their fierce surprise
    A tone Satanic in;
And bearded bushmen tread
Around the sleeper's head —
"See here — the bloke is dead."
    "Now, where's his pannikin?"

They read his words and weep,
And lay him down to sleep
Where wattle branches sweep
    A style mechanic in;
And, reader, that's the way
The poets of today
Spin out their little lay
    About a pannikin.

# The Protest

I say 'e *isn't* Remorse!
    'Ow do I know?
Saw 'im on Riccarton course
    Two year ago!
Think I'd forget any 'orse?
    *Course* 'e's The Crow!

Bumper Maginnis and I,
    After a "go",
Walkin' our 'orses to dry,
    I says, "Hello!
What's that old black goin' by?"
    Bumper says, "Oh!
That's an old cuddy of Flanagan's
    — Runs as The Crow!"

Now they make out 'e's Remorse.
    Well, but I *know*.
Soon as I came on the course
    I says, " 'Ello!
    'Ere's the old Crow."
Once a man's seen any 'orse,
    'Course 'e must know.
Sure as there's wood in this table,
    I say 'e's The Crow.

*(Cross-examined by the Committee)*

'Ow do I know the moke
    After one sight?
S'posin' you met a bloke
    Down town at night,
Wouldn't you know 'im again
    when you met 'im?
    That's *'im* all right!

What was the brand on 'is 'ide?
    *I* couldn't say.
Brands can be transmogrified.
    That ain't the way —
It's the *look* of a 'orse and the
       way that 'e moves
    That I'd know any day.

What was the boy on 'is back?
    Why, 'e went past
All of a minute, and off down the track.
    — "The 'orse went as fast?"
True, so 'e did! But, my eyes, what a treat!
    'Ow can I notice the 'ands and the seat
Of each bumble-faced kid of a boy that I meet?
    Lor'! What a question to ast!

*(Protest Dismissed)*

# An Evening in Dandaloo

It was while we held our races —
Hurdles, sprints and steeplechases —
   Up in Dandaloo,
That a crowd of Sydney stealers,
Jockeys, pugilists and spielers
Brought some horses, real heelers,
   Came and put us through.

Beat our nags and won our money,
Made the game by no means funny,
   Made us rather blue;
When the racing was concluded,
Of our hard-earned coin denuded
Dandaloonies sat and brooded
   There in Dandaloo.

          \* \* \* \*

Night came down on Johnson's shanty
Where the grog was no means scanty,
   And a tumult grew
Till some wild, excited person
Galloped down the township cursing,
"Sydney push have mobbed Macpherson,
   Roll up, Dandaloo!"

Great St Denis! what commotion!
Like the rush of stormy ocean
   Fiery horsemen flew.
Dust and smoke and din and rattle,
Down the street they spurred their cattle
To the war-cry of the battle,
   "Wade in, Dandaloo!"

So the boys might have their fight out,
Johnson blew the bar-room light out,
　　Then, in haste, withdrew.
And in darkness and in doubting
Raged the conflict and the shouting,
"Give the Sydney push a clouting,
　　Go it, Dandaloo!"

Jack Macpherson seized a bucket,
Every head he saw, he struck it —
　　Struck in earnest, too;
And a man from Lower Wattle,
Whom a shearer tried to throttle,
Hit out freely with a bottle,
　　There in Dandaloo.

Skin and hair were flying thickly,
When a light was fetched, and quickly
　　Brought a fact to view —
On the scene of the diversion
Every single, solid person
Came along to help Macpherson —
　　*All* were Dandaloo!

When the list of slain was tabled,
Some were drunk and some disabled,
　　Still we found it true.
In the darkness and the smother
We'd been belting one another;
Jack Macpherson bashed his brother
　　There in Dandaloo.

So we drank, and all departed —
How the "mobbing" yarn was started
　　No one ever knew —
And the stockmen tell the story
Of that conflict fierce and gory,
How we fought for love and glory
　　Up in Dandaloo.

It's a proverb now, or near it —
At the races you can hear it,
    At the dog fights, too;
Every shrieking, dancing drover,
As the canines topple over,
Yells applause to Grip or Rover,
    "Give him 'Dandaloo'!"

And the teamster slowly toiling
Through the deep black country soiling
    Wheels and axles, too,
Lays the whip on Spot and Banker,
Rouses Tarboy with a flanker —
"Redman! Ginger! Heave there! Yank her!
    Wade in, Dandaloo!"

# *A Ballad of Ducks*

The railway rattled and roared and swung
  With jolting carriage and bumping trucks.
The sun, like a billiard red ball, hung
In the Western sky: and the tireless tongue
Of the wild-eyed man in the corner told
This terrible tale of the days of old,
And the party that ought to have kept the ducks.

"Well, it ain't all joy bein' on the land
With an overdraft that'd knock you flat;
And the rabbits have pretty well took command;
But the hardest thing for a man to stand
Is the feller who says, 'Well, I told you so!
You should ha' done this way, don't you know!'
I could lay a bait for a man like that.

"The grasshoppers struck us in ninety-one
And what they leave — well, it ain't *de luxe*.
But a growlin' fault-findin' son of a gun
Who'd lent some money to stock our run —
I said they'd eaten what grass we had —
Says he, 'Your management's very bad,
You had a right to have kept some ducks!'

"To have kept some ducks! And the place was white!
Wherever you went you had to tread
On grasshoppers guzzlin' day and night;
And when with a swoosh they rose in flight,
If you didn't look out for yourself they'd fly
Like bullets into your open eye
And knock it out of the back of your head.

"There isn't a turkey or goose or swan,
Or a duck that quacks, or a hen that clucks,
Can make a difference on a run
When a grasshopper plague has once begun;

264

'If you'd finance us,' I says, 'I'd buy
Ten thousand emus and have a try;
The job,' I says, 'is too big for ducks!

" 'You must fetch a duck when you come to stay;
A great big duck — a Muscovy toff —
Ready and fit,' I says, 'for the fray;
And if the grasshoppers come our way
You turn your duck into the lucerne patch,
And I'd be ready to make a match
That the grasshoppers eats his feathers off!'

"He came to visit us by and by,
And it just so happened one day in Spring
A kind of a cloud came over the sky —
A wall of grasshoppers nine miles high,
And nine miles thick, and nine hundred wide,
Flyin' in regiments, side by side,
And eatin' up every living thing.

"All day long, like a shower of rain,
You'd hear 'em smackin' against the wall,
Tap, tap, tap, on the window pane,
And they'd rise and jump at the house again
Till their crippled carcases piled outside.
But what did it matter if thousands died —
A million wouldn't be missed at all.

"We were drinkin' grasshoppers — so to speak —
Till we skimmed their carcases off the spring;
And they fell so thick in the station creek
They choked the waterholes all the week.
There was scarcely room for a trout to rise,
And they'd only take artificial flies —
They got so sick of the real thing.

"An Arctic snowstorm was beat to rags
When the hoppers rose for their morning flight
With a flapping noise like a million flags:
And the kitchen chimney was stuffed with bags
For they'd fall right into the fire, and fry
Till the cook sat down and began to cry —
And never a duck or a fowl in sight!

"We strolled across to the railroad track —
Under a cover, beneath some trucks,
I sees a feather and hears a quack;
I stoops and I pulls the tarpaulin back —
Every duck in the place was there,
No good to them was the open air.
'Mister', I says, 'There's your blanky ducks!' "

# Tommy Corrigan

*Died August 13, 1894*

Y ou talk of riders on the flat, of nerve and dash and pace!
Not one in fifty has the nerve to ride a steeplechase.
It's gay enough while horses pull and take their fences strong,
To rush a flyer to the front and bring the field along;
But what about the last half mile, with horses blown and beat —
When every jump means all you know to keep him on his feet!
When any slip means sudden death — with wife and child to keep,
It needs some pluck to draw the whip and flog him at the leap.
But Corrigan would ride them out by danger undismayed,
He never flinched from fence or wall, he never was afraid.

With easy seat and nerve of steel, light hand and cheery face,
He held the rushing horses back and made the sluggards race,
He gave the shirkers extra heart, he steadied down the rash,
He rode great clumsy, boring brutes and chanced the fatal smash,
He got the rushing Wymlet home that never jumped at all,
But clambered over every fence and clouted every wall;
But ah! you should have heard the cheers that shook the members' stand
Whenever Tommy Corrigan weighed out to ride Lone Hand!

They were, indeed, a splendid pair — the great upstanding horse,
The gamest jockey on his back that ever faced a course,
Though weight was big and pace was hot and jumps were stiff and tall,
"You follow Tommy Corrigan" was passed to one and all.
And every man in Ballarat raised all he could command
To put on Tommy Corrigan when riding old Lone Hand.

But now we'll keep his memory green while horsemen come and go,
We may not see his like again where silks and satins glow;
We'll drink to him in silence, boys, he's followed down the track
Where many a good man went before, but never one came back.
And let us hope in that far land, where shades of brave men reign,
That gallant Tommy Corrigan will ride Lone Hand again.

# The Reveille

Trumpets of the Lancer Corps
  Sound a loud reveille;
Sound it over Sydney shore,
Send the message far and wide
Down the Richmond River side.
Boot and saddle, mount and ride,
  Sound a loud reveille.

Whither go ye, Lancers gay,
  With your bold reveille?
O'er the ocean far away
From your sunny southern home,
Over leagues of trackless foam
In a foreign land to roam,
  With your bold reveille.

When we hear our brethren call,
  Sound a clear reveille.
Then we answer, one and all,
Answer that the world may see,
Of the English stock are we,
At their side we still will be,
  Sound a bold reveille.

English troops are buried deep.
  Sound a soft reveille.
In this foreign land asleep,
Underneath Majuba Hill,
Lying sleeping very still,
Nevermore those squadrons will
  Answer to reveille.

Onward without fear or doubt,
  Sound a bold reveille.
'Till that shame is blotted out.
While our Empire's bounds are wide,
Britons all stand side by side,
Boot and saddle, mount and ride.
  Hear the bold reveille.

# The Maori's Wool

Now, this is just a simple tale to tell the reader how
They civilised the Maori tribe at Rooti-iti-au.

\* \* \* \*

The Maoris are a mighty race — the finest ever known;
Before the missionaries came they worshipped wood and stone;
They went to war and fought like fiends, and when the war was done
They pacified their conquered foes by eating every one.
But nowadays about the *pahs* in idleness they lurk,
Prepared to smoke or drink or talk — or anything but work.
Around the hills their flocks of sheep are fed on tribal lands —
A communistic ownership that no one understands.
The richest tribe in all the North in sheep and horse and cow
Were those who led their simple lives at Rooti-iti-au.

'Twas down to town at Wellington a noble Maori came,
A Rangatira of the best, Rerenga was his name —
(The word "Rerenga" means a "snag" — but until he was gone
This didn't strike the folk he met — it struck them later on.)
He stalked into the Bank they call the "Great Financial Hell",
And told the Chief Financial Fiend the tribe had wool to sell.
The Bold Bank Manager looked grave — the price of wool was high.
He said, "We'll lend you what you need — we're not disposed to buy.
You ship the wool to England, Chief! You'll find it's good advice,
And meanwhile you can draw from us the local market price."
The Chief he thanked him courteously and said he wished to state
In all the Rooti-iti tribe his *mana* would be great,
But still their tribe were simple folk who might not understand
This strange financial jugglery which gave them cash in hand
Before the wool was sold at all; and even after sale
Perhaps they mightn't get the price — the notion turned him pale!
So off he started home again, with trouble on his brow,
To lay the case before the tribe at Rooti-iti-au.

They held a great *korero* in the Rooti-iti clan,
With speeches lasting half a day from every leading man.
They called themselves poetic names — "lost children in a wood";
They said the Great Bank Manager was *"Kapai"* — extra good!

And so they sent Rerenga down, full-powered and well-equipped,
To draw as much as he could get, and let the wool be shipped,
And wedged into a "Cargo Tank", full up from stern to bow —
A mighty clip of wool went Home from Rooti-iti-au.

It was the Bold Bank Manager who drew a heavy cheque;
Rerenga cashed it thoughtfully, then clasped him round the neck.
A hug from him was not at all a thing you'd call a lark,
You see, he lived on mutton-birds and dried remains of shark.
But still it showed his gratitude, and, as he pouched the pelf,
"I'll *'haka'* for you, sir," he said. "In honour of yourself!"
The *haka* is a striking dance — the sort they don't allow
In any place more civilised than Rooti-iti-au.

He *"haka'd"* most effectively — then, with an airy grace
Rubbed noses with the Manager, and vanished into space.
But when the Wool-return came back, ah me, what sighs and groans!
For every bale of Maori wool was loaded up with stones!
Yes — thumping great New Zealand rocks among the wool they found;
On every rock the Bank had lent just seven pence a pound.
And now the Bold Bank Manager, with trouble on his brow,
Is searching vainly for the chief from Rooti-iti-au.

# Sunrise on the Coast

Grey dawn on the sandhills — the night wind has drifted
   All night from the rollers a scent of the sea;
With the dawn the grey fog his battalions has lifted,
   At the scent of the morning they scatter and flee.

Like mariners calling the roll of their number
   The sea fowl put out to the infinite deep.
And far overhead — sinking softly to slumber —
   Worn out by their watching, the stars fall asleep.

To eastward where resteth the dome of the skies on
   The sea line stirs softly the curtain of night;
And far from behind the enshrouded horizon
   Comes the voice of a God saying, "Let there be light."

And lo, there is light! Evanescent and tender,
   It glows ruby-red where 'twas now ashen grey;
And purple and scarlet and gold in its splendour —
   Behold, 'tis that marvel, the birth of a day!

# Song of the Pen

Not for the love of women toil we, we of the craft,
    Not for the people's praise.
Only because our Goddess made us her own, and laughed,
    Claiming us all our days.

Claiming our best endeavour, body and heart and brain,
    Given with no reserve.
Niggard is she towards us, granting us little gain,
    Still we are proud to serve.

Not unto us is given choice of the tasks we try —
    Gathering grain or chaff.
One of her favoured servants toils at an epic high,
    One — that a child may laugh.

Yet if we serve her truly in our appointed place,
    Freely she doth accord
Unto her faithful servants always this saving grace;
    Work is its own reward!

# A Late
# Collection

# The Bushfire

### An Allegory

'Twas on the famous Empire run,
    Whose sun does never set,
Whose grass and water, so they say,
    Have never failed them yet —
They carry many million sheep,
    Through seasons dry and wet.

They call the homestead Albion House,
    And then, along with that,
There's Welshman's Gully, Scotchman's Hill,
    And Paddymelon Flat:
And all these places are renowned
    For making jumbucks fat.

And the out-paddocks — holy frost!
    There wouldn't be no sense
For me to try and tell you half —
    They really are immense;
A man might ride for days and weeks
    And never strike a fence.

But still for years they never had
    Been known a sheep to lose;
Old Billy Gladstone managed it,
    And you can bet your shoes
He'd scores of supers under him,
    And droves of jackaroos.

Old Billy had an eagle eye,
    And kept his wits about —
If any chaps got trespassing
    He quickly cleared 'em out;
And coves that used to "work a cross",
    They hated him, no doubt.

But still he managed it in style,
    Until the times got dry,

And Billy gave the supers word
　　To see and mind their eye —
"If any paddocks gets a-fire
　　I'll know the reason why."

Now on this point old Bill was sure,
　　Because, for many a year,
Whenever times got dry at all,
　　As sure as you are here,
The Paddymelon Flat got burnt,
　　Which Bill thought rather queer.

He sent his smartest supers there
　　To try and keep things right.
No use! The grass was always dry —
　　They'd go to sleep at night,
And when they woke they'd go and find
　　The whole concern alight.

One morning it was very hot —
　　The sun rose in a haze;
Old Bill was cutting down some trees
　　(One of his little ways);
A black boy came hot-foot to say
　　The Flat was in a blaze.

Old Bill he swears a fearful oath
　　And lets the tommy fall —
Says he: "I'll take this business up,
　　And fix it once for all;
If this goes on, the cursed run
　　Will send us to the wall."

So he withdrew his trespass suits —
　　He'd one with Dutchy's boss —
In prosecutions criminal
　　He entered *nolle pros.*,
But these were neither here nor there —
　　They always meant a loss.

And off to Paddymelon Flat
　　He started double-quick
Drayloads of men with lots of grog
　　Lest heat should make them sick,

And all the strangers came around
    To see him do the trick.

And there the fire was flaming bright,
    For miles and miles it spread,
And many a sheep and horse and cow
    Were numbered with the dead —
The super came to meet Old Bill,
    And this is what he said:

"No use, to try to beat it out,
    'Twill dry you up like toast,
I've done as much as man can do,
    Although I never boast;
I think you'd better chuck it up,
    And let the jumbucks roast."

Then Bill said just two words: "You're sacked,"
    And pitches off his coat,
And wrenches down a blue-gum bough
    And clears his manly throat,
And into it like threshing wheat
    Right sturdily he smote.

And beat the blazing grass until
    His shirt was dripping wet;
And all the people watched him there
    To see what luck he'd get,
"Gosh! don't he make the cinders fly,"
    And, "Golly, don't he sweat!"

But though they worked like Trojans all,
    The fire still went ahead
So far as you could see around;
    The very skies were red,
Sometimes the flames would start afresh,
    Just where they thought it dead.

His men, too, quarrelled 'mongst themselves,
    And some coves gave it best
And some said, "Light a fire in front,
    And burn from east to west" —
But Bill, he still kept sloggin' in,
    And never took no rest.

Then, through the crowd a cornstalk kid
    Come ridin' to the spot;
Says he to Bill, "Now take a spell,
    You're lookin' very 'ot,
And if you'll only listen, why,
    I'll tell you what is what.

"These coves as set your grass on fire,
    There ain't no mortal doubt,
I've seen 'em ridin' here and there,
    And pokin' round about;
It ain't no use your workin' here,
    Until you finds them out.

"See yonder, where you beat the fire —
    It's blazin' up again,
And fires are starting right and left
    On Tipperary plain,
Beating them out is useless quite,
    Unless Heaven sends the rain."

Then Bill, he turns upon the boy,
    "Oh, hold your tongue, you pup!"
But a cinder blew across the creek
    While Bill stopped for a sup,
And fired the Albion paddocks, too —
    It was a bitter cup;
Old Bill's great heart was broke at last,
    He had to chuck it up.

*Moral*

The run is England's Empire great,
    The fire is the distress
That burns the stock they represent —
    Prosperity you'll guess.
And the blue-gum bough is the Home Rule Bill
    That's making such a mess.

And Ireland green, of course I mean
    By Paddymelon Flat;

All men can see the fire, of course,
    Spreads on at such a bat,
But who are setting it alight,
    I cannot tell you that.

But this I think all men will see,
    And hold it very true —
"Don't quarrel with effects until
    The *cause* is brought to view."
What is the cause? That cornstalk boy —
    He seemed to think he knew.

# The Maori Pig Market

In distant New Zealand, whose tresses of gold
    The billows are ceaselessly combing,
Away in a village all tranquil and old
I came on a market where porkers were sold —
    A market for pigs in the gloaming.

And Maoris in plenty in picturesque rig
    The lands of their forefathers roaming,
Were weighing their swine, whether little or big,
For purchasers paid by the weight of the pig —
    The weight of the pig in the gloaming.

And one mighty chieftain, I grieve to relate,
    The while that his porker was foaming
And squealing like fifty — that Maori sedate,
He leant on the pig just to add to its weight —
    He leant on the pig in the gloaming.

Alas! For the buyer, an Irishman stout —
    O'Grady, I think, his cognomen —
Perceived all his doings, and, giving a shout,
With the butt of his whip laid him carefully out
    By the side of his pig in the gloaming.

A terrible scrimmage did straightway begin,
    And I thought it was time to be homing,
For Maoris and Irish were fighting like sin
'Midst war-cries of "Pakeha!" "Batherashin!"
While the pigs did their best to lend tone to the din
    As I fled from the spot in the gloaming.

# *Behind the Scenes*

The actor struts his little hour,
   Between the limelight and the band;
The public feel the actor's power,
   Yet nothing do they understand
Of all the touches here and there
   That make or mar the actor's part,
They never see, beneath the glare,
   The artist striving after art.

To them it seems a labour slight
   Where nought of study intervenes;
You see it in another light
   When once you've been behind the scenes.

For though the actor at his best
   Is, like a poet, born not made,
He still must study with a zest
   And practise hard to learn his trade.
So, whether on the actor's form
   The stately robes of Hamlet sit,
Or as Macbeth he rave and storm,
   Or plays burlesque to please the pit,

'Tis each and all a work of art,
   That constant care and practice means —
The actor who creates a part
   Has done his work behind the scenes.

# Reconstruction

### *From a Farmer's Point of View*

S o, the bank has bust its boiler! And in six or seven year
   It will pay me all my money back — of course!
But the horse will perish waiting while the grass is germinating,
   And I reckon I'll be something like the horse.

There's the ploughing to be finished and the ploughmen want their pay,
   And I'd like to wire the fence and sink a tank;
But I own I'm fairly beat how I'm going to make ends meet
   With my money in a reconstructed bank.

"It's a safe and sure investment!" But it's one I can't afford,
   For I've got to meet my bills and pay the rent,
And the cash I had provided (so these meetings have decided)
   Shall be collared by the bank at three per cent.

I can draw out half my money, so they tell me, from the Crown;
   But — it's just enough to drive a fellow daft —
My landlord's quite distressed, by this very bank he's pressed,
   And he'll sell me up, to pay his overdraft.

There's my nearest neighbour, Johnson, owed this self-same bank a debt,
   Every feather off his poor old back they pluck't,
For they set to work to shove him, and they sold his house above him,
   Lord! They never gave *him* time to reconstruct.

And their profits from the business have been twenty-five per cent,
   Which, I reckon, is a pretty tidy whack,
And I think it's only proper, now the thing has come a cropper,
   That they ought to pay a little of it back.

I have read about "reserve funds", "banking freeholds", and the like,
   Till I thought the bank had thousands of as*sets*,
And it strikes me very funny that they take a fellow's money
   When they haven't got enough to pay their debts.

And they say they've lent my money, and they can't get paid it back.
    I know their rates per cent were tens and twelves;
And if now they've made a blunder after scooping all this plunder,
    Why, they ought to fork the money out themselves.

So all you bank shareholders, if you won't pay what you owe,
    You will find that on your bank will fall a blight;
And the reason is because it's simply certain that deposits
    Will be stopped, the bank will bust, and serve you right!

# The Ghost of the Murderer's Hut

My horse had been lamed in the foot
    In the rocks at the back of the run,
So I camped at the Murderer's Hut,
    At the place where the murder was done.

The walls were all spattered with gore,
    A terrible symbol of guilt;
And the bloodstains were fresh on the floor
    Where the blood of the victim was spilt.

The wind hurried past with a shout,
    The thunderstorm doubled its din
As I shrank from the danger without,
    And recoiled from the horror within.

When lo! at the window a shape,
    A creature of infinite dread;
A thing with the face of an ape,
    And with eyes like the eyes of the dead.

With the horns of a fiend, and a skin
    That was hairy as satyr or elf,
And a long, pointed beard on its chin —
    My God! 'Twas the Devil himself.

In anguish I sank on the floor,
    With terror my features were stiff,
Till *the thing* gave a kind of a roar,
    Ending up with a resonant "Biff!"

Then a cheer burst aloud from my throat,
    For the thing that my spirit did vex
Was naught but an elderly goat —
    Just a goat of the masculine sex.

When his master was killed he had fled,
    And now, by the dingoes bereft,
The nannies were all of them dead,
    And only the billy was left.

So we had him brought in on a stage
    To the house where, in style, he can strut,
And he lives to a fragrant old age
    As the Ghost of the Murderer's Hut.

# *The Matrimonial Stakes*

I wooed her with a steeplechase, I won her with a fall,
   I made her heartstrings quiver on the flat
When the pony missed his take-off, and we crashed into the wall;
    Well, she simply *had* to have me after that!

It awoke a thrill of int'rest when they pulled me out for dead
    From beneath the shattered ruins of a horse;
And although she *looked* indiff'rent when I landed — on my head —
    In the water, it appealed to her, of course!

When I won the Flappers' Flatrace it was "all Sir Garneo",
    For she praised the way I made my final run.
And she thought the riding won it — for how *could* the poor girl know
    That a monkey could have ridden it and won!

Then they "weighed me in" a winner — it's not often that occurs!
    So I didn't let my golden chances slip,
For I showed her all the blood-marks where I jabbed him with the spurs,
    And the whip-strokes where I hit him with the whip.

Then I asked her if she loved me, and she seemed inclined to shirk
    For a moment, so I took her by the head
(So to speak) and rushed her at it; and she seemed to like the work
    When she kissed me, though she blushed a rosy red.

She's a mouth as soft as velvet, and she plenty has of heart,
    I could worship every little step she takes;
And the saddling-bell is ringing, so we're going to the start,
    Certain winners for the Matrimonial Stakes!

# Sydney Cup, 1899

### An Outside Tip

Of course they all say if this Bobadil starts
    He'll settle 'em all in a flash:
For the pace he can go will be breaking their hearts,
    And he ends with the "Bobadil dash".
But there's one in the race is a fancy of mine
    Whenever the distance is far —
Crosslake! He's inbred to the Yattendon line,
    And we know what the Yattendons are.

His feet are his trouble: they're tender as gum!
    If only his feet are got straight,
If the field were all Bobadils — let 'em *all* come
    So long as they carry the weight.
For a three-year-old colt with nine-three on his back —
    Well, he needs to be rather a star!
And with seven stone ten we will trust the old black,
    For we know what the Yattendons are.

He is sired by Lochiel, which ensures that his pace
    Is enough, and a little to spare.
But the blood that will tell at the end of the race
    Is the blood of the Yattendon mare.
And this "Bobby" will find, when the whips are about,
    It's a very fast journey and far.
And there's just the least doubt — will he battle it out?
    But we *know* what the Yattendons are.

In the rest of the field there are some that can stay,
    And a few that can fly — while they last.
But the old black outsider will go all the way,
    And finish uncommonly fast.
If his feet last him out to the end of the trip —
    Bare-footed or shod with a bar —
If he once get this Bobadil under the whip,
    Then he'll show what the Yattendons are.

# The Federal Bus Conductor
## and the Old Lady

Now 'urry, Mrs New South Wales, and come along of us,
We're all a-goin' ridin' in the Federation 'bus.
A fam'ly party, don't you know — yes, Queensland's comin', too.
You can't afford it! Go along! We've kep' box seat for you.
The very one of all the lot that can afford it best,
You'll only have to pay your share the same as all the rest.

You say your sons is workin' men, and can't afford to ride!
Well, *all* our sons is workin' men, a-smokin' up outside.
You think you might be drove to smash by some unskilful bloke!
Well, ain't we all got necks ourselves? And we don't want 'em broke.
You bet your life we're not such fools but what we'll do our best
To keep from harm — for harm to one is harm to all the rest.

Now, don't go trudgin' on alone, but get aboard the trap;
That basket, labelled "Capital", you take it in your lap!
It's nearly time we made a start, so let's 'ave no more talk:
You 'urry up and get aboard, or else stop out and walk.
We've got a flag; we've got a band; our 'orses travels fast;
Ho! Right away, Bill! Let 'em go! The old 'un's come at last!

# The Lost Leichhardt

*An English scientific society is fitting out
a pioneering party to search for traces of the
lost explorer Leichhardt*

Another search for Leichhardt's tomb,
 Though fifty years have fled
Since Leichhardt vanished in the gloom,
  Our one Illustrious Dead!

But daring men from Britain's shore,
  The fearless bulldog breed,
Renew the fearful task once more,
  Determined to succeed.

Rash men, that know not what they seek,
  Will find their courage tried.
For things have changed on Coopers Creek
  Since Ludwig Leichhardt died.

Along where Leichhardt journeyed slow
  And toiled and starved in vain;
These rash excursionists must go
  Per Queensland railway train.

Out on those deserts lone and drear
  The fierce Australian black
Will say — "You show it pint o' beer,
  It show you Leichhardt track!"

And loud from every squatter's door
  Each pioneering swell
Will hear the wild pianos roar
  The strains of "Daisy Bell".

The watchers in those forests vast
  Will see, at fall of night,
Commercial travellers bounding past
  And darting out of sight.

About their path a fearful fate
    Will hover always near.
A dreadful scourge that lies in wait —
    The Longreach Horehound Beer!

And then, to crown this tale of guilt,
    They'll find some scurvy knave,
Regardless of their quest, has built
    A pub on Leichhardt's grave!

\* \* \* \*

Ah, yes! Those British pioneers
    Had best at home abide,
For things have changed in fifty years
    Since Ludwig Leichhardt died.

# Investigating Flora

'Twas in scientific circles
    That the great Professor Brown
Had a world-wide reputation
    As a writer of renown.
He had striven finer feelings
    In our natures to implant
By his *Treatise on the Morals*
    *Of the Red-eyed Bulldog Ant.*
He had hoisted an opponent
    Who had trodden unawares
On his *Reasons for Bare Patches*
    *On the Female Native Bears.*
So they gave him an appointment
    As instructor to a band
Of the most attractive females
    To be gathered in the land.

'Twas a "Ladies' Science Circle" —
    Just the latest social fad
For the Nicest People only,
    And to make their rivals mad.
They were fond of "science rambles"
    To the country from the town —
A parade of female beauty
    In the leadership of Brown.
They would pick a place for luncheon
    And catch beetles on their rugs;
The Professor called 'em "optera" —
    *They* called 'em "nasty bugs".
Well, the thing was bound to perish
    For no lovely woman can
Feel the slightest real interest
    In a club without a Man —
The Professor hardly counted
    He was crazy as a loon,
With a countenance suggestive
    Of an elderly baboon.

But the breath of Fate blew on it
 With a sharp and sudden blast,
And the "Ladies' Science Circle"
 Is a memory of the past.
There were two-and-twenty members,
 Mostly young and mostly fair,
Who had made a great excursion
 To a place called Dontknowwhere,
At the crossing of Lost River,
 On the road to No Man's Land.
There they met an old selector,
 With a stockwhip in his hand,
And the sight of so much beauty
 Sent him slightly "off his nut";
So he asked them, smiling blandly,
 "Would they come down to the hut?"
"I am come," said the Professor,
 In his thin and reedy voice,
"To investigate your flora,
 Which I hear is very choice."
The selector stared dumbfounded,
 Till at last he found his tongue:
"To investigate my Flora!
 Oh, you howlin' Brigham Young!
Why, you've two-and-twenty wimmen —
 Reg'lar slap-up wimmen, too!
And you're after little Flora!
 And a crawlin' thing like you!
Oh, you Mormonite gorilla!
 Well, I've heard it from the first
That you wizened little fellers
 Is a hundred times the worst!
But a dried-up ape like you are,
 To be marchin' through the land
With a pack of lovely wimmen —
 Well, I cannot understand!"

"You mistake," said the Professor,
 In a most indignant tone —
While the ladies shrieked and jabbered
 In a fashion of their own —

"You mistake about these ladies,
 I'm a lecturer of theirs;
I am Brown, who wrote the *Treatise*
 *On the Female Native Bears*!
When I said we wanted flora,
 What I meant was native flowers."
"Well, you *said* you wanted *Flora*,
 And I'll swear you don't get ours!
But here's Flora's self a-comin',
 And it's time for you to skip,
Or I'll write a treatise on you,
 And I'll write it with the whip!
Now, I wants no explanations;
 Just you hook it out of sight,
Or you'll charm the poor girl some'ow!"
 The Professor looked in fright:
She was six feet high and freckled,
 And her hair was turkey-red.
The Professor gave a whimper,
 And threw down his bag and fled,
And the Ladies' Science Circle,
 With a simultaneous rush,
Travelled after its Professor,
 And went screaming through the bush!

At the crossing of Lost River,
 On the road to No Man's Land,
Where the grim and ghostly gum trees
 Block the view on every hand,
There they weep and wail and wander,
 Always seeking for the track,
For the hapless old Professor
 Hasn't sense to guide 'em back;
And they clutch at one another,
 And they yell and scream in fright
As they see the gruesome creatures
 Of the grim Australian night;
And they hear the mopoke's hooting,
 And the dingo's howl so dread,
And the flying foxes' jabber
 From the gum trees overhead;

295

While the weird and wary wombats,
 In their subterranean caves,
Are a-digging, always digging,
 At those wretched people's graves;
And the pike-horned Queensland bullock,
 From his shelter in the scrub,
Has his eye on the proceedings
 Of the Ladies' Science Club.

# Fed Up

I ain't a timid man at all, I'm just as brave as most,
I'll take my chance in open fight and die beside my post;
But riding round the 'ole day long as target for a Krupp,
A-drawing fire from Koppies — well, I'm fair fed up.

It's wonderful how few get hit, it's luck that pulls us through;
Their rifle fire's no class at all, it misses me and you;
But when they sprinkle shells around like water from a cup
From that there blooming pom-pom gun — well, I'm fed up.

We never get a chance to charge, to do a thrust and cut,
I'll have to chuck the Cavalry and join the Mounted Fut.
But after all — What's Mounted Fut? I saw them t'other day,
They occupied a koppie when the Boers had run away.
The Cavalry went riding on and seen a score of fights,
But there they kept them Mounted Fut three solid days and nights —
Three solid starving days and nights with scarce a bite or sup,
Well! after that on Mounted Fut I'm fair fed up.

And tramping with the Footies ain't as easy as it looks,
They scarcely ever see a Boer except in picture books.
They do a march of twenty mile that leaves 'em nearly dead,
And then they find the bloomin' Boers is twenty miles ahead.
Each Footy is as full of fight as any bulldog pup,
But walking forty miles to fight — well, I'm fed up!

So after all I think that when I leave the Cavalry
I'll either join the ambulance or else the A.S.C.;
They've always tucker in the plate and coffee in the cup,
But bully beef and biscuits — well! I'm fair fed up!

# Commandeering

Our hero was a Tommy with a conscience free from care,
And such an open countenance that when he breathed the air
He mopped up all the atmosphere — so little went to spare
You could hardly say he breathed, he "commandeered" it.

For nowadays you'll notice when a man is "on the make",
And other people's property is anxious for to take,
We never use such words as "steal", or "collar", "pinch", or "shake".
No, the fashion is to say we "commandeered" it.

And our simple-minded hero used to grumble at his lot,
Said he, "This commandeerin's just a little bit too hot,
A fellow has to carry every blooming thing he's got;
Whatever he puts down they'll commandeer it."

So after much anxiety our simple-minded elf
He thought he'd do a little commandeering for himself,
And the first thing that he noticed was a bottle on a shelf
In a cottage, so he thought he'd commandeer it.

"What ho!" says he, "a bottle, and, by George, it's full of beer,
And no commanding officer to come and interfere.
Here's my own blooming health," says he, "I'm on the commandeer."
And without another word he commandeered it.

\* \* \* \*

On his subsequent proceedings we must draw a little veil,
For the Boers had left some sheep dip in that bottle labelled "Ale";
But the doctor said he'd shift it — if all other methods fail,
We must use the stomach pump and commandeer it.

# The Rum Parade

*Tune: "Ballyhooley"*

Now ye gallant Sydney boys, who have left your household joys
    To march across the sea in search of glory,
I am very much afraid that you do not love parade,
    But the rum parade is quite another story.
For the influenza came and to spoil its little game,
    They ordered we should drink a curious mixture;
Though at first it frightened some, when they found it mostly rum,
    Parade became a very pleasant fixture.

## Chorus

So it's forward the Brigade, if they'll hold a rum parade
    At Pretoria there's nothing to alarm ye;
And it's easy to be seen if they leave out the quinine,
    Ye'll be there before the blessed British Army.

Then a corporal he come and he said I drank the rum,
    But the quinine never reached its destination;
For begob he up and swored that I threw it overboard,
    Sure my heart was filled with grief and indignation.
For I'm different to some, I prefer quinine to rum,
    And I only take the rum just as a favour,
And it's easy to be seen I'm so fond of the quinine,
    That I keep it lest the rum should spoil its flavour.

When we get to Africay we'll be landed straight away,
    And quartered with the troops of Queen Victoria;
And we hope they'll understand that the moment that we land
    We are ready for a march upon Pretoria.
And we'll pay off all the scores on old Kruger and his Boers,
    And just to prove our manners aren't a failure,
And to show we are not mean, shure we'll give them the quinine,
    And drink the rum in honour of Australia.

# *Now Listen to Me and I'll Tell You My Views*

Now listen to me and I'll tell you my views concerning the African war,
And the man who upholds any different views, the same is a rotten
Pro-Boer!
(Though I'm getting a little bit doubtful myself, as it drags on week after week:
But it's better not ask any questions at all — let us silence all doubts with a
shriek!)

And first let us shriek the unstinted abuse that the Tory Press prefer —
De Wet is a madman, and Steyn is a liar, and Kruger a pitiful cur!
(Though I think if Oom Paul — as old as he is — were to walk down the
Strand with his gun,
A lot of these heroes would hide in the sewers or take to their heels and run!
For Paul he has fought like a man in his day, but now that he's feeble
and weak
And tired, and lonely, and old and grey, of course it's quite safe to shriek!)

And next let us join in the bloodthirsty shriek, Hooray for Lord Kitchener's
"bag"!
For the fireman's torch and the hangman's cord — they are hung on the
English Flag!
In the front of our brave old army! Whoop! the farmhouse blazes bright.
And their women weep and their children die — how dare they presume
to fight!
For none of them dress in a uniform, the same as by rights they ought.
They're fighting in rags and in naked feet, like Wallace's Scotchmen fought!
(And they clothe themselves from our captured troops — and they're
catching them every week;
And they don't hang *them* — and the shame is ours, but we cover the shame
with a shriek!)

And, lastly, we'll shriek the political shriek as we sit in the dark and doubt;
Where the Birmingham Judas led us in, and there's no one to lead us out.
And Rosebery — whom we depended upon! Would only the Oracle speak!
"You go to the Grocers," says he, "for your laws!" By heavens! it's time
to shriek!

# A Nervous Governor-General

We read in the press that Lord Northcote is here
    To take up Lord Tennyson's mission.
'Tis pleasant to find they have sent us a Peer,
    And a man of exalted position.
It's his business to see that the Radical horde
    From loyalty's path does not swerve us;
But his tastes, and the task, don't seem quite in accord
    For they say that His Lordship is nervous.

Does he think that wild animals walk in the street,
    Where the wary marsupial is hopping?
Does he think that the snake and the platypus meet
    And "bail up" the folk who go shopping?
And that boomerangs fly round the scared passer-by
    Who has come all this way to observe us.
While the blackfellow launches a spear at his eye?
    — No wonder His Lordship is nervous.

Does he think that with callers he'll be overtasked,
    From a baronet down to a barber?
Does he dream of the number of times he'll be asked
    "What he thinks of our Beautiful Harbour?"
Does he sadly reflect on the sorrows that ding
    Round his task? (From such sorrows preserve us!)
He must hear John See speak and O'Sullivan sing,
    — It's enough to make any man nervous.

Does he think he'll be waked in the dead of the night
    From Melbourne to go willy-nilly,
To live at the Federal Capital site
    At Tumut or Wagra-go-billy?
Well, the Melbournites *may* let the Capital go
    (Here we wink with one eye, please observe us!)
But not in a hurry! By no means! Oh, no!
    He has not the least need to be nervous!

# The Premier and the Socialist

The Premier and the Socialist
　　Were walking through the State:
They wept to see the Savings Bank
　　Such funds accumulate.
"If these were only cleared away,"
　　They said, "it would be great."

"If three financial amateurs
　　Controlled them for a year,
Do you suppose," the Premier said,
　　"That they would get them clear?"
"I think so," said the Socialist;
　　"They would — or very near!"

"If we should try to raise some cash
　　On assets of our own,
Do you suppose," the Premier said,
　　"That we could float a loan?"
"I doubt it," said the Socialist,
　　And groaned a doleful groan.

"Oh, Savings, come and walk with us!"
　　The Premier did entreat;
"A little walk, a little talk,
　　Away from Barrack Street;
My Socialistic friend will guide
　　Your inexperienced feet."

"We do not think," the Savings said,
　　"A Socialistic crank,
Although he chance just now to hold
　　A legislative rank,
Can teach experienced Banking men
　　The way to run a Bank."

The Premier and the Socialist
　　They passed an Act or so
To take the little Savings out
　　And let them have a blow.

"We'll teach the Banks," the Premier said,
    "The way to run the show.

"There's Tom Waddell — in Bank Finance
    Can show them what is what.
I used to prove not long ago
    His Estimates were rot.
But that — like many other things —
    I've recently forgot.

"Advances on a dried-out farm
    Are what we chiefly need,
And loans to friends of Ms.L.A.
    Are very good, indeed,
See how the back-block Cockatoos
    Are rolling up to feed."

"But not on us," the Savings cried,
    Falling a little flat,
"We didn't think a man like you
    Would do a thing like that;
For most of us are very small,
    And none of us are fat."

"This haughty tone," the Premier said,
    "Is not the proper line;
Before I'd be dictated to
    My billet I'd resign!"
"How brightly," said the Socialist,
    "Those little sovereigns shine."

The Premier and the Socialist
    They had their bit of fun;
They tried to call the Savings back
    But answer came there none,
Because the back-block Cockatoos
    Had eaten every one.

# The Man from Goondiwindi, Q.

## I

This is the sunburnt bushman who
Came down from Goondiwindi, Q.

## II

This is the Push from Waterloo
That spotted the sunburnt bushman who
Came down from Goondiwindi, Q.

## III

These are the wealthy uncles — two,
Part of the Push from Waterloo
That spotted the sunburnt bushman who
Came down from Goondiwindi, Q.

## IV

This is the game, by no means new,
Played by the wealthy uncles — two,
Part of the Push from Waterloo
That spotted the sunburnt bushman who
Came down from Goondiwindi, Q.

## V

This is the trooper dressed in blue
Who busted the game by no means new
Played by the wealthy uncles — two,
Part of the Push from Waterloo
That spotted the sunburnt bushman who
Came down from Goondiwindi, Q.

# VI

This is the magistrate who knew
Not only the trooper dressed in blue,
But also the game by no means new,
And likewise the wealthy uncles — two,
And ditto the Push from Waterloo
That spotted the sunburnt bushman who
Came down from Goondiwindi, Q.

# VII

This is the tale that has oft gone through
On Western plains where the skies are blue,
Till the native bear and the kangaroo
Have heard of the magistrate who knew
Not only the trooper dressed in blue,
But also the game by no means new,
And likewise the wealthy uncles — two,
And ditto the Push from Waterloo
That spotted the sunburnt bushman who
Came down from Goondiwindi, Q.

# *A Motor Courtship*

Into her presence he gaily pranced,
A very fat spark, and a bit advanced.

With a Samson tread on the earth he trod,
He was stayed and gaitered, and fifty odd.

And she was a tulip just unfurled,
The sweetest thing in the motor world.

Her body was one of which poets dreamed;
Eighteen — twenty, or so she seemed.

Her air was haughty, her spirit proud,
But properly governed, as all allowed.

"Pity," he said, "my sad condition;
My heart's in a state of advanced ignition.

"Ask me to do some desperate deed,
And I'll do it at once at my topmost speed."

"Sir," said the maiden, "pray be seated;
I fear from your bearing you're somewhat heated.

"And I trust that a timely lubrication
Of throttle will cool your circulation."

As a well-made mixture she indicated,
With joy and gladness he radiated.

"Oh, come," said he, "in this soft spring weather,
Let us run over the world together!"

But she slipped his clutch with a gesture mocking,
"Your heart," she said; "I can hear it knocking.

"You haven't the gear at my pace to last;
Both men and motors — I like them fast.

"And I think that in me you have missed your mission;
You are only an old-style tube-ignition!"

With a sidelong motion he left the place;
For weal or woe he was off his base.

He drove his car to the cliffs of Dover,
Made one short circuit and ran her over.

And the stormy Petrol her rest is taking,
Where only the wild waves do the "brakeing".

# "We're All Australians Now"

Australia takes her pen in hand,
　　To write a line to you,
To let you fellows understand,
　　How proud we are of you.

From shearing shed and cattle run,
　　From Broome to Hobson's Bay,
Each native-born Australian son,
　　Stands straighter up today.

The man who used to "hump his drum",
　　On far-out Queensland runs,
Is fighting side by side with some
　　Tasmanian farmer's sons.

The fisher-boys dropped sail and oar
　　To grimly stand the test,
Along that storm-swept Turkish shore,
　　With miners from the west.

The old state jealousies of yore
　　Are dead as Pharaoh's sow,
We're not State children any more
　　We're all Australians now!

Our six-starred flag that used to fly,
　　Half-shyly to the breeze,
Unknown where older nations ply
　　Their trade on foreign seas,

Flies out to meet the morning blue
　　With Vict'ry at the prow;
For that's the flag the Sydney flew,
　　The wide seas know it now!

The mettle that a race can show,
　　Is proved with shot and steel,
And now we know what nations know
　　And feel what nations feel.

The honoured graves beneath the crest
    Of Gaba Tepe hill,
May hold our bravest and our best,
    But we have brave men still.

With all our petty quarrels done,
    Dissensions overthrown,
We have, through what you boys have done,
    A history of our own.

Our old world diff'rences are dead,
    Like weeds beneath the plough,
For English, Scotch, and Irish-bred,
    They're all Australians now!

So now we'll toast the Third Brigade,
    That led Australia's van,
For never shall their glory fade
    In minds Australian.

Fight on, fight on, unflinchingly,
    Till right and justice reign.
Fight on, fight on, till Victory
    Shall send you home again.

And with Australia's flag shall fly
    A spray of wattle bough,
To symbolise our unity,
    We're all Australians now.

# *Australia Today — 1916*

They came from the lower levels
    Deep down in the Brilliant mine;
From the wastes where the whirlwind revels,
    Whirling the leaves of pine.

On the Western plains, where the Darling flows,
    And the dust storms wheel and shift,
The teamster loosened his yokes and bows,
    And turned his team adrift

On the Western stations, far and wide,
    There's many an empty pen,
For the "ringers" have cast the machines aside
    And answered the call for men.

On the lucerne flats where the stream runs slow,
    And the Hunter finds the sea,
The women are driving the mowers now,
    With the children at their knee.

For the men have gone, as a man must go,
    At the call of the rolling drums;
For the men have sworn that the Turks shall know
    When the old battalion comes.

Column of companies by the right,
    Steady in strong array,
With the sun on the bayonets gleaming bright,
    The battalion marched away.

They battled, the old battalion,
    Through the toil of the training camps,
Sweated and strove at lectures,
    By the light of the stinking lamps.

Marching, shooting, and drilling;
    Steady and slow and stern;
Awkward and strange, but willing
    All of their job to learn.

Learning to use the rifle;
    Learning to use the spade;
Deeming fatigue a trifle
    During each long parade.

Till at last they welded
    Into a concrete whole,
And there grew in the old battalion
    A kind of battalion's soul.

Brotherhood never was like it;
    Friendship is not the word;
But deep in that body of marching men
    The soul of a nation stirred.

And like one man with a single thought
    Cheery and confident;
Ready for all that the future brought,
    The old battalion went.

Column of companies by the right,
    Steady in strong array,
With the sun on the bayonets gleaming bright,
    The battalion marched away.

How shall we tell of their landing
    By the hills where the foe were spread,
And the track of the old battalion
    Was marked by the Turkish dead?

With the dash that discipline teaches,
    Though the hail of the shrapnel flew,
And the forts were raking the beaches,
    And the toll of the dead men grew.

They fixed their grip on the gaunt hillside
    With a pluck that has won them fame;
And the home-folks know that the dead men died
    For the pride of Australia's name.

Column of companies by the right,
    To the beat of the rolling drums;
With honours gained in a stirring fight
    The old Battalion comes!

# The Army Mules

Oh the airman's game is a showman's game for we all of us watch him go
With his roaring soaring aeroplane and his bombs for the blokes below,
Over the railways and over the dumps, over the Hun and the Turk,
You'll hear him mutter, "What ho, she bumps," when the Archies get to work.
But not of him is the song I sing, though he follow the eagle's flight,
And with shrapnel holes in his splintered wing comes home to his roost at
night.
He may silver his wings on the shining stars, he may look from the throne on
high,
He may follow the flight of the wheeling kite in the blue Egyptian sky,
But he's only a hero built to plan, turned out by the Army schools,
And I sing of the rankless, thankless man who hustles the Army mules.

Now where he comes from and where he lives is a mystery dark and dim,
And it's rarely indeed that the General gives a D.S.O. to him.
The stolid infantry digs its way like a mole in a ruined wall;
The cavalry lends a tone, they say, to what were else but a brawl;
The Brigadier of the Mounted Fut like a cavalry Colonel swanks
When he goeth abroad like a gilded nut to receive the General's thanks;
The Ordnance man is a son of a gun and his lists are a standing joke;
You order, "Choke arti Jerusalem one" for Jerusalem artichoke.
The Medicals shine with a number nine, and the men of the great R.E.,
Their Colonels are Methodist, married or mad, and some of them all the
three;
In all these units the road to fame is taught in the Army schools,
But a man has got to be born to the game when he tackles the Army mules.

For if you go where the depots are as the dawn is breaking grey,
By the waning light of the morning star as the dust cloud clears away,
You'll see a vision among the dust like a man and a mule combined —
It's the kind of thing you must take on trust for its outlines aren't defined,
A thing that whirls like a spinning top and props like a three-legged stool,
And you find its a long-legged Queensland boy convincing an Army mule.
And the rider sticks to the hybrid's hide like paper sticks to a wall,
For a "magnoon" Waler is next to ride with every chance of a fall,
It's a rough-house game and a thankless game, and it isn't a game for a fool,
For an army's fate and a nation's fame may turn on an Army mule.

And if you go to the front-line camp where the sleepless outposts lie,
At the dead of night you can hear the tramp of the mule train toiling by.
The rattle and clink of a leading-chain, the creak of the lurching load,
As the patient, plodding creatures strain at their task in the shell-torn road,
Through the dark and the dust you may watch them go till the dawn is grey in
     the sky,
And only the watchful pickets know when the "All-night Corps" goes by.
And far away as the silence falls when the last of the train has gone,
A weary voice through the darkness calls: "Get on there, men, get on!"
It isn't a hero, built to plan, turned out by the modern schools,
It's only the Army Service man a-driving his Army mules.

## *Moving On*

In this war we're always moving,
  Moving on;
When we make a friend another friend has gone;
Should a woman's kindly face
Make us welcome for a space,
Then it's boot and saddle, boys, we're
  Moving on.

In the hospitals they're moving,
  Moving on;
They're here today, tomorrow they are gone;
When the bravest and the best
Of the boys you know "go west",
Then you're choking down your tears and
  Moving on.

# Hawker, the Standard Bearer

The grey gull sat on a floating whale,
    On a floating whale sat he,
And he told his tale of the storm and the gale,
And the ships that he saw with steam and sail,
    As he flew by the Northern Sea.

"I have seen a sign that is strange and new,
    That I never before did see:
A flying ship that roared as it flew,
The storm and the tempest driving through,
It carried a flag and it carried a crew,
    Now what would that be?" said he.

"And the flag was a Jack with stars displayed,
    A flag that is new to me;
For it does not ply in the Northern trade,
But it drove through the storm-wrack unafraid,
    Now, what is that flag?" said he.

"I have seen that flag that is starred with white,"
    Said a southern gull, said he,
"And I saw it fly in a bloody fight,
When the raider *Emden* turned in flight,
    And crashed on the Cocos lee."

"And who are these folk whose flag is first
    Of all the flags that fly
To dare the storm and the fog accurst,
Of the great North Sea where the bergs are nursed,
    And the Northern Lights ride high?"

"The Australian folk," said a lone sea-mew,
    "The Australian flag," said he.
"It is strange that a folk that is far and few
Should fly their flag where there never flew
    Another flag!" said he.

"I have followed their flag in the fields of France,
   With its white stars flying free,
And no misfortune and no mischance
Could turn them back from their line of advance,
   Or the line that they held," said he.

"Wherever there's ever a rule to break,
   Wherever they oughtn't to be,
With a death to dare and a risk to take,
A track to find or a way to make,
   You will find them there," said he.

"They come from a land that is parched with thirst,
   An inland land," said he,
"On risk and danger their breed is nursed,
And thus it happens their flag is first
   To fly in the Northern Sea."

"Though Hawker perished, he overcame
   The risks of the storm and the sea,
And his name shall be written in stars of flame,
On the topmost walls of the Temple of Fame,
   For the rest of the world to see."

# *Boots*

*"The Australian boots were the best of any issued to the Allied forces."*

We've travelled per Joe Gardiner, a humping of our swag
    In the country of the Gidgee and Belar.
We've swum the Di'mantina with our raiment in a bag,
    And we've travelled per superior motor car,
But when we went to Germany we hadn't any choice,
    No matter what our training or pursuits,
For they gave us no selection 'twixt a Ford or Rolls de Royce
    So we did it in our good Australian boots.

They called us "mad Australians"; they couldn't understand
    How officers and men could fraternise,
They said that we were "reckless", we were "wild, and out of hand",
    With nothing great or sacred to our eyes.
But on one thing you could gamble, in the thickest of the fray,
    Though they called us volunteers and raw recruits,
You could track us past the shell holes, and the tracks were all one way
    Of the good Australian ammunition boots.

The Highlanders were next of kin, the Irish were a treat,
    The Yankees knew it all and had to learn,
The Frenchmen kept it going, both in vict'ry and defeat,
    Fighting grimly till the tide was on the turn.
And our army kept beside 'em, did its bit and took its chance,
    And I hailed our newborn nation and its fruits,
As I listened to the clatter on the cobblestones of France
    Of the good Australian military boots.

# The Old Tin Hat

In the good old days when the Army's ways were simple and unrefined,
With a stock to keep up their chins in front, and a pigtail down behind,
When the only light in the barracks at night was a candle of grease or fat,
When they put the extinguisher on the light, they called it the Old Tin Hat.

Now, a very great man is the C. in C., for he is the whole of the show —
The reins and the whip and the driver's hand that maketh the team to go —
But the road he goes is a lonely road, with ever a choice to make,
When he comes to a place where the roads divide, which one is the road to take.
For there's one road right, and there's one road wrong, uphill, or over the flat,
And one road leads to the Temple of Fame, and one to the Old Tin Hat.

And a very great man is the man who holds an Army Corps command,
For he hurries his regiments here and there as the C. in C. has planned.
By day he travels about in state and stirreth them up to rights,
He toileth early and toileth late, and sitteth up half the nights;
But the evening comes when the candle throws twin shadows upon the mat,
And one of the shadows is like a wreath, and one like an Old Tin Hat.

And a very proud man is the Brigadier at the sound of the stately tread
Of his big battalions marching on, as he rides with his staff ahead.
There's never a band to play them out, and the bugle's note is still,
But he hears two tunes in the gentle breeze that blows from over the hill.
And one is a tune in a stirring key, and the other is faint and flat,
For one is the tune of "My new C.B." and the other, "My Old Tin Hat".

And the Colonel heading his regiment is life and soul of the show,
It's "Column of Route", "Form troops", "Extend", and into the fight they go;
He does not duck when the air is full of the "wail of the whimpering lead",
He does not scout for the deep dugout when the 'planes are overhead;
He fears not hog, nor devil, nor dog, and he'd scrap with a mountain cat,
But he goeth in fear of the Brigadier, and in fear of the Old Tin Hat.

# That Half-Crown Sweep

*A Tale of the Territory*

The run of Billabong-go-dry
    Is just beyond Lime Burner's Gap;
Its waterhole and tank supply
    Is excellent — upon the map.
But, lacking nature's liquid drench,
    The station staff are wont to try
With "Bob-in Sweeps" their thirst to quench,
    Or nearly quench, at Bong-go-dry.

The parson made five-yearly rounds
    That soil of arid souls to delve,
He wrote, "I'll come for seven pounds,
    Or I could stop away for twelve."
But lack of lucre brought about
    The pusillanimous reply:
"Our luxuries are all cut out,
    You'll have to come to Bong-go-dry."

Now rabbit skins were very high —
    There'd been a kind of rabbit rush —
And what with traps and sticks they'd shy,
    The station blacks were very flush,
And each was taught his churchman's job,
    "When that one parson's plate comes roun'
No good you put in sprat or bob,
    Too quick you put in harp-a-crown."

The parson's word was duly kept,
    He came and did his bit of speak;
The boss remarked he hadn't slept
    So sound and well for many a week.
But Gilgai Jack and Monkey Jaw
    Regarded preaching as a crime
Against good taste; they said, "What for
    That one chap yabber all the time?"

Proceedings ceased: the boss's hat
    Was raked from underneath his chair;
The coloured congregation sat
    And waited with expectant air.
At last from one far-distant seat
    Where Gilgai's Mary'd been asleep,
There came a kind of plaintive bleat,
    "Say, boss! Who won the harp-crown sweep?"

# A Dog's Mistake

*In Doggerel Verse*

He had drifted in among us as a straw drifts with the tide,
He was just a wand'ring mongrel from the weary world outside;
He was not aristocratic, being mostly ribs and hair,
With a hint of spaniel parents and a touch of native bear.

He was very poor and humble and content with what he got,
So we fed him bones and biscuits, till he heartened up a lot;
Then he growled and grew aggressive, treating orders with disdain,
Till at last he bit the butcher, which would argue want of brain.

Now the butcher, noble fellow, was a sport beyond belief,
And instead of bringing actions he brought half a shin of beef,
Which he handed on to Fido, who received it as a right
And removed it to the garden, where he buried it at night.

'Twas the means of his undoing, for my wife, who'd stood his friend,
To adopt a slang expression, "went in off the deepest end",
For among the pinks and pansies, the gloxinias and the gorse
He had made an excavation like a graveyard for a horse.

Then we held a consultation which decided on his fate:
'Twas in anger more than sorrow that we led him to the gate,
And we handed him the beef-bone as provision for the day,
Then we opened wide the portal and we told him, "On your way."

# Shearing with a Hoe

The track that led to Carmody's is choked and overgrown,
 The suckers of the stringybark have made the place their own;
The mountain rains have cut the track that once we used to know
When first we rode to Carmody's, a score of years ago.

The shearing shed at Carmody's was slab and stringybark,
The press was just a lever beam, invented in the Ark;
But Mrs Carmody was cook — and shearers' hearts would glow
With praise of grub at Carmody's, a score of years ago.

At shearing time no penners-up would curse their fate and weep,
For Fragrant Fred — the billy-goat — was trained to lead the sheep;
And racing down the rattling chutes the bleating mob would go
Behind their horned man from Cook's, a score of years ago.

An owner of the olden time, his patriarchial shed
Was innocent of all machines or gadgets overhead:
And pieces, locks and super-fleece together used to go
To fill the bales at Carmody's, a score of years ago.

A ringer from the Western sheds, whose fame was wide and deep,
Was asked to take a vacant pen and shear a thousand sheep.
"Of course, we've only got the blades!" "Well, what I want to know:
*Why don't you get a bloke to take it off 'em with a hoe?"*

# The Silent Shearer

Weary and listless, sad and slow,
   Without any conversation,
Was a man that worked on The Overflow,
   The butt of the shed and station.

The shearers christened him Noisy Ned,
   With an alias "Silent Waters",
But never a needless word he said
   In the hut, or the shearers' quarters.

Which caused annoyance to Big Barcoo,
   The shed's unquestioned ringer,
Whose name was famous Australia through
   As a dancer, fighter and singer.

He was fit for the ring, if he'd had his rights
   As an agent of devastation;
And the number of men he had killed in fights
   Was his principal conversation.

"I have known blokes go to their doom," said he,
   "Through actin' with haste and rashness:
But the style that this Noisy Ned assumes,
   It's nothing but silent flashness.

"We may just be dirt, from his point of view,
   Unworthy a word in season;
But I'll make him talk like a cockatoo
   Or I'll get him to show the reason."

Was it chance or fate, that King Condamine,
   A king who had turned black tracker,
Had captured a baby porcupine,
   Which he swapped for a "fig tobacker"?

With the porcupine in the Silent's bed
   The shearers were quite elated,
And the things to be done, and the words to be said,
   Were anxiously awaited.

323

With a screech and a howl and an eldritch cry
    That nearly deafened his hearers
He sprang from his bunk, and his fishy eye
    Looked over the laughing shearers.

He looked them over and he looked them through
    As a cook might look through a larder;
"Now, Big Barcoo, I must pick on you,
    You're big, but you'll fall the harder."

Now, the silent man was but slight and thin
    And of middleweight conformation,
But he hung one punch on the Barcoo's chin
    And it ended the altercation.

"You've heard of the One-round Kid," said he,
    "That hunted 'em all to shelter?
The One-round Finisher — that was me,
    When I fought as the Champion Welter.

"And this Barcoo bloke on his back reclines
    For being a bit too clever,
For snakes and wombats and porcupines
    Are nothing to me whatever.

"But the golden rule that I've had to learn
    In the ring, and for years I've tried it,
Is only to talk when it comes your turn,
    And never to talk outside it."

# The Billy-Goat Overland

Come all ye lads of the droving days, ye gentlemen unafraid,
I'll tell you all of the greatest trip that ever a drover made,
For we rolled our swags, and we packed our bags, and taking our lives in hand,
We started away with a thousand goats, on the billy-goat overland.

There wasn't a fence that'd hold the mob, or keep 'em from their desires;
They skipped along the top of the posts and cake-walked on the wires.
And where the lanes had been stripped of grass and the paddocks were nice
        and green,
The goats they travelled outside the lanes and we rode in between.

The squatters started to drive them back, but that was no good at all,
Their horses ran for the lick of their lives from the scent that was like a wall:
And never a dog had pluck or gall in front of the mob to stand
And face the charge of a thousand goats on the billy-goat overland.

We found we were hundreds over strength when we counted out the mob;
And they put us in jail for a crowd of thieves that travelled to steal and rob:
For every goat between here and Bourke, when he scented our spicy band,
Had left his home and his work to join in the billy-goat overland.

# Black Harry's Team

No soft-skinned Durham steers are they,
  No Devons plump and red,
But brindled, black, and iron-grey
  That mark the mountain-bred;
For mountain-bred and mountain broke,
  With sullen eyes agleam,
No stranger's hand could put a yoke
  On old Black Harry's team.

Pull out, pull out, at break of morn
  The creeks are running white,
And Tiger, Spot, and Snailey-horn
  Must bend their bows by night;
And axles, wheels and flooring boards
  Are swept with flying spray
As, shoulder-deep, through mountain fords
  The leaders feel their way.

He needs no sign of cross or kirn
  To guide him as he goes,
For every twist and every turn
  That old black leader knows.
Up mountains steep they heave and strain
  Where never wheel has rolled,
And what the toiling leaders gain
  The body bullocks hold.

Where eaglehawks their eyries make,
  On sidelings steep and blind,
He rigs the good old-fashioned brake —
  A tree tied on behind.
Up mountains, straining to the full,
  Each poler plays his part —
The sullen, stubborn, bullock pull
  That breaks a horse's heart.

Beyond the furthest bridle track
    His wheels have blazed the way;
The forest giants, burnt and black,
    Are earmarked by his dray.
Through belts of scrub where messmates grow
    His juggernaut has rolled,
For stumps and saplings have to go
    When Harry's team takes hold.

On easy grade and rubber tyre
    The tourist car goes through;
They halt a moment to admire
    The far-flung mountain view.
The tourist folk would be amazed
    If they could get to know
*They take the track Black Harry blazed*
    *A hundred years ago.*

# The Weather Prophet

" 'Ow can it rain," the old man said,
   "with things the way they are?
You've got to learn off ant and bee,
    and jackass and galah;
And no man never saw it rain,
    for fifty years at least.
Not when the blessed parakeets are
    flyin' to the East!"

The weeks went by, the squatter wrote
    to tell his bank the news.
"It's still as dry as dust," he said,
    "I'm feeding all the ewes;
The overdraft would sink a ship,
    but make your mind at rest,
It's all right now, the parakeets
    are flyin' to the West."

# Buffalo Country

Out where the grey streams glide,
Sullen and deep and slow,
And the alligators slide
From the mud to the depths below
Or drift on the stream like a floating death,
Where the fever comes on the south wind's breath,
There is the buffalo.

Out on the big lagoons,
Where the Regia lilies float,
And the Nankin heron croons
With a deep ill-omened note,
In the ooze and the mud of the swamps below
Lazily wallows the buffalo,
Buried to nose and throat.

From the hunter's gun he hides
In the jungles dark and damp,
Where the slinking dingo glides
And the flying foxes camp;
Hanging like myriad fiends in line
Where the trailing creepers twist and twine
And the sun is a sluggish lamp.

On the edge of the rolling plains
Where the coarse cane grasses swell,
Lush with the tropic rains
In the noontide's drowsy spell,
Slowly the buffalo grazes through
Where the brolgas dance, and the jabiru
Stands like a sentinel.

All that the world can know
Of the wild and the weird is here,
Where the black men come and go
With their boomerang and spear,
And the wild duck darken the evening sky
As they fly to their nests in the reed beds high
When the tropic night is near.

# Castlebar

Bidding good morrow to all our cares,
    Riding along with a joyful heart,
Little we reck of the world's affairs,
    All that we ask is a decent start.
Though the jumps are big and the distance far
We will get to the finish on Castlebar.

Little Blue Peter goes sailing by;
    Little Blue Peter may stand or fall,
For his rider reckons no man can die
    Till his day comes round — so he chances all!
And away to the front where the good ones are
Go Little Blue Peter and Castlebar.

Bay and chestnut and brown and black,
    I hear in the timber their hoof beats drum,
As I clear the fence on the Prospect track
    I turn in the saddle and watch them come.
But the chestnut horse with the big white star,
Why isn't he following Castlebar?

Dear little woman with eyes of blue,
    With lissom figure and easy grace,
I turn in the saddle and long for you
    As the field sweeps on at a rattling pace.
But I know that away on the heights afar
Your heart is following Castlebar.

# Here's Luck

*A Toast at a Hunt Club Dinner*

It chanced one day I watched a steeplechase,
    And one horse singled out and led them all
Across the fences at a rattling pace
    Until he hit a fence and took a fall.
His rider laughed and muttered with a smile —
"Well, anyhow, I led 'em for a while."

And this the text is for my theme tonight —
    A moral that the wisest men have sung;
Our life is very short — and swift the flight
    Of time — so, comrades, go it while you're young.
And when old age comes on you'll find it good
To think you made the running while you could.

There's nothing now too solid or too high
    For some of you to take and chance a spill;
But we must funk the fences bye and bye,
    When limbs grow stiff and hands have lost their skill.
In wintry age we'll seek the hearthstone's blaze;
So let us make the most of youth's bright days.

So now, my friends, good luck and may you keep
    Stout hearts and true and honest kindly mirth,
When drawing nearer to the last great leap
    That lands us on the other side of earth,
Where many a gallant horseman and brave steed
Has gone before to give us all a lead.

# Queensland Mounted Infantry

There's a very well-built fellow, with a swinging sort of stride,
  About as handy sort as I have seen.
A rough and tumble fellow that is born to fight and ride
  And he's over here a-fighting for the Queen.

He's Queensland Mounted Infantry — compounded 'orse and foot.
  He'll climb a cliff or gallop down a flat.
He's cavalry to travel but he's infantry to shoot.
  And you'll know him by the feathers in his hat!

# Cape Mounted Rifles

*Tune: "Botany Bay"*

Now, when you've done talking of trifles,
    I'll sing you a song of the war —
A song of the Cape Mounted Rifles,
    The dandy South African Corps.
Though some of us haven't a penny,
    And others have acted the goat,
Yet, take us all round, there ain't many
    Will tread on the tail of our——

## Chorus

Pom, pom, pom, pom, torralido
Pom, pom, pom, pom, tooralay.
Yes, take us all round, there ain't many
Will tread on the tail of our coat.

They told us to stop on the border:
    We thought we were out of the hunt.
But quietly, they sent us an order —
    "The rifles are wanted in front."
And up in the front did they set us
    To fight all the Dutchmen afloat,
But ne'er a Commando that met us
    Could tread on the tail of our ——

They sent us with Colonel Dalgety
    To fight with De Wet and old Steyn.
We've fought and we've beat them already —
    We'll fight and we'll beat them again.
Oom Paul has been picking up trifles —
    With millions of cash he's afloat —
If he meets with the Cape Mounted Rifles
    They'll jump for the tail of his coat!

# *Maxims of War*

Firstly, when fighting the Dutchman, make it your cardinal rule —
Think he's a rogue if it please you: *never believe he's a fool.*

Never be needlessly reckless — he who does this is a dunce —
Stopping a bullet is easy — but you don't stop 'em well more than once.

Make better use of your cover — don't ride about in full view.
God made the kopjes for Dutchmen — likewise he made 'em for you.

Parties of twenty for scouting — easy to see and to smother:
Neither can fight nor keep hidden — neither one thing nor the other.

If reconnoitring a kopje, you feel the least shadow of doubt,
Send up one man to inspect it — send up a Rimington scout!
Don't send a *troop* as a target for Dutchmen to hustle about.

Never hold more than you've need of — kopjes all round you are strown.
If they can't help you, they'll hurt you — leave 'em severely alone.

If you should find a position, when it would suit you to fight,
Keep it! Don't shift! If you leave it, the Boers will come down in the night.
Then you'll go back and they'll shoot you — and serve you most
    damnably right!

Why should you load up with "Bully", bringing your transport to grief?
Look at the veldt all around you, stocked with the primest of beef!

Finally, never get jumpy — e'en though the fighting is hot!
Think of how often you're shot at — think of how seldom you're shot!

# Our Own Flag

They mustered us up with a royal din,
    In wearisome weeks of drought.
Ere ever the half of the crops were in,
    Or the half of the sheds cut out.

'Twas down with saddle and spurs and whip;
    The swagman dropped his swag.
And we hurried us off to an outbound ship
    To fight for the English flag.

The English flag — it is ours in sooth
    We stand by it wrong or right.
But deep in our hearts is the honest truth
    We fought for the sake of a fight.

And the English flag may flutter and wave
    Where the World-wide Oceans toss,
But the flag the Australian dies to save
    Is the flag of the Southern Cross.

If ever they want us to stand the brunt
    Of a hard-fought, grim campaign,
We will carry our own flag up to the front
    When we go to the wars again.

# Campin' Round Coonamble

*Written when reporting for* The Sydney Morning Herald *on the shearing troubles at Coonamble.*

C ampin' round Coonamble,
   Keepin' up the strike,
Through the black soil country
   Plugging on the "bike";
Half a thousand shearers,
   What had we to gain
Campin' round Coonamble,
   Campin' in the rain?

Twenty bob a hundred
   Shearing with machines!
Good enough in these times
   We know what it means —
Sinking tanks and fencing,
   Shearing's better pay
Twenty bob a hundred,
   Twenty bob a day!

Every little farmer
   Up Monaro side
Sends the boys a-shearing,
   Hoping to provide
Something for the homestead;
   All his hopes are vain,
While we're round Coonamble,
   Campin' in the rain.

Up at old man Tobin's,
   First pen on the right,
Don't I know his wethers,
   Know 'em all by sight!
Many a year I shore 'em
   Like to shear again,
Better game than campin',
   Campin' in the rain.

What's the use of talking
    Five-and-twenty bob,
While there's hundreds hungry
    Looking for a job?
Darling Harbour casuals,
    Hollow in the cheek,
Cadging from the Government
    Two days' work a week.

When with peal of trumpets,
    And with beat of drums,
Labour's great millennium
    Actually comes;
When each white Australian,
    Master of his craft,
Keeps a foreign servant
    Just to do the graft;

When the price of shearing
    Goes to fifty bob,
And there's no man hungry
    Looking for a job;
Then, if they oppress us,
    Then we'll go again
Campin' round Coonamble,
    Campin' in the rain.

# A Grain of Desert Sand

Beneath the blue Egyptian skies,
With ramp and roller, guide and stay,
I saw the Pryamids arise
And I shall see them pass away.

I watched when Alexander passed;
I saw Napoleon's flag unfurled —
The greatest and perhaps the last
Of men whose footsteps shook the world.

To each his hour of pride and place,
Arab and Persian, Greek and Jew;
Mahomet trod upon my face,
Darius spurned me with his shoe.

And yet I am not Priest or King,
Sultan or Chief in high command.
I am that one unchanging thing,
A grain of desert sand.

# Song of Murray's Brigade

Small birds singing in the tree tops tell
    Where runs the river of my home;
And the wistful wishing of the folk who love us well
    And follow us wherever we may roam.

And our hearts go back to the folk beside the river
    To the land where the sheep and cattle roam.
It's a long, long job, but we'll finish it together
    For every mile we travel leads us home.

No songs greet us for the birds are mute
    The aeroplane's the only thing to fly.
Upward to the pilot send a special brand salute
    For we may need him badly bye and bye.

Soldiers singing as their fancies come
    New songs, old songs, they sang another day.
Thus they sing and march to the beating of the drum
    Till orders come to put the drums away.

And our hearts go back to the folk beside the river
    To the land where the sheep and cattle roam.
It's a long, long job, but we'll finish it together
    For every mile we travel leads us home.

# *The Uplift*

When the drays are bogged and sinking, then it's no use sitting thinking,
 You must put the teams together and must double-bank the pull.
When the crop is light and weedy, or the fleece is burred and seedy,
   Then the next year's crop and fleeces may repay you to the full.

   So it's lift her, Johnny, lift her,
   Put your back in it and shift her,
While the jabber, jabber, jabber of the politicians flows.
   If your nag's too poor to travel
   Then get down and scratch the gravel
For you'll get there if you walk it — if you don't, you'll feed the crows.

Shall we waste our time debating with a grand young country waiting
For the plough and for the harrow and the lucerne and the maize?
   For it's work alone will save us in the land that fortune gave us
There's no crop but what we'll grow it; there's no stock but what we'll raise.

   When the team is bogged and sinking
   Then it's no use sitting thinking.
There's a roadway up the mountain that the old black leader knows:
   So it's lift her, Johnny, lift her,
   Put your back in it and shift her,
Take a lesson from the bullock — he goes slowly, but he goes!

# THE ANIMALS
# NOAH FORGOT

# The Animals Noah Forgot
## Prologue — Australian Scenery

### The Mountains

A land of sombre, silent hills, where mountain cattle go
By twisted tracks, on sidelings steep, where giant gum trees grow
And the wind replies, in the river oaks, to the song of the stream below.

A land where the hills keep watch and ward, silent and wide awake
As those who sit by a dead campfire, and wait for the dawn to break,
Or those who watched by the Holy Cross for the dead Redeemer's sake.

A land where silence lies so deep that sound itself is dead
And a gaunt grey bird, like a homeless soul, drifts, noiseless, overhead
And the world's great story is left untold, and the message is left unsaid.

### The Plains

A land, as far as the eye can see, where the waving grasses grow
Or the plains are blackened and burnt and bare, where the false mirages go
Like shifting symbols of hope deferred — land where you never know.

Land of plenty or land of want, where the grey Companions dance,
Feast or famine, or hope or fear, and in all things land of chance,
Where Nature pampers or Nature slays, in her ruthless, red, romance.

And we catch a sound of a fairy's song, as the wind goes whipping by,
Or a scent like incense drifts along from the herbage ripe and dry
— Or the dust storms dance on their ballroom floor, where the bones of
the cattle lie.

# An Emu Hunt

West of Dubbo the west begins
    The land of leisure and hope and trust,
Where the black man stalks with his dogs and gins
And Nature visits the settlers' sins
    With the Bogan shower, that is mostly dust.

When the roley-poley's roots dry out
    With the fierce hot winds and the want of rain,
They come uprooted and bound about
And dance in a wild fantastic rout
    Like flying haystacks across the plain.

And the horses shudder and snort and shift
    As the bounding mass of weed goes past,
But the emus never their heads uplift
As they look for roots in the sandy drift,
    For the emus know it from first to last.

Now, the boss's dog that had come from town
    Was strange to the wild and woolly west,
And he thought he would earn him some great renown
When he saw, on the wastes of the open down,
    An emu standing beside her nest.

And he said to himself as he stalked his prey
    To start on his first great emu hunt,
"I must show some speed when she runs away,
For emus kick very hard, they say;
    But I can't be kicked if I keep in front."

The emu chickens made haste to flee
    As he barked and he snarled and he darted round,
But the emu looked at him scornfully
And put an end to his warlike glee
    With a kick that lifted him off the ground.

And when, with an injured rib or two,
    He made for home with a chastened mind,
An old dog told him, "I thought you knew
An emu kicks like a kangaroo,
    And you can't get hurt — *if you keep behind*."

# Benjamin Bandicoot

If you walk in the bush at night,
  In the wonderful silence deep,
By the flickering lantern light
    When the birds are all asleep
You may catch a sight of old Skinny-go-root,
Otherwise Benjamin Bandicoot.

With a snout that can delve and dig,
    With claws that are strong as steel,
He roots like a pigmy pig
    To get his evening meal,
For creeping creatures and worms and roots
Are highly relished by bandicoots.

Under the grass and the fern
    He fashions his beaten track
With many a twist and turn
    That wanders and doubles back,
And dogs that think they are most astute
Are baffled by Benjamin Bandicoot.

In the depth of the darkest night,
    Without a star in the sky,
He'll come to look at a light,
    And scientists wonder why:
If the bush is burning it's time to scoot
Is the notion of Benjamin Bandicoot.

# A Bush Lawyer

When Ironbark the turtle came to Anthony's lagoon
    The hills were hid behind a mist of equinoctial rain,
The ripple of the rivulets was like a cheerful tune
    And wild companions waltzed among the grass as tall as grain.

    But Ironbark the turtle cared no whit for all of these;
    The ripple of the rivulets, the rustle of the trees
    Were only apple sauce to him, or just a piece of cheese.

Now, Dan-di-dan the water rat was exquisitely dressed,
    For not a seal in Bass's Straits had half as fine a coat,
And every day he combed and brushed his golden-yellow vest,
    A contrast with the white cravat he wore beneath his throat.

    And Dan-di-dan the water rat could move with ease and grace,
    So Ironbark appeared to him a creature out of place,
    With iron-plated overcoat and dirty little face.

A crawfish at the point of death came drifting down the drains.
    Said he, "I'm scalded to the heart with bathing near the bore."
The turtle and the water rat disputed his remains,
    For crawfish meat all day they'd eat, and then they'd ask for more.

    Said Dan-di-dan, "The prize is mine, for I was fishing here
    Before you tumbled down the bank and landed on your ear."
    "I wouldn't care," the turtle said, "if you'd have fished a year."

So Baggy-beak the Pelican was asked to arbitrate;
    The scales of justice seemed to hang beneath his noble beak.
He said, "I'll take possession of the subject of debate";
    He stowed the fish inside his pouch and then began to speak.

    "The case is far from clear," he said, "and justices of note" —
    But here he snapped his beak and flapped his piebald overcoat —
    "Oh dear," he said, "that wretched fish has slithered down my throat."

"But still," he said, "the point involved requires a full debate.
    I'll have to get the lawyer birds and fix a special day.
*Ad interim* I rule that costs come out of the estate."
    And Baggy-beak the Pelican got up and flew away.

    So both the pair who went to law were feeling very small.
    Said they, "We might have halved the fish and saved a nasty brawl;
    For half a crawfish isn't much, but more than none at all."

# Camouflage

Beside the bare and beaten track of travelling flocks and herds
The woodpecker went tapping on, the postman of the birds,
"I've got a letter here," he said, "that no one's understood,
Addressed as follows: 'To the bird that's like a piece of wood.'

"The soldier bird got very cross — it wasn't meant for her;
The spurwing plover had a try to stab me with a spur:
The jackass laughed, and said the thing was written for a lark.
I think I'll chuck this postman job and take to stripping bark."

Then all the birds for miles around came in to lend a hand;
They perched upon a broken limb as thick as they could stand,
And just as old man eaglehawk prepared to have his say
A portion of the broken limb got up and flew away.

Then, casting grammar to the winds, the postman said, "That's him!
The boobook owl — he squats himself along a broken limb,
And pokes his beak up like a stick; there's not a bird, I vow,
Can tell you which is boobook owl and which is broken bough.

"And that's the thing he calls his nest — that jerry-built affair —
A bunch of sticks across a fork; I'll leave his letter there.
A cuckoo wouldn't use his nest, but what's the odds to him —
A bird that tries to imitate a piece of leaning limb!"

# A Change of Menu

Now the new chum loaded his three-nought-three,
    It's a small-bore gun, but his hopes were big.
"I am fed to the teeth with old ewe," said he,
    "And I might be able to shoot a pig."
And he trusted more to his nose than ear
To give him warning when pigs were near.

Out of his lair in the lignum dark,
    Where the wild duck nests and the bilbie digs,
With a whoof and a snort and a kind of bark
    There rose the father of all the pigs:
And a tiger would have walked wide of him
As he stropped his tusks on a leaning limb.

Then the new chum's three-nought-three gave tongue
    Like a popgun fired in an opera bouffe:
But a pig that was old when the world was young
    Is near as possible bullet-proof.
(The more you shoot him the less he dies,
Unless you catch him between the eyes.)

So the new chum saw it was up to him
    To become extinct if he stopped to shoot;
So he made a leap for a gidgee limb
    While the tusker narrowly missed his boot.
Then he found a fork, where he swayed in air
As he gripped the boughs like a native bear.

The pig sat silent and gaunt and grim
    To wait and wait till his foe should fall:
For night and day were the same to him,
    And home was any old place at all.
"I must wait," said he, "till this sportsman drops;
I could use his boots for a pair of strops."

The crows that watch from the distant blue
    Came down to see what it all might mean;
An eaglehawk and a cockatoo
    Bestowed their patronage on the scene.
Till a far-off boundary rider said
"I must have a look — there is something dead."

Now the new chum sits at his Christmas fare
    Of a dried-up chop from a tough old ewe.
Says he, "It's better than native bear
    And nearly as tender as kangaroo.
An emu's leg I can masticate,
But pork," says he, "is the thing I hate."

# The Diggers

*B*ristling Billy the porcupine,
  *A person that nobody liked,*
*Sinking a shaft on an ant-bed mine,*
*Came on a burrowing lizard's line,*
    *And the lizard was badly spiked.*
*"You're a blundering fool," said the snake's half-brother —*
*And that was how one thing led to another.*

Weary Willie the wombat king
    Said he was champion excavator;
But the Bristler said, "You ain't no such thing;
    You couldn't dig up a new pertater!"
So a match was made on their mining skill —
Bristling Billy and Weary Will.

Both of the creatures were stout as steel,
    With knife-like claws that could dig for ever.
The wombat dug with the greater zeal,
    But he hadn't the style or the action clever
Of Bristling Billy, who looked a winner
Till he struck some ants, and he stopped for dinner.

Down where the ants had hid their young
    Underground in a secret tunnel,
Scooping them up with his sticky tongue
    Into his mouth that was like a funnel:
"Why should I dig for your wagers scanty,"
Said he, "when I'm feeling so full and ant-y?"

A kangaroo who had lost his cash
    Was wild at this most absurd come-uppance.
"Now listen, you poor ant-eating trash,
    I'd give you a kick in the ribs for twopence!"
"Well, when I've finished with this here diet,"
Said Bristling Billy, "you come and try it."

*Bristling Billy the porcupine,*
  *A person that nobody likes,*
*Wanders away on his lonely line,*
  *Rattles his fearful spikes.*
*Says he, "There's none of you long-haired squibs*
*Is game to give me a kick in the ribs."*

# *Flying Squirrels*

On the rugged water shed
    At the top of the bridle track
Where years ago, as the old men say,
The splitters went with a bullock dray,
    But never a dray came back.

At the time of the gum tree bloom,
    When the scent in the air is strong,
And the blossom stirs in the evening breeze,
You may see the squirrels among the trees,
    Playing the whole night long.

Never a care at all
    Bothers their simple brains;
You can see them glide in the moonlight dim
From tree to tree and from limb to limb,
    Little grey aeroplanes.

Each like a dormouse sleeps
    In the spout of a gum tree old,
A ball of fur with a silver coat;
Each with his tail around his throat
    For fear of his catching cold.

These are the things he eats,
    Asking his friends to dine:
Moths and beetles and newborn shoots,
Honey and snacks of the native fruits,
    And a glass of dew for wine.

# Frogs in Chorus

The chorus frogs in the big lagoon
  Would sing their songs to the silvery moon.
Tenor singers were out of place,
For every frog was a double bass.
But never a human chorus yet
Could beat the accurate time they set.
The solo singer began the joke;
He sang, "As long as I live I'll croak,
Croak, I'll croak,"
And the chorus followed him: "Croak, croak, croak!"

The poet frog, in his plaintive tone,
Sang of a sorrow was all his own;
"How shall I win to my heart's desire?
How shall I feed my spirit's fire?"
And the solo frog in his deepest croak,
"To fire your spirit," he sang, "eat coke,
Coke, eat coke,"
And the chorus followed him: "Coke, coke, coke!"

The green frog sat in a swampy spot
And he sang the song of he knew not what.
"The world is rotten, oh cursed spite,
That I am the frog that must set it right.
How shall I scatter the shades that lurk?"
And the old man bullfrog sang, "Get work,
Work, get work,"
And the chorus followed him: "Work, work, work!"

The soaring spirits that fain would fly
On wings of hope to the starry sky
Must face the snarls of the jealous dogs,
For the world is ruled by its chorus frogs.

# Fur and Feathers

The emus formed a football team
    Up Walgett way;
Their dark-brown sweaters were a dream
But kangaroos would sit and scream
    To watch them play.

"Now, butterfingers," they would call,
    And such-like names;
The emus couldn't hold the ball
— They had no hands — but hands aren't all
    In football games.

A match against the kangaroos
    They played one day.
The kangaroos were forced to choose
Some wallabies and wallaroos
    That played in grey.

The rules that in the west prevail
    Would shock the town;
For when a kangaroo set sail
An emu jumped upon his tail
    And fetched him down.

A whistler duck as referee
    Was not admired.
He whistled so incessantly
The teams rebelled, and up a tree
    He soon retired.

The old marsupial captain said,
    "It's do or die!"
So down the ground like fire he fled
And leaped above an emu's head
    And scored a try.

Then shouting, "Keep it on the toes!"
    The emus came.
Fierce as the flooded Bogan flows
They laid their foemen out in rows
    And saved the game.

On native pear and Darling pea
    They dined that night:
But one man was an absentee:
The whistler duck — their referee —
    Had taken flight.

# High Explosive

'Twas the dingo pup to his dam that said,
"It's time I worked for my daily bread.
Out in the world I intend to go,
And you'd be surprised at the things I know.

"There's a wild duck's nest in a sheltered spot,
And I'll go right down and I'll eat the lot."
But when he got to his destined prey
He found that the ducks had flown away.

But an egg was left that would quench his thirst,
So he bit the egg and it straightway burst.
It burst with a bang, and he turned and fled,
For he thought that the egg had shot him dead.

"Oh, mother," he said, "let us clear right out
Or we'll lose our lives with the bombs about;
And it's lucky I am that I'm not blown up —
It's a very hard life," said the dingo pup.

# The Lung Fish

The Honourable Ardleigh Wyse
   Was every fisherman's despair;
He caught his fish on floating flies,
   In fact he caught them in the air,
And wet-fly men — good sports, perhaps —
He called "those chuck-and-chance-it chaps".

And then the Fates that sometimes play
   A joke on such as me and you
Deported him up Queensland way
   To act as a station jackaroo.
The boundary rider said, said he,
"You fish dry fly? Well, so do we.

"These barramundi are the blokes
   To give you all the sport you need:
For when the big lagoons and soaks
   Are dried right down to mud and weed
They don't sit there and raise a roar,
They pack their traps and come ashore.

"And all these rods and reels you lump
   Along the creel from day to day
Would only give a man the hump
   Who does his fishing Queensland way.
For when the barramundi's thick
We knock 'em over with a stick.

"The black boys on the Darwin side
   Will fill a creek with bitter leaves
And when the fish are stupefied
   The gins will gather 'em in sheaves.
Now tell me, could a feller wish
A finer way of catchin' fish?"

The stokehold of the steamship *Foam*
    Contains our hero, very sick,
A-working of his passage home
    And brandishing a blue-gum stick.
"Behold," says he, "the latest fly;
It's called the Great Australian Dry."

# Morgan's Dog

Morgan the drover explained,
    As he drank from his battered quart-pot,
Many a slut have I trained;
    This is the best of the lot.

Crossing these stringybark hills,
    Hungry and rocky and steep
This is the country that kills
    Weakly and sore-footed sheep.

Those that are healthy and strong
    Battle away in the lead,
Carting the others along,
    Eating the whole of the feed.

That's where this little red slut
    Shows you what's bred in the bone;
Works it all out in her nut,
    Handles it all on her own.

Backwards and forwards she'll track,
    Gauging the line at a glance,
Keeping the stronger ones back,
    Giving the tailers a chance.

Weary and hungry and lame,
    Sticking all day to her job,
Thin as a rabbit, but game,
    Working in front of the mob.

\* \* \* \*

Tradesmen, I call 'em, the dogs,
    Those that'll work in a yard;
Bark till they're hoarser than frogs,
    Makin' 'em savage and hard.

Others will soldier and shirk
    While there's a rabbit to hunt:
This is an artist at work;
    Watch her — out there — in the front.

# *Old Man Platypus*

Far from the trouble and toil of town,
    Where the reed beds sweep and shiver,
Look at a fragment of velvet brown —
Old Man Platypus drifting down,
    Drifting along the river.

And he plays and dives in the river bends
    In a style that is most elusive;
With few relations and fewer friends,
For Old Man Platypus descends
    From a family most exclusive.

He shares his burrow beneath the bank
    With his wife and his son and daughter
At the roots of the reeds and the grasses rank;
And the bubbles show where our hero sank
    To its entrance under water.

Safe in their burrow below the falls
    They live in a world of wonder,
Where no one visits and no one calls,
They sleep like little brown billiard balls
    With their beaks tucked neatly under.

And he talks in a deep unfriendly growl
    As he goes on his journey lonely;
For he's no relation to fish nor fowl,
Nor to bird nor beast, nor to horned owl;
    In fact, he's the one and only!

# Swinging the Lead

*Army term for malingering*

Said the soldier to the Surgeon, "I've got noises in me head
And a kind o' filled up feeling after every time I'm fed;
I can sleep all night on picket, but I can't sleep in my bed."
    And the Surgeon said,
    "That's Lead!"

Said the soldier to the Surgeon, "Do you think they'll send me back?
For I really ain't adapted to be carrying a pack
Though I've humped a case of whisky half a mile upon my back."
    And the Surgeon said,
    "That's Lead!"

"And my legs have swelled up cruel, I can hardly walk at all,
But when the Taubes come over you should see me start to crawl;
When we're sprinting for the dugout, I can easy beat 'em all."
    And the Surgeon said,
    "That's Lead!"

So they sent him to the trenches where he landed safe and sound,
And he drew his ammunition, just about two fifty round:
"Oh, Sergeant, what's this heavy stuff I've got to hump around?"
    And the Sergeant said,
    "That's Lead!"

# *Weary Will*

The strongest creature for his size
   But least equipped for combat
That dwells beneath Australian skies
   Is Weary Will the Wombat

He digs his homestead underground,
   He's neither shrewd nor clever;
For kangaroos can leap and bound
   But wombats dig for ever.

The boundary rider's netting fence
   Excites his irritation;
It is to his untutored sense
   His pet abomination.

And when to pass it he desires,
   Upon his task he'll centre
And dig a hole beneath the wires
   Through which the dingoes enter.

And when to block the whole they strain
   With logs and stones and rubble,
Bill Wombat digs it out again
   Without the slightest trouble.

The boundary rider bows to fate,
   Admits he's made a blunder,
And rigs a little swinging gate
   To let Bill Wombat under.

So most contentedly he goes
   Between his haunt and burrow:
He does the only thing he knows,
   And does it very thorough.

# White Cockatoos

Now the autumn maize is growing,
　　Now the corn-cob fills,
Where the Little River flowing
　　Winds among the hills.
Over mountain peaks outlying
　　Clear against the blue
Comes a scout in silence flying,
　　One white cockatoo.

Back he goes to where the meeting
　　Waits among the trees.
Says, "The corn is fit for eating;
　　Hurry, if you please."
Skirmishers, their line extending,
　　Shout the joyful news;
Down they drop like snow descending,
　　Clouds of cockatoos.

At their husking competition
　　Hear them screech and yell.
On a gum tree's high position
　　Sits a sentinel.
Soon the boss goes boundary riding;
　　But the wise old bird,
Mute among the branches hiding,
　　Never says a word.

Then you hear his strident squalling:
　　"Here's the boss's son,
Through the garden bushes crawling,
　　Crawling with a gun.
May the spiny cactus bristles
　　Fill his soul with woe;
May his knees get full of thistles.
　　Brothers, let us go."

Old Black Harry sees them going,
  Sketches Nature's plan:
"That one cocky too much knowing,
  All same Chinaman.
One eye shut and one eye winkin' —
  Never shut the two;
Chinaman go dead, me thinkin',
  Jump up cockatoo."

# Why the Jackass Laughs

The Boastful Crow and the Laughing Jack
Were telling tales of the outer back:
"I've just been travelling far and wide,
At the back of Bourke and the Queensland side;
There isn't a bird in the bush can go
As far as me," said the old black crow.

"There isn't a bird in the bush can fly
A course as straight or a course as high.
Higher than human eyesight goes
There's sometimes clouds — but there's always crows,
Drifting along for a scent of blood
Or a smell of smoke or a sign of flood.
For never a bird or a beast has been
With a sight as strong or a scent as keen.
At fires and floods I'm the first about,
For then the lizards and mice run out:
And I make my swoop — and that's all they know —
I'm a whale on mice," said the Boastful Crow.

The Bee-birds over the homestead flew
And told each other the long day through
"The cold has come, we must take the track."
"Now, I'll make you a bet," said the Laughing Jack,
"Of a hundred mice, that you dare not go
With the little Bee-birds, my Boastful Crow."

Said the Boastful Crow, "I could take my ease
And fly with little green birds like these.
If they went flat out and they did their best
I could have a smoke and could take a rest."
And he asked of the Bee-birds circling round:
"Now, where do you spike-tails think you're bound?"
"We leave tonight, and our present plan
Is to go straight on till we reach Japan.

"Every year, on the self-same day,
We call our children and start away,
Twittering, travelling day and night,
Over the ocean we take our flight;
And we rest a day on some lonely isles
Or we beg a ride for a hundred miles
On a steamer's deck, and away we go:
We hope you'll come with us, Mister Crow."

But the old black crow was extremely sad.
Said he: "I reckon you're raving mad
To talk of travelling night and day,
And how in the world do you find your way?"
And the Bee-birds answered him, "If you please,
That's one of our own great mysteries."

Now, these things chanced in the long ago
And explain the fact, which no doubt you know,
That every jackass high and low
Will always laugh when he sees a crow.

# OTHER VERSE

# Barney Devine

*Tune: "Paddy McGhee"*

Where are you roving now, Barney Devine,
Shearing or droving now, what is your line?
Oh, but it's years since the last that we heard,
Never a mailman has brought us a word.

### Chorus

Anyhow, anywhere, country or town,
Making the money or knocking it down.
Drought or wet weather, in rain or in shine,
Here's a long life to you, Barney Devine!

Say, are you shearing away in the west,
You that were always the fastest and best,
Shearing a hundred with never a scratch!
Where was the shearer could turn out their match?

Out on the cattle camps waiting for light,
Watching the stock in the hush of the night,
Singing your songs of the bush and its ways,
Telling your tales of the wandering days.

Far, far away though you happen to roam,
Ne'er you'll forget them the old folks at home,
Sadly they wait for a word or a line
Won't you come back to them, Barney Devine?

# The Scapegoat

We have all of us read how the Israelites fled
    From Egypt with Pharaoh in eager pursuit of 'em,
And Pharaoh's fierce troop were all put "in the soup"
    When the waters rolled softly o'er every galoot of 'em.
The Jews were so glad when old Pharaoh was "had"
That they sounded their timbrels and capered like mad.
You see he was hated from Jordan to Cairo —
Whence comes the expression "to buck against faro".

For forty long years, 'midst perils and fears
In deserts with never a tramline to follow by,
The Israelite horde went roaming abroad
Like so many sundowners "out on the wallaby".
When Moses, who led 'em, and taught 'em, and fed 'em,
Was dying, he murmured, "A rorty old hoss you are:
I give you command of the whole of the band" —
And handed the Government over to Joshua.

But Moses told 'em before he died,
"Wherever you are, whatever betide,
Every year as the time draws near
By lot or by rote choose you a goat,
And let the high priest confess on the beast
The sins of the people the worst and the least,
Lay your sins on the goat! Sure the plan ought to suit yer,
Because all your sins are 'his troubles' in future.
Then lead him away to the wilderness black
To die with the weight of your sins on his back:
Of thirst let him perish alone and unshriven,
For thus shall your sins be absolved and forgiven!"

'Tis needless to say, though it reeked of barbarity
This scapegoat arrangement gained great popularity.
By this means a Jew, whate'er he might do,
Though he burgled, or murdered, or cheated at loo,
Or meat on Good Friday (a sin most terrific) ate,
Could get his discharge, like a bankrupt's certificate;
Just here let us note — *Did they choose their best goat?*

374

It's food for conjecture, to judge from the picture
By Hunt in the Gallery close to our door, a
Man well might suppose that the scapegoat they chose
Was a long way from being their choicest Angora.

In fact I should think he was one of their weediest:
'Tis a rule that obtains, no matter who reigns,
When making a sacrifice, offer the seediest;
Which accounts for a theory known to my hearers
Who live in the wild by the wattle beguiled,
That a "stag" makes quite good enough mutton for shearers.
Be that as it may, as each year passed away,
A scapegoat was led to the desert and freighted
With sin (the poor brute must have been overweighted)
And left there — to die as his fancy dictated.

The day it has come, with trumpet and drum.
With pomp and solemnity fit for the tomb
They lead the old billy-goat off to his doom:
On every hand a reverend band,
Prophets and preachers and elders stand
And the oldest rab*bi*, with a tear in his eye,
Delivers a sermon to all standing by.
(We haven't his name — whether Cohen or Harris, he
No doubt was the "poisonest" kind of a Pharisee.)
The sermon was marked by a deal of humility
And pointed the fact, with no end of ability,
That being a Gentile's no mark of gentility,
And, according to Samuel, would certainly d ——n you well.
Then, shedding his coat, he approaches the goat
And, while a red fillet he carefully pins on him,
Confesses the whole of the Israelites' sins on him.
With this eloquent burst he exhorts the accurst —
"Go forth in the desert and perish in woe,
The sins of the people are whiter than snow!"
Then signs to his pal "for to let the brute go".
(That "pal" as I've heard, is an elegant word,
Derived from the Persian "Palaykhur" or "Pallaghur"),
As the scapegoat strains and tugs at the reins
The Rabbi yells rapidly, "Let her go, Gallagher!"

The animal, freed from all restraint
Lowered his head, made a kind of a feint,
And charged straight at that elderly saint.
So fierce his attack and so very severe, it
Quite floored the Rabbi, who, ere he could fly,
Was rammed on the — no, not the back — but just near it.
The scapegoat he snorted, and wildly cavorted,
A light-hearted antelope "out on the ramp",
Then stopped, looked around, got the "lay of the ground",
And made a beeline back again to the camp.
The elderly priest, as he noticed the beast
So gallantly making his way to the east,

Says he, "From the tents may I never more roam again
If that there old billy-goat ain't going home again.
He's hurrying, too! This never will do.
Can't somebody stop him? I'm all of a stew.
After all our confessions, so openly granted,
He's taking our sins back to where they're not wanted.
We've come all this distance salvation to win agog,
If he takes home our sins, it'll burst up the Synagogue!"

He turned to an Acolyte who was making his bacca light,
A fleet-footed youth who could run like a crack o' light.
"Run, Abraham, run! Hunt him over the plain,
And drive back the brute to the desert again.
The Sphinx is a-watching, the Pyramids frown on you,
From those granite tops forty cent'ries look down on you —
Run, Abraham, run! I'll bet half-a-crown on you."
So Abraham ran, like a man did he go for him,
But the goat made it clear each time he drew near
That he had what the racing men call "too much toe" for him.

The crowd with great eagerness studied the race —
"Great Scott! isn't Abraham forcing the pace —
And don't the goat spiel? It is hard to keep sight on him,
The sins of the Israelites ride mighty light on him.
The scapegoat is leading a furlong or more,
And Abraham's tiring — I'll lay six to four!
He rolls in his stride; he's done, there's no question!"
But here the old Rabbi brought up a suggestion.
('Twas strange that in racing he showed so much cunning),

"It's a hard race," said he, "and I think it would be
A good thing for someone to take up the running."
As soon said as done, they started to run —
The priests and the deacons, strong runners and weak 'uns
All reckoned ere long to come up with the brute,
And so the whole boiling set off in pursuit.
And then it came out, as the rabble and rout
Streamed over the desert with many a shout —
The Rabbi so elderly, grave, and patrician,
Had been in his hot youth a bold metallician,
And offered, in gasps, as they merrily spieled,
"Any price, Abraham! Evens the field!"
Alas! the whole clan, they raced and they ran,
And Abraham proved him an "even-time" man,
But the goat — now a speck they could scarce keep their eyes on —
Stretched out in his stride in a style most surprisin'
And vanished ere long o'er the distant horizon.
Away in the camp the bill-sticker's tramp
Is heard as he wanders with paste, brush, and notices,
And paling and wall he plasters them all,
"I wonder how's things gettin' on with the goat," he says,
Then pulls out his bills, "Use Solomon's Pills":
"Great Stoning of Christians! To all devout Jews! you all
Must each bring a stone — Great sport will be shown;
Enormous Attractions! And prices as usual!
Roll up to the Hall!! Wives, children and all,
For naught the most delicate feelings to hurt is meant!!"
Here his eyes opened wide, for close by his side
Was the scapegoat: And eating the latest advertisement!
One shriek from him burst — "You creature accurst!"
And he ran from the spot like one fearing the worst.
His language was chaste, as he fled in his haste,
But the goat stayed behind him — and "scoffed up" the paste.

With downcast head, and sorrowful tread,
The people came back from the desert in dread.
"The goat — was he back there? Had anyone heard of him?"
In very short order they got plenty word of him.
In fact as they wandered by street, lane and hall,
"The trail of the serpent was over them all."
A poor little child knocked out stiff in the gutter,

Proclaimed that the scapegoat was bred for a "butter".
The bill-sticker's pail told a sorrowful tale,
The scapegoat had licked it as dry as a nail;
He raced through their houses, and frightened their spouses,
But his latest achievement most anger arouses,
For while they were searching, and scratching their craniums,
One little Ben Ourbed, who looked in the flow'r-bed,
Discovered him, eating the Rabbi's geraniums.

### Moral

The moral is patent to all the beholders —
Don't shift your own sins on to other folks' shoulders;
Be kind to dumb creatures and never abuse them,
Nor curse them nor kick them, nor spitefully use them:
Take their lives if needs must — when it comes to the worst,
But don't let them perish of hunger or thirst.
Remember, no matter how far you may roam
That dogs, goats, and chickens, it's simply the dickens,
Their talent stupendous for "getting back home".
Your sins, without doubt, will aye find you out,
And so will a scapegoat, he's bound to achieve it,
But, die in the wilderness! Don't you believe it!

# The Ballad of Ashantie Pagoda

*or How the Brigadier Got the Order of the Nile
and the Servian White Eagle*

I write that he who reads may run
    Of Colonel Ashantie Pagoda
Who thought no day was well begun
    Unless begun with whisky-soda.

And when he entertained a friend
    All thoughts of slumber proudly scorning
He thought no day should have an end
    Till half past four o'clock next morning.

Though poor his gain in worldly gear
    He lived his life upon the level.
His soldiers said he stood in fear
    Of neither hog nor dog nor devil.

And when he moved against the Turk
    They paused in intervals of drinking
To whisper, "There'll be dirty work
    At the crossroads, tonight I'm thinking."

The Brigadier whom he obeyed
    Was what is called a "Regimental".
His gallantry had been displayed
    In actions at The Continental.

He'd gained distinctions orthodox
    The D.S.O. and Croix de Wowsers
By ordering all Lieutenants' socks
    Should match the colour of their trousers.

At camp inspections he was great
    For dixie lids he knew the right wash.
At lectures he would rise and state
    The road to fame is paved with whitewash.

But when he moved against the Turk
    To mop 'em up and put 'em through it

379

He didn't know the fighting work
    So old Pagoda had to do it.

Now let us hear a story true
    About a fight as soldiers view it —
They know but little what they do
    And know still less of why they do it.

But even toads have jewels bright
    Within their heads, so some old stager
May get an inkling of a fight
    — Let's hear the Squadron Sergeant-Major.

"The whole kaboose moved out at dawn
    — Column of route, our squadron leadin'
And never yet since I was born
    Have I seen anything more bleedin'.

" 'Twas just what always is the case
    The rest was told to halt and set there
While we was sent to some wrong place
    And then mistook the road to get there.

"We marches twenty miles, I guess,
    With hills and rocks around us scowlin' —
Talk of a howling wilderness
    So help me, you could hear it howlin'.

"We had no guides and we was sore
    To find some Turks that we could score on;
We caught some Bedouin who swore
    They didn't know there was a war on.

"We perished on until I think
    We must have crossed the Turkish borders
And not a bloomin' drop to drink
    And not a bloomin' word of orders.

"The Colonel says to me, 'Here, you,
    You're always there when trouble's brewin'.
Ride up that hill and have a view
    And see if you can see what's doin'.'"

"So up I goes and there I sees
    The finest sight that you could show me

For there was Turks as thick as bees
    All squatted in the plain below me.

"So when we're gettin' off to fire
    A chap comes ridin' hell for leather
Says he, 'Your orders are retire
    The Turks is too strong altogether.'

" 'We've fought all day, we're fightin' still!'
    'You must retire, you can't pursue 'em.'
'Right,' says old Ashantie, 'I will
    I'll bloomin' well retire right through 'em.

" 'See here,' says he, 'You sons of guns.
    This force,' says he, 'We've ridden round 'em —
We've looked all day for Turks and Huns
    And now thank Gawd at last we've found 'em.

" 'Our road to Camp Headquarters goes
    Direct across that Turk position
So I'm entitled, I suppose,
    To go straight home with that permission.

" 'Fix bay'nets, walk march, open out!
    Now, boys, go at 'em, hell for leather!'
We fixes spikes and gives a shout
    And charges down the hill together.

"Good Lord, you should have heard the din
    The rattlin' tins, the horses fallin',
And just as we was closin' in
    The Jackos and the Germans squallin'.

"We gives 'em nothin'! Strike me blue
    They thought we was a whole division.
Before they'd formed we'd ridden through
    The camp and captured the position.

"They turned it in: three thousand head
    Of Turkish prisoners there we counted
And old Pagoda grinned and said
    'Well, cavalry's some use when mounted.'

"They'd been there fighting all day long
    The Brigadier'd already wired

381

To say the Turks was far too strong
    An all our troops had been retired!

"He had to cancel all he'd sent
    The wires grew hot with telegraphin',
And those who tumbled what it meant
    Were fit to split their sides with laughin'."

Here ends the Sergeant's story true
    Of how we captured Turks in plenty
The rest was done by G.H.Q.
    See G.R.O. 1/19/20.

The Brigadier Commanding Force
    Is hereby warmly complimented,
A whole Brigade of Turkish horse
    He first attacked, then circumvented.

The Nile Boil, and the Servian Stain
    Are his to wear within our borders,
But Ashantie will "please explain"
    For misinterpreting his orders!

# Uncle Bill

## *The Larrikin's Lament*

My Uncle Bill! My Uncle Bill!
How doth my heart with anguish thrill!
For he, our chief, our Robin Hood,
Has gone to jail for stealing wood!
With tears and sobs my voice I raise
To celebrate my uncle's praise;
With all my strength, with all my skill,
I'll sing the song of Uncle Bill.

Convivial to the last degree,
An open-hearted sportsman he.
Did midnight howls our slumbers rob,
We said, "It's uncle 'on the job'."
When sounds of fight rang sharply out,
Then Bill was bound to be about,
The foremost figure in "the scrap",
A terror to the local "trap".
To drink, or fight, or maim, or kill,
Came all alike to Uncle Bill.
And when he faced the music's squeak
At Central Court before the beak,
How carefully we sought our fob
To pay his fine of forty bob!
Recall the happy days of yore
When Uncle Bill went forth to war!
When all the street with strife was filled
And both the traps got nearly killed.
When the lone cabman on the stand
Was "stoushed" by Bill's unaided hand,
And William mounted, filled with rum,
And drove the cab to kingdom come.
Remember, too, that famous fray
When the "Black-reds", who hold their sway
O'er Surry Hills and Shepherd's Bush,
Descended on the "Liver Push".

Who cheered both parties long and loud?
Who heaved blue metal at the crowd!
And sooled his bulldog, Fighting Bet,
To bite, haphazard, all she met?
And when the mob were lodged in gaol
Who telegraphed to me for bail?
And — here I think he showed his sense —
Who calmly turned Queen's evidence?

Enough! I now must end my song,
My needless anguish, why prolong?
From what I've said, you'll own, I'm sure,
That Uncle Bill was pretty "pure",
So, rowdies all, your glasses fill,
And — drink it standing — "Uncle Bill".

# *Unforgotten*

Oh Captain Cook he was a sailor
    Sail, oh, sail away,
He sailed until he found Australia
    Sail to Sydney Bay,
For the wind blows fair, and the wind blows free
And Sydney town's the town for me
The brave old town by the Southern Sea
    Sail, oh, sail away.

Oh Kingsford Smith, the aviator
    Fly, oh, fly away
He was the air's great navigator
    Fly to Sydney Bay,
And he steered his course by the stars and skies
And no man knows where now he lies
Till trumpets sound and the dead arise
    Fly, oh, fly away.

Sir John Monash, he fought in Flanders
    Fight to keep us free
The wisest man of our commanders
    Fight by land and sea
And we'd scorn to flinch from a foe's attack
Had we the soul of Monash back
To fly his flag on the well-worn track
    Fight for victory.

# *The Lost Drink*

I had spent the night in the watch-house —
   My head was the size of three —
So I went and asked the chemist
   To fix up a drink for me;
And he brewed it from various bottles
   With soda and plenty of ice,
With something that smelt like lemon,
   And something that seemed like spice.

It fell on my parching palate
   Like the dew on a sunbaked plain,
And my system began to flourish
   Like the grass in the soft spring rain;
It wandered throughout my being,
   Suffusing my soul with rest,
And I felt as I "scoffed" that liquid
   That life had a new-found zest.

I have been on the razzle-dazzle
   Full many a time since then
But I never could get the chemist
   To brew me that drink again.
He says he's forgotten the notion —
   'Twas only by chance it came —
He's tried me with various liquids
   But oh! they are not the same.

We have sought, but we sought it vainly,
   That one lost drink divine;
We have sampled his various bottles,
   But somehow they don't combine:
Yet I know when I cross the River
   And stand on the Golden Shore
I shall meet with an angel chemist
   To brew me that drink once more.

# The Duties of an Aide-de-Camp

Oh, some folk think vice-royalty is festive and hilarious,
  The duties of an A.D.C. are manifold and various,
So listen, whilst I tell in song,
The duties of an *aide-de-cong*.

   Whatsoever betide
   To the Governor's side
We must stick — or the public would eat him —
   For each bounder we see
   Says, "Just introduce me
To His Lordship — I'm anxious to meet him."

   Then they grab at his paw
   And they chatter and jaw
Till they'd talk him to death — if we'd let 'em —
   And the folk he has met,
   They are all in a fret,
Just for fear he might chance to forget 'em.

   When some local King Billy
   Is talking him silly,
Or the pound-keeper's wife has waylaid him,
   From folks of that stamp
   When he has to decamp —
We're his aides to decamp — so we aid him.

   Then some feminine beauty
   Will come and salute ye,
She may be a Miss or a Madam,
   Or a man comes in view,
   Bails you up, "How de do!"
And you don't know the fellow from Adam!

387

But you've got to keep sweet
    With each man that you meet,
And a trifle like this mustn't bar you,
    So you clutch at his fin,
    And you say, with a grin,
"Oh, delighted to see you — how *are* you?"


    Then we do country shows
    Where some prize-taker blows
Of his pig — a great, vast forty-stoner —
    "See, my Lord! aint he fine!
    How is that for a swine!"
When it isn't a patch on its owner!


    We fix up the dinners
    For parsons and sinners
And lawyers and bishops and showmen,
    And a judge of the court
    We put next to a "sport",
And an Orangeman next to a Roman.


    We send invitations
    To all celebrations,
Some Nobody's presence entreating,
    And the old folks of all
    We invite to a ball,
And the young — to a grandmothers' meeting.


    And when we go dancing,
    Like cart-horses prancing,
We plunge where the people are thickenin';
    And each gay local swell
    Thinks it's "off" to dance well,
So he copies our style — ain't it sickenin'!


    Then at banquets we dine
    And swig cheap, nasty wine,
But the poor *aide-de-camp* mustn't funk it —
    And they call it champagne,
    But we're free to maintain,
That he feels real pain when he's drunk it.

Then our horses bestriding
    We go out a-riding
Lest our health by confinement we'd injure;
    You can notice the glare
    Of the Governor's hair
When the little boys say, "Go it, Ginger!"

    Then some wandering lords —
    They so often are frauds —
This out-of-way country invading,
    If a man dresses well
    And behaves like a swell,
Then he's somebody's cook masquerading.

    But an out-and-out ass
    With a thirst for the glass
And the symptoms of drink on his "boko",
    Who is perpetually
    Pursuing the ballet,
He is *always* the "true Orinoco".

    We must slave with our quills —
    Keep the cash — pay the bills —
Keep account of the liquor and victuals —
    So I think you'll agree
    That the gay A.D.C.
Has a life that's not *all* beer and skittles!

# The Quest Eternal

O west of all that a man holds dear, on the edge of the Kingdom Come,
Where carriage is far too high for beer, and the pubs keep only rum,
On the sunburnt ways of the Outer Back, on the plains of the darkening
    scrub,
I have followed the wandering teamster's track, and it always led to a pub.

There's always in man some gift to show, some power he can command,
And mine is the Gift that I always know when a pub is close at hand;
I can pick them out on the London streets, though most of their pubs are queer,
Such solid-looking and swell retreats, with never a sign of beer.

In the march of the boys through Palestine when the noontide fervour
    glowed,
Over the desert in thirsty line our sunburnt squadrons rode.
They looked at the desert lone and drear, stone ridges and stunted scrub,
And said, "We should have had Ginger here, I bet he'd have found a pub!"

We started out in the noonday heat on a trip that was fast and far,
We took in one each side of the street to balance the blooming car,
But then we started a long dry run on a road we did not know,
In the blinding gleam of the noonday sun, with the dust as white as snow.

For twenty minutes without a drink we strove with our dreadful thirst,
But the chauffeur pointed and said, "I think," I answered "I saw it first!"
A pub with a good old-fashioned air, with bottles behind the blind,
And a golden tint in the barmaid's hair — I could see it all — in my mind —

Ere ever the motor ceased its roar, ere ever the chauffeur knew,
I made a dash for the open door and madly darted through.
I looked for the barmaid, golden-crowned as they were in the good old time,
And — shades of Hennessy! — what I found was a wowser selling "lime!"
And the scoundrel said as he stopped to put on his lime-washed boots a rub,
"The Local Option voted it shut, it ain't no longer a pub!"

'Twas then I rose to my greatest heights in dignified retreat
(The greatest men in the world's great fights are those who are great in defeat).
I shall think with pride till the day I die of my confidence sublime,
For I looked the wowser straight in the eye, and asked for a pint of lime.

# The Wreck of the Golfer

It was the Bondi golfing man
   Drove off from the golf house tee,
And he had taken his little daughter
   To bear him company.

"Oh, Father, why do you swing the club
   And flourish it such a lot?"
"You watch it fly o'er the fences high!"
   And he tried with a brassey shot.

"Oh, Father, why did you hit the fence
   Just there where the brambles twine?"
And the father he answered never a word,
   But he got on the green in nine.

"Oh, Father, hark from behind those trees,
   What dismal yells arrive!"
" 'Tis a man I ween on the second green,
   And I've landed him with my drive."

"Oh, Father, why does the poor Chinee
   Fall down on his knees and cry?"
"He taketh me for his Excellency,
   And he thinks once hit twice shy."

So on they fared to the waterhole,
   And he drove with a lot of dash,
But the balls full soon in the dread lagoon
   Fell down with a woeful splash.

"Oh, Father, why do you beat the sand
   Till it flies like the carded wool?"
And the father he answered never a word,
   For his heart was much too full.

"Oh, Father, why are they shouting 'fore'
    And screaming so lustily?"
But the father he answered never a word,
    A pallid corpse was he.

For a well-swung drive on the back of his head
    Had landed and laid him low.
Lord save us all from a fate like this
    When next to the links we go.

# *They Met in the Hall at a Charity Ball*

They met in the hall, at a Charity Ball,
  Patronised by the pink of Society,
They were both in a state, I grieve to relate,
  That the Clergyman calls insobriety.

He wanted to know was she *comme il faut*,
  Or whether her manner was shadylike,
And he wondered in doubt, as she lowered a stout,
  In a style more proficient than ladylike.

He asked might he call, the night after the Ball,
  If she'd pardon his impetuosity,
She embraced him and said, "You must come home to bed,
  Just to show there is no animosity."

She sang him a song, as they rattled along,
  There were verses a little bit blue in it,
And a story she told of adventures of old,
  With a queer situation or two in it.

When they went to repose, and he threw off his clothes,
  In his anxious excitement to doss it, he
Was knocked when she bid him fork out two quid,
  Just to show there was no animosity.

'Twas a little bit rough, but he forked out the stuff,
  Though he thought it was very absurd of her,
Then she went down below, for a moment or so,
  And that was the last that he heard of her.

For a big-shouldered lout came and lumbered him out,
  And used him with awful ferocity,
He was very much hurt, but they chucked him his shirt,
  *Just to show there was no animosity.*

# Typographical

*A Ballad of Burdens*

The Editor wrote his political screed
    In ink that was fainter and fainter;
He rose to the call of his country's need,
And in spiderish characters wrote with speed,
    A column on "Cutting the Painter".

The "reader" sat in his high-backed chair,
    For literals he was a hunter;
But he stared aghast at the column long
Of the editorial hot and strong,
For the comp. inspired by some sense of wrong
    Had headed it "Gutting the Punter".

# Ten Little Jackaroos

Ten little Jackaroos at riding wished to shine,
  One rode the Corkscrew colt, and then there were nine.

Nine little Jackaroos mending up a gate
One knew how to use the adze — and then there were eight.

Eight little Jackaroos riding home at even
One took a short cut and then there were seven.

Seven little Jackaroos playing up their tricks
One kicked the Boss's dog and then there were six.

Six little Jackaroos learnt to bullock drive
One stroked a bullock's leg and then there were five.

Five little Jackaroos baking in a store
One mistook the arsenic tin and then there were four.

Four little Jackaroos went to fell a tree
One waited till she cracked and then there were three.

Three little Jackaroos feeling rather blue
Started hitting beers to leg, and then there were two.

Two little Jackaroos learnt to fight like fun
One fought the shearer's cook and then there was one.

One little Jackaroo working all alone
He learnt some common sense, and then there was none.

# *A Rule of the A.J.C.*

Come all ye bold trainers attend to my song,
    It's a rule of the A.J.C.
You mustn't train ponies, for that's very wrong
    By the rules of the A.J.C.
You have to wear winkers when crossing the street,
For fear that a pony you'd happen to meet;
If you hear one about, you must beat a retreat —
    That's a rule of the A.J.C.

And all ye bold owners will find without fail
    By the rules of the AJ.C.,
The jockey boys' fees you must pay at the scale —
    It's a rule of the A.J.C.
When your horse wins a fiver, you'll laugh, I'll be bound,
But you won't laugh so much by the time that you've found
That the fee to the boy is exactly ten pound!
    That's a rule of the A.J.C.

And all ye bold "Books" who are keeping a shop,
    In the rules of the A.J.C.,
There's a new regulation that says you must stop!
    That's a rule of the A.J.C.
You must give up your shop with its pipes and cigars
To an unlicensed man who is thanking his stars,
While *you* go and bet in the threepenny bars —
    That's a rule of the A.J.C.

And all ye small jockeys who ride in a race,
    In the rules of the A.J.C.
If owners' instructions are "Don't get a place",
    By the rules of the A.J.C.,
You must ride the horse out — though, of course, if you do
You will get no more mounts, it's starvation to you.
But, bless you, you'll always find plenty to chew
    In the rules of the A.J.C.

# Shakespeare on the Turf

**An Unpublished Drama**

*A Winter's Turf Tale*
*As the public have "stood" uncomplainingly the publication of a portrait of*
*the Supreme Being, they may accept the following drama as the work of*
*William Shakespeare.*

## SCENE I

SCENE: The saddling paddock at a racecourse.
*Citizens, Battlers, Toffs, Trainers, Flappers, Satyrs, Bookmakers and*
*Turf Experts.*

*Enter Shortinbras, a Trainer, and two Punters.*

FIRST PUNTER: Good Shortinbras, what thinkest thou of the Fav'rite?

SHORTINBRAS (*aside*): This poltroon would not venture a ducat
on David to beat a dead donkey; a dull and muddy-mettled rascal.
(*To Punter*): Aye marry Sir, I think well of the Favourite.

PUNTER: And yet I have a billiard marker's word
That in this race to-day they back Golumpus,
And when they bet, they tell me, they will knock
The Favourite for a string of German Sausage.

SHORTINBRAS: Aye, marry, they would tell thee, I've no doubt,
It is the way of owners that they tell
To billiard markers and the men on trams
Just when they mean to bet. Go back it, back it!

(*Tries to shuffle off; but Punter detains him.*)

PUNTER: Nay, good Shortinbras, what thinkest thou of Golumpus?
Was it not dead last week?

SHORTINBRAS: Marry, sir, I think well of Golumpus.
'Tis safer to speak well of the dead: betimes they rise again.

(*Sings*)

397

They pulled him barefaced in the mile,
    Hey, Nonny, Nonny.
The Stipes were watching them all the while;
And the losers swear, but the winners smile,
    Hey, Nonny, Nonny.

*Exit Shortinbras.*

SECOND PUNTER: A scurvy knave! What meant he by his prate
    Of Fav'rite and outsider and the like?
    Forsooth he told us nothing. Follow him close.
    Give him good watch, I pray you, till we see
    Just what he does his dough on. Follow fast.

*Exeunt Punters.*

# SCENE II

*The same. Bookmakers call: "Seven to Four on the Field!"*
*"Three to One, Bar One!" "Ten to One, Golumpus."*
*Enter Two Heads.*

FIRST HEAD: How goes the Battle? Did thou catch the last?

SECOND HEAD: Aye, marry did I, and the one before,
But this has got me beat. The Favourite drifts,
And not a single wager has been laid
About Golumpus. Thinkest thou that both are dead?

*Re-enter Punters.*

PUNTER: Good morrow, Gentlemen. I have it cold
Straight from the owner, that Golumpus goes
Eyes out to win today.

FIRST HEAD: Prate not to me of owners. Hast thou seen
The good red gold Go in. The Jockey's Punter
Has he put up the stuff, or does he wait
To get a better price. Owner say'st thou?
The owner does the paying, and the talk;
Hears the tale afterwards when it gets beat
And sucks it in as hungry babes suck milk.
Look you how ride the books in motor cars
While owners go on foot, or ride in trams,

Crushed with the vulgar herd and doomed to hear
From mouths of striplings that their horse was stiff,
When they themselves are broke from backing it.

## SCENE III

*Enter an Owner and a Jockey.*

OWNER: 'Tis a good horse. A passing good horse.

JOCKEY: I rode him yesternoon: it seemed to me
That in good truth a fairly speedy cow
Might well outrun him.

OWNER: Thou froward varlet; must I say again,
That on the Woop Woop course he ran a mile
In less than forty with his irons on!

JOCKEY: Then thou should'st bring the Woop Woop
course down here.

OWNER: Thou pestilential scurvy Knave. Go to!

*Strikes him.*
*Alarms and excursions. The race is run and Shortinbras enters, leading in the
winner.*

FIRST PUNTER: And thou hast trained the winner, thou thyself,
Thou complicated liar. Didst not say
To back Golumpus or the Fav'rite!

SHORTINBRAS: Get work! For all I ever had of thee
My children were unfed, my wife unclothed,
And I myself condemned to menial toil.

PUNTER: The man who keeps a winner to himself
Deserves but death. *(Kills him)*

*Enter defeated Owner and Jockey.*

OWNER: Thou whoreson Knave: thou went into a trance
Soon as the barrier lifted and knew naught
Of what occurred until they neared the post.
*(Kills him)*
*Curtain falls on ensemble of punters, bookmakers, heads and surviving
jockeys and trainers.*

CURTAIN

# Not On It

The new chum's polo pony was the smartest pony yet —
The owner backed it for the Cup for all that he could get.
The books were laying fives to one, in tenners; and you bet
    He was on it.

The bell was rung, the nags came out their quality to try,
The band played, "What Ho! Robbo!" as our hero cantered by,
The people in the Leger Stand cried out, "Hi, mister, hi!
    Are you on it?"

They watched him as the flag went down; his fate is quickly told —
The pony gave a sudden spring, and off the rider rolled.
The pony finished first all right, but then our hero bold
    Was not on it.

# Johnny Riley's Cow

### *A Ballad of Federation*

Come all you Federationists and hearken to me now —
   I've a story will instruct you very highly.
'Tis about a free selector and his Federation cow
   And the free selector's name was Johnny Riley.
He was farming forty acres on the Upper Murray side,
Where the river's very shallow and it isn't very wide,
And his cow could cross the river every single time she tried.
   "Bad scran, to such a cow," said Johnny Riley.

"Sure, I belong to Sydney-side and when she goes across
   'Tis a loss to New South Wales," said Johnny Riley.
"Are all the Sydney merchants to be saddled with a loss
   To propitiate a cow," said Johnny Riley,
"For she splashes through the river, just to feed on foreign ground,
And never pays the tax at all, be jabers, I'll be bound,
I owe them darn Victorians about a thousand pound
   In fines for that there cow," said Johnny Riley.

"And I'm down on Federation — it will cripple New South Wales —
   But the cow don't seem to care," said Johnny Riley.
"For what will come to Sydney, if the Murray traffic fails
   And the Riverina trade?" said Johnny Riley.
"I've argued and expounded but they can't be made to see
That it makes no shade of odds at all to folks like you and me:
The Sydney landlords may be hurt, but what's the odds?" said he.
   "She's a narrow-minded cow," said Johnny Riley.

"You see the cow is Queensland-bred and doesn't care a pin
   If the Sydney rents or Melbourne's rise more highly —
To keep our country's union back for landlords is a sin;
   That's the verdict of the cow," said Johnny Riley.
"It's Australia for Australians — one people east and west —
And all may do as I do — travel where the grass is best.
Free trade with one another and protection from the rest.
   She's a narrow-minded cow," said Johnny Riley.

So, here's luck to Johnny Riley and his Federation cow!
    Their example we should value very highly.
" 'Twixt Melbourne town and Sydney it's a narrow-minded row,
    For the trade is none so much," said Johnny Riley.
"If Sydney gets the capital and Melbourne gets the trade
From Riverina stations — well, a fair exchange is made."
"And the twenty yards of river, we'll no longer be afraid
    When we cross it," says the cow to Johnny Riley.

# The Ballad of G.R. Dibbs

This is the story of G.R.D.,
Who went on a mission across the sea
To borrow some money for you and me.

This G.R. Dibbs was a stalwart man
Who was built on a most extensive plan,
And a regular staunch Republican.

But he fell in the hands of the Tory crew
Who said, "It's a shame that a man like you
Should teach Australia this nasty view.

"From her mother's side she should ne'er be gone,
And she ought to be glad to be smiled upon,
And proud to be known as our hanger-on."

And G.R. Dibbs, he went off his peg
At the swells who came for his smiles to beg
And the Prince of Wales — who was pulling his leg

And he told them all when the wine had flown,
"The Australian has got no land of his own,
His home is England, and there alone."

So he strutted along with the titled band
And he sold the pride of his native land
For a bow and a smile and a shake of the hand.

And the Tory drummers they sit and call:
"Send over your leaders great and small;
For the price is low, and we'll buy them all

"With a tinsel title, a tawdry star
Of a lower grade than *our* titles are,
And a puff at a Prince's big cigar."

And the Tories laugh till they crack their ribs
When they think how they purchased G.R. Dibbs.

# The Ballad of M.T. Nutt
## and His Dog

The Honourable M.T. Nutt
    About the bush did jog,
Till, passing by a settler's hut,
    He stopped and bought a dog.

Then started homewards full of hope,
    Alas, that hopes should fail!
The dog pulled back and took the rope
    Beneath the horse's tail.

The Horse remarked, "I would be soft
    Such liberties to stand!
Oh dog," he said, "Go up aloft,
    Young man, go on the land!"

# The Dam that Keele Built

*Being the History of the Cataract Dam in Verse*

This is the dam that Keele built
This is the stream that brought the water
 to fill the dam that Keele built;

This is the Water and Sewer Brigade,
That measured the stream that brought the water
 to fill the dam that Keele built.

This is the Engineer by Trade —
Head of the Water and Sewer Brigade —
Who measured the stream that brought the water
 to fill the dam that Keele built.

These are the Calculations made
By the Eminent Engineer by Trade,
Head of the Water and Sewer Brigade,
Who measured the stream that brought the water
 to fill the dam that Keele built.

This is the Scornful Mr Wade,
Who sneered at the Calculations made
By the Eminent Engineer by Trade,
Head of the Water and Sewer Brigade,
Who measured the stream that brought the water
 to fill the dam that Keele built.

This is the Minister quite dismayed,
At the sight of the Scornful Mr Wade,
Who sneered at the Calculations made
By the Eminent Engineer by Trade,
Head of the Water and Sewer Brigade,
Who measured the stream that brought the water
 to fill the dam that Keele built.

This is the Sydneyite afraid
That a serious blunder will be made,
Because of the Minister, quite dismayed,
At the sight of the Scornful Mr Wade,
Who sneered at the Calculations made
By the Eminent Engineer by Trade,
Head of the Water and Sewer Brigade,
Who measured the stream that brought the water
    to fill the dam that Keele built.

# *The Ballad of that P.N.*

The shades of night had fallen at last,
When through the house a shadow passed,
That once had been the Genial Dan,
But now become a desperate man,
At question time he waited near,
And on the Premier's startled ear
A voice fell like half a brick —
"Did ye, or did ye not, pay Crick
    Did ye?"

By land and sea the Premier sped,
But found his foe where'er he fled,
The sailors swore — with whitened lip —
That Neptune swam behind the ship:
When to the stern the Premier ran,
Behold, 'twas no one else but Dan,
And through the roaring of the gale
That clarion voice took up the tale,
"Ahoy there! Answer, straight and slick!
Did not the Ministry pay Crick
    Did they?"

In railway trains he sought retreat,
But soon, from underneath the seat,
With blazing eye and bristling beard,
His ancient enemy appeared,
And like a boiling torrent ran
The accents of the angry Dan —
"Tell me, John See, and tell me quick
Did not ye pay your shares to Crick
    Did ye?"

# The Dauntless Three

*With Apologies to the Shade of Macaulay*

Chris Watson, of the Parliament,
　　By his Caucus Gods he swore
That the great Labor Party
　　Should suffer wrong no more.
By his Caucus Gods he swore it,
　　And named a trysting day,
And bade his Socialists ride forth,
East and west and south and north,
　　To summon his array.

East and west and south and north
　　The Socialists ride fast,
And every town in New South Wales
　　Has heard their trumpet's blast.
Shame to the false elector
　　Who lingers in his hole,
While Watson and his myrmidons
　　Are riding to the poll.

Then up spake brave Horatius Gould,
　　And a Liberal proud was he,
"Now, who will stand on either hand
　　And face the foe with me?"
Then out spake bold Herminius Millen,
　　And Walker out spake he,
"We will abide on either side
　　And win a seat with thee."

" 'Tis well," quoth brave Horatius,
　　"As thou sayest, so let it be."
And straight against the proletaire
　　Forth went the dauntless three.
　　*(Issue impending)*

408

# The Deficit Demon

*A Political Ballad*

It was the lunatic poet escaped from the local asylum,
Loudly he twanged on his banjo and sang with his voice like a saw-mill,
While as with fervour he sang there was borne o'er the shuddering wildwood,
Borne on the breath of the poet a flavour of rum and of onions.

He sang of the Deficit Demon that dwelt in the Treasury Mountains,
How it was small in its youth and a champion was sent to destroy it:
Dibbs he was called, and he boasted, "Soon will I wipe out the Monster,"
But while he was boasting and bragging the monster grew larger and larger.

One day as Dibbs bragged of his prowess in daylight the Deficit met him,
Settled his hash in one act and made him to all men a byword,
Sent him, a raving ex-Premier, to dwell in the shades of oblivion,
And the people put forward a champion known as Sir Patrick the Portly.

As in the midnight the tom-cat who seeketh his love on the house top,
Lifteth his voice up in song and is struck by the fast whizzing brickbat,
Drops to the ground in a swoon and glides to the silent hereafter,
So fell Sir Patrick the Portly at the stroke of the Deficit Demon.

Then were the people amazed and they called for the champion of champions
Known as Sir 'Enry the Fishfag unequalled in vilification.
He is the man, said the people, to wipe out the Deficit Monster,
If nothing else fetches him through he can at the least talk its head off.

So he sharpened his lance of Freetrade and he practised in loud-mouthed
        abusing,
"Poodlehead", "Craven", and "Mole-eyes" were things that he purposed to
        call it,
He went to the fight full of valour and all men are waiting the issue,
Though they know not his armour nor weapons excepting his power of
        abusing.

Loud sang the lunatic poet his song of the champions of valour
Until he was sighted and captured by fleet-footed keepers pursuing,
To whom he remarked with a smile as they ran him off back to the madhouse,
"If you want to back Parkes I'm your man — here's a cool three to one on
        the Deficit."

# *El Mahdi to the Australian Troops*

And wherefore have they come, this warlike band,
That o'er the ocean many a weary day
Have tossed; and now beside Suakim's Bay,
With faces stern and resolute, do stand,
Waking the desert's echoes with the drum —
Men of Australia, wherefore have ye come?

To keep the Puppet Khedive on his throne,
To strike a blow for tyranny and wrong,
To crush the weak and aid the oppressing strong!
Regardless of the hapless Fellah's moan,
To force the payment of the Hebrew loan,
Squeezing the tax like blood from out the stone?

And fair Australia, freest of the free,
Is up in arms against the freeman's fight;
And with her mother joined to crush the right —
Has left her threatened treasures o'er the sea,
Has left her land of liberty and law
To flesh her maiden sword in this unholy war.

Enough! God never blessed such enterprise —
England's degenerate Generals yet shall rue
Brave Gordon sacrificed, when soon they view
The children of a thousand deserts rise
To drive them forth like sand before the gale —
God and the Prophet! Freedom will prevail.

410

# The Fitzroy Blacksmith

*With Apologies to Longfellow*

Under the spreading deficit,
 The Fitzroy Smithy stands;
The smith, a spendthrift man is he,
 With too much on his hands;
But the muscles of his brawny jaw
 Are strong as iron bands.

Pay out, pay out, from morn till night,
 You can hear the sovereigns go;
Or you'll hear him singing "Old Folks at Home",
 In a deep bass voice and slow,
Like a bullfrog down in the village well
 When the evening sun is low.

The Australian going "home" for loans
 Looks in at the open door;
He loves to see the imported plant,
 And to hear the furnace roar,
And to watch the private firms smash up
 Like chaff on the threshing-floor.

Toiling, rejoicing, borrowing,
 Onward through life he goes;
Each morning sees some scheme begun
 That never sees it close.
Something unpaid for, someone done,
 Has earned a night's repose.

# *The Incantation*

A darkened cave. In the middle a cauldron boiling.
Enter the three witches.

1ST WITCH: Thrice hath the Federal Jackass brayed.

2ND WITCH: Once the Bruce-Smith War-horse neighed.

3RD WITCH: So Georgie comes, 'tis time, 'tis time,
Around the cauldron to chant our rhyme.

1ST WITCH: In the cauldron boil and bake
Fillet of a tariff snake,
Home-made flannels — mostly cotton,
Apples full of moths, and rotten,
Lamb that perished in the drought,
Starving stock from "furthest out",
Drops of sweat from cultivators,
Sweating to feed legislators.
Grime from a white stoker's nob,
Toiling at a nigger's job.
Thus the great Australian Nation,
Seeks political salvation.

ALL: Double, double, toil and trouble,
Fire burn, and cauldron bubble.

2ND WITCH: Heel-taps from the threepenny bars,
Ash from Socialist cigars.
Leathern tongue of boozer curst
With the great Australian thirst,
Two-up gambler keeping dark,
Loafer sleeping in the park —
Drop them in to prove the sequel,
All men are born free and equal.

ALL: Double, double, toil and trouble,
Fire burn, and cauldron bubble.

3RD WITCH: Lung of Labour agitator,
Gall of Isaacs turning traitor;
Spleen that Kingston has revealed,
Sawdust stuffing out of Neild;
Mix them up, and then combine
With duplicity of Lyne,
Alfred Deakin's gift of gab,
Mix the gruel thick and slab.

ALL: Double, double! Boil and bubble!
Heav'n help Australia in her trouble.

HECATE: Oh, well done, I commend your pains,
And everyone shall share i' the gains,
And now about the cauldron sing,
Enchanting all that you put in.
Round about the cauldron go,
In the People's rights we'll throw,
Cool it with an Employer's blood,
Then the charm stands firm and good,
And thus with chaos in possession,
Ring in the coming Fed'ral Session.

# Gone Down

To the voters of Glen Innes 'twas O'Sullivan that went,
  To secure the country vote for Mister Hay.
So he told 'em what he'd borrowed, and he told 'em what he'd spent,
Though extravagance had blown it all away.
Said he, "Vote for Hay, my hearties, and wherever we may roam
We will borrow, undismayed by Fortune's frown!"
When he got his little banjo, and he sang them "Home, Sweet Home!"
Why, it made a blessed horse fall down.

Then he summoned his supporters, and went spouting through the bush,
To assure them that he'd build them roads galore,
If he could but borrow something from the "Plutocratic Push",
Though he knew they wouldn't lend him any more.
With his Coolangatta Croesus, who was posing for the day
As a Friend of Labour, just brought up from town:
When the Democratic Keystone told the workers, "Vote for Hay",
Then another blessed horse fell down!

When the polling day was over, and the promising was done —
The promises that never would be kept —
Then O' Sullivan came homeward at the sinking of the sun,
To the Ministerial Bench he slowly crept.
When his colleagues said, "Who won it? Is our banner
    waving high?
Has the Ministry retained Glen Innes Town?"
Then the great man hesitated, and responded with a sigh —
"There's another blessed seat gone down!"

# Jimmy Dooley's Army

*A Political Ballad by our Bolshevik Bard*

There's a dashin' sort of boy
Which they call his Party's Joy,
And his smile-that-won't-come-off would quite disarm ye;
And he played the leadin' hand
In the Helter-Skelter Band,
Known as Jimmy Dooley's Circulating Army.
When the rank and file they found,
They were marchin' round and round,
They one and all began to act unruly;
And the letter that he wrote,
Sure it got the Labor goat,
So we set ourselves to deal with Captain Dooley.

### Chorus

Whill-il-loo. High Ho!
We'll all be there you know,
The repartees and ructions they will charm ye;
And we'll see which we prefer,
Is it Dooley or McGirr,
To take command of Jimmy Dooley's Army.

When we're marchin' to the poll,
And we're under his control,
We sometimes feel a trifle unsalubrious;
For by one and all 'twas said
That if our objective's Red,
To call it claret-coloured makes us dubious.
Sure, the Fat Men one fine day
They chanced to come our way,
And we thought that we should bate them well and trooly;
But we let them pass us by
And not half a brick did fly,
'Twas then we tore our tickets up on Dooley.

## Chorus

Whill-il-loo. High Ho!
We'll all be there you know,
The repartees and ructions they will charm ye;
And we'll see which we prefer,
Is it Dooley or McGirr,
To take command of Jimmy Dooley's Army.

# The Ballad of Cockatoo Dock

Of all the docks upon the blue
There was no dockyard, old or new,
To touch the dock at Cockatoo.

Of all the ministerial clan
There was no nicer, worthier man
Than Admiral O'Sullivan.

Of course we mean E. W.
O'Sullivan, the hero who
Controlled the dock at Cockatoo.

To workmen he explained his views —
"You need not toil unless you choose,
Your only work is drawing screws."

And sometimes to their great surprise
When votes of censure filled the skies
He used to give them all a rise.

"What odds about a pound or two?"
Exclaimed the great E. W.
O'Sullivan at Cockatoo.

The dockyard superintendent, he
Was not at all what he should be —
He sneered at all this sympathy.

So when he gave a man the sack
O'Sullivan got on his track
And straightway went and fetched him back.

And with a sympathetic tear
He'd say, "How dare you interfere,
You most misguided engineer?

"Your sordid manners please amend —
No man can possibly offend
Who has a Member for a friend.

"With euchre, or a friendly rub,
And whisky from the nearest 'pub',
We'll make the dockyard like a club.

"Heave ho, my hearties, play away,
We'll do no weary work today.
What odds — the public has to pay!

"And if the public should complain
I'll go to Broken Hill by train
To watch McCarthy making rain."

And there, with nothing else to do
No doubt the great E. W.
Will straightway raise McCarthy's screw.

# Macbreath

*A Tragedy as Played at Ryde*

| | |
|---|---|
| Macbreath | Mr Henley |
| Macpuff | Mr Terry |
| The Ghost | |

## ACT I

*TIME:* The day before the election.
*SCENE:* A Drummoyne tram running past a lunatic asylum.
All present are Reform Leaguers and supporters of Macbreath.
They seat themselves in the compartment.

MACBREATH: Here, I'll sit in the midst.
Be large in mirth. Anon we'll all be fitted
With Parliamentary seats.
*(Voter approaches the door.)*
There's blood upon thy face.

VOTER: 'Tis Thompson's, then.

MACBREATH: Is he thrown out? How neatly we beguiled
The guileless Thompson. Did he sign a pledge agreeing to retire?

VOTER: Aye, that he did.

MACBREATH: Not so did I!
Not on the doubtful hazard of a vote
By Ryde electors, cherry-pickers, oafs,
That drive their market carts at dread of night
And sleep all day. Not on the jaundiced choice
Of folks who daily run their half a mile
Just after breakfast, when the steamer hoots
Her warning to the laggard — not on these
Relied Macbreath, for if these rustics' choice
Had fall'n on Thompson, I should still have claimed
A conference. But hold! Is Thompson out?

VOTER: My Lord, his name is mud. That I did for him
I paid my shilling and I cast my vote.

419

MACBREATH: Thou art the best of all the shilling voters.
Prithee, be near me on election day
To see me smite Macpuff — and now we shan't
Be long —
*(Ghost of Thompson appears.)*
What's this? A vision!
Thou canst not say I did it! Never shake
Thy gory locks at me. Run for some other seat,
Let the woods hide thee. Prithee, chase thyself!
*(The ghost of Thompson disappears, and Macbreath revives himself with
a great effort.)*
Leaguers all,
Mine own especial comrades of Reform,
All amateurs and no professionals,
So many worthy candidates I see,
Alas that there are only ninety seats.
Still, let us take them all — and Joe Carruthers,
Ashton, and Jimmy Hogue, and all the rest,
Will have to look for work! Oh, joyous day,
To-morrow's poll will make me M.L.A.

## ACT II

*TIME:* Election day.
*SCENE:* Macbreath's committee rooms.

MACBREATH: Bring me no more reports: let them all fly;
Till Labour's platform to Kyabram come
I cannot taint with fear. How go the votes?

*Enter First Voter*

FIRST VOTER: May it please my Lord,
The cherry-pickers' vote is two to one
Towards Macpuff: and all our voters say
The ghost of Thompson sits in every booth,
And talks of pledges.

MACBREATH: What a polished liar!
And yet the dead can vote! *(Strikes him.)*
What if it should be!
*(Ghost of Thompson appears to him suddenly.)*

GHOST: The Pledge! The Pledge!

MACBREATH: I say I never signed the gory pledge.
*(Ghost disappears. Enter a Messenger.)*
Thou com'st to use thy tongue. Thy story quickly!

MESSENGER: Gracious, my Lord,
I should report that which I know I saw,
But know not how to do it.

MACBREATH: Well, say on!

MESSENGER: As I did stand my watch in Parliament
I saw the Labour platform come across
And join Kyabram — Loans were overthrown —
The numbers were reduced — extravagance
Is put an end to by McGowen's vote.

MACBREATH: The devil damn thee black, thou cream-faced loon!
Where got'st thou this fish yarn?

MESSENGER: There's nearly forty —

MACBREATH: Thieves, fool?

MESSENGER: No, members, will be frozen out of work!

MACBREATH: Aye, runs the story so! Well, well, 'tis sudden!
These are the uses of the politician,
A few brief sittings and another contest;
He hardly gets to know th' billiard tables
Before he's out ...

*(Alarums and Harbour excursions; enter Macpuff at the head
of a Picnic Party.)*

MACPUFF: Now, yield thee, tyrant!
By that fourth party which I once did form,
I'll take thee to a picnic, there to live
On windfall oranges!

MACBREATH: ... Nay, rather death!
Death before picnic fare! Lay on, Macpuff,
And damned be he who first cries Hold, enough!
*(They fight. Macbreath is struck on the back of the head by some blue metal
from Pennant Hills Quarry. He falls. The referee counts, "One, two, three,
eight, nine, ten — out!")*

421

MACPUFF: Kind voters all, and worthy gentlemen,
Who rallied to my flag to-day, and made me
Member for Thompson, from my soul I thank you.
There needs no trumpet blast, for I can blow
Like any trombone. Prithee, let us go!
Thanks to you all who shared this glorious day,
Whom I invite to dance at Chowder Bay!

CURTAIN

# A Job for McGuinness

*A man named McGuinness and his wife are leaving
Australia because the man can get no work, though his wife is
offered plenty of employment at washing and cooking.*

Oh, it's dreadful to think in a country like this
    With its chances for work — and enjoyment
That a man like McGuinness was certain to miss
    Whenever he tried for employment.

He wrote to employers from Bondi to Bourke,
    From Woolloomooloo to Glen Innes,
But he found — though his wife could get plenty of work —
    There was never a job for McGuinness.

But perhaps — later on — when the Chow and the Jap
    Begin to drift down from the tropics,
When a big yellow stain spreading over the map
    Provides some disquieting topics,

Oh, it's then when they're wanting a man that will stand
    In the trench where his own kith and kin is,
With a frown on his face and a gun in his hand —
    Then there might be a job for McGuinness!

# Ave Caesar

Long ago the Gladiators,
    When the call to combat came,
Marching past the massed spectators,
    Hailed the Emp'ror with acclaim!
Voices ringing with the fury
    Of the strife so soon to be,
Cried, *"O Caesar, morituri*
    *salutamus te!"*

Nowadays the massed spectators
    See the unaccustomed sight —
Legislative gladiators
    Marching to their last great fight;
Young and old, obscure and famous,
    Hand to hand and knee to knee —
Hear the war-cry, *"Salutamus*
    *morituri te!"*

Fight! Nor be the fight suspended
    Till the corpses strew the plain.
Ere the grisly strife be ended
    Five and thirty must be slain.
Slay and spare not, lest another
    Haply may discomfit thee:
Brother now must war with brother —
    *"Salutamus te!"*

War-worn vet'ran, skilled debater,
    Trickster famed of bridge and road,
Now for each grim gladiator
    Gapes Oblivion's drear abode.
Should the last great final jury
    Turn their thumbs down — it must be!
*"Ave, Caesar, morituri*
    *salutamus te!"*

# Our Underpaid Army

Napoleon made his Marshals out of mud,
And Cromwell's Ironsides were mostly tanners:
But nowadays our officers have blood,
And lots of cash, and regulation manners:
And each must own a wardrobe so extensive
That dying for one's country comes expensive.

The "Tommy" simply doesn't care a groat,
The war is barred to him from rising higher:
For how could he with cheap and shabby coat
To hold his own with social swells aspire,
He lacks the three great aids to high position
Viz. Money, Petticoat or Politician!

The Cavalry look down on "Mounted Fut"
And "Mounted Fut" at Infantry will snigger,
And Infantry esteem themselves a cut
Above the C.I.V. — the humble figure
That drives a squadron cart, cries as he passes,
"Hi! Clear de way dere, you dashed lower classes!"

And nowadays each little cheap success
Is quite enough to set the country yelling,
With big black headlines in the daily press
And D.S.O.s thrown out like pom-poms shelling.
With people drinking, Mafficking and bawling,
Our frenzied self-laudation is appalling!

When Wellington sent news of Waterloo
A quarter-page of print was all he needed.
He praised his soldiers in a line or two
And twenty pages-full of "Killed" succeeded.
But nowadays we go into hysterics
Over "one bullet wound and two enterics".

No matter who goes "in" or who goes "out"
Or whether Liberal or whether Tory
Midleads the country, still beyond all doubt
It's just the same old melancholy story.

The army isn't open to the Nation,
It's sacred ground for some rich man's relation.

There is *no* hope: the whole concern is worked
In the sole interest of the "upper classes"
Enquiries will be resolutely Burked
And die unheeded when the clamour passes.
The word reform makes leading people shiver
They hold their prey like we held Eland's River.

The Army knows! They knew the worthless man
And who got drunk! And who was simply silly,
They likewise know that by the present plan
The eye-glassed impotent from Piccadilly
Gets most rewards! — In silence they abide it.
They talk within the mess but not outside it!

And some folks hoped that when old Kandahar
Took charge, we might see some great reformation.
But no! Reform seems every bit as far
As ever. Think what consternation
There'd be in Mayfair if he recommended
That all incompetents should be suspended.

We know how Remount men were sent away
For horses, and the scandals so unhappy!
And some were shrewd enough — too shrewd, they say —
But most were what they call "A dear good chappie".
But business training! Why, they never had one!
If sent to buy a pie they'd buy a bad one.

Clear out the titled men! Let men come in
Who are not asked to pay for being shot at
Make idle luxury an army sin
Some faint reform might then perhaps be got at.
But until then — I don't wish to alarm ye
But until then you'll never have an army!

But what am I against the social clique
A field-mouse in a foreign furrow straying,
But all the same I'll raise my valiant squeak
And say the thing that badly needeth saying,
There are no doubt some faults in a democracy
But Lord preserve us from an aristocracy!

# The Ballad of the Carpet Bag

*The political season being now upon us, the following
ballad may be appropriate*

Ho! Darkies, don't you hear dose voters cryin',
    Pack dat carpetbag!
You must get to de Poll, you must get there flyin';
    Pack dat carpet bag!
You must travel by de road, you must travel by de train,
And the things what you've done you will have to explain,
And the things what you've promised, you must promise 'em again.
    Pack dat carpet bag!

Hear dem voters callin'!
    Pack de clean boiled rag.
For there's grass in the west, and the rain am fallin'.
    Pack dat carpet bag!

You must pack up a volume of *Coghlan's Figures*,
    Pack dat carpet bag!
And a lot o' little jokes to amuse those niggers.
    Pack dat carpet bag!
You must wheedle all de gals with a twinkle of your eye,
You must bob down your head when de eggs begin to fly.
Oh! those eggs what they're saving, and they'll throw 'em by and by.
    Pack dat carpet bag!

Hear dem voters callin'!
    Pack de clean boiled rag.
For there's grass in the west, and the rain am fallin'.
    Pack dat carpet bag!

You must get upon a stump, you must practise speakin',
    Pack dat carpet bag!
You must follow Georgie Reid or Alfred Deakin.
    Pack dat carpet bag!
You must come to de scratch, or you're bound to fail,
For it ain't any time to be sittin' on de rail,
Or de votes that you'll get — they won't keep you out o' jail.
    Pack dat carpet bag!

Hear dem voters callin'!
    Pack de clean boiled rag.
For there's grass in the west, and the rain am fallin',
    Pack dat carpet bag!

And supposin' that you're beat, and you feel like cryin',
    Pack dat carpet bag!
You must hustle back to work — just to keep from dyin'.
    Pack dat carpet bag!
You must travel second-class when you travel by de train,
For you haven't got a pass on de end of your chain,
While the other fellow's packing for de great campaign.
    Pack dat carpet bag!

Hear dem voters callin'!
    Pack de clean boiled rag.
For there's grass in the west, and the rain am fallin'.
    Pack dat carpet bag!

# Tom Collins — A Political Ballad

W ho never drinks and never bets,
   But loves his wife and pays his debts
And feels content with what he gets?
   Tom Collins.

Who has the utmost confidence
That all the banks now in suspense
Will meet their paper three years hence?
   Tom Collins.

Who reads the *Herald* leaders through,
And takes the *Evening News* for true,
And thought the *Echo*'s jokes were new?
   Tom Collins.

Who is the patriot renowned
So very opportunely found
To fork up Dibbs's thousand pound?
   Tom Collins.

# The Seven Ages of Wise

*A Post-Shakespearian Fragment*

Parliament's a stage,
  And all the Politicians merely players!
They have their exits and their entrances,
And Wise doth in his time play many parts,
His acts being seven changes.

  First the Runner,
With spiked shoe he spurns the cinder track,
And just for once runs straight.

  The next the Student,
Burning the midnight oil with Adam Smith
For Cobden medals.

  Next the youthful member,
With shining morning face, creeping between
Two seasoned leaders into place and power
Before his whiskers grow.

  The next the bravo.
Jealous of greater men, he cries: "Ha, Ha!
Beware Bernardo's dagger!" — and would strike
His friend i' th' back.

  Then comes a sudden change.
Once more a child, he comes with quick-turned coat,
New friends, new doctrines, and new principles,
Lets Friedman loose, and wrecks the Government.
Then leads the horny-handed sons of toil
By many a specious promise to their doom
In Arbitration Courts.

Last scene of all,
That ends this strange, disastrous history.
He aims at Judgeships and Commissionerships,
But, failing, passes on to mere oblivion.
*Sans* place, *sans* power, *sans* pay, *sans* everything.

# The Sausage Candidate

*A Tale for the Elections*

Our fathers, brave men were and strong,
      And whisky was their daily liquor;
They used to move the world along
      In better style than now — and quicker.
Elections then were sport, you bet!
      A trifle rough, there's no denying
When two opposing factions met
      The skin and hair were always flying.

When "cabbage-trees" could still be worn
      Without the question, "Who's your hatter?"
There dawned a bright election morn
      Upon the town of Parramatta.
A man called Jones was all the go —
      The people's friend, the poor's protector;
A long, gaunt, six-foot slab of woe,
      He sought to charm the green elector.

Now, Jones had one time been trustee
      For his small niece, and he — the villain! —
Betrayed his trust most shamefully,
      And robbed the child of every shillin'.
He used to keep accounts, they say,
      To save himself in case of trouble;
Whatever cash he paid away
      He always used to charge it double.

He'd buy the child a cotton gown
      Too coarse and rough to dress a cat in,
And then he'd go and put it down
      And charge the price of silk or satin!
He gáve her once a little treat —
      An outing down the harbour sunny —
And Lord! the bill for bread and meat,
      You'd think they all had eaten money!

432

But Jones exposed the course he took
    By carelessness — such men are ninnies.
He went and entered in his book
    "Two pounds of sausages — *two guineas.*"
Now this leaked out, and folk got riled,
    And said that Jones, "he didn't oughter"
But what cared Jones? he only smiled —
    Abuse ran off his back like water.

And so he faced the world content:
    His little niece — he never paid her:
And then he stood for Parliament,
    Of course he was a rank free trader.
His wealth was great, success appeared
    To smile propitious on his banner,
But Providence it interfered
    In this most unexpected manner.

A person — call him Brown for short —
    Who knew the story of this stealer,
Went calmly down the town and bought
    Two pounds of sausage from a dealer,
And then he got a long bamboo
    And tied the sausage tightly to it;
Says he, "This is the thing to do,
    And I am just the man to do it.

"When Jones comes out to make his speech
    I won't a clapper be, nor hisser,
But with this long bamboo I'll reach
    And poke the sausage in his 'kisser'.
I'll bring the wretch to scorn and shame,
    Unless those darned police are nigh:
As sure as Brown's my glorious name,
    I'll knock that candidate kite-high."

The speech comes on — beneath the stand
    The people push and surge and eddy
But Brown waits calmly close at hand
    With all his apparatus ready;
And while the speaker loudly cries,
    "Of ages all, this is the boss age!"

Brown hits him square between the eyes,
    Exclaiming, "What's the price of sausage?"

He aimed the victuals in his face,
    As though he thought poor Jones a glutton.
And Jones was covered with disgrace —
    Disgrace and shame, and beef and mutton.
His cause was lost — a hopeless wreck
    He crept off from the hooting throng;
Protection proudly ruled the deck,
    Here ends the sausage and the song.

# Policeman G.

*Air: "Widow McGrath"*

To Policeman G. the Inspector said:
"When you pass the 'shops' you must turn your head;
If you took a wager, that would be a sin;
So you'll earn no stripes if you run them in."
   Mush-a-ring-tiy-ah,
   Fol-de-diddle-doh!

To the House Committee, the Inspector said:
" 'Tis a terrible thing how the gamblers spread,
For they bet on the Steeple, and they bet on the Cup,
And the magistrates won't lock them up."
   Mush-a-ring-tiy-ah,
   Fol-de-diddle-doh!

But Policeman G., as he walks his beat,
Where the gamblers are — up and down the street —
Says he: "What's the use to be talkin' rot —
If they'd make me a sergeant, I could cop the lot!"
   With my ring-tiy-ah,
   Fol-de-diddle-doh!

"But, bedad if you start to suppress the 'shop',
Then the divil only knows where you're going to stop;
For the rich and the poor, they would raise a din,
If at Randwick I ran fifty thousand in."
   Mush-a-ring-tiy-ah,
   Fol-de-diddle-doh!

"Though ye must not box — nor shpit — nor bet,
I'll find my way out to Randwick yet;
For I'm shtandin' a pound — and it's no disgrace —
On Paddy Nolan's horse — for the Steeplechase!"
   Mush-a-ring-tiy-ah,
   Fol-de-diddle-doh!

# Who is Kater Anyhow?

*"Mr Henry Edward Kater, of Moss Vale,
son-in-law of the late William Forster,
has been appointed a member of the New South Wales
Legislative Council." Daily paper*

Why, oh why was Kater lifted
From the darkness, where he drifted
All unknown, and raised to honour,
Side by side with Dick O'Connor,
In the Council, free from row?
Who *is* Kater, anyhow?

Did he bid our armies rally,
Like the recent Billy Dalley?
Did he lend a Premier money,
Like — (No libels here, my sonny. — Ed. B.)
Was he, like John Davies, found
Very useful underground?

Not at all! his claim to glory
Rests on quite another story.
All obscure he might have tarried,
But he managed to get married —
And (to cut the matter shorter)
Married William Forster's daughter.

So when Henry Edward Kater
Goes to answer his Creator,
Will the angel at the wicket
Say, on reading Kater's ticket —
"Enter! for you're no impostor,
Son-in-law of Billy Forster!"

# The Rhyme of the O'Sullivan

*Pro Bono Publico*
     Went out the streets to scan,
And marching to and fro
     He met a seedy man,

Who did a tale unfold
     In solemn tones and slow,
And this is what he told
     *Pro Bono Publico.*

"For many years I led
     The people's onward march;
I was the 'Fountain Head',
     The 'Democratic Arch'.

"In more than regal state
     I used to sit and smile,
And bridges I'd donate,
     And railways by the mile.

"I pawned the country off
     For many million quid,
And spent it like a toff —
     So help me, Bob, I did.

"But now those times are gone,
     The wind blows cold and keen;
I sit and think upon
     The thing that I have been.

"And if a country town
     Its obligation shirks,
I press for money down
     To pay for water works.

"A million pounds or two
     Was naught at all to me —
And now I have to sue
     For paltry £ s d!

"Alas, that such a fate
    Should come to such a man,
Who once was called the Great —
    The great O'Sullivan!"

With weary steps and slow,
    With tears of sympathy
*Pro Bono Publico*
    Went sadly home to tea.

Remarking, as he went,
    With sad and mournful brow,
"The cash that party spent —
    I wish I had it now!"

# *To George Lambert*

*An Essay on Australian Art and Literature
In recognition of Lambert's really excellent
portrait of Mrs Paterson*

Come all ye men of paint and pen,
    Who toil with hand and brain.
Forsake the town and take the brown
    And dusty roads again,
The tracks that we old-timers know,
Who·showed you all the way to go
With Clancy of the Overflow
    Across the Black Soil Plain.

# Old Schooldays

Awake, oh Muse, the echoes of a day
Long past, the ghosts of mem'ries manifold —
Youth's memories that once were green and gold
But now, alas, are grim and ashen grey.

The drowsy schoolboy wakened up from sleep,
First stays his system with substantial food,
Then off for school with tasks half understood,
Alas, alas, that cribs should be so cheap!

The journey down to town — 'twere long to tell
The storm and riot of the rabble rout;
The wild Walpurgis revel in and out
That made the ferry boat a floating hell.

What time the captive locusts fairly roared:
And bulldog ants, made stingless with a knife,
Climbed up the seats and scared the very life
From timid folk, who near jumped overboard.

The hours of lessons — hours with feet of clay
Each hour a day, each day more like a week:
While hapless urchins heard with blanched cheek
The words of doom "Come in on Saturday".

The master gowned and spectacled, precise,
Trying to rule by methods firm and kind
But always just a little bit behind,
The latest villainy, the last device.

Born of some smoothfaced urchin's fertile brain
To irritate the hapless pedagogue,
And first involve him in a mental fog
Then "have" him with the same old tale again.

The "bogus" fight that brought the sergeant down
To that dark corner by the old brick wall,
Where mimic combat and theatric brawl
Made noise enough to terrify the town.

440

But on wet days the fray was genuine,
When small boys pushed each other in the mud
And fought in silence till thin streams of blood
Their dirty faces would incarnadine.

The football match or practice in the park
With rampant hoodlums joining in the game
Till on one famous holiday there came
A gang that seized the football for a lark.

Then raged the combat without rest or pause,
Till one, a hero, Hawkins unafraid
Regained the ball, and later on displayed
His nose knocked sideways in his country's cause.

Before the mind quaint visions rise and fall,
Old jokes, old sports, old students dead and gone:
And some that lead us still, while some toil on
As rank and file, but "Grammar" children all.

And he, the pilot, who has laid the course
For all to steer by, honest, unafraid —
Truth is his beacon light, so he has made
The name of the old School a living force.

# *A Triolet*

Of all the sickly forms of verse,
    Commend me to the triolet.
It makes bad writers somewhat worse:
Of all the sickly forms of verse
That fall beneath a reader's curse,
    It is the feeblest jingle yet.
Of all the sickly forms of verse,
    Commend me to the triolet.

# The Hypnotist

A man once read with a mind surprised
Of the way that people were "hypnotised";
By waving of hands you produced, forsooth,
A kind of trance where men told the truth!
His mind was filled with a wond'ring doubt;
He grabbed his hat and he started out,
He walked the street and he made a "set"
At the first half-dozen folk he met.
He "tranced" them all, and without a joke
'Twas much as follows the subjects spoke:

### First Man

"I am a doctor, London-made,
Listen to me and you'll hear displayed
A few of the tricks of the doctor's trade.
'Twill sometimes chance when a patient's ill
That a dose, or draught, or a lightning pill,
A little too strong or a little too hot,
Will work its way to a vital spot.
And then I watch with a sickly grin
While the patient 'passes his counters in'.
But when he has gone with his fleeting breath
I certify that the cause of death
Was something Latin, and something long,
And who is to say that the doctor's wrong!
So I go my way with a stately tread
While my patients sleep with the dreamless dead."

### Next, Please

"I am a barrister, wigged and gowned;
Of stately presence and look profound.
Listen awhile till I show you round.
When courts are sitting and work is flush
I hurry about in a frantic rush.

I take your brief and I look to see
That the same is marked with a thumping fee;
But just as your case is drawing near
I bob serenely and disappear.
And away in another court I lurk
While a junior barrister does your work;
And I ask my fee with a courtly grace,
Although I never came near the case.
The loss means ruin to you, maybe,
But nevertheless *I must have my fee!*
For the lawyer laughs in his cruel sport
While his clients march to the Bankrupt Court."


## Third Man


"I am a banker, wealthy and bold —
A solid man, and I keep my hold
Over a pile of the public's gold.
I am as skilled as skilled can be
In every matter of £ s. d.
I count the money, and night by night
I balance it up to a farthing right:
In sooth, 'twould a stranger's soul perplex
My double entry and double checks.
Yet it sometimes happens by some strange crook
That a ledger-keeper will 'take his hook'
With a couple of hundred thousand 'quid',
And no one can tell how the thing was did! "


## Fourth Man


"I am an editor, bold and free.
Behind the great impersonal 'We'
I hold the power of the Mystic Three.
What scoundrel ever would dare to hint
That anything crooked appears in print!
Perhaps an actor is all the rage,
He struts his hour on the mimic stage,
With skill he interprets all the scenes —
And yet next morning I give him beans.

I slate his show from the floats to flies,
Because the beggar won't advertise.
And sometimes columns of print appear
About a mine, and it makes it clear
That the same is all that one's heart could wish —
A dozen ounces to every dish.
But the reason we print those statements fine
Is — the editor's uncle owns the mine."

## The Last Straw

"A preacher I, and I take my stand
In pulpit decked with a gown and band
To point the way to a better land.
With sanctimonious and reverent look
I read it out of the sacred book
That he who would open the golden door
Must give his all to the starving poor.
But I vary the practice to some extent
By investing money at twelve per cent,
And after I've preached for a decent while
I clear for 'home' with a lordly pile.
I frighten my congregation well
With fear of torment and threats of hell,
Although I know that the scientists
Can't find that any such place exists.
And when they prove it beyond mistake
That the world took millions of years to make,
And never was built by the seventh day
I say in a pained and insulted way
That 'Thomas also presumed to doubt',
And thus do I rub my opponents out.
For folks may widen their mental range,
But priest and parson, they never change."

With dragging footsteps and downcast head
The hypnotiser went home to bed,
And since that very successful test
He has given the magic art a rest;
Had he tried the ladies, and worked it right,
What curious tales might have come to light!

445

## Our Mat

It came from the prison this morning,
   Close-twisted, neat-lettered, and flat;
It lies the hall doorway adorning,
   A very good style of a mat.

Prison-made! how the spirit is moven
   As we think of its story of dread —
What wiles of the wicked are woven
   And spun in its intricate thread!

The letters are new, neat and nobby,
   Suggesting a masterly hand —
Was it Sikes, who half-murdered the bobby,
   That put the neat D on the "and"?

Some banker found guilty of *laches* —
   It's always called *laches,* you know —
Had Holt any hand in those Hs?
   Did Bertrand illumine that O?

That T has a look of the gallows,
   That A's a triangle, I guess;
Was it one of the Mount Rennie fellows
   Who twisted the strands of the S?

Was it made by some "highly connected",
   Who is doing his spell "on his head",
Or some wretched woman detected
   In stealing her children some bread?

Does it speak of a bitter repentance
   For the crime that so easily came?
Of the wearisome length of the sentence,
   Of the sin, and the sorrow, and shame?

A mat! I should call it a sermon
    On sin, to all sinners addressed;
It would take a keen judge to determine
    Whether writer or reader is best.

Though the doorway be hard as a pavestone,
    I rather would use it than that —
I'd as soon wipe my boots on a gravestone,
    As I would on that Darlinghurst mat!

# *The Angel's Kiss*

An angel stood beside the bed
Where lay the living and the dead.

He gave the mother — her who died —
A kiss that Christ the Crucified

Had sent to greet the weary soul
When, worn and faint, it reached its goal.

He gave the infant kisses twain,
One on the breast, one on the brain.

"Go forth into the world," he said,
"With blessings on your heart and head,

"For God, who ruleth righteously,
Hath ordered that to such as be

"From birth deprived of mother's love,
I bring His blessing from above;

"But if the mother's life he spare
Then she is made God's messenger

"To kiss and pray that heart and brain
May go through life without a stain."

The infant moved towards the light,
The angel spread his wings in flight.

But each man carries to his grave
The kisses that in hopes to save
The angel or his mother gave.

# General Drought and General Rain

Parched are the plains and bare,
Dusty and eaten out:
Animals everywhere
Perish in dumb despair;
For the land is held in the iron grip
Of the enemy General Drought!

Who shall deliver us?
Who shall assuage our pain?
Men in their bitter grief,
Pray that they get relief,
That help may come from the friendly hand
Of our ally, General Rain.

Look at those flying mists
Sweeping across the plain!
These are the lads of the Light Brigade,
Light but fearless and undismayed;
They are the van of the first attack
Of the valiant General Rain.

Now are the Light Brigade
Baffled and beaten back:
But the blast of the rain-wind fifing clear,
Rallies its forces far and near
Onto the grand attack.

Out of the stormy south
To the sound of the thunder's drum,
Peal upon peal, and crash on crash,
To the heliograph of the lightning flash,
The big battalions come!

Look at those big black clouds,
Gathering out at sea!
Never the swiftest war horse yet
Moved as they move, all stern and set,
On to their victory!

Never a Maxim Gun
Shoots like the stinging hail,
Never the blast of a fifer rings
Clear as the call that the storm wind sings
As the foe begins to fail.

Now may our thanks ascend
Over the smiling plain.
Thanks let us give that the foe falls back,
Crushed by the might of the fierce attack
Of the valiant General Rain.

# I Joined a Contingent

I joined a contingent and went to the war
  In search of promotion and pay,
For I fancied the pastime of hunting the Boer
    Would suit me at five bob a day.
But, riding along, I heard something go *wheeuw* —
    A bullet passed close to my head —
So I sprang to the ground like a hero so true,
    And I lay there and shammed to be dead.

*Spoken*

Yes, you can talk about your V.C. and all that.
Wait till you've heard a bullet go like this, *wheeuw*,
close past your head. The officer shouted out:
"Forwards, Forwards!", so I lay there and said to
myself, "Well, he doesn't want me — I'm not
a forward, I'm a full-back."

But they called me a white-livered cur,
A Mounted Australian Cur;
But, after all's said,
I'm alive and they're dead,
And that's what I greatly prefer!
I'm alive, so I'm gay
With my five bob a day
As a Mounted Australian Cur.

My grandmother taught me a little refrain —
    A sort of a nursery rhyme —
"If you fight till you're slain, you cannot fight again —
    If you run you can run every time."
And this piece of wisdom I gathered from her,
    Which, somehow, I never forgot:
"It will hurt you, no doubt, to be branded a cur,
    But it hurts you much more to be shot."

*Spoken*

Yes, a lot of our poor fellows got shot. And what's
the good of five bob a day to a dead man?

The officer says to me, "You're a white-livered cur,"
he says. "You're a silly ass," I says. "You'll get
somebody hurt, lettin' the Boer shoot at us like this.
A man's a fool to follow you," I says.
"You'll be shot tomorrow morning by a firing
squad," he says. "No, I won't," I says.
"I'll go home tonight. I'm tired of the war," I says.

But they called me a white-livered cur,
A Mounted Australian Cur;
But, after all's said,
I'm alive and they're dead,
And that's what I greatly prefer!
I'm alive, so I'm gay
On my five bob a day
As a Mounted Australian Cur.

# What Have the Cavalry Done?

What have the cavalry done?
  Cantered and trotted about,
Routin' the enemy out,
Causin' the beggars to run!
And we tramped along in the blazin' heat,
Over the veldt on our weary feet.
Tramp, tramp, tramp
Under the blazin' sun,
With never the sight of a bloomin' Boer,
'Cause they'd hunted 'em long before —
That's what the cavalry done!

What have the gunners done
Battlin' every day,
Battlin' any way.
Boers outranged 'em, but what cared they?
"Shoot and be damned," said the R.H.A.!
See! when the fight grows hot,
Under the rifles or not,
Always the order runs,
"Fetch up the bloomin' guns!"

And you'd see them great gun horses spring
To the "action front" — and around they'd swing.
Find the range with some queer machine
"At four thousand with fuse fourteen.
Ready! Fire number one!"
Handled the battery neat and quick!
Stick to it, too! How *did* they stick!
Never a gunner was seen to run!
Never a gunner would leave his gun!
Not though his mates dropped all around!
Always a gunner would stand his ground.
Take the army — the infantry,
Mounted rifles, and cavalry,
Twice the numbers I'd give away,
And I'd fight the lot with the R.II.A.,
For they showed us how a corps *should* be run,
That's what the gunners done!

# Cassidy's Epitaph

Here lies a bloke who's just gone West,
    A Number One Australian;
He took his gun and did his best
    To mitigate the alien.
So long as he could get to work
    He needed no sagacity;
A German, Austrian, or Turk,
    Were all the same to Cassidy.

Whenever he could raise "the stuff"
    — A liquor deleterious —
The question when he'd have enough
    Was apt to be mysterious.
'Twould worry prudent folks a lot
    Through mental incapacity;
If he could keep it down or not,
    Was all the same to Cassidy.

And when the boys would start a dance,
    In honour of Terpsichore,
'Twas just an even-money chance
    You'd find him rather shickery.
But once he struck his proper stride,
    And heard the band's vivacity,
The jazz, the tango, or the slide
    Was all the same to Cassidy.

And now he's gone to face the Light,
    With all it may reveal to him,
A life without a drink or fight
    Perhaps may not appeal to him;
But when St Peter calls the roll
    Of men of proved tenacity,
You'll find the front-rank right-hand man
    Will answer: "Here ... Cassidy."

# Bandy Burke

Our sergeant-major is Bandy Burke.
    Of course he couldn't afford
To take a commission — he does the work
    And the credit goes to a Lord.

These officer blokes can follow the hunt
    Or shine in a fencing school,
But we like to know that the man in front
    Is more than a titled fool.

And if you gave us an open choice
    When it comes to some deadly work,
We'd sooner follow the well-known voice
    Of bellerin' Bandy Burke.

For Bandy Burke has hair on his chest
    As rough as a badger's wool.
And you'll hear his voice right over the rest,
    Like the roar of an angry bull.

But after dark when the pipes are lit,
    And the stars come one by one,
You'll hear him talk to the boys a bit,
    And show them how things are done.

He's only a farmer — like this De Wet —
    But he knows his army work;
And the very best officers you can get
    Are the fellows like Bandy Burke.

# *No Class*

Oh! When we took Pretoria we thought the war was done;
  We thought to do some marching past and finish up the fun;
But wandering over Africa and trampin' down the grass
In search of Christian De Wet — well, that's no class.

We thought this here De Wet was something better than the rest,
The way he took those yeomanry was equal to the best,
We haven't got no grudge for that, we let the matter pass,
But burnin' all our letters up — well, that's no class.

The grub we get it ain't the sort to make us extra fat,
We don't expect no pigeon pie or anything like that;
But trek ox grown too old to work and starving on the grass
And ne'er a fire to cook it with — well, that's no class.

So where we go and what we do is hidden from our sight,
We have to starve, we have to tramp, we have to rouse and fight —
A kind of endless pilgrimage that we must make, alas!
"With Hunter, all round Africa! Per boot! No class!"

# The Dry Canteen

There were three soldiers who went to the war,
   *(Chorus)* Well, why not?
They'd arms and legs and plenty of jaw,
*(Chorus)* All they'd got!
They reckoned the first three years were the worst
And anything's yours if you see it first,
Whatever you do, take care of your thirst.
*(Chorus)* Well, why not?

And they made their way to the dry canteen,
*(Chorus)* Well, why not?
The drinks all tasted of gasoline,
*(Chorus)* All they'd got!
They handed the orderly bloke a wink,
He made them up a gallon of drink,
The sort for turning an elephant pink.
*(Chorus)* Well, why not?

There were three horses were hanging outside,
*(Chorus)* Well, why not?
Said they, "We'll take the three for a ride."
*(Chorus)* All they'd got!
They galloped the garrison through and through,
The sergeant ran like a kangaroo,
They reckoned the sergeant-major flew.
*(Chorus)* Well, why not?

The corporal came and gathered 'em in,
*(Chorus)* Well, why not?
Said he, "Who handed you rum and gin?"
*(Chorus)* All ye got!
They sorted 'em out and removed their caps:
"We run this place to oblige you chaps,
The colonel may shorten your lives, perhaps."
*(Chorus)* Perhaps not!

The colonel told 'em, "You're due for the clink,"
*(Chorus)* Well, why not?
"For filling yourselves with hinkey pink,"
*(Chorus)* All ye got!
"But listen, my boys, you're under the whip
And I might perhaps forgive your slip,
If you put me wise where you got that nip."
*(Chorus)* Well, why not?

# Index of Titles

459

460

461

# *Index of First Lines*